Joss Wood's passion for putting black letters on a white screen is only matched by her love of books and travelling (especially to the wild places of southern Africa) and, possibly, by her hatred of ironing and making school lunches.

Joss has written over sixteen books for the Mills & Boon KISS, Mills & Boon Presents and, most recently, Mills & Boon Desire lines.

After a career in business lobbying and local economic development, Joss now writes full-time. She lives in KwaZulu-Natal, South Africa, with her husband and two teenage children, surrounded by family, friends, animals and a ridiculous amount of books.

Joss is a member of the RWA (Romance Writers of America) and ROSA (Romance Writers of South Africa).

Maverick
Millionaires

JOSS WOOD

MILLS & BOON

First Published in Great Britain 2018
by Mills & Boon, an imprint of HarperCollins*Publishers*
1 London Bridge Street, London, SE1 9GF

MAVERICK MILLIONAIRES © 2018 Harlequin Books S. A.

Trapped With The Maverick Millionaire © 2016 Joss Wood
Pregnant By The Maverick Millionaire © 2016 Joss Wood
Married To The Maverick Millionaire © 2016 Joss Wood

ISBN: 978-0-263-26700-6

05-0318

MIX
Paper from
responsible sources
FSC™ C007454

FSC
www.fsc.org

Printed and bound in Spain
by CPI, Barcelona

TRAPPED WITH THE MAVERICK MILLIONAIRE

JOSS WOOD

To the "Book Sisters," Romy Sommers,

Rae Rivers and Rebecca Crowley. All are fantastic authors but are also funny, supportive and kind.

Basically, you rock!

Prologue

Rory Kydd, dressed in a too-small T-shirt and battered pajama bottoms, walked into the kitchen of her sister's luxurious kitchen and looked at the dark screen of the TV sitting on the counter.

Her best friend, Troy, had texted to tell her the Vancouver Mavericks had won and there had been high drama during the post-game interview. She was tempted to turn on the TV to see what he was talking about but, because she had a paper due and exams looming—and because she was trying not to think about one Maverick player in particular—she decided to have a cup of coffee and go back to the books. But even if she didn't give in to temptation, it couldn't be denied, team newbies Kade Webb, Quinn Rayne and Mark "Mac" McCaskill were a handful both on and off the ice, and Vancouver had three new heroes.

Three young, unfairly talented and, it had to be said, stupidly good-looking heroes.

And the best-looking of the bunch, in her opinion, was dating her older sister Shay.

Rory poured herself a cup of coffee and leaned her butt against the counter. Shay and Mac made perfect sense, she told herself. Again. Shay was a model and a TV presenter. Mac was the supertalented, superfine center for the city's beloved hockey team. They were the perfect age, she was twenty-three and Mac a year older, and, according to the press, because they were both beautiful and successful, a perfect match.

It was all perfectly perfect.

Except that Rory wasn't convinced.

And that wasn't because Mac made her toes tingle and her stomach jump. It had nothing to do with her insane attraction to the man. No, she'd spent enough time around Shay and Mac to see the cracks in their relationship, to know the bloom was off the rose and Shay was acting like a loon. Judging by Mac's wary, closed-off expression whenever Rory saw them together, Shay had him on the Crazy Express.

Rory would bet her last dollar Shay was feeling desperate, calling and texting relentlessly whenever they were apart. Since they both had such demanding careers, they were apart *a lot*.

Rory knew why Shay was insecure, why she couldn't trust a man. Rory had grown up in the same house as Shay. The difference between them was that Shay kept hoping there was one man out there who could be faithful and monogamous.

Rory was pretty damn sure that, like unicorns and the yeti, such a creature didn't exist.

Rory scowled and wrapped her hands around her mug. Shay hadn't told Mac why she was acting crazy, Rory was pretty sure of that. To complicate matters further, Rory and Mac had somehow become friends. Sadly, that was all they could ever be. He was too good-looking, too much of a celebrity, too far out of her league. She was a college student. He was a successful player, both on and off the ice… Oh, and that other little thing—*he was her sister's boyfriend!*

Besides all that, Mac treated Rory as he would a younger sister. He teased her, argued with her and made her laugh. So she'd caught him watching her with a brooding look on that sexy face once or twice but she wasn't an idiot, she knew it didn't mean anything. He'd probably wanted to talk to her about Shay, wanted advice on how to deal with her volatility. Rory *never* wanted to have that conversation.

A couple of nights ago, he'd given her a lift home from work and she'd been surprised when he didn't mention Shay. Why he'd waited for Rory to finish her waitressing shift was still a mystery but sitting in his sports car, shoulder to shoulder, saying next to nothing, had been the best twenty minutes of her life.

He'd walked her to the door of her lousy apartment building—the same building that currently had no heat—and he'd stood there looking down at her. Something in his expression had heat swirling in her stomach; he'd looked like a man about to kiss a woman. But she knew that had to be her imagination working overtime. He was dating Shay, tall, slim, stunning.

But, just for a moment, she'd thought he'd wanted to kiss her, to taste her, to yank her into his arms… Rory sighed. It wasn't possible. He was dating her sister. He was permanently off-limits; messing in Shay's relationship was a line she would not cross. Thinking about Mac, like that, was a flight of fancy she had no right to take. Enough of that now.

Rory heard the front door open and she waited for Shay's yell that she was home. It didn't come, and Rory heard heavy footsteps on the wooden floor, a tread that couldn't possibly belong to her sister. The saliva in her mouth dried up and her heart rolled; there was only one other person who had a key to Shay's apartment and he was the one person Rory didn't want to be alone with.

In her pajamas, with crazy hair, sans makeup and bra-less.

Mac appeared in the doorway to the kitchen, scowled at her and ran a hand over his tired face. He had a light bruise on his jaw—he'd obviously traded blows on the ice—and the beginnings of a black eye but his injuries looked superficial. It was the emotion she saw in his dark eyes that held her rooted to the spot; he looked frustrated and wound up.

"Where's your sister?" he demanded, his deep, rough voice rumbling over her skin.

"Hello to you too." Rory shrugged and his frown deepened at her response. "I have no idea where she is. Are you okay?"

Mac let out a low, humorless laugh. "Hell, no, I'm screwed." He scowled at her and placed his hands on his hips. "Why are you here?"

"Heat's out in my apartment. Shay said I could sleep here so I don't freeze."

"Just my friggin' luck," Mac muttered.

"Jeez, what's your problem?" Rory asked him as he shrugged out of his expensive leather jacket and tossed it onto the granite counter. A long-sleeved black T-shirt clung to his broad chest and fell, untucked, over well-fitting jeans. He looked hot and tired and so damn sexy she could jump him right now, right where he stood.

Sister's boyfriend, she reminded herself as he walked over to the fridge, pulled out a microbrewed beer and cracked the top. He took a long swallow, sighed and, closing his eyes, placed the bottle against his forehead.

"Bitching, horrible, freakin' revolting day."

She wouldn't have thought the big badass of the Mavericks could sound so melodramatic. "It couldn't have been that dire—you won the game."

Mac's ink-blue eyes lasered into hers. "Did you watch?" he asked, his question as pointed as a spear tip.

Rory shook her head. "Nah, had to study. Why?"

"Because I was wondering why my head was still attached to my neck."

Rory narrowed her eyes. "What did you do?"

Instead of answering, he gave her a long look. Then he placed his bottle on the center island and walked toward her. He gripped the counter, one hand on either side of her body. He was like a big human cage, she thought.

Up close and personal, she could see the slight tinge of auburn in his stubble, notice how long his eyelashes were, could see a faded scar on his top lip. And man, he smelled so good. She wanted to stand on her toes and kiss that scar, run her lips over that bruise on his jaw, kiss his eye better.

Sister's boyfriend, sister's boyfriend…she had no right to be standing this close to Mac, tasting his breath, feeling his heat. Playing with fire, coloring outside the lines was something her father did, his worst trait, yet despite that sobering thought she couldn't make herself move away, was unable to duck under Mac's arm. Even though Mac belonged to Shay, Rory wanted just one kiss from him. She wanted to know what he tasted like, how strong his arms felt around her, how it felt to be plastered against that solid wall of muscle. *Just one kiss*...

Gray eyes clashed with blue as his mouth hovered above hers. As she stood there, *so* close and *so* personal, she knew exactly what he'd do, how she'd feel...

His lips would slide across hers, cool, strong...smart. She'd open her mouth to protest, to say they couldn't do this—or to let him in, who knew—and he wouldn't hesitate. As his tongue slid into her mouth, his hand on her lower back would pull her into him and his other hand would delve beneath the elastic of her flannel bottoms to cup a butt cheek. His kiss would turn deeper and wetter and her hands would burrow under his loose T-shirt and explore the muscles of his back, his shoulders, his fabulously ripped stomach.

She'd think that it was wrong but she wouldn't be able to stop herself. Mac would, ever so slowly, pull her T-shirt up to expose her too-small breasts and she'd whimper into his mouth and push her hips against him, needing to rub herself against his hard, hard erection. He'd be what a man felt like, strong, hot, in control...

"I just saw our entire kiss in your eyes. God, that was so hot," Mac growled, and she tasted his sweet breath on her lips again.

"We can't, it's wrong." Rory pushed the words up her throat, past her teeth, through her lips. Four words and she felt like she'd run a marathon.

Mac's eyes stayed locked on hers and, in case she missed the desire blazing there, his erection nudging her knee let her know how much he wanted her. Mac wanted her…he really did. Tall, built, smelling great, gorgeous… how was she supposed to resist him?

Sister's boyfriend, sister's boyfriend…

Rory placed her hands on his pecs and pushed. Mac stepped back but as he did, he lifted his hand to run his knuckle over her cheek. That small, tender action nearly shattered her resolve and she had to grab the edge of the counter with both hands to keep from launching herself into his arms, wrapping her legs around his hips and feasting on that fallen-angel mouth.

So this was primal lust, crazy passion. She wasn't sure she liked how out of control it made her feel. Squirmy, hot, breathless…it was intensely tempting to throw caution to the wind and get lost in the moment. Did having such a flammable reaction to Mac mean that she was more like her dad than she thought? Ugh. This wasn't going to happen, she decided. From this point on she would not kiss, touch or think about her sister's boyfriend. This stopped. Now.

Rory held up a hand. "Back up."

Mac took two steps back and she could breathe. She felt the craziness recede. He jammed his hands into the pockets of his jeans and sent her a brooding look. "That was…"

"Wrong? Crazy? A betrayal of my sister?"

Mac frowned. "Let's not get carried away here. We didn't even kiss."

"We wanted to!"

"But we didn't so let's not get too caught up in the melodrama." Mac picked up his beer, sipped and sighed. His head snapped up and Rory heard the front door closing, heard her sister kicking off her heels. Rory tried to keep her face blank but she felt like her brain and heart were on fire as guilt and shame pricked her skin.

We didn't actually kiss but I really, really wanted to...

"You're here." Shay tossed the words at Mac as she stepped into the kitchen. Rory frowned. Shay didn't walk up to Mac and kiss him. It was what she did, every single time she saw him, whether they'd been apart five minutes or five weeks.

Mac made no effort to touch Shay either. He just stood there wearing that inscrutable face Rory knew he used when he wanted to avoid a scene.

But a scene, she knew it like she knew her own signature, was what they were about to have. Why?

Rory turned her eyes to her sister's face. She recognized that expression, a mixture of betrayal, broken trust, hurt and humiliation. God, she looked devastated.

"What the hell, Mac?" Shay's shout bounced off the walls.

Rory's gaze jumped around the room. How could Shay know? Did she have cameras in the apartment? X-ray vision? A girlfriend's gut instinct?

Mac held his hands up. "I'm sorry, Shay, for all of it. I never meant to hurt you."

"Yet you're doing such a fine job of it." Shay wiped her eyes with the back of her wrist. "There were easier ways to get rid of me, Mac. You didn't have to humiliate me on national TV."

Rory looked at Mac and then at Shay. Okay, maybe this conversation had nothing to do with Rory and the almost-kiss. "What are you talking about? What did he do?"

Shay let out a laugh that held absolutely no amusement. "You haven't seen it?"

"Seen what?"

Shay's laugh was brittle. "Well, you're probably the only person in the city—the country—who hasn't!" She lunged for the remote on the counter and jabbed her finger on the buttons to get the TV to power up. While she flipped through channels, Rory snuck a look at Mac. He gripped the bridge of his nose with his finger and thumb and he looked utterly miserable.

Sad, sorry and, to be frank, at the end of his rope.

"And in today's sports news, Maverick's center Mac McCaskill was caught on an open mic commenting on sex, monogamy and hot women."

Rory snapped her head up and looked at the screen. Footage of the post-match news appeared on the screen. Quinn, Kade and Mac lounged behind a table draped with the Maverick's logo. Kade said something that was too low to hear and the three of them laughed.

"The blonde reporter in the third row is seriously hot." Quinn's voice was muffled and she could just hear his words.

"Did you see the redhead?" Kade demanded, his voice equally muted. "I have a thing for redheads."

"You have a thing for all women." Mac's voice was clear and loud; obviously his was the only microphone that was live. Oh…shoot.

"Like you do. When are you going to give up this relationship BS and start playing the field again?" Quinn demanded. "It's not like you're particularly happy with your ball and chain."

"I'm not and you're right, monogamy sucks," Mac said, looking past Quinn. Rory recognized that smile, the appreciation in his eyes. "Your blonde from the third row is very hot."

"Shay is also hot," Kade pointed out.

"Yeah but she's crazy. Besides, I'm bored with tall and built. I'm thinking that petite might be a nice change of pace— Why is Vernon gesturing to me to shut up?"

Then a rash of swear words was followed by: "My mic is on!"

Rory looked at Shay, who'd dropped into a chair at the kitchen table with a vacant look in her eyes. She'd stopped crying and she looked like she'd checked out, mentally and emotionally. Mac picked up his jacket from the counter and walked over to stand in front of Shay. He bent his knees so he could look directly into her face.

"I'm sorry I spoke behind your back and I'm so sorry that I hurt you, Shay. It wasn't my intention. I take full responsibility for running my mouth off. Not my finest moment and I *am* very sorry."

When Shay looked through him and didn't respond, he slowly stood up and placed his apartment key on the counter. Rory looked at her broken, desperately sad sister, grabbed Mac by the arm and pulled him into the hall, feeling as if her gray eyes must be full of angry lightning.

When their eyes met, he lifted one broad shoulder. "Told you I was screwed," he said.

"So you came over here to screw me?" she demanded, thinking about that almost-kiss, fury clogging her throat.

Mac's flashing eyes met hers. "Believe it or not, I'm not that much of a bastard. I didn't even know you would be here."

"What were you thinking, Mac?" she demanded, insanely angry. On behalf of her sister, but also because Rory had trusted him just as Shay had. "You've done so many interviews, you know how mics work."

"I wasn't thinking, dammit!"

Red dots appeared in front of Rory's eyes. "Did you plan this? Was the smack talk an easy way to get out of your relationship with Shay?"

"Contrary to the evidence, I am better than that."

Rory snorted. "You could've fooled me. First you insult my sister, then you almost kiss me? What was *that* about?"

Mac let out a harsh, angry breath. "I knew when I left that news conference that I was toast. I regret what I said. I came here to apologize to Shay but found you instead—"

"So you were angry and frustrated and I was there, a handy way to let off some steam!" Rory interrupted.

Mac's curses filled the small hallway.

Rory drilled a finger into his chest. "How many times have you cheated on Shay? Because that move with me was far too practiced to be your first time!" The red dots turned scarlet and her chest tightened.

Mac stepped back and anger sparked in his eyes. "I'm only going to say this once. I never cheated on your sister. And, babe, you wanted to kiss me as much as I wanted to kiss you! I'll take full responsibility for being a prick on national television but I *will not* take *all* the blame for what almost happened in there."

Guilt swamped her. She knew he was right and she hated it. She didn't want to shoulder *any* of the blame; it would be a lot easier if she could just blame him for everything: for being too sexy, for making her want something she had no right to want.

Mac raked his fingers through his hair. "Look, why don't we let this situation settle down and I'll call you? We can have coffee, chat. Sort this out?"

Pick up where we left off?

That wasn't going to happen. There was no way she could date someone who'd dated—*slept with*—her sister, who'd almost cheated on her. Someone who'd made Rory so crazy with lust that she'd almost betrayed her sister! He would've kissed her had she not stopped him. He would've cheated...of that she was categorically convinced.

She could never trust him.

Ever.

"Don't bother. I'm not interested." Rory walked around him, yanked open the front door and gestured for him to leave. "Go. You've created enough havoc for one evening, for one lifetime."

Mac, with a final inscrutable look, walked out of the Kydd sisters' lives. *Good riddance*, Rory thought. The last thing either of them needed was a cheating, backstabbing man in their lives.

Rory turned and saw her sister standing in the kitchen doorway. She'd heard every word of their conversation. So she'd stopped the kiss. That meant little. The truth remained: she wanted Shay's man, wanted him badly. They both knew she was more like their dirtbag father than either of them had thought possible. Shay was going to strip layers of skin off her and Rory deserved it.

"You two almost kissed? You had a moment?"

Facing her sister, she couldn't deny the truth. "Yes. I'm really sorry."

"Okay then. Thanks for getting rid of him," Shay told Rory in a cold and hard voice. "Now get the hell out of my apartment and my life."

One

Ten or so years later...

Rory made her way to a small table by the window in the crowded cafeteria of St. Catherine's Hospital, juggling a stack of files, her bag and a large blueberry smoothie. Dumping the files on the table, she took a berry-flavored hit before pulling out a chair and dropping into it. She'd been on the go since before seven, had missed lunch and was now running on fumes. She had two more patients to see. She might be able to get home before eight.

An early night. Bliss.

Her cell phone chimed and Rory squinted at the display, smiling when she saw her sister's name.

"Sorry, something just came up. I'll call you right back," Shay stated before disconnecting.

Rory smiled, grateful that she and Shay were really

close, a minor miracle after the McCaskill incident. Mac running his mouth off and his subsequent breakup with Shay had been the first major media storm involving one of the three most famous Mavericks. It had been the catalyst for the city's fascination with anything to do with Mac, Quinn and Kade.

Shay had been swept up into the madness; she'd been stalked and hassled by reporters and photographers for months. Her life had been a living hell. Unfortunately, because she refused to talk to Rory, Shay had weathered the media attention by herself. She'd lost weight and, as Rory had found out years later, she'd come close to a breakdown. Rory was so grateful the incident was solidly behind them; the man-slut captain of the Mavericks professional ice hockey team was not worth losing sleep, never mind a sister, over.

Except that she did, frequently, still lose sleep thinking about him. Rory sighed. He was her fantasy man, the man she always thought of when she was alone and well, she hated to admit it…horny. She wondered and she imagined and the fact that she did either—both—annoyed the pants off her.

The jerk.

Her cell rang again, Rory answered and Shay said a quick hello. "Sorry, as you picked up the delivery guy arrived."

"No worries, what's up?"

"Dane sent me two dozen red roses."

And, judging by Shay's frantic voice, this was a problem? "Okay, lucky you. Why are you freaking out?"

"Two dozen red roses? Who sends his wife of eight months two dozen red roses? He must be cheating on me."

Here we go again, Rory thought, exasperated. *I haven't*

had enough coffee to cope with Shay's insecurities. Thanks again, Dad, for the incredible job you did messing up your daughters' love lives.

Rory sucked on her straw musing about the fact that she and Shay had different approaches to life and love. She was closed off to the idea of handing her heart over to a man, yet Shay had never given up on love. She had eventually, she was convinced, caught the last good guy in the city. The fact that Dane was calm and strong enough to deal with Shay's insecurities made Rory love him more.

"He must be having an affair. Nobody can work as much as he does," Shay fretted.

"Shay! Princess!" Rory interrupted her mumblings. "Stop obsessing, you're getting yourself into a state. You're a gorgeous blonde ex-model and you still look like a million dollars. Dane married you and you promised to trust him."

Shay sighed. "I did, didn't I?"

"Look at your wedding photos. Look at how he's looking at you…like you're the moon and stars and everything that's perfect." In spite of her cynicism when it came to romance, Rory couldn't help feeling a little jealous every time Dane looked at her sister, love blazing from his eyes. What must it feel like to have someone love you that much, someone so determined to make you happy? Logically, she knew the risk wasn't worth it, but…damn, seeing that look punched her in the heart every time.

"Dane is in the middle of a big case—some gang shooting, remember? And he's the homicide detective in charge—and sending you roses is his way of reminding you that he loves you."

"So, no affair?"

"No affair, Shay." And if there was—there wasn't!—but if there was then Rory would take Dane's own weapon and shoot him with it.

Rory said goodbye to her sister, shot off a text to Dane suggesting Shay might need a little extra attention—she and her brother-in-law worked as a team to keep Shay's insecurities from driving them both nuts—and looked down at the folders. She needed to make notes and read over the files of the two patients she was about to see.

She so wanted her own practice. Craydon's Physiotherapy patients were channeled through the system like cans on a conveyor line. There was little time for proper one-on-one care and she was providing patients with only enough treatment to see them through to the next session. Sometimes she wondered if she was doing any good at all.

If she had her own place, she'd slow it down, take more time, do some intensive therapy. But setting up a new practice required cash she didn't have, premises she couldn't afford. She'd just have to keep saving… Maybe one day.

She had barely looked over the first file when her cell rang again. This time it was a number she did not recognize. She answered the call with a cautious hello.

"Rory? Kade Webb, from the Vancouver Mavericks. We met a long time ago."

Kade Webb? Why on earth would he be calling her? "I remember…hi. What can I do for you?"

Kade didn't waste time beating around the bush. "I have a player in St. Catherine's, in The Annex Clinic, and I'd like you to take a look at his chart, assess his injury and tell me what you think."

Rory frowned, thinking fast. "Kade, the Mavericks

have a resident physiotherapist. I know because my bosses would kill for the Mavericks' contract. Why me?"

"Because you have an excellent track record in treating serious sports injuries," Kade replied. "Will you do it? Take a look and let me know what you think?"

"I—"

"Thanks. I'll call you back in a couple of hours."

Rory wanted to tell him that she had patients, that it was against company policy, but he was gone. Argh! She had questions, dammit! Who was the player? What room he was in? Did he know that she was coming? Had Kade spoken to her bosses about this?

Infuriating man, she thought as she stood up and gathered her possessions. It was said that Kade, like his two partners in crime, could charm the dew off roses and the panties off celibates. He hadn't bothered to use any of that charm on her, Rory thought with an annoyed toss of her head.

Not that she would've responded to it, but it would've been nice for him to try.

Mac McCaskill, you stupid idiot, Rory thought.

She'd had many variations of the thought over the past decade, some expressed in language a lot more colorful, but the sentiment was the same. However, this was the first time in nearly a decade that she wasn't mocking his tendency to jump from one gorgeous woman to another or shaking her head over the fact that he was, essentially, a man-slut.

As much as his social life irritated her, she felt sorry for him. He was an exceptionally talented player and as she looked at the notes on his chart, she realized his arm was, to use nontechnical terms, wrecked. For a player of his caliber that was a very scary situation.

"Rory, what are you doing in here?"

Rory, standing next to Mac's bed, flipped a glance over her shoulder and smiled, relieved, when she saw her best friend stepping into Mac's private room. If it had been someone other than Troy she would've had to explain herself.

This was all kinds of wrong, she thought. There were protocols around patient visits and she shouldn't be in Mac's room, looking at his chart, assessing his injury. She should've refused Kade's request, but here she was again, flouting the rules. What was it about McCaskill that made her do that?

"I need to get the mat on him, need to get his circulation restored as soon as possible," she said with urgency.

As a therapist, she wanted the best for him. Even if he was the man who'd hurt her sister. Even if her heart rate still kicked up from just looking at him.

"You're not authorized to treat him and if you're caught we'll both be fired." Troy closed the door behind him, his handsome face creased with worry.

"I'll take full responsibility," Rory retorted. "It's his *arm*, Troy. The arm he needs to slap those pucks into the net at ninety miles an hour."

"Mac usually reaches speeds of a hundred plus miles an hour," Troy, the sports fanatic, corrected her, as she'd counted on him doing.

"Exactly and the mat will start helping immediately," Rory retorted.

"Jobs, fired, on the streets," Troy muttered. Yet he didn't protest when she pulled a mat from her bag and placed the control box it was connected to on Mac's bedside table. When the lights brightened, she very gently wrapped the mat around Mac's injured arm. He didn't stir and Rory relaxed; he was solidly asleep and would be for a while.

Troy was right to worry. Earlier, she'd hesitated and had stood outside of his room, debating whether to go in. Partly because of that almost-kiss years ago, partly because she knew she shouldn't be there, despite Kade's request.

The bottom line was that Mac was a sportsman who needed her expertise and her mat. It was crucial to get his blood flowing through the damaged capillaries to start the healing process. The longer she delayed, the longer he would take to recover. Healing, helping, was what she did, who she was, and she'd fight the devil himself to give a patient what he needed, when he needed it.

Besides, there was little chance of her being discovered in Mac's room. The Annex Clinic was an expensive, private ward attached to St. Catherine's, the hospital situated in the exclusive Vancouver suburb of West Point Gray. Every patient admitted into The Annex had two things in common: they were ridiculously wealthy and they wanted total privacy. Each patient had their own private nurse, and Rory had lucked out because Troy was assigned to room 22.

Not only would he keep her interference a secret, but because he was in the room with her, Rory resisted the urge to run her hand through Mac's thick hair, over his strong jaw shaded with stubble.

He looked as good as he had years ago. Maybe better.

His beard was dark but when he grew it out, it glinted red in the sun. As did his dark brown hair. The corners of his eyes had creases that weren't there a decade ago. He looked, if she ignored his bandaged arm, stronger, fitter and more ripped than he had at twenty-four.

She was a professional, she reminded herself, and she shouldn't be mentally drooling over the man.

"How did you even know he was admitted?" Troy demanded.

"Are you sure he's asleep?" she asked Troy, ignoring his question.

"Morphine. He was in severe pain and it was prescribed." Troy looked at his watch. "Getting back to my point, he only came out of surgery two hours ago and was injured no more than six hours ago. How did you know he was here?"

Rory stood back from the bed and pushed her hands into her lower back as she stretched and explained that Kade, who'd taken on the CEO responsibilities and duties when the owner/manager of the Vancouver Mavericks died, had called and asked her to check on Mac and give her professional opinion.

Troy frowned, worried. "Which is?"

"It's bad, Troy."

Troy swore and Rory knew his disappointment and concern would be shared by most of the residents of Vancouver, Mavericks and Canucks fans alike. Mac was a hell of a player and respected for his leadership and skill. Maverick fans would be devastated to lose their captain for a couple of matches. To lose him for the season would be a disaster. Losing him forever would be a tragedy. But she'd treated enough sport stars to know the impact of his injury, both physical and emotional, would be tremendous.

"How did the surgery go?" Rory asked Troy.

"Good." Troy cleared his throat. "We really could get

fired, Rorks. Even though I know the voodoo blanket helps, it's still a form of treatment and you're not authorized. I like my job."

Rory knew he was right, but she still rolled her eyes at her best friend. "As I've explained to you a million times before, the blanket is not voodoo! It sends electromagnetic signals that stimulate the pumping of the smallest blood vessels. It will help normalize the circulation in this injured area. Kade asked me to be here. He'll work it out. It'll be okay, Troy."

When Troy narrowed his bright green eyes, Rory looked away. "This will run for the next thirty minutes," she said. "Why don't you go get some coffee?"

She needed to be alone with Mac, to get her thoughts—and her reaction to him—under control.

"Ok, I'll be back in thirty."

Troy sent her a worried smile and left the room. When the door closed behind him, she turned back to Mac and couldn't resist the impulse to place her hand on his chest, directly over his heart. Under the thin cotton of the hospital gown she felt the warmth of his skin.

She kept her hand there, trying not to wish she could run it over his hard stomach, down the thick biceps of his uninjured arm. He was so big, his body a testament to a lifetime dedicated to professional sports, to being the hardest, toughest, fastest player on the ice.

She glanced toward the end of the bed at his chart. Reading the chicken scrawl again wouldn't change a damn thing. Essentially, Mac had pulled a tendon partly off the bone and injured a ligament. The surgeons doubted he'd regain his former strength anytime soon, if ever.

That would kill him. Even in the short time they'd known each other, she'd understood that hockey was what

Mac did, who he was. He'd dedicated the last fourteen years to the Mavericks. He was their star player, their leader, the reason fans filled the arena week after week. He was their hope, their idol, the public face of the well-oiled machine Kade managed.

With his crooked smile, his aloof but charming manner and incredible prowess on the ice, he was the city's favorite, regularly appearing in the press, usually with a leggy blonde on his arm. Speculating about when one of the Mavericks Triumvirate—Mac, their captain, Kade as CEO and Quinn as Acting Coach (the youngest in the NHL but widely respected) were all hot and single—would fall in love and settle down was a citywide pastime.

A part of him belonged to the city but Rory doubted that anyone, besides his best friends, knew him. From that time so long ago she knew that Mac, for all his charm, was a closed book. Very little was known about his life before he was recruited to play for the Mavericks. Even Shay hadn't known more than what was public knowledge: he was raised by a single mother who died when he was nineteen, he was a scholarship kid and he didn't talk about his past.

They had that in common. Rory didn't talk about her past either.

Rory adjusted the settings on the control box and Mac shifted in his sleep, releasing a small pain-filled moan. He would hate to know that she'd heard him, she thought. Mac, she remembered, had loathed being sick. He'd played with a broken finger, flu, a sprained ankle, a hurt knee. He'd play through plagues of locusts and an asteroid strike.

Rory looked at his injured arm and sighed. He wouldn't

be able to play through this. How was she supposed to tell Kade that?

A big, hot hand touched her throat and a thumb stroked her jaw. Her brain shut down when he touched her and, just like she had in Shay's kitchen, she couldn't help responding. She allowed her head to snuggle into his hand as he slowly opened his eyes and focused on her face. His fabulous eyes, the deep, dark blue of old-fashioned bottled ink, met hers.

"Hey," he croaked.

"Hey back," Rory whispered, her fingers digging into the skin on his chest. She should remove herself but, once again, she stayed exactly where she was.

So nothing much had changed then. She hadn't grown up at all.

"They must have given me some powerful drugs because you seem so damn real."

Rory shuddered as his thumb brushed over her bottom lip. He thought he was imagining her, she realized.

"Helluva dream… God, you're so beautiful." Mac's hand drifted down her throat over her collarbone. His fingers trailed above the cotton of her tunic to rest on the slight swell of her breast. His eyes, confused and pain-filled, stayed on her face, tracing her features and drinking her in.

Then he heaved in a sigh and the blue deepened to midnight. "My arm is on fire."

"I know, Mac." Rory touched his hair, then his cheek, and her heart double-tapped when he turned his face into her palm, as if seeking comfort. She tried to pull her hand away but Mac slapped his hand on hers to keep her palm against his cheek. Everyone, even the big, bold

Mac, needed support, a human connection. At the moment she was his.

"It's bad, isn't it?"

What should she say? She didn't want to lie to him, but she had no right to talk to him about his injuries. She shouldn't even be here. "You'll be okay, Mac. No matter what, you'll be okay."

Pain—the deep, dark, emotional kind—jumped into his eyes. His hand moved to her wrist and he pulled her down until her chest rested on his. Her mouth was a quarter inch from his. God, this was so wrong. She shouldn't be doing this. Despite those thoughts ricocheting through her head she couldn't help the impulse to feel those lips under hers, to taste him.

Just once to see if the reality measured up to her imagination.

This would be the perfect time, *the only time*, to find out. She could stop wondering and move the hell past him, past the kiss they'd never shared.

There was no one in the room with them. Nobody would ever know.

His injured state hadn't affected his skills, Rory thought as he took control of the kiss, tipping her head to achieve the precise angle he wanted. His tongue licked its way into her mouth, nipping here, sliding there. Then their tongues met and electricity rocketed through her as she sank into him.

It was all she'd dreamed about. And a lot more.

Rory had no idea how long the kiss lasted. She was yanked back to the present when Mac hissed in pain. Stupid girl! He'd had surgery only hours before! He was in a world of hurt. Mac, she noticed, just lay there, his hand on her thigh and his eyes closed. He was so still. Had he fallen back to sleep? Rory looked down at his big tanned hand and licked her top lip, tasting him there.

It had been just two mouths meeting, tongues dancing, but his kisses could move mountains, part seas, redesign constellations. It had been that powerful. Kissing Mac was an out-of-body experience.

The universe knew what it was doing by keeping them apart. She wasn't looking for a man and she certainly wasn't looking for a man like Mac. Too big, too bold, too confident. A celebrity who had never heard of the word *monogamy*.

He was exactly what she didn't need. Unfaithful. She was perfectly content to fly solo, she reminded herself.

The machine beeped to tell her the program had ended, and Rory started to stand up. The hand squeezing her thigh kept her in place. When she looked at Mac, his eyes were still closed but the corners of his mouth kicked up into a cocky smile.

"Best dream ever," he said before slipping back into sleep.

Two

He'd been dreaming of Rory, something he hadn't done in years, Mac realized as he surfaced out of a pain-saturated sleep. She'd been sitting cross-legged on his bed, her silver-gray eyes dancing. Wide smile, firm breasts, golden-brown hair that was so long, he remembered, that it flirted with her butt...five foot three of petite perfection.

In his dream he'd been French-kissing her and it had felt...man...amazing! Slow, hot, sexy—what a kiss should really be. Okay, he'd had far too many drugs if he was obsessing about a girl he'd wanted to kiss a lifetime ago. Mac shoved his left hand through his hair before pushing himself up using the same hand, trying but failing to ignore the slamming pain in his other arm as he moved.

This was bad. This was very, very bad.

Half lying, half sitting, he closed his eyes and fought the nausea gathering in his throat. Dimly aware of people entering his private hospital room, he fought the pain, pushed down the nausea and concentrated on those silver eyes he'd seen in his dream. The way her soft lips felt under his...

He had been dreaming, right?

"Do you need something for the pain, Mr. McCaskill?"

Mac jerked fully awake and looked into the concerned face of a guy a few years younger than him.

"I'm Troy Hunter, your nurse," he said. "So, some meds? You're due."

"Hell yes," Mac muttered. He usually hated drugs but he slowly rolled onto his good side, presenting his butt to be jabbed as Kade and Quinn walked into the room. "Hey, guys."

Troy glanced at Mac's visitors with his mouth dropped open, looking like any other fan did when the three of them were together...awestruck.

Tall and rock solid, in both stature and personality, Mac wasn't surprised to see Kade and Quinn and so soon after his surgery. They were his friends, his one-time roommates, his colleagues...his family. They were, in every way that counted, his brothers.

After giving him the injection, Troy pulled up Mac's shorts and stood back to look at him, his face and tone utterly professional. "Let's get you sorted out. I need to do my boring nurse stuff and then I'll leave you to talk." He looked more closely at Mac. "You look uncomfortable."

Mac nodded. He was half lying and half sitting but the thought of moving made him break out in a cold sweat. "Yeah, I am."

"I can remedy that." Troy, with surprising ease and

gentleness for a man who was six-three and solid, maneuvered Mac into a position he could live with. While Troy wound a blood pressure cuff around Mac's arm, Kade sat down in the chair on the opposite side of the bed, his expression serious.

"We would appreciate your discretion as to Mac's condition," he told Troy. That voice, not often employed, usually had sponsors, players and random citizens scattering.

Troy, to his credit, didn't look intimidated. "I don't talk about my patients. Ever."

Kade stared at Troy for a long time before nodding once. "Thank you."

They waited in silence until Troy left the room and then Kade turned to him and let out a stream of profanity.

Here it comes, Mac thought, resigned.

"What were you thinking, trying to move that fridge yourself? One call and one of us would've been there to help you!"

Mac shrugged. "It wasn't that heavy. It started to fall and I tried to catch it."

"Why the hell can't you just ask for help?" Quinn demanded. "It's serious, Mac, career-ending serious."

Mac felt the blood in his face drain away. When he could speak, he pushed the words out between dry lips. "That bad, huh?"

Kade looked as white as Mac imagined himself to be. "That bad."

"Physiotherapy?" Mac demanded.

"An outside chance at best," Quinn answered him. He didn't sugarcoat his words, and Mac appreciated it. He needed the truth.

Kade spoke again. "We've found someone to work

with you. She's reputed to be the best at sports rehabilitation injuries."

Neither of his friends met his eyes, and his heart sank to his toes. He knew that look, knew that he wouldn't like what was coming next.

"Who? Nurse Ratched?" he joked.

"Rory Kydd," Kade told him, his face impassive.

"Rory? *What?*" he croaked, not liking the frantic note in his voice. It was bad enough seeing Rory in his dreams but being her patient would mean hitting the seventh level of hell.

There was a reason why he never thought of her, why he'd obliterated that day from his memory. He'd publicly humiliated himself and the world had seen him at his worst. Rory'd had a front-row seat to the behind-the-scenes action.

Saying what he had on that open mic had been bad enough but almost kissing his about-to-be ex's sister was unforgiveable. At the time he'd been thinking of Rory a lot, had been, strangely, attracted to Shay's petite but feisty younger sister. But he should never have caged her in, tempting them both. He knew better than to act on those kinds of feelings, even if his relationship with Shay had been sliding downhill.

His mother's many messy affairs had taught him to keep his own liaisons clean, to remove himself from one situation before jumping into another. He'd forgotten those lessons the moment Rory looked at him with her wide, lust-filled eyes. His big brain shut down as his little brain perked up…

In the months afterward he hadn't missed Shay—too needy, too insecure—but he had missed talking to, teasing, laughing with Rory. She'd been, before he mucked it up, his first real female friend.

That day he'd also unwittingly created a media superstorm and a public persona for himself. He'd been branded a player, a party-hard, commitment-phobic prick whose two objectives in life were to play with a puck and to chase skirts.

They had it half right…

Yes, he liked the occasional party and was commitment-phobic. Yes, he loved to play with a puck and yeah, he had sex, but not as much or with as many woman as was suggested in the tabloids. These days he was a great deal more discriminating about who he took into his bed, and it had been a couple of months since he'd been laid.

He looked down at his arm and scowled. It seemed like it would be a few more.

Quinn gripped the railing at the end of the bed with his massive hands. "Rory is the best and God knows you need the best. We need her because everything we've worked toward for the past five years is about to slip from our fingers because you were too pigheaded to ask for help!"

Kade frowned at their hotheaded friend. "Take it easy, Quinn. It wasn't like he did it on purpose."

No, but it was his fault. Mac tipped his head up to look at the ceiling. He'd failed again today, failed his team, his friends, his future.

And it looked like, once again, Rory would be there to witness it.

There had to be another option. "Find someone else! Anyone else!"

"Don't be a moron!" Quinn told him.

Kade, always the voice of reason, stepped between them before they started to yell. "You'll work with her while we do damage control on our end."

Mac rested his head on his pillow, feeling the sedative effects of whatever the nurse had stuck in him. Ignoring the approaching grogginess, he sucked in some deep breaths and forced his brain to work.

Dammit, why did Vernon Hasselback have to die before they'd concluded the deal they'd all been discussing for the past decade? It was a simple plan: when the time was right he and Kade and Quinn would buy the franchise from Vernon. They'd been working toward this since they were all rookie players and they'd hammered out a detailed plan to raise the cash, which included using their player fees and endorsement money to invest in business opportunities to fund their future purchase of the franchise. The strategy had worked well. Within a decade they had a rock-solid asset base and were, by anyone's standards, ridiculously wealthy. Money wasn't an issue. They could buy the franchise without breaking much of a sweat. But to take the team and its brand to the next level they needed a partner who brought certain skills to the table. Someone who had bigger and better connections in all facets of the media, who could open the doors to mega-sponsorship deals, who had merchandising experience.

Unfortunately, because Vernon died in the bed of his latest mistress, his widow and the beneficiary of his entire estate wasn't inclined to honor his wishes about passing the mantle on to the three of them. Myra wanted to sell the franchise to a Russian billionaire who'd acquired six sports teams in the past two years and was rebranding them to be generic, cardboard cutouts of the teams they once were and mouthpieces for his bland corporation. Kade had convinced Myra to give them some time but they knew she was impulsive and impatient. She would use any setback as an excuse to sell the franchise out from under them, and Mac's injury was a very big setback.

"No one can know how badly I'm injured."

Kade and Quinn nodded. "I'm very aware of that," Kade said. "I also have a potential investor on the hook. He's a loaded Mavericks fan, meets all our requirements and runs a massive media empire so nothing can jeopardize our negotiations. You are one of the reasons he wants to buy the team. He knows you only have a few more years left at this level and he wants you to spend that time mentoring the rookie talent."

So, no additional pressure then. Mac pushed the drowsiness away. "So I have to start playing with his team when the season opens."

"Essentially," Quinn replied, blowing air into his cheeks. "If not sooner."

Mac clenched his jaw in determination. It was the same attitude that had won the team the Stanley Cup two years ago, that had taken him from being just another rookie to one of the most exciting players of his generation. When he decided he was going to do something, achieve something, win something, nothing and nobody got in his way.

"Then I will be on the ice when the season opens."

If that meant working with Rory, so be it. Yes, he'd embarrassed himself a very long time ago. It happened and it was time to move the hell on. He refused to give in or give up—not while there was a chance of getting what he wanted.

"Set up the physio and let's get this party started."

Kade smiled. "You had surgery earlier today. How about getting some sleep first?"

"Are you convinced Rory is the best?" he asked with slightly slurred words.

Kade nodded. "Yeah, she is."

"Get her. Offer her what she needs so she can concentrate on me…" Stupid drugs, Mac thought, making him say the wrong thing. "On my arm. Not me."

Quinn placed a hand on Mac's good shoulder and squeezed. "Go to sleep, bud."

Mac managed a couple more words before slipping off into sleep. "Offer her whatever it takes…"

Rory paused outside the door to Mac's room the next day and hoisted her bag over her shoulder. She pushed her hand through her layered, choppy bob before smoothing out a crease that had appeared in her white and navy tunic, thinking that it had already been a weird day and it wasn't even mid-morning yet. Her day had started with Kade contacting her at the crack of dawn, demanding a meeting to discuss Mac and his injury. She'd told him she could only give Mac her assessment of his injuries and if Mac wanted Kade there, then that was his prerogative. Kade had seemed more amused than annoyed by her crisp tone and had followed up his demands by telling her he had a proposition for her…one that she'd want to hear.

That was intriguing enough to get her to meet with them during her morning break.

Just knock on the door and get this meeting over with, Rory told herself. *You are not nineteen anymore and desperately infatuated with your sister's boyfriend. You're a highly qualified professional who is in high demand. He's a patient like any other.*

Except none of her patients kissed her like he did, or flooded her system with take-me-quick hormones with one look from his navy eyes.

God, you are ridiculous, Rory thought, not amused.

Not allowing herself another minute to hesitate, she briskly knocked on the door, and when she heard his command to enter, she stepped inside. She ignored Mac's two friends standing on either side of his bed and her gaze immediately landed on his face. She told her libido to calm down and gave Mac a *professional* once-over. He was wearing a V-neck T-shirt and someone, probably Troy, had removed the right sleeve. His injured arm was bandaged from wrist to shoulder and was supported by a sling. Clear, annoyed and very wary eyes met hers.

Mac, she also noticed, was in pain but he was fighting his way through it.

Rory looked at his friends, good-looking guys, and smiled. "Hello, Kade. Quinn." Rory stepped toward the bed. "Mac. It's been a while."

Rory held her breath, waiting to see if he remembered the kiss they'd shared, whether he'd say anything about her being in his room the night before. His face remained inscrutable and the look in his eyes didn't change. Thank God, he didn't remember. That would make her life, and this experience, easier.

Or as easy as it could possibly be.

"Rory."

Her name on his lips, she'd never thought she'd hear it again. She desperately wished it wasn't under such circumstances. Rory gathered her wits and asked Quinn to move out of her way. When he did, she stepped up to the bed and pulled the smaller of the two blankets from her bag and placed the control box on the bedside table.

"What are you doing?" Mac demanded. "You're here to talk, not to fuss."

Rory looked him in the eye and didn't react to his growl. "And we will talk, after I set this up."

"What is it?" Kade demanded from his spot on the other side of the bed.

Rory explained how the blanket worked and gently tucked the mat around Mac's injured arm. She started the program, stepped back and folded her arms. "You need some pain meds," she told Mac.

"I'm fine," Mac muttered, his tone suggesting she back off. That wasn't going to happen. The sooner Mac learned that she wasn't easily intimidated, the better. The trick with difficult patients, and obstinate men, was to show no fear.

"You either take some meds or I walk out this door," Rory told him, her voice even. Her words left no doubt that she wasn't bluffing. She picked up the two pills that sat next to a glass of water and waited until Mac opened his hand to receive them. He sent her a dirty look, dry swallowed them and reluctantly chased them down with water from the glass she handed to him.

"You're not a martyr, nor a superhero, so take the meds on schedule," she told him in her best no-nonsense voice. Rory held his hot look and in his eyes she saw frustration morph into something deeper, darker, sexier.

Whoo boy! Internal temperature rising...

"You cut your hair," Mac said, tipping his head to the side.

"Quite a few times in the past decade," Rory replied, her voice tart. One of them had to get this conversation back on track and it looked like she'd been elected.

Fantastic kiss aside, Mac was a potential patient, nothing more, nothing less. She'd be professional if it killed her. She deliberately glanced at her watch and lifted her arched eyebrows. "I have another patient in thirty minutes…so let's skip the small talk and you can tell me why I'm really here."

"I need a physiotherapist."

"Obviously." Rory shrugged. "You're going to need a lot of therapy to get your arm working properly."

"I don't want it to work properly. I want it to be as good as new," Mac stated. "In two months' time."

"In your dreams." Okay, everyone knew Mac was determined but he wasn't stupid. "That's not going to happen. You know that's not possible."

Mac pulled on his stubborn expression. "It *is* going to happen and I'll be back on the ice with or without your help."

Rory sent Kade and Quinn a "help me" look but they just stood there. She was on her own, it seemed. "McCaskill, listen to me. You half ripped a tendon off the bone. It was surgically reattached. We don't know how much damage you've done to the nerves. This injury needs time to heal—"

"I don't have time," Mac told her. "I've got a couple of months and that's it."

Rory shoved her hands into her hair in sheer frustration. "You can sit out another couple of months—you are not indispensable!"

Dammit, her voice was rising. Not good. Do not let him rattle you!

"Two months and I need to be playing. That's it, Rory, that's all the time I've got," Mac insisted. "Now, either I get you to help me do that or I take my chances on someone else."

"Someone you will railroad into allowing you to do what you want, when you want, probably resulting in permanent damage." This was how he'd be in a relationship, she thought. All bossy and stubborn and determined to have his way.

After a lifetime of watching her father steamroll their mother, those weren't characteristics she'd ever tolerate.

"Maybe," was all Mac said.

Rory placed her hands on the bed and leaned forward, brows snapping together. "Why are you doing this, Mac? You have enough money, enough accolades to allow you to sit out a couple of months, a couple of seasons. This is not only unnecessary, it's downright idiotic!"

Mac pulled in a deep breath. For a split second she thought that he might explain, that he'd give her a genuine, responsible reason for his stance. Then his eyes turned inscrutable and she knew it wouldn't happen. "I play. That's what I do."

Rory shook her head, disappointed. He was still the same attention-seeking, hot-dogging, arrogant moron he'd been in his twenties. Did he really believe the hype that he was indispensable and indestructible?

"You're ridiculous, that's what you are," Rory said as she straightened. She sent his friends a blistering look. "You're supporting him in this?"

Kade and Quinn nodded, reluctantly, but they still nodded. Right, so it seemed like she was the only clear thinker in the room. She had to try one more time. "It's one season! You'd probably not even miss the entire season…"

Mac looked resolute. "I have to be there, Rory."

Mac had a will of iron. He was going to play, come hell or high water. She wouldn't be able to change his mind.

"It's my choice and I'll live with the consequences," Mac told her. "I'm not the type to create a storm and then bitch when it rains."

There was no doubting the sincerity in his words. Now, responsibility was something her father had never grasped, she thought. He'd been a serial adulterer and when he got caught—and he *always* got caught—there were a million reasons why it wasn't his fault. And, really, why was she thinking about her father? *Honestly, woman, concentrate!*

She might not agree with what Mac wanted to do, it was a colossal mistake in her professional opinion, but it seemed he was prepared to accept the consequences of his decisions. She had to respect that. But didn't have to be party to his madness.

She dropped her eyes from his face to look at the control box. "There's still twenty minutes to go. I'll ask Troy to disconnect the mat and pack it away. Have a nice life."

Rory turned around and walked toward the door, thinking that her bosses at Craydon's Physiotherapy would throw a hissy fit if they found out she'd turned down the opportunity to treat the great Mac McCaskill.

A part of her wanted to stay, to carry on trying to convince him—them—why this was the stupidest plan in history. *But you're not the jackass whisperer,* her brain informed her.

She had her hand on the door when Mac spoke again. "Rory, dammit...wait!"

Rory turned and saw the silent conversation taking place between the three friends. Kade nodded, Quinn looked frustrated but resigned and Mac looked annoyed.

Well, tough.

"Why can't anything ever be easy with you?" he muttered, and Rory lifted an eyebrow. This from the man who'd dissed Shay on national television and created a public scandal with her sister at the center? Who'd—sort of—made a move on Rory, thereby causing a riff between her and Shay that took many months to heal? Seriously?

"It isn't my job to make things easy for you," Rory retorted. "If there's nothing else…?"

"Hell yes, there's a big something else!" Mac snapped. "And if you repeat it I'll blow a gasket."

Rory just stared at him. The Kydd girls didn't blab. If they did they could've made themselves a nice chunk of change selling their Mac stories to the tabloids.

Mac rubbed the back of his neck with his good hand and proceeded to explain how his being hurt could materially affect the Mavericks. Rory listened, shocked, as Mac dissected the implications of his injury. "If Chenko buys the team, Kade will be replaced as CEO, Quinn's coaching contract won't be renewed and if I'm injured, I'm too old for them to give me another chance. The Mavericks will be turned into another corporate team—and I will *not* let that happen."

Rory took a moment to allow his words to make sense. When they did, her jaw tightened. The Mavericks were a Vancouver institution that had been owned by the Hasselbacks for generations and she knew—thanks to listening to Troy's rants on the subject over the years—that when corporate businesses took over sports teams, the magic dissipated. Traditions were lost; fans were disappointed; the players lost their individuality. It became soulless and clinical. She kept her eyes on Mac, pale-faced and stressed. "And if you do play?"

"Then we have a chance of saving the team."

"How?" Rory demanded.

"It's complicated, and confidential, but we need a particular type of partner, one who has the connections and skills in PR, merchandising, sponsorships. Even though we are retaining control, we are asking for a lot of money for a minor share and we have to accept that I am the face of the team and an essential part of the deal. I have to play." Mac rubbed his forehead with the tips of his fingers, his gesture indicating pain or frustration or exhaustion. Probably all three. "This isn't about me, not this time. Or, at least, it isn't all about me. If I could take the time off I would, I'm not that arrogant. But I need to get back on the ice and, apparently, you're my best bet."

Rory bit her bottom lip, knowing what he was asking was practically impossible. "The chance of you being able to play in two months' time is less than ten percent, Mac. Practically nonexistent."

"I can do it, Rory. You just need to show me how."

She nearly believed him. If anybody could do it then it would be him.

"Mac, you could do yourself some permanent damage."

Mac pressed his lips together. "Again, my choice, my consequences."

God, why did that have to resonate so deeply with her? Okay, so this wasn't *all* about him and his career. A part of it was, of course it was, but she knew how much the Mavericks meant to him. There had been many reports about the bond he shared with his mentor, the now dead owner of the team. The *cheating* dead owner of the Mavericks—dying in his mistress's bed.

Don't think about that, she told herself. With her history of a having a serial cheater for a father, it was a sure way to get her blood pressure spiking.

She had to disregard the emotion around this decision, try to forget he was attempting to save his team, his friends' jobs and the traditions of the Mavericks, which were an essential part of the city's identity. She had to look at his injury, his need and his right to treatment. If this were any other sportsman and not Mac, would she be trying to help him? Yeah, she would.

And really, if she didn't help Mac, Troy might never speak to her again.

She nodded reluctantly. "Okay. I'll help you, as much as I can."

Mac, to her surprise, didn't look jubilant or excited. He just looked relieved and wiped out. "Thank you," he quietly said.

Rory turned to Kade. "You need to contact my office, sign a formal contract with my employers."

Kade grimaced. "Yeah, that's the other thing…we'd like to cut out the middleman."

Rory lifted up her hands in frustration. Was nothing going to be simple today? "What does that mean?"

Kade jerked his head in Mac's direction and Rory saw that his head was back against his pillow and his eyes were closed. "Let's carry on this discussion outside and I'll fill you in."

"Why do I know that you're about to complicate my life even further?" Rory demanded when they were standing in the passage outside Mac's room.

"Because you are, obviously, a very smart woman," Kade said, placing a large hand on her shoulder. "Let's go get some coffee and we'll sort this mess out."

That sounded like an excellent idea since she desperately needed a cup of liquid sanity.

Three

Rory walked into the diner situated around the corner from St. Catherine's Hospital and scanned the tables, looking for her best friend. It had only been an hour since Kade had laid out his terms, and she needed Troy to talk her off the ledge…

Dressed in skinny jeans and a strappy white crop top, she ignored the compliments coming from a table of construction workers on her left. She waved at Troy and smiled at grumbles behind her when they saw her breakfast companion—huge, sexy and, not that they'd ever realize it, gay. With his blond hair, chiseled jaw and hot bod, he had guys—and girls—falling over him and had the social life of a boy band member.

Unlike her who, according to Mr. Popular, partied like a nun.

Troy stood up as she approached and she reached up

to place a kiss on his cheek. He'd changed out of his uniform into jeans and a T-shirt but he still looked stressed.

"Rough night? Is Mac being a pain in your backside?" she asked him.

"He's not a problem at all. I was at the home until late. My mom had a bad episode."

Rory sent him a sympathetic look. Troy's mom suffered from dementia and most of his cash went to funding the nursing home he'd put her into. Unfortunately the home wasn't great, but it was the best he could afford.

Rory had decided a long time ago that when she opened her clinic Troy would be her first hire, at a salary that would enable him to move his mom out of that place into a nicer home. Hopefully, if they did well, he could also move out of his horrible apartment and buy a decent car. "Sorry, honey."

Troy shrugged as they sat down on opposite sides of the table. "You look as frazzled as I do. What's up?"

"So much," Rory replied. "Let's order and I'll tell you a story." She pushed the folder she'd been carrying toward Troy. "Look at this."

After they ordered, Rory tapped the file with her index finger. "Read."

"Mark McCaskill?" Troy looked at the label. "Why do you have Open Mac's file?"

Rory pulled a face as the waitress poured them coffee. She'd always loathed that nickname since it was a play on the microphone incident from so long ago, something she didn't need to be constantly reminded of. Then again, his other nickname, PD—short for Panty Dropper—was even worse. "If you're not going to read it then fill me in on all the gossip about him."

Troy frowned. "Why?"

"I'll explain." She waved her hand. "Go. Center and captain of the Vancouver Mavericks hockey team. Incredible player, one of the very best. Dates a variety of women. What else?"

Troy rested his forearms on the table, his face pensive. "Well, he's spokesperson for various campaigns, epilepsy being one of them. He sits on the boards of a few charities, mostly relating to children. He's also, thanks to investing in bars, restaurants and food trucks, one of the wealthiest bachelors in town. He's also supremely *haawwwt*," Troy added. "And surprisingly nice, even though I know how stressed he must be wondering if this injury will keep him out for the season."

Mac—nice? Yeah, sure.

Troy flicked the file open and flipped through the pile of papers. "You're treating him?"

Rory nodded and Troy looked confused. "But this isn't a Craydon file," he added, referring to the distinctive yellow-and-blue patient files used at the physiotherapy practice she worked for. "What gives, Rorks?"

Rory folded her arms across her chest and tapped her foot, her big, silver-gray eyes tight with worry. How much to tell him? As much as she could, she decided, he was her best friend. She trusted him implicitly and valued his judgment. Still, sharing didn't come easily to her so she took a moment to work out what to say. "Mac and I have a…history."

Troy's snort was disbelieving. "Honey, you're not his type. He dates tall, stacked, exotic gazelles."

Rory scowled. She knew what type of woman Mac dated. She saw them every time she opened a newspaper or magazine. "I know that I am short, and flat-chested," Rory snapped. "You don't need to rub it in."

"I didn't mean it like that," Troy quietly stated. "Yeah, you're short but you have a great figure, you know that you do. And there's nothing wrong with your chest."

"Like you'd know," Rory muttered.

"I know that you desperately need some masculine hands on your boobs and on other more exciting parts of your body. It's been a year, eighteen months, since you've had some action?"

Actually it was closer to two years, but she'd rather die than admit that to Mr. Cool. "Can we concentrate on my McCaskill problem please?"

"He's a problem?"

"You've forgotten that Shay was dating him during the open-mic disaster."

Troy's mouth dropped open. "I *did* forget that. He said he was bored with her, that monogamy was for the birds."

"Yep. Obviously that's a position he still holds."

Troy leaned back so the waitress could put their food down. He frowned at Rory's sarcastic comment. "Honey, that was a long time ago and he was young. Shay's moved on…what's the problem?"

"He's a man-slut. It annoys me."

"It shouldn't. He didn't cheat on *you*," Troy pointed out, and Rory stared down at her plate.

No, he'd almost cheated on her sister with her. The intention had been there. He would've cheated if Rory hadn't stopped him. He was just like her father and exactly the last person in the world she should be attracted to.

It made absolutely no sense at all.

She'd never told Troy—or anyone—what had happened between her and Mac and she still couldn't. Hurting her sister hadn't been her finest moment.

"Okay, admittedly, Mac is not the poster boy for love and commitment so I kind of get your antipathy to him since you have such a huge issue with infidelity," Troy said after taking a sip of his coffee.

"Doesn't everyone?" Rory demanded. "Have issues with it?"

"No. And if they do, they don't take it to the nth degree like you do. Hell, Rorks, I recall you not accepting a date from a perfectly nice guy because you said he had a 'cheating face.'"

Rory ignored his air quotes and lifted her nose in the air. "Okay, maybe that was wrong of me."

"Wrong of you? It was properly ridiculous."

Troy tapped the folder before he attacked his eggs. "Tell me how this came about."

Rory filled him in and Troy listened, fascinated.

"So, they want you, widely regarded as the best sports rehab physio in the area, to work on Mac. Why didn't they just approach the clinic directly and hire you that way?"

She'd asked Kade the same question. "They are going to keep the extent of Mac's injury a secret from the public and the fans. They'll admit that he's pulled a muscle or something minor but they don't want it getting out that his injury is as bad as it is."

"Why the secrecy?"

"Sorry, I can't tell you that." Troy, to his credit, didn't push. "Kade asked me to take a leave of absence from the clinic to treat Mac."

Troy's eyebrows lifted. "Seriously?"

"Yeah."

"And you said yes, no, hell, no?"

"Thanks to the fact that I am a workaholic, I have

nearly two and a half months of vacation due to me that I have to either use or lose."

Troy just looked at her, waiting for her to continue.

"Kade offered me twenty grand for six weeks and another thirty if I get Mac back into condition by the time the season starts in two months."

"Fifty K?" Troy's mouth fell open. After a moment of amazed silence he spoke again. "With that sort of money you could open your own practice like you've been dreaming of doing."

And, more important, she could employ him. Rory nodded. "Yeah. I want to set up a clinic that isn't a conveyor belt of only treating the patient's pain—"

"No need to go on, I've been listening to you ramble on about your clinic for years." Troy's smile was full of love. "And Kade's offer will allow you to establish this clinic without having to take a loan or use the money you were saving for a house."

"Essentially."

"It sounds like a no-brainer, Rorks," Troy said quietly.

Rory sucked her bottom lip between her teeth. It did, didn't it? "Except for two rather major points."

"Which are?"

"First, I am stupidly, crazily attracted to Mac. Nobody makes my blood move like he does." She glared at Troy. "Don't you dare laugh! How am I supposed to treat him when all I want to do is crawl all over him?"

Troy hooted, vastly amused.

"Second, and more important, I don't think I can fix him, Troy, and especially not in two months." Troy stopped laughing and stared at her.

"I don't think he's got a hope in hell."

"Except that you are forgetting one thing..." Troy

cocked his head at her and slowly smiled. "When Mac McCaskill decides he wants something, he'll move hell and high water to get it. Everyone knows that if Mac says he is going to do something, he'll get it done. He doesn't know what *failure* means."

Yet he'd failed Shay and, in a roundabout way, failed her. He wasn't anywhere as perfect as Troy thought him to be.

The next morning Rory knocked on Mac's door and stuck her head inside after he told her to come in.

"I'm in the bathroom, I'll be with you in a sec," Mac called, so Rory sat down in the visitors' chair, her bag at her feet. Inside the folder that she placed on her knees was a signed contract to be Mac's physiotherapist for the next two months.

A little over two months...nine or so weeks. Rory felt panic bubble in her throat and she rubbed her hands over her face. She wasn't sure if she was scared, excited or horrified. A clinic, the last piece of a down payment for a house, a job for Troy, she reminded herself.

If she continued to save as she'd been doing, it would take another two years to gather what they were prepared to pay her in two months. This was a once-in-a-lifetime deal and she would be a moron to turn to it down. As she'd explained to Troy, there was just one little problem—she had to work with Mac, around Mac, *on* Mac. The chemistry between them hadn't changed. She was as attracted to him as she had been at nineteen, possibly even more. Young Mac had been charismatic and sexy and charming but Mac-ten-years-on was a potent mix of power, strength and determination that turned her to jelly. Kade might be the Mavericks' CEO, and Quinn was no pushover, but yesterday in this same room, Mac, despite his pain, was their undisputed leader. He had, thanks to his mental strength, pushed through pain and taken charge of the meeting.

Mac was determined and had a will to win that was second to none. He was also a rule breaker and a risk taker and utterly bullheaded.

Exactly the type of man she always avoided. They were fun and interesting and compelling, but they broke hearts left, right and center. Sometimes, as was the case with her father, they broke the same hearts over and over again.

She was too smart to let that happen to her.

Mac hated to take orders, but if she had any hope of fixing his arm, then he had to listen to her, do as she said when she said it. That would be a challenge. Mac, alpha male, was overly confident about his own abilities. She'd seen him in action; if he wanted to run a six-minute mile, he did it. If he wanted to improve the speed on his slap shot, he spent hours and hours on the ice until he was satisfied. If Mac wanted to fix his arm, he would work on it relentlessly. Except that muscles and injuries needed time to heal and, especially since his injury was so serious, he had to be careful. If he pushed the recovery process he could suffer irreversible damage and his career would be over. Permanently.

Yet if he wasn't healed in two months, the Mavericks, as Vancouver knew them, would be gone, and while she might have a brand-new shiny clinic, she might not have any clients if she couldn't fix the great Mac McCaskill.

Rock, meet hard place.

"Rory."

Rory snapped her head up to see Mac standing in the

doorway of the bathroom, wearing nothing more than a pair of designer denims and a deep scowl. His hair was wet and he'd wrapped a plastic bag around his arm to keep it dry. He hadn't managed the buttons on his jeans and through the open flaps she could see the white fabric of his, thank goodness, underwear. His chest was damp and a continent wide, lightly covered in brown hair in a perfect *T* that tapered into a fine trail of hair that crossed those fabulous washboard abs.

Sexy, almost-naked man in open blue jeans, Rory thought… *I could so jump you right now.*

Mac tried to button his jeans with one hand and swore creatively. Very creatively, Rory thought. She'd never before heard that combination of words strung together.

"Sorry," Mac muttered when he lifted aggravated eyes to meet hers. "But I am so damn frustrated I could punch something."

Rory placed the folder on the table next to her and slowly stood up. "Want some help?"

Mac looked at his watch and then scowled in the direction of the door. He looked as uncomfortable as she felt.

"Kade was supposed to come and help me get dressed and drive me home…"

"You've been discharged?"

"Yeah. The more time I spend here, the better the chances are of the press finding me." Mac lifted a muscled, tanned shoulder. "Besides, it's just my arm, the rest of me works just fine."

And looks pretty good too. Okay, get a grip, Kydd. You're a professional, remember? Try to act like one.

She rocked on her heels. "So, do you want some help?"

Mac looked at the door again and released a heavy sigh. "Yeah. Please."

Rory tried to keep her face blank as she reached for the flaps of his jeans. *Just get it done, fast*, she told herself, so she grabbed the first button and slotted it through its corresponding hole, brushing something that felt very masculine in the process, and not as soft as it should be. Keeping her head down, she moved on to button number two and repeated the action, very conscious of the growing bulge beneath her hands. She was flushed by the time she slotted in the last button, and she stepped back and pushed her hair out of her eyes.

She would not acknowledge his halfway-there erection. It was a conditioned response and something he couldn't help. Her hands were fiddling around his crotch; she could've been three hundred pounds with a mustache and he would've been turned on. It wasn't personal.

But damn, he was impressive... *Ignore, ignore, ignore.*

"Whoever packed for you was an idiot. Elasticized track pants or shorts would've been a better option," she stated, feeling hot from the inside out.

Mac ignored her comment and reached out to hold a strand of her hair. "I loved your long hair but this style works for you too."

"Uh..." Her brain needed oxygen. She couldn't think when he was so close, when she could smell the soap on his skin, could count every individual eyelash, see the different shades of dark blue in his eyes. What had he said? Something about her hair...

"Thanks."

Mac pushed her hair behind her ear and his fingers brushed her skin, and Rory couldn't help but shiver. This wasn't good, she thought, taking a huge step backward. He was dangerous, working with him was dangerous...

she shouldn't do this. It was a train wreck waiting to happen.

Clinic, house, practice, dream, her brain reminded her.

Shay, Mac cheating, men are inherently faithless, her soul argued. *Attraction leads to love and love leads to betrayal. Not happening.*

Rory jammed her hands into the back pockets of her jeans and nodded at Mac's bare feet. "Shoes?"

"Flip-flops," Mac replied, walking over to the bed and picking up a royal blue, V-necked T-shirt. He pulled the opening over his head and managed to slide his un-injured arm through the corresponding opening. Then he looked at his injured, immobile arm and cursed again.

"There's an art to dressing yourself when you're injured," she told him. Idiot that she was, she got up close and personal with him again, but this time she tried to avoid touching him as she pulled the shirt up and over his head. Shaking it out, she found the sleeve to his injured arm and gently slid the shirt up and over so that it bunched around his shoulder. He ducked his head through the opening, shoved his other arm through and the fabric fell down his chest.

It was wrong to hide such a work of art, Rory thought.

"Thanks."

Rory looked up at him, her head barely scraping his shoulder. God, he was big, six foot three of solid, sexy man. "Anything else?"

Mac shook his head. "No. I'm okay." He sat down on the edge of the bed and gestured to the chair she'd been sitting on earlier. "Take a seat, we need to talk."

Rory wasn't under any illusion that his quietly stated words were anything other than an order. Her spine straightened and her mouth tightened. Since there were, actually, a few things she had to say to him, she sat down and crossed her legs.

"You've had a little time to read over my chart, to assess the damage." Mac stretched out his long legs and sent her a hard look. "Thoughts?"

Rory pulled in a breath. "I presume you don't want me to sugarcoat it for you?"

"Hell, no."

Okay, then. "You ripped the lateral ulnar collateral ligament, luckily not completely from the bone, and it was surgically repaired. You also sprained the radial collateral ligament and the annular ligament."

"Which means?" Mac demanded, impatient.

"You're in a lot of pain and the injuries won't be easy to fix."

Mac's expression hardened. "Oh, they will be fixed. How much time does it normally take?"

She hated these types of questions; there were too many variables. Like bruised, broken and battered hearts, there was no time frame for recovery. "C'mon, Mac, you know better than to ask me that! Some people heal quicker, some never do. I can't answer that!"

"Can it be done in two months?" Mac pushed for an answer.

Rory tipped her head back to look at the ceiling. "I think you are asking for a miracle."

"Miracles happen," Mac calmly stated. "What can I do to jump-start the healing process?"

Rory thought for a minute. "My electromagnetic mat, for a start. We'll do treatments three or four times a day. It's noninvasive and will get the blood moving through the damaged capillaries. Anti-inflammatory drugs to take the swelling down.

"When *I* think it's time, we will start doing exercises," Rory added, and as she expected Mac's scowl deepened.

"I'm a professional player, I can take the pain," Mac said through gritted teeth. He wasn't listening to her, Rory realized. Did men like him ever listen to what they didn't want to hear?

"It's not about what you can endure, McCaskill!" Rory snapped. "It's about not making a very bad injury ten times worse! You will start exercising that arm when I say you can, with the exercises I approve, and not a minute before."

Mac glared at her and she kept her face impassive. "I'm not joking, Mac, this point is not up for negotiation."

Mac rubbed the back of his neck with his free hand. "Look, Rory, I'm not trying to be a jerk but a lot is riding on me being able to play in nine or so weeks."

"I understand that, but what you don't understand is that if you push, you might never play ever again! Is that a risk you are prepared to take?"

For a moment, Mac looked desolate, then his inscrutable expression fell back into place. He didn't respond to her question but she knew she'd made her point. "I don't want you to pussyfoot around me. You push me and you push me hard. As soon as you can."

He didn't allow for weakness, Rory thought, his body had to function how he wanted it to. She suspected he carried that trait into his relationships. His way or the highway…

Reason number fifty-four why they would never have managed to make a relationship work.

Going back to their actual conversation and pushing aside the craziness in her head, Rory realized that was the only concession he was prepared to make and she mentally declared their argument a draw. Good enough for her. She stood up to leave and gestured to the folder on the table. "I've signed your contract and I've been released from my job for ten weeks. We need to set up a schedule for when it's convenient for me to see you. To check on your mobility, to wrap your arm in the mat."

Mac shifted on the bed. "Where do you live?"

"I have an apartment in Eastside."

"I live in Kitsilano, not far from here actually. Commuting to my place three or four times a day is unnecessary. I have a spare room. You should move in."

Yeah, no way. Ever. That was far more temptation than she could handle. She needed to keep as much distance between them as she possibly could and if that meant trekking across town daily, or three or four times a day, then that was what she would do. She and Mac together in a house, alone, was asking for trouble. Trouble she needed like a hole in her heart.

Rory slowly shook her head.

"C'mon, Rory, it's not a big deal." Mac was obviously used to women moving in to his house on a regular basis but she wasn't going to follow those lemmings off a cliff. Nope, she'd deal with the devil if it meant the chance to run her own clinic, to treat her patients the way she wanted to, but she'd keep this particular devil at a safe distance.

"I'll live with the driving." She pulled her cell from her back pocket. "What's your address?"

Mac told her and also gave her his cell number, handing his phone to her so she could input hers into his state-of-the-art phone. When they were done, Rory looked at the door. She should leave. She picked up her bag and pulled it over her shoulder. "I'll see you later this evening. Around five?"

Mac nodded. She was almost at the door when Mac spoke again. "Are we not going to discuss it? At all? Pretend it didn't exist?"

Rory turned around slowly and lifted her hands. "What's the point? You insulted her on national television, we almost kissed, my sister heard us talking. She had to deal with a broken heart while she was stalked and hassled by the press. And she didn't talk to me for months."

Mac's jaw tightened and his lips thinned. "I'm sorry, I didn't think of that."

"You weren't thinking at all that day," Rory told him, her voice tart. "Admittedly, I wasn't either." Rory exhaled. "Look, it happened a long time ago and there's nothing to talk about."

Mac released a laugh that was heavy with derision and light on joy. "You're right. Nothing...except that the chemistry hasn't gone away. We're still attracted to each other."

She wished she could deny it but that would be a bald-faced lie, and she suspected Mac could still read her like a book. "I don't sleep with my patients."

Mac didn't look convinced. "You think we can resist each other? We'll be spending an enormous amount of time together and biology is biology."

"Unlike you, I can control myself," Rory told him primly.

Mac lifted an arrogant eyebrow. "Really? You think chemistry like ours just evaporates?" Mac snorted. "So if I kiss you, right here, right now...you can resist me?"

Rory rolled her eyes. "I know you find this hard to believe but there are women who can."

Mac smiled slowly. "You're not one of them."

Unfortunately he was probably right. Not that Rory would allow him to put his theory to the test. He'd already kissed her once and, despite the fact that he'd been as high as a kite, the kiss had blown her boots off. There was no way she would confirm his suspicions.

"Get over yourself, McCaskill. You're confusing me with those pretty, brainless bunnies that drop in and out of your life."

Mac took a step closer and his hurt arm brushed her chest. "Jealous?"

She wasn't even going to ask herself that question, mostly because she wasn't a hundred percent convinced that she wasn't jealous. Rory made an effort to look condescending. For good measure, she patted his cheek. "Bless your delusional little heart."

Mac's eyes darkened with fury, or lust, who knew, and he wrapped his good arm around her waist and pulled her up onto her toes, slamming his mouth against hers. No drugs affected his performance this time. This was Mac, pure and undiluted.

He didn't tease or tangle. The kiss was hard, demanding, harsh and urgent. *Hot.* On his lips she could taste her own bubblegum-flavored lip balm mixed with his toothpaste and the stringent tang of the mouthwash he must've used earlier. Rory felt his hand drop down her back to palm her butt, kneading her cheek until she was squirming, trying to get closer, needing to climb inside his mouth, his skin, to feel wrapped up within his heat...

Mac jerked back. "Dammithell." These words were followed by a string of others and it took Rory a minute to realize that his pale face and harsh breathing wasn't a result of the kiss, but from her bumping his injured arm.

She winced and lifted her hands to do something to help. When he took another step back she realized she'd done more than enough. Of everything.

Rory watched as Mac slowly straightened, as his breathing evened out. When she was sure he wasn't about to fall over, she slapped her hands on her hips. "That's not happening again. Ever."

One corner of Mac's mouth lifted to pull his lips up into a cocky smile. "Of course it won't," he replied, his voice oozing sarcasm. "Because we have no chemistry and you can resist me."

Lord give me patience. Rory yanked the door open and barreled into the passageway. *Because if You give me strength I'm going to need bail money, as well.*

Four

She'd had her hand on his crotch.

His life was currently a trash fire—messy and ugly—and all he could think about was how Rory's fingers felt brushing across his junk, how much he wanted her hand encircling his erection, how nobody had ever managed to set his blood on fire like that pint-size fairy who needed her attitude adjusted.

Mac glared at the half-open door, dropped into the chair and leaned his head back against the wall. He was not having a good day; it was just another day from hell in a series of hellish days in Hell City. He hadn't felt this crazy since that disaster ten years ago.

Wah, wah, wah... Admittedly, he sounded like a whiny ten-year-old, but wasn't he allowed to? Just this once? He hadn't been this unsure of his future since he'd hitched a ride out of his hometown fifteen years ago. And even then, he hadn't been that worried. He'd made excellent grades in school and a rare talent on the ice had translated into a full scholarship to college. He'd then been recruited to play for the Mavericks and earned serious money. By investing in companies and start-ups, he'd earned more. Considerably more. He was, by anyone's definition, a success. He was living the life, incredibly wealthy, popular, successful.

Despite his rocky upbringing, he believed he was, mostly, a functioning adult, fully committed to steering his own ship. He had an active social life; he genuinely liked women, and while he didn't "do" commitment, he wasn't the player everyone assumed him to be. Sure, he'd dated one or two crackpots but he'd managed to remain friends with most of the women he'd dated.

So, if he was a successful adult, why was he so insanely pissed off right now? Bad things happened to good people all the time…

He'd be handling this better if his fight with the fridge had only impacted his own life, his own career. Like that long ago incident with Shay, his actions had not only hurt himself but could hurt people he cared about too. He knew what it felt like to be collateral damage. He'd been the collateral damage of his mother's bad choices and perpetual negativity.

To this day, he could still hear her lack of enthusiasm for anything he said or did. His mother was the reason he had no intention of settling down. In his head commitment equaled approval and he'd be damned if he ever sought approval from a woman again. He didn't want it and he didn't need it…

Wanting approval was like waiting to catch a boat at an airport. Constantly hopeless. Endlessly disappointing.

It was far easier not to give people, a woman, the opportunity to disappoint him. Rory—funny, loyal, interesting—was a problem. He didn't care for the fact that he *liked* her, that this blast from his past excited him more than he thought possible.

You are overthinking this, idiot. This is just about sex, about lust, about attraction.

It had to be because he wouldn't allow it to be anything else.

That being said, he was playing with fire in more ways than one. Yes, Rory might be the best physiotherapist around and eminently qualified to treat him, but she was also his famous ex's sister. If the press found out about this new connection, they would salivate over the story. If they then found out he and Rory were attracted to each other they'd think they'd died and gone to press heaven.

There were many reasons to downplay his injury, but the thought of putting Rory through the same hell Shay experienced at the hands of those rabid wolves made him feel sick. *Not happening*, he decided.

Not again.

Thank God she'd refused his asinine suggestion to move in with him. Wasn't that a perfect example of how his brain shut down whenever she was around? If she moved in he'd give them, mmm, maybe five minutes before they were naked and panting.

He had no choice but to keep his attraction to her under control, keep his distance—emotionally and physically. He had to protect himself and protect her, and the only way to do both was to put her in the neutral zone—that mental zone he'd created for people, events, stuff that didn't, or shouldn't, impact him.

So he'd put her there, but he wasn't convinced, in any way, shape or form, that she'd actually remain there.

Rory stood on the pavement outside Mac's Kitsilano home, the key Mac had given her earlier in her hand. The house wasn't what she'd expected. She'd thought he'd have a blocky, masculine home with lots of concrete and steel. She hadn't expected the three-story with its A-pitched roof, painted the color of cool mist with dark gray accents. It looked more like a home and less like the den of sin she'd expected.

Rory walked up the steps to the front door, slid the key into the lock and entered the house, stopping to shove the key back into the front pocket of her jeans. There was good art on the wall, she noticed as she moved farther into the living area, and the leather furniture was oversize and of high quality. A massive flat-screen TV dominated one wall, and apart from a couple of photographs of the three Maverick-teers, there wasn't anything personal in the room. Mac had no hockey memorabilia on display, nothing to suggest he was the hottest property on ice. She'd expected his walls to be covered with framed jerseys and big self-portraits. Instead his taste ran to original art and black-and-white photographs.

"Rory?" Mac's voice drifted down the stairs. "Come on up. Top floor."

She walked back into the hallway and up the stairs. She reached the second floor, looked down the passage and wished she could explore. Instead she jogged up the short, second flight that ended at the entrance to an expansive bedroom. The high pitch of the roof formed the paneled ceiling. The room was dominated by a massive king-size messy but empty bed. Rory looked around and saw Mac sprawled on a long sofa on the far side of the room. His head rested against the arm and his eyes were closed. Pain had etched deep grooves next to his mouth. His normally tanned skin was pale and he was taking long, slow, measured breaths.

His eyes didn't open but his mouth did. "Hey, were there any press people outside when you let yourself in?"

"No, why?"

"Just asking."

Rory dropped her gaze and her eyebrows lifted at his unbuttoned white shirt, his unzipped gray suit pants and his bare feet. An aqua tie lay on the seat next to him, on top of what was obviously a matching suit jacket. Black shoes and socks sat on the wood coffee table in front of him.

Oh, hell, no! "Going somewhere?"

"Planning on it."

"The only place you are going is back to bed." Rory folded her arms against her chest. "You need a full-time nurse, McCaskill."

If she moved in then she could stop him from making stupid decisions. But would she be able to stop *herself* from making stupid decisions, like sleeping with him?

"I don't need a nurse, I need a morphine drip," Mac responded, finally opening his eyes and squinting at her.

"Would you care to explain why you are all dressed up when you should be in bed, resting that injury?" Rory demanded, annoyed. This was what she'd been worried about. Mac thought that he was a superhero, that the usual consequences of surgery and injury didn't apply to him.

Despite the fact that he was a very intelligent man, the wheel was turning but the hamster seemed to be dead.

"Don't give me grief, Rory," Mac said, sounding exhausted. "Trust me, there is no place I'd rather be than in bed but something came up."

"A wine auction? A ball? A poker game?" Rory asked, her eyebrows lifting. Mac was very active on the Vancouver social scene and he was, with the women who spun in and out of his life, invited to all the social events.

Mac, despite his pain, managed to send her an annoyed glance. "Myra Hasselback, current owner of the Mavericks, is holding an end-of-season cocktail party for the sponsors, management and staff. I can't miss it. As Captain, I am expected to be there."

"But…" Rory looked from him to his arm and back again. "Does she know that you are hurt?"

Mac's smile was grim. "Oh, she knows, but she doesn't know how bad it is. Kade told her it's a slight sprain, nothing for her to worry about. She told Kade to tell me she was looking forward to seeing me tonight. Besides, she knows I would move heaven and earth to be at the cocktail party. It's a tradition that was important to Vernon." Mac sat up slowly. "She'd suspect something if I wasn't there."

"Judging by your pale face and pain-filled eyes she's going to suspect something anyway." Rory sighed her frustration. "What do the other two Maverick-teers have to say on the subject?"

"They wanted me to fake a stomach bug or an allergic reaction to medication."

"Not a bad idea. Why not go with that?"

Mac looked uncomfortable. "I suppose I could but I don't want to give her an excuse to arrive on my doorstep after the party is over to check on me."

"She's done that before?" Rory asked.

Mac looked uncomfortable, and not from the pain. "Yeah, once or twice."

Rory turned his words over, recalling the thirty-year difference between Myra and her dead husband. Ah, the widow wanted naked comforting.

Rory wanted to ask if he'd slept with Myra but she mentally slapped her hand across her mouth. She had no right to ask that but... *But* nothing. She had no right to know.

"Anyway, about the party, I need to be there. The speculation will be endless if I don't attend. It would raise a lot of questions, questions I do not want to answer." Mac looked stubborn. "No, it's better for me to act like everything is normal as far as I possibly can. So, will you please help me finish getting dressed?"

"I'm not happy about this, Mac."

"I know. I'm not either."

But he'd go, Rory realized. He needed rest and time for that injury to heal but he would do what he always did. If this was his intended pace, they were in for some serious problems.

Rory walked across his bedroom to stand in front of the huge windows and watched a container ship navigate the sound. But her thoughts weren't on the gorgeous view, they were on that stubborn man who didn't know the meaning of the words *slow down, take it easy*. To heal, Mac needed rest and lots of it. It was that simple, that imperative.

That difficult.

Dammit, she was going to *have* to move in here. His arm, his career, the Mavericks were at risk and she was balking because he had the ability to melt the elastic on her panties. She was better, stronger, a great deal more professional than that.

She was a smart, independent, focused woman who could say no to what wasn't good for her. Who could, who *would*, keep their relationship strictly professional.

"Don't even think about it. You are not now, or ever, going to move in."

Dammit! Had he started reading her mind now? When? How? "But you suggested it earlier."

"I changed my mind. It would be a terrible idea. Moving on, are you going to help me or not?" Mac demanded, sounding irritable.

She wanted to be petty and tell him to go to hell but she knew he was stubborn enough to dress himself. *One fight at a time*, Rory thought.

"Yes. If you take some painkillers," Rory stated, her tone discouraging any arguments. "You look like a breath of wind could blow you over, Mac, and there is no way anyone will believe you have a slight sprain if you walk into that room looking like that. Painkillers…that's my demand."

"They make me feel like hell. Spacey and out of control," Mac muttered.

"I have some in my bag. They aren't as strong as yours but they'll take the edge off." Rory looked at her watch. "What time do you need to leave for this party?"

"Kade and Quinn should be here any moment." A door slammed below them and the corner of Mac's mouth kicked up. "Speaking of the devil and his sidekick…"

"Who is the devil and who is the sidekick?" Rory asked.

"Depends on the occasion. We all have our moments."

Now *that* she could believe. Rory jammed her hands

into the pockets of her jeans and rocked on her heels. "I'll run downstairs to get those painkillers and one of your sidekicks can come back up and help you dress."

"Aw, they aren't as pretty as you. Nor do they smell as good."

"I'm not so sure…they are both very pretty and they do smell good," she teased.

Mac sent her a narrow-eyed look. "Do not flirt with my friends."

He sounded jealous. But that was probably just her imagination running off again.

"Why on earth not?" Rory asked, deliberately ignoring the heat building between her legs and the thump-thump of her heartbeat.

"I wouldn't like it," Mac growled.

Rory forced herself to do a massive eye roll as she edged her way to the door. "I think you are confusing me with someone who might actually give a damn."

"Rory?"

When she turned, Mac did a slow perusal of her body. She felt like he'd plugged her into the electricity grid. "Seriously, no flirting."

"Seriously, you're an idiot." Rory made a big production of her sigh. "They really should invent a vaccine to prevent that."

The next morning Mac, dressed in a T-shirt and a pair of sweatpants, walked into his kitchen and, ignoring his two friends sitting at his table, headed straight for the coffeepot. Filling a cup to the brim, he gulped a sip, shuddered, swallowed another mouthful and prayed the caffeine would hit his system in the next thirty seconds. He felt like death warmed over. His arm was on fire, his head was pounding and he wanted to climb back into bed and sleep for a week. He supposed being out last night and pretending he was fine contributed to his less than stellar mood.

As did the drugs and the anesthetic, he realized. It always took time for drugs to work their way out of his system. He felt like a wet blanket was draped over his head. He'd work through it, as he always did.

He jerked his head at his friends and looked around the kitchen. "Where's Rory?"

"She went home," Quinn replied, taking a donut from the box on the table and biting into it.

"But…" Mac frowned, looking toward the front door. "I thought she was here earlier. She wrapped that mat thing around my arm."

"She was. Now she's gone," Quinn replied, stretching out his long legs. "Need anything? I can make eggs."

Mac shook his head, smiling internally. Quinn, their resident badass, was a nurturer at heart, intent on making the world around him better and brighter for the people he loved. There weren't many people he showed his softer side to. To the world he was an adrenaline-addicted bad boy, speed-freak player, but his family and close friends knew he would move heaven and earth for the people he loved.

"I'm good, thanks."

Kade pushed back his chair and pulled back the cuff of his shirt to look at his watch. It was new, Mac realized, and damn expensive. "I've got to get moving, my morning is crazy."

"Can you give me fifteen minutes?" Mac asked, picking up his coffee. "We need to talk."

He didn't want to do this. Frankly he was considering abdicating all his rights to adulthood at this point and going back to bed, but he leaned against the counter and held his cup in his good hand.

"What's up?" Quinn asked.

"This situation is a classic cluster…" Mac allowed his words to trail away and rubbed the back of his neck. He needed air. This kitchen was far too small for three six-foot-plus men.

"Let's go outside." Mac placed his cup on the table and grabbed a donut. Maybe a sugar rush would make him feel better. He took one bite, grimaced and tossed the donut back into the box.

Kade and Quinn exchanged a long, worried look, which made Mac grind his back teeth. He was about to knock some heads together—okay, he couldn't beat up a worm at the moment but the thought was there—when Kade stood up and walked over to the open doors that led to the small patio. Mac followed him out into the sunshine and Quinn lumbered to his feet to do the same.

They looked over the houses below them, across False Creek and toward the Lions Gate Bridge and the mountains beyond. God, he loved this city and its endless, changing views. He couldn't think of living anywhere else; this was home. He'd had offers from teams all over the continent but he'd never been willing to be traded, and Vernon had kept him, and Kade and Quinn. Unless they managed to buy the Mavericks, that would all change. Mac didn't mind change, as long it was the change *he* wanted.

"I'm really worried about the press finding out about my injury," Mac quietly stated.

Kade rested his forearms on the railing and cocked his head to look at Mac. "We put out a press release stating you have a minor injury and that you should be fine soon."

Not good enough, Mac decided. "There's too much at stake."

Quinn frowned. "But only the three of us and Rory know the truth. The doctors and nurses are bound by patient confidentiality. I think we'll be okay."

Mac rubbed his chin. "Until the press realizes I am spending an enormous amount of time with my ex-girlfriend's sister."

It took a minute for the implications of that scenario to register with his friends. When it did, they both looked uneasy. Kade rubbed his chin. "That was the incident that started their obsession with what we do, who we date."

Mac felt a spurt of guilt. "Yeah. And if they find out about Rory, how will we explain why we are spending time together?" He frowned. "I will not tell them we are seeing each other, in any capacity. God, that would open up a nasty can of worms, not only for Rory but for Shay, as well."

"And even if you told them she was your physio, that statement would raise questions as to why we aren't using our resident physios, why we need her to treat you," Kade said. "Especially since your injury is supposed to be a minor one."

"Bingo."

Quinn swore. "What's that saying about lies and tangles we weave?"

"Shut up, Shakespeare." Kade stood up, looking worried. So was Mac. He'd spent most of the night thinking about how they could avoid this very wide, imminent pitfall.

Quinn leaned his hip against the railing and narrowed

his eyes. "We've painted ourselves into a corner. We've downplayed your injury and said you'll be fine in a couple of weeks. When you are not fine in a week or two, how are we going to explain that?"

"I have a solution," Mac said. "I don't like it—in fact, I hate it. I need to be here, working with you on the deal to purchase the team. But it's all I can think of…"

"Well?" Quinn demanded, impatient.

"I need to get out of the city."

Kade tapped his finger against his chin. "Yeah, but any fool can see you are more badly injured than we say you are. We got away with lying once, only because the injury was brand-new, but we can't keep shoveling that story. Your eyes are dull, you can tell you are on hectic painkillers."

"I'll stop the drugs," Mac insisted.

"Now who is being stupid?" Quinn demanded.

"Last night you hadn't taken the proper pain meds and you looked like a walking corpse," Kade said. "The point is that people will notice and that will lead to complications. I think your instinct is right. It's best for you to leave. We can tell Myra, the press, anyone who cares that you are taking an extended vacation."

Mac swore. "I have no idea where to go. There's nowhere I *want* to go."

"The chalet in Vail?" Quinn suggested.

"No snow, and even if there was, I couldn't ski. Torture."

"An African safari?"

"Done that." God, didn't he sound like a spoiled brat?

"What about the Cap de Mar property?" Kade persisted.

He'd already considered Puerto Rico and he'd immediately dismissed that idea. Too hot, too isolated, too sexy…

"Are you nuts?" Mac rolled his eyes.

"No," Kade replied, his voice calm as he ticked off points on his fingers. "Not big on ice hockey so you'll be able to fly under the radar. Two, there's sun, sea and beaches…where's the problem? Three, you love it there. Four, Rory will go with you and she'll do her treatment there."

A vision of Rory dressed in nothing more than four triangles flipped onto the big screen of his brain and he shuddered with lust. This wasn't a good idea. The property was empty, the cove would be deserted, he and Rory would be alone and living together. Whenever he thought of Cap de Mar he thought about sunny days and sensual nights, warm, clear seas and sex…

"You have to go, Mac," Kade said, deeply serious.

Mac knew it was a reasonable option. Hell, he'd brought up the idea of leaving. But he couldn't help feeling like he had as a kid. Powerless over his situation.

"My life sucks," Mac grumbled.

"Yeah, poor baby. You're heading for a luxury house on a Caribbean island with a hot chick." Quinn mocked him by rubbing his eyes like a toddler. "Boo hoo."

Mac still had the use of his good arm. A well-placed punch to Quinn's throat would relieve a lot of his frustration.

Kade ignored Quinn. "I like the idea of you heading to the beach house for all the reasons I mentioned and one more."

"Uh-huh?"

"Nobody will know where you are so you'll be free of the media."

"Always a bonus," Mac agreed.

"And if something happens between you and Rory then they won't pick up on that either," Kade added.

Mac held Kade's mocking glare. Okay, yeah, of course that was a factor. He would try to resist her but his will-power where she was concerned wasn't a sure thing.

"It's not going to happen," he said, but he wasn't sure whether he was trying to convince his friends or himself.

Quinn laughed. "You're going to take one look at Rory in her bikini and be all 'let me show you the view from my room.'"

A punch to the throat would definitely shut Quinn up and would make Mac feel so much better, he mused.

Five

"Sorry, I'm late." Rory picked up her e-reader from her coffee table and shoved it into her tote bag.

"We've got time." Mac, standing by the window, looked at his watch. "Not a lot but some. And if the jet misses its time slot, we'll just request another."

Private jets and time slots. Rory tried not to look impressed. But she was. She was traveling to the Caribbean in *style*. Rory tried to think calmly. She'd done most of her packing last night but she'd thought she'd have time to finish up this morning. Thanks to Troy's mom going walkabout from her nursing home, that hadn't happened. She and Troy had spent three hours looking for her and had eventually tracked her down in a garden center sitting on a bench between two cherry trees. Rory was glad Troy's mom was okay but her temporary disappearance had put a serious dent in Rory's schedule.

"Passport and credit card," Mac told her. "You can buy anything else you need there."

So spoke the man with far too much disposable income, Rory thought. She held up her hand in a silent gesture for him to be quiet. She needed to think, and him standing in her little apartment, looking so hot, wasn't helping. All she could think about was that she was leaving the country with a sexy man who just had to breathe to turn her on.

Her eyes dropped to his arm, which rested in a black sling. He was injured, she reminded herself.

You could go on top...

Rory slapped her hand across her forehead.

"Tell me about Puerto Rico," Rory said, hoping the subject would distract her from thinking about straddling Mac, positioning herself so that...argh!

"It's an island in the Caribbean," Mac replied.

"Don't be a smart-ass. Tell me about the house where we're staying."

Mac leaned his shoulder into the wall and crossed his legs at the ankles. It was so wrong that he looked at home in her apartment, like he had a right to be there. "The house is situated about thirty-five minutes from San Juan, on a secluded cove near only two other houses. It's three stories, mostly open-plan and it has glass folding doors that open up so you feel like you are part of the beach and sea.

"The owners of the other two properties are off-island at the moment so we'll be the *only* people using the cove." Mac added.

Rory swallowed at the low, sexy note in his voice. She'd be alone with Mac, on a Caribbean island, with warm, clear water and white beaches and palm trees.

Utterly and absolutely alone. She wasn't sure whether the appropriate response was to be thrilled or terrified.

Or both.

Sex and business don't mix! He's your patient!

Sun, sea, sexy island…sexy man.

Get a grip, Kydd. Not liking the cocky look in his eyes, the glint that suggested he knew exactly what she was thinking, she lifted her nose. "Well, at least we won't disturb the neighbors with your screams of pain when we start physio."

"Or your screams of pleasure when I make you fall apart in my arms," Mac replied without a second's hesitation.

Rory's heart thumped in her chest but she kept her eyes locked on his, refusing to admit he rattled her. Instead of making her furious, as it should, his comments made her entire body hum in anticipation. Her body was very on board with that idea.

Rory folded her arms and rocked on her heels. "I hate it when you say things like that."

"No, you don't. You want to hate it because it turns you on." Mac looked up at the ceiling. When he looked back at her, his expression was rueful. "Ignore me, ignore that."

She couldn't do as he asked. They needed to address the pole dancing, come-and-get-me-baby elephant gyrating in the room. "Mac, I don't know what you think is going to happen in Puerto Rico, but us sleeping together can't happen, won't happen."

"I know why *I* think it shouldn't happen. I have a few solid reasons for thinking it would be a hell of a mistake, but I'm interested in hearing yours."

Rory bit the inside of her lip. God, she couldn't tell

him she thought he was just like her dad, unfaithful. That the fact he'd dated her sister bugged her. Or her personal favorite: that he drove her crazy.

Rory thought fast and latched onto the first reasonable excuse that popped into her head. "I'm on sticky ground here. I shouldn't treat you and sleep with you—that would be crossing some pretty big lines. I have to maintain professional boundaries with clients. I can't misuse or abuse my position of authority—"

"You have no position of authority over me," Mac scoffed.

"The point remains—" Rory gritted her teeth "—that if I engage in any nonprofessional behavior I can be pulled up before the board."

Mac stared at her, his face inscrutable. "Okay, for the sake of argument, may I point out that you'll be in a foreign country and nobody but us will know? And you're on holiday."

"I'd know," Rory said, her voice resolute. "You might be a rule breaker, Mac, but that's not a risk I'm willing to take."

"You're lying, Rory. Besides, last I checked, physiotherapists are allowed private lives." Mac shook his head. "Not buying it."

So much for using that as an excuse to keep some distance between them. Rory hated the fact that he could look past her cool, professional shell and see below the surface. And he was right. Nobody would believe she'd bullied Mac into having a relationship he didn't want to have. Yeah, sleeping with Mac wouldn't be professional but it wasn't a death sentence either.

She'd forgotten how damn complicated men could be.

"So what is your reason why we shouldn't scratch this particular itch?"

"God, I wish there was just one." Mac dropped a curse and rubbed the back of his neck. "But I can't remember any of them because I am too damn busy thinking about how you taste, how good you feel in my arms. I want to feel that, *feel you*, again. It's not smart, or sensible, but… to hell with being sensible and smart!"

"Mac—"

"Come here, Rorks."

She could say no, should say no, but she found herself walking toward him. Stopping when she was a foot from him, she tipped her head up to look at his face. His jaw held that sexy stubble, and the corners of his mouth suggested he was amused, but his eyes told her everything she needed to know. He was as turned on as she was.

Crazy chemistry.

Mac lifted his good hand, gripped the edge of her collar and pulled her toward him. Rising on her tiptoes, she kept her eyes locked on his, deciding whether she should kiss him or not. "I just want one kiss, Rory," Mac murmured, doing his mind reading thing again. "Stop thinking for a second and *be*."

He had a way of cutting to the heart of the problem. He was right; she was making far too big a deal of this. It didn't have to mean anything! Kissing him just made her feel good. Like chocolate or a foot rub.

"That's it, babe, stop thinking and kiss me."

Rory moved her head so her lips moved across his ear, under his short sideburns, through his surprisingly soft stubble, slowly, so slowly, making her way to his mouth. Mac's hand clenched her waist and she heard the low growl in the back of her throat as her tongue darted out to taste the skin on his jaw, to explore the space where his top and bottom lip met. She felt his erection against her hip and knew she had maybe five seconds before he exploded and all hell—possibly heaven—broke loose.

Rory moved her lips over his, her teeth gently scraping his upper lip, her hand grasping the back of his neck. She kept her tongue away, wondering how long he would wait before he took control of the kiss. Five seconds passed and then another ten. Rory sucked on his bottom lip.

He muttered something against her lips, something harsh and hot and sexy, and his big hand gripped her butt and lifted her up and into him. The time for playing, for teasing, was over. She'd never experienced a kiss so… sexual, Rory realized. This wasn't a prelude to sex. This was just another version of the act. His tongue pushed inside and retreated, swirled and sucked, and Rory felt her panties dampen as she unconsciously ground herself against his erection, frustrated by the layers of fabric between them.

She wanted to get naked. Now.

"Plane waiting. Puerto Rico," Mac muttered after wrenching his mouth off hers.

"You said you could get another time slot and the island isn't going anywhere." Rory snuck her hands under his shirt and scraped her nails across the skin covering the hard muscles of his abs.

"Rory…" Mac muttered a curse and slapped his good hand on hers to keep it from sliding lower. She looked up at him and half smiled at the seventy-shades-of-crazy look on his face. She'd put that look on his face, she thought, amazed. This sexy man looked like he couldn't go without her for one more heartbeat.

"We really should stop," Mac muttered. "We shouldn't take this any further."

"Why not?"

Mac looked rueful. "One reason would be because someone has been pounding on your door for the last minute. At least."

Rory jerked back, surprised. Really? She hadn't heard a damn thing. As the bells in her head stopped ringing she heard the *rat-tat-tat* on her doorjamb. Her heart dropped to the floor; there was only one person who used that particular combination on her door. As a child she'd considered it their secret code, as an adult—about to get lucky—it irritated the hell out of her.

"Problem?" Mac asked as she stepped away from him and pushed a hand into her hair.

"Yes, no...my father." Rory pulled a face. She lifted a hand, waved it toward her front door and grimaced. "Give me a sec, okay?"

Bad timing, Dad, she thought as she crossed the room to the door. Or maybe he'd arrived just in time to save her from making a very silly mistake. Either way, why was he here? She'd called her mother last night, told her that she'd be out of the country for the foreseeable future. Her parents lived in a suburb twenty minutes from here, and since they weren't close, Rory couldn't understand why her father had made the trek to see her.

Rory checked the peephole to make sure it was her father and opened the door. "Dad."

David Kydd had that sheepish look on his face that she was sure had charmed many a woman into his bed over the years. "There's my girl." He leaned forward to kiss her and Rory allowed him to brush her cheek. Since he wasn't one for spontaneous gestures of affection, Rory had to wonder what he was up to.

Okay, she was cynical, but being cynical protected her. She'd learned that if she had no expectations of him then she couldn't be disappointed by his behavior.

"Can I come in?" David asked.

Rory kept her body in the open space of the door so he couldn't look into the apartment and see Mac. Her father was a fan and she didn't want to spend the next hour listening to hockey talk. And, even if she begged him, she wasn't sure her Dad would keep quiet about seeing Mac at her place. Her Dad wasn't the soul of discretion at the best of times.

"It's not a good time. I told Mom last night that I was leaving the city for a while and I need to get to the airport."

"She told me." David gave her another of his sheepish grins. "I thought I'd make the offer to feed your animals or water your plants."

"I don't have pets or plants." As he was well aware. Rory narrowed her eyes at him. "Why are you really here?"

David dropped his eyes and shifted from foot to foot. Eventually he muttered an answer. "Your mother and I are going through a rough time."

Rory felt that familiar, piercing pain shoot through her heart. A rough time… How often had she heard that phrase over the years? *A rough time* meant her mother had caught him again—sexting, cheating, an internet relationship…who knew? He was a master at all of them.

Rory knew how it worked. Her parents would separate for a month or six weeks. Her dad would get bored with his latest conquest and beg her mother to take him back. She liked the begging, liked the attention, and they swore to make it work this time.

"Anyway, we thought that since you wouldn't be here for a while, I could move in to your place until you get back," David suggested, utterly blasé.

"No," Rory told him, her expression brittle. He needed to leave her, and her apartment, out of any games he was playing.

Rory stepped backward and rubbed her forehead with her fingertips. "I've got to go. I'm late as it is."

"Rory, come on," David pleaded.

"Sorry." Rory closed the door in his face and rested her forehead against the wood, trying to hold back the tears threatening to fall. She needed a minute to find her center, to process what had just happened.

She heard her father's footsteps as he walked away from her door. There went the reason why she found it difficult, impossible really, to trust that someone she allowed herself to love would not lie to her or abandon her. How could she put her faith in love after witnessing her parents' skewed perception of the emotion all her life? As a product of their twisted love, was she even worthy of being in a monogamous relationship? If such a thing even existed.

She was so damn confused about the meaning of love and marriage. Why did her parents stay together after all this drama? What did they get out of it? Their love, their marriage, their entire married life had been a sham, an illusion...

Love was a sham, an illusion...

"Rorks? You okay?"

Dammit. She'd temporarily forgotten Mac was in the room. He'd witnessed that silly conversation. She turned slowly. How could she explain this without going into the embarrassing details? She managed to find a smile, unaware that it didn't come anywhere near her eyes. "Sorry about that." She made herself laugh. "My folks, slightly touched."

Mac's skeptical look told her he didn't buy her breezy attitude. Yet there was something in his eyes that suggested sympathy, that made her want to confide in him, to tell him why her parents drove her batty. She had the strange idea that he might understand.

Rory bit the inside of her cheek, confused and feeling off-kilter. Since meeting Mac again, her life had done a one-eighty. She felt like she was standing in a fun house. The reflections didn't make sense...

"Excuse me a sec," Rory said before walking through her bedroom to the bathroom. Grabbing the counter in an iron-fisted grip, she stared at herself in the mirror.

What was she doing? Thinking? She simply wasn't sure and she wished she had more than five minutes to figure it out. This thing between her and Mac was getting out of hand, and she needed, more than anything, to control it, to understand it.

She was about to fly away with him and how was she going to resist him?

It was just sex, she told herself. Sex was physical. It wasn't a promise to hand over her heart. If she slept with Mac she would be sharing her body, not her soul, and she wouldn't be risking anything emotional. Could she be laid-back about such an intimate act? She would have to be, because love wasn't an option. She wasn't interested, and Mac wasn't the type of guy a girl should risk her heart on anyway.

But...

But it would be cleaner, smarter, less complicated if she didn't sleep with him. Passion and chemistry like theirs was crazy. Her libido was acting like a wild and uncontrollable genie. A genie who would be impossible to get back in the bottle if she popped the cork. It was far better to keep the situation, and her lust, contained.

Rory pointed her index finger at her reflection and scowled. "Do not let him pop your cork, Kydd."

In his seat, Mac scowled at his computer screen through his wire-rimmed glasses and wished he could concentrate. He needed to make sense of these balance sheets and read the profit and loss statements for a couple of sports bars they owned in Toronto. How was he supposed to do that when his mind was filled with Rory? He turned his head sideways to look at her and smiled when he saw she'd curled up in her seat and fallen asleep. He picked up a lock of hair that had fallen over her eyes and gently tucked it behind her ear.

So much more beautiful than she'd been at nineteen.

Mac pulled off his glasses and rubbed his eyes, conscious of the fiery throb in his arm. His head ached in sympathy. Truth be told, he was relieved to be leaving the city and to stop pretending he was fine. He could take the pain tablets, zone out and try not to worry about Myra and the investor and the fans and, God, whether the press would find out how serious his injury actually was and how much pain he was living with.

Rory let out a breathy sigh and he looked at her again, his stomach churning with the need to have her. That need worried him.

With her, he didn't feel in control and he hated that sensation. In his real life, he dated to get laid. He and the woman both had fun and then they moved on. He understood how much it hurt to have unmet expectations so he made no promises, offered no hope to the women who slept with him. In his world, sex didn't involve talking, sharing, caring. In that world, conversation took place horizontally; bodies spoke, not mouths.

He didn't confide in any of his lovers. He never shared his feelings, and the one guarantee his lovers had was that he'd always leave.

He never allowed anyone to get too close; he'd learned a long time ago to be his own champion, his own motivator. His mother hadn't believed in or supported him so he didn't expect anyone else to either.

Rory was different. She made him feel more, made him say more, want more. He was out of his depth with her and flailing...

Mac rubbed his temples with his fingertips. He was definitely losing it. *Flailing? Over a woman?* God, he sounded like a fool.

Irritated with himself and his introspection, he picked up his tablet computer and swiped his finger across the screen, immediately hitting the link for his favorite news site. Instead of focusing on the US elections or the migrant crisis in Europe, the headlines detailed the breakup of a famous Hollywood golden couple after ten years and fostering six kids.

Mac had been caught in the same type of media hype, on less of a global scale admittedly, and it had sucked.

Phoenix is currently being treated for depression and begs the media to give her some privacy, he read. He'd heard that Shay had suffered with depression during their breakup and the constant press attention had made the situation ten times worse. He couldn't do that to Rory, couldn't risk her like that. Yeah, it was Puerto Rico. Yes, they would be flying under the radar. But it just took one determined paparazzo, one photograph, and their world would implode.

Not happening. He had to keep his hands off her.

"You look like your brain is going to explode," Rory softly said.

Mac rolled his head on his shoulders and watched as she stretched. "It feels that way," he admitted, knowing he had to address this longing for her. Now or never, he thought.

You won't die if you don't have sex. You might think you are going to, but you won't.

Mac rubbed his temples again. "Look, Rory, I've been thinking."

Rory sent him an uncertain look. "Uh-huh?"

"Despite my smart comments about us sleeping together and that hot kiss, maybe it would be better if we didn't. Sleep together, that is."

He couldn't help noticing the immediate flash of relief in her eyes. So something had shifted in her after that bizarre conversation with her father. When she'd returned from the bathroom, sexy Rory had disappeared and had been replaced with enigmatic Rory. He still didn't know what to make of that.

"Want to clue me in on why you've had a change of heart?"

You scare the crap out of me? When I'm with you I feel like I am on shifting sand? I don't want to see you hurt or scared or feeling hunted?

Yeah, he couldn't admit to any of the above.

So he fudged the truth. "My arm is killing me. I'd like to get to the house and chill, take my meds and just zone out for a while. I want to relax and not have to worry about you or keeping you happy, in bed or out." Mac stared past her to look out the window. "I'd like us to play it cool, just be friends." Because he was a man and believed in keeping his options open, he tacked on a proviso. "For now?"

Rory didn't answer, her gray eyes contemplative. "Sure. Fine."

Mac watched her out of the corner of his eye and sighed. *Fine.* God, he hated that word, especially when a woman stated it in that hard-to-read way. What did it actually mean? Was she okay with waiting? Was she pissed? Did she actually want to say "Screw you"?

Sometimes, most times, women made no sense. At all.

Six

Rory loved the Cap de Mar beach house. Shortly after her arrival, she claimed one of the smaller guest rooms, partly because it had an excellent view of the U-shaped bay and mostly because it was a floor below and a long way from the massive master suite.

She pulled on a bikini, a pair of shorts and a T-shirt and, walking barefoot, she set out to explore the house. As Mac had said, the living areas, sitting and dining room and the kitchen were all open-plan, leading onto a massive balcony filled with comfortable chairs and day-beds either under the balcony roof or under umbrellas. Tucked into the corner of the balcony was a huge Jacuzzi and she could easily imagine sitting in that tub watching the sun go down.

It was mid-afternoon now, Rory thought, resting her elbows on the railing and looking down into the sparkling pool below her. In a perfect world she'd like to take a swim, lie in the sun and then sit on the beach with a glass of white wine in her hand and wait for the sun to paint the horizon in Day-Glo colors. That, she thought, would be a wonderful end to a rather difficult day...

Rory saw a movement out of the corner of her eye and saw Mac step out of his bedroom through the doors that led straight onto this balcony. He'd shucked his jeans and shirt and pulled on a pair of board shorts. He hadn't bothered with a shirt. Why should he? He had a torso to die for.

The rest of him was pretty spectacular too.

Rory huffed out a sigh. She had to corral her overexcited hormones. Speaking of hormones, she'd been caught flat-footed at Mac's suggestion they postpone sleeping together. She hadn't expected Mac would let his arm get in the way of pleasure, or that he was humble enough to admit he was in pain and needed some time.

Mac, barefoot, walked over and gestured to the cove. "Nice, isn't it?"

"Gorgeous," Rory agreed. "It almost feels like we are part of the beach."

Mac half smiled. "That was the intention when I designed it. I wanted to bring the outdoors in."

"You designed this?"

Mac sat down on a daybed and leaned back, placing his good hand under his head. His biceps bulged, his shoulder flexed and the rest of him rippled as he swung his legs up onto the cushions. "Yeah."

She remembered something about him and architecture, about studying it in college. When he was dating Shay, he'd just completed some business courses and Rory had been super impressed that he'd managed to study and still play for the Mavericks. He hadn't needed to study further; he was earning enough with his salary and endorsements that, if he invested it properly, he could live comfortably for a very long time.

This wasn't living comfortably, Rory thought, looking around. This was living large. An island home on a secluded beach translated into big-boy money. She recalled what Troy had said about him and his friends investing in property and businesses, and her curiosity had her asking, "How many properties do you own? How many businesses do you have?"

Mac looked at her from below half-closed eyes. "Enough." He yawned and dropped his arm to pick up a pillow and shove it behind his head. "You want a statement of my assets and liabilities, Rory?"

Rory flushed. Okay, admittedly, she had no right to ask him that; they weren't lovers. They weren't even friends. And she'd rather die than ask any of her other clients such a personal question.

"Kade, Quinn and I have our own projects but a lot of our assets are held together in a partnership, and all the assets we share have to generate an income, this house included. It's our rule. If it doesn't make money, we ditch it. That is why we get to use this property but, for the most part, it's rented out. Not so much during the summer months because it's so damn hot and it's hurricane season."

Rory darted a quick look toward the endlessly blue horizon. "Hurricanes?"

"They happen," Mac replied. "They aren't that bad. A lot of wind, a lot of rain."

"Super," Rory said drily.

Mac shifted in his seat and winced when he moved his injured arm, trying to find a more comfortable position.

"Did you take your painkillers and the anti-inflammatory pills?" Rory demanded.

"Yes, Mom, that's why I'm feeling so damn sleepy," Mac murmured. He waved a hand toward the house. "Food and drinks in the kitchen. I asked our rental agent to arrange for someone to stock the place. I've also arranged for someone to come and clean and do laundry a couple of times a week. Otherwise we're on our own."

On our own was a phrase she did not need to hear.

"Okay," Rory said, watching him fight sleep.

"Jeep in the garage. Keys in the kitchen. San Juan is thirty-five minutes away, north. Casinos, restaurants five minutes away, south." Mac yawned again. "Make yourself at home."

"Will do," Rory said, but she doubted he'd heard her because he'd drifted off to sleep. He still had a frown on his face as she moved an umbrella closer to him so he could sleep in the shade. Her thumb moved over the creases on his forehead and she wondered what was making him worry. Their deal to buy the Mavericks franchise, his injury, being alone with Rory in this house?

She might have her fair share of problems but Mac had his too.

He wasn't always who she expected him to be, Rory admitted. Sure, he could be overconfident about his abilities and about the effect he had on her, but he was also honest enough to admit that their attraction was a two-way street. She affected him just as badly. She didn't know Mac well, not yet, and because he was so damn reticent, she probably never would. But she did know he wasn't the arrogant jerk he'd been ten years ago. He was ambitious and determined, but he wasn't selfish. He was smart and loyal and, yes, infuriating.

It was a surprise to realize that she *liked* him. A lot. And that liking had nothing to do with his masculine face and sculpted muscles.

There was a great deal more to Mac McCaskill than his pretty packaging. Dammit.

With every conversation they shared he shattered another of her preconceptions. If they continued these conversations, she'd start to like him a little more than she should, and there was a possibility she would feel more for him than lust and attraction.

She couldn't let that happen. She would have to try to ignore him, try to avoid him. Because falling in lust with him was one thing, falling in *like* with him was another.

Falling in love with him would be intolerable.

So she simply wouldn't.

A week after landing in San Juan, Rory and Mac watched the sun go down in the small fishing village of Las Croabas. She was full to bursting from demolishing a massive bowl of crab seviche. She was relaxed and a little buzzy. The single glass of wine couldn't be blamed for that, she thought. No, it was a combination of the spectacular sunset—God was painting the sky with vivid purples and iridescent oranges—and the equally magnificent man who sat opposite her, hair ruffled by the balmy evening breeze.

A lovely sunset, a rustic restaurant, a really hot guy with a girl eating dinner…they could be an advertisement for romance, Rory thought. There would be no truth in that advertisement. Mac hadn't laid a finger on her since they'd arrived in Puerto Rico and he hadn't kissed her again. Truthfully, she hadn't given him any opportunity to do either as she'd made a point of spending as little time with him as she possibly could without shirking her duties.

But a girl had to eat, and over dinner she'd intercepted a couple of intense looks from him, which made her think he'd catch her if she decided to jump him.

Which she wouldn't. But the will-he-won't-he anticipation was, admittedly, very hot and incredibly sexy.

"There's something I have to tell you," Mac said.

That sounded ominous, Rory thought. "What is it?"

"There's a hurricane on the way." He lifted his seviche-filled fork to his mouth.

"A big one?" she squawked, half lifting her butt off her seat and whipping around to inspect the horizon. It was still cloud-free. Shouldn't there be clouds?

Mac shrugged. "Big enough."

"How big is *big enough*?" Rory demanded. How could he eat? A natural phenomena was about to smack them in the face. "When will it arrive? Should we evacuate? Are there bunkers?"

Mac sent her a puzzled glance. "It's a hurricane, not a nuclear bomb, Rorks."

"You're not giving me any information!" Rory wailed. She tried to recall what she'd read about preparing for a hurricane and, unfortunately, it wasn't a lot. Or anything at all. "Don't we need to put boards up or something?"

"I've arranged to have some guys come over tomorrow to put the boards up. Stupid, because I could do them if it wasn't for this arm!"

"I'm sure I can do it," Rory bravely suggested. She didn't know if she could but she thought she should offer.

Mac smiled at her. "No offense, Rorks, but it'll take them a couple of hours and it would take you two weeks."

"Why do people always say 'no offense' and then go on to offend you?" Rory grumbled.

"How often have you wielded a hammer?"

Rory lifted her nose at his smirk. "I pound in my own hooks to hang pictures." Well, she had once and had lost a fingernail in the process. Troy then banned her from using tools. He'd fixed her cupboard door, replaced the broken tile in her shower, fixed the leaky pipe under her sink. Troy also changed the tires on her car, made a mean chicken parmesan and removed spiders. He'd be her perfect husband if he only liked girls. And if she was even marginally attracted to him.

"Liar," Mac said cheerfully.

His ability to see through her annoyed the pants off her. Actually, the way he looked, his deep voice, his laugh—all of it made her want to drop her pants, but that was another story entirely. "Tell me about the hurricane!"

Mac dug his fork into his salad. "I'm not sure what you want to know. There's a hurricane approaching. It'll probably hit land around midnight tomorrow night. There will be wind, rain. We'll be fine."

Rory scowled at him. "You are so annoying."

Mac's lips twitched. "I try." He dumped some wine into their glasses, picked hers up and handed it to her. "Drink. We might as well enjoy the gorgeous night before we die."

Rory rolled her eyes. "If you're going to be a smart-ass, there has to be some smart involved. Otherwise you just sound like an ass." She took the glass from his hand, looked into his amused eyes and sighed. "I'm overreacting, aren't I?"

Mac lifted his glass to his lips, sipped and swallowed. "Just a little." He sent her another quick, quirky smile. "We'll be fine. If I thought we were in danger, I'd be making arrangements to get you out of here."

Rory nodded and took a large sip of her wine. Okay, then. Maybe she could cope with the hurricane. She glanced at the sky. "Tomorrow night, huh?"

Mac lifted his hand and rubbed his thumb across her bottom lip. He lingered there, pressing the fullness before moving from her lip and drifting up and over her cheekbone. She watched as his eyes deepened, turned a blue-black in the early evening light. Rory tossed a look at the beach and wished she could jump up from the table and walk—run—away.

She'd been doing that for the last week, finding any excuse to avoid him. She left his presence when she felt the spit drying up in her mouth, when she felt the first throb between her legs. Because Mac spent most of his time shirtless, she'd spent a lot of time walking away from him. She'd run to the beach, run *on* the beach, had started canoeing and snorkeling again. She'd also taken a lot of cold showers.

She was *so* pathetic.

"You can't run off in the middle of a meal," Mac told her, his eyes dancing.

Rory lifted her nose and tried to look puzzled. "Sorry?"

"You've been avoiding me, running away every time something sparks between us," Mac said conversationally, dropping his hand from her face and popping an olive from his salad into his mouth.

"Uh—"

"You're not alone. Every time you do therapy on me,

I have to stop myself from grabbing you and kissing you senseless."

Rory groaned and dropped her chin to her chest.

Mac twisted his fingers in hers. "Your hands touch me and I inhale your scent—you smell so damn good—and my brain starts to shut down. It's not just you, Rory."

Rory picked up her glass and sipped, trying to get some moisture back into her mouth. "Ah… I'm not sure what to say."

"Avoiding each other makes it worse. It's driving me crazy. I barely sleep at night because I want you in my bed." Mac's voice raised goose bumps all over her skin. "What are we going to do about this…situation, Rory?"

Rory touched the top of her lip with the tip of her tongue and her eyelids dropped to half-mast. Couldn't he see the big fat take-me-now sign blazing from her forehead in flashing neon?

She blew out a breath and sent him a rueful shrug. Mac seemed to have a hard time taking his eyes off her mouth. He was enjoying the anticipation, too, she realized when his gaze slammed into hers, his eyes hot and filled with passion.

"How the hell am I supposed to resist you?" he demanded.

Rory rolled her shoulders and gripped his wrist.

"I don't do relationships," Mac growled.

"I don't either," Rory softly replied. "But I can't stop wondering whether we'll be as good together as all the kisses we've shared suggest."

Mac shot up and with one step he was standing in front of her and pulling her to her feet. Keeping his injured arm hanging at his side, he used his other arm to yank her into his hard chest. His mouth slammed against hers.

His tongue slid once, then twice over her lips, and she immediately opened her mouth and allowed him inside. He tasted of wine and sex and heat, and Rory pushed into him so she could feel her nipples touch his chest through the thin fabric of their cotton shirts. She sighed when his erection nudged her stomach, and she linked her hands at the back of his neck to stop herself from reaching down and encircling him. Kissing in a public place was one thing, but heavy petting was better done in a more private setting.

"You taste so damn good," Mac muttered against her lips, his hand sliding over her butt. "And you feel even better."

"Kiss me again," Rory demanded, tipping her head to the side so he could change the angle of the kiss, go deeper and wetter.

"If I kiss you again I don't know if I'm gonna be able to stop," Mac replied, resting his forehead on hers.

"Who asked you to?"

Mac half laughed and half groaned. "You're not helping, Rorks." He stepped back and pushed her hair, curly from the humidity, from her eyes. "Let's take a step back here, think about this a little more. Make damn sure it's what we want."

Rory glanced down, saw the evidence of his want and lifted an eyebrow. "We both want it, McCaskill."

"Yeah, but what we want is not always good for us," Mac said, suddenly somber. He picked up her hand and rubbed the ball of his thumb across her knuckles. "We're here for a little while longer, Rory. I don't want to muck this up. There are consequences."

"I'm on the pill and I expect you to use a condom."

"Noted. But those aren't the consequences I'm worrying about."

Rory cocked her head. "Okay, what are you talking about?"

"I don't want either of us to regret this in the morning, to feel awkward, to feel we've made a colossal mistake." Mac looked uncharacteristically unsure of himself as he tugged at the collar of his white linen button-down shirt. "Taking you to bed would be easy, Rory. Making love to you would be a pleasure. In the morning we're both still going to be here. You still need to treat me and we have to live together. I don't want it to get weird between us."

Those were all fair points. "Anything else?"

Mac looked around them, frowned and rocked on his heels. "We're flying under the radar here but if just one person sees us, snaps a photo—we're toast. If it gets out that you're my physio, or that we're sleeping together and you are my ex's sister, it'll be news."

She hauled in a sharp breath. Wow, she hadn't even considered that.

"The media will go nuts and you'll be at the center of it, like Shay was," Mac added.

The thought made her want to heave. She'd never felt comfortable in the limelight and couldn't think of anything worse than being meat for the media's grinder.

"They will wonder why you—the best physiotherapist around—are treating me and why are you doing it in secret. They'll dig until they find out the truth," Mac said.

Rory dropped her head to look at the floor.

"Are you prepared to risk all that, Rory? Can you deal with the consequences of the worst-case scenario?"

"It won't happen." Rory bit her bottom lip.

"Probably not, but what if it does? Can you deal?"

"Can you?" Rory demanded. "You have more to lose than I do."

"Yeah, don't think that I haven't realized that," Mac muttered, and pinched the bridge of his nose with his finger and thumb. When he opened his eyes, she saw the ruefulness, the touch of amusement, in his gaze.

"Yet I still want you. I'm really hoping to get over it," he added. His tone invited her to help him break the tension, to get over this awkward, emotion-tinged moment. He picked up his wineglass, drained the contents and looked at his empty glass. "See, you're driving me to drink."

Rory bumped her wineglass against his. "I feel your pain. You should try living inside my head."

Mac dropped a quick, hard kiss on her mouth. "Help me out and be sensible about this, Rorks. I'm relying on you to be the adult here because I have little or no sense when it comes to wanting you."

Well, that comment didn't help!

Seven

The next day Rory stood on the beach in front of the house and knew Mac was watching her from the balcony, his good hand gripping the railing, his expression brooding. She tilted her face up and looked for the sun, now hidden behind gloomy, dark clouds. She'd been, maybe obsessively, glued to the Weather Channel, and she knew the hurricane was about twelve hours away. It would slam into them later tonight.

The wind had already picked up and was whipping her hair around her head and pushing her sarong against her thighs. The sea, normally gentle, was choppy and rough, and foam whipped across the surface of the ocean. It looked nothing like the warm friend who had been sharing his delights and treasures with her on a daily basis.

Everything was changing, Rory thought. She picked a piece of seaweed off her ankle, tossed it and watched the wind whisk it away. Like she'd have to face the hurricane, she couldn't run away from Mac anymore. She couldn't hide. She couldn't avoid him or the passion he whipped up in her.

He was right, she had a choice to make...hell, she'd already made the choice. She knew it. He knew it... If she gave him the slightest hint, like breathing, he'd do her in a New York minute.

What she had to do now was stand strong and ride the winds, hoping she'd come out with as little damage as possible when it all ended. Her desire—no, her *need*—for him was too strong, too compelling. She just had to ride the crazy as best she could and hope she could stop the lines between lust and like—she absolutely refused to use any other *L* word—from smudging together.

She turned and looked back at the house and across the sand, across the shrubs that separated the beach from his house, their eyes met. Even at a distance she could see and feel his desire for her, knew that hers was in her heated eyes, on her face, in every gesture she made.

She couldn't run away anymore so she ran to him, into that other hurricane rapidly bearing down on her, one that was even scarier than the one approaching from the sea.

She couldn't wait another second, another minute. Her resistance had petered out. Her need for him was greater than her desire to protect herself. This was it, this was now...

Rory picked up the trailing ends of her sarong and pulled the fabric up above her knees and belted across the sand. The wind tossed her hair into her eyes and she grabbed the strands blowing in her face, holding them out of her eyes so she could watch Mac, watch for that moment when he realized she wasn't running away from the storm but running to him, running into the tempest she knew she'd find in his touch.

He wasn't an idiot so he caught on pretty quickly. She knew it by the way he straightened, the way his appreciative glance became predatory, anticipatory. But he just stood on the balcony, waiting for her to fly to him. She knew he was waiting for her to change her mind, like she'd been doing, to avoid the steps that led from the path directly to where he was standing. He was expecting her to veer off and enter the house, access her room via the second set of stairs farther along.

She wanted to yell at him that she wouldn't change her mind, that she wanted him intensely, crazily, without thought. She hurtled up the steps and bolted onto the balcony, skidding to a stop when he leaned his hip against the railing and jammed his hand into the pocket of his expensive khaki shorts.

What if she'd read the situation wrong? What if he'd changed his mind? Rory flushed with embarrassment and dropped her gaze, looking at her cherry-red toes. She'd picked the color because she thought it was vibrant, sexy, because she could imagine him taking her baby toe, exquisitely sensitive and tipped with red, into his hot mouth…

Rory let out a small moan and closed her eyes.

"You okay?" Mac asked, and when she heard the amusement in his voice she flushed again. God, she must look like an idiot. She *was* an idiot.

"Fine."

Mac's penetrating gaze met hers. "On the beach, you made a decision."

She rocked on her heels. "Yep."

"You're sure?"

"Yep."

He didn't move toward her. Was he waiting for her to make the first move? Unsure, it had been so damn long since she'd danced this dance, she looked around for a temporary distraction because she had no idea what to do, to say. "Storm is on its way."

Mac's eyes didn't leave her face. "I know. Are you scared?"

Of this? Of liking you too much? Of making a mistake? Absolutely terrified.

"I'm a hurricane virgin," she admitted, trying for a light tone but hearing only her croaky voice.

"I have a plan to distract you," Mac softly stated, moving so he stood so close to her that his chest brushed her cotton shirt. He pushed his thigh between her legs as he placed his wineglass on the table next to him. "But in order for the distraction to work we have to practice, often."

Rory closed her eyes in relief and smiled. "Really? It'll have to be very good to distract me from the storm."

"That's why we have to practice." Mac placed his hand on her hip, sliding it under the fabric of her sarong, his hand making contact with the bare skin at her waist. Rory looked at his mouth and stood on her toes, reaching up so her lips met his. His mouth softened, his eyes closed and his long lashes became smudges on his cheeks. She felt him holding back, felt the tension as his mouth rested on hers, as if he were savoring the moment, taking stock. She placed her hand on his waist and flicked her tongue out to trace his lips, to encourage him to let go, to come out and play.

Mac exploded. His good arm went around her back and she was pulled flush against him as his mouth plundered hers in a kiss that was all heat and passion and pent-up frustration. His tongue twisted around hers and his hand pushed the fabric of her sarong down her hips. The knot in the fabric impeded his progress. He pulled back and hissed in frustration.

"You're going to have to help me, honey," he said, his voice rough and growly. He swore. "I want to rip everything off you but that's not gonna happen. Get naked, please?"

Rory, her hands now linked around his neck, dropped her head back so she could look into his frustrated face. Against her stomach she felt the hard, long line of his erection and she noticed the fine tremors skittering under his skin. He was half insane with wanting her and she liked him like that. Maybe she could drive him a little crazier...

It would be fun to try. "I think you need to get naked first," she said, stepping back.

"Uh, no." Mac gripped the hand that started to undo the buttons on his shirt. "If that happens then this is going to be over a lot sooner than we'd like."

Rory placed a kiss on the V just below his throat. "I'm not going to let that happen. I intend to go very, very slowly." She carried on with separating the buttons from their holes and then she pushed the sides of his shirt apart and placed her hands on his pecs, his flat nipples underneath her palms. Mac's hand reached between them to echo her movement by placing his hand on her breast.

"No bare skin," he complained.

Rory reached for her thin cotton shirt and pulled it over her head to reveal her strapless bikini top. Allowing him a moment to look, she pushed his shirt off his shoulder and gently maneuvered the shirt down his hurt arm, dropping kisses on the still-bruised skin. "You sure you can do this?" she murmured, her mouth against his biceps.

"My arm hurts, not the rest of me. Well, another part of me is aching, too, but in the best way possible." He tugged at the edge of her tangerine bikini top, looking impatient. "Take this off. Take it all off."

Rory reached behind her with one hand and undid the snap. The top fell forward and Mac pulled the fabric down, and she allowed it to drop to the ground as she watched him peruse her. His fingers drifted over her already puckered nipples and she sucked in a breath when he dropped his head so that his lips closed over her in a deep, seductive kiss.

She could feel her nipple on the roof of his mouth and shuddered as his tongue swept over her, once, twice. She was supposed to be making him crazy, she thought, yet he was the one pushing her. Dropping her head back, she threaded one hand into his hair to hold him in place as he put one knee on the daybed next to him to align his mouth perfectly with her chest. Moving away, he dropped a hot kiss onto her sternum before turning his mouth to the neglected nipple on her other breast. Rory pulled the knot of her sarong apart and pushed her bikini bottoms down her hips, forgetting about them as they fell to the floor.

She felt Mac stiffen as he looked down. What would he see? A flat stomach with a faded appendix scar, a narrow landing strip and short legs? She'd far prefer he touch rather than look.

"Mac," she groaned. God, she'd waited ten long years for him to touch her there yet he kept his forehead between her breasts, huffing like a freight train.

"Getting there," Mac muttered. "God, you're gorgeous. I could look at you forever."

"I'd prefer you use your hands and mouth," Rory told him, pushing his hand between her legs. She couldn't wait, she was burning with need.

Mac's hard, knowing fingers found her bud and had her arching her back. She felt the insistent throbbing that told her she was so very close to losing it. It took one sliding finger and she was exploding, bucking, sobbing and laughing, tumbling along that fantastically ferocious wave of pure, cosmic pleasure.

When her pleasure tapered off, leaving her lady parts still tingling, she realized she was half sitting on Mac's thighs, his mouth was on her breast and his erection was tenting his pants. Climbing off him, she helped him push his shorts over his hips so he was free to her touch. She wrapped her hands around him and smiled at his shudder and desperate groan.

He pulled her hands away one at a time and held her wrists behind her back with one hand. "I'm so close. If you squeeze me once…"

Rory shrugged. "Not a problem." Actually, she'd love to see him lose control.

"Hell, no," Mac said, dropping his lips to pull the skin beneath her ear. "I want to be inside you. I need to be inside you."

"Okay," Rory told him, her hand drifting across his eight-pack. "God, you have the most amazing body."

His erection jumped at her words and his mouth slammed onto hers. Pulling her down to the daybed, he lay on his back and Rory flung a leg over him, immediately settling her happy spot on his hard shaft. She was going to come again. Woo-hoo, lucky her.

"Condom," she gasped, needing him to slide on home.

Mac lifted his hips and pushed his hand under the cushion next to his thigh. He cursed when he came up empty.

"Try the other side," he huffed, and Rory leaned sideways to pat the space under the cushion. Feeling the cool foil packets, she pulled a condom loose, and instead of one, she held a four-pack in her hand. She looked down and then lifted an eyebrow in Mac's direction.

"Confident, aren't you?" she asked.

"Prepared. I have them stashed all over the house," Mac admitted, grabbing a condom and lifting the packet to his teeth to open it. He cursed at his clumsiness and Rory took it from him.

"So, when did you put the packet of condoms there, McCaskill?" she asked as she rolled the latex down his shaft.

Mac grinned. "Ten minutes after we arrived. Though, to be fair, I've had this fantasy about making love to you since the day we met."

Rory jerked at his words. Which time? Years ago or weeks ago? Then the questions disappeared as Mac pushed into her, stretching and filling and completing her.

She rose and fell, easily matching his rhythm. He filled her cold and empty spaces, she thought, as he speared up into her. She glanced down and saw him watching her, his eyes deep and dark and determined. "Come for me, baby."

Not able to refuse him, Rory shattered around him, and from a place far away she felt his last thrust, felt him pulse against her as her followed her over the cliff.

Rory collapsed against his chest. His good arm wrapped around her as she turned her face into his neck.

She inhaled the scents of the fragrant, perfumed air and sex, felt his thumping heart beneath hers, the rough texture of his chest hair beneath her cheek.

This place, here in his embrace, was the place she felt safest. Happiest. The place she most wanted to be.

Dammit.

Mac had always liked hurricanes. The power extreme weather contained was thrilling. He'd experienced two storms on the island before and neither had done much damage. He expected this storm would be more of the same.

He stood on the veranda and watched the sky darken. The wind was picking up and he mentally took inventory of his hurricane supplies. They had enough water and food for three days, adequate lighting for when the power went off and he had, and knew how to use, his extensive first-aid kit. They were ready for the storm; the boards were up courtesy of a couple of young guys from the village who'd made short work of the task. They'd also moved the outside furniture into the store rooms next to the garage and generally made themselves useful. They would be fine and if it was just him, he'd jump into bed with a good book and let the storm do its thing, but Rory was acting like it was the hour before the world ended. He turned his head and saw that she sat where he'd left her, in the corner of the couch, her arms clutching a pillow in a death grip, her eyes wide and scared.

"Relax, we'll be fine," he told her.

"We're on the edge of a beach with a hurricane approaching…which means big waves and big wind. I think I've got a right to panic," Rory retorted. "Will you please come inside?"

Mac lifted his face to the sky, enjoying the rain-tinged wind on his face. "I built this house to be, as much as possible, hurricane-proof."

"Don't you have a shelter?"

"That's for tornadoes, not hurricanes." Mac told her, walking back into the room. He lifted a bottle of wine and aimed the opening at her glass. "Have some wine, try to relax."

"Huh." Rory gulped from her glass and her anxious eyes darted to the rapidly darkening sky.

He needed to distract her or else she'd soon be a basket case. The wind howled and the lights flickered. Rory pushed herself farther into the corner of the couch. He sat down next to her, put his feet up onto the coffee table and placed his hand on her thigh beneath the edge of her shorts. More sex would be a great distraction, he thought, but Rory's white face and tense body suggested she might kick him if he proposed that. Besides, they'd done it three times since noon. She needed some time to recover.

And that meant talking. Dammit. Not his best talent. Maybe he'd get lucky and she'd start.

He was given a temporary reprieve when his cell phone buzzed. Picking it up, he saw a message from Quinn, checking whether they were okay, and he quickly replied. He picked up Rory's cell phone and tossed it into her lap. "I suggest you let your friends and family know there is a hurricane and you are safe. They tend to freak if you don't. And the cell towers sometimes go down during storms so we might lose our signal."

Rory nodded quickly and her fingers flew across the keypad. Within thirty seconds her phone buzzed and she was smiling at the message on the screen. "It's Shay, suggesting I climb under a bed with a bottle of vodka."

Shay…now there was a subject they'd been avoiding. He sipped his wine and rested his head on the back of the couch. "Did you take flak because we almost kissed?"

Rory tapped her finger against her glass. "You have no idea. She refused to talk to me for six months and it took us a while to find our groove again."

Mac frowned. "Look, I admit I wasn't exactly Prince Charming that night, I messed up in numerous ways but, God, we were young, and nothing happened!" Mac waited a beat. "Even if that open-mic incident hadn't happened, she knew we were on our way out—"

"She'd mentioned she thought she was approaching her expiry date," Rory interjected, her voice dry.

Mac winced. "Look, I can understand her thinking I'm a douche, but why couldn't she forgive you?"

Rory's eyes flicked to his face and went back to studying her wine. "The reason why Shay has such massive insecurities and the reason why I am not good at relationships is the same."

Wait. Why would she think that she wasn't good at relationships? She was open and friendly and funny and smart, who wouldn't want to be in a relationship with her? Well, he wouldn't…but he didn't want to be in a relationship with anyone so he didn't count. She had to be better at relationships than he was; then again, pretty much ninety percent of the world's population was. "How do you know that you are bad at relationships?"

Rory's laugh was brittle. She looked him in the eye and tried, unsuccessfully, to smile. "I can date, I can flirt, I can do light and fluffy, but I suck at commitment. I drive men crazy."

He couldn't imagine it. Here he was, the King of Easily Bored, and he was as entranced with Rory as he'd been from the beginning. "How?"

Rory waved his question away. "When I think things are getting hot or heavy or too much to deal with—when I get scared—I take the easy way out and I run. I just disappear."

There was a message in her statement and he was smart enough to hear it. When she thought their time was over she'd make like Casper and fade away. Good to know, he thought cynically. Thinking back, he remembered what she'd said earlier. "You said there was a reason why you and Shay act like you do. Will you tell me what it is?"

He was as surprised as she looked at his question. He hadn't intended to ask that. Did he really want to know the answer? It seemed he did, he reluctantly admitted. Rory was, when she let go, naturally warm and giving, and he wondered why she felt the need to protect herself.

"Well, that's a hell of a subject to discuss during a hurricane," Rory replied, tucking her feet under her. "Actually, it's a hell of a subject at any time."

"We can talk about something else, if you prefer." Mac backtracked to give her, and him, an out of the conversation. He stood and walked over to the open balcony doors, holding his flashlight in his hand. Unable to resist the power of the approaching storm, he stepped outside and let the rapidly increasing wind slam into him. He leaned forward, surprised that the wind could hold him upright as the rain smacked his face like icy bullets.

Hello, Hurricane Des, Mac thought as he stepped back into the house and closed and bolted the doors behind him. The lights flickered and he checked that the hurricane lamp and matches were on the coffee table. They would probably lose power sooner rather than later. Mac resumed his seat, linked his hands across his stomach and looked at Rory. "Want to talk about something else?"

Rory shrugged and pulled the tassels of the pillow through nervous fingers. He knew it wasn't only the crazy wind slamming into the house that made her nervous. The power dropped, surged and died.

"Perfect," Rory muttered.

Within a minute Mac had the hurricane lamps casting a gentle glow across the room and smiled at Rory's relieved sigh. "My parents are hugely dysfunctional..."

"Aren't they all?"

Rory cocked an eyebrow at his interruption but he gestured for her to continue. "When I was thirteen, I was in the attic looking for an old report card—I wanted to show Shay that I was better at math than she was." Rory tipped her head. "Strange that I remember that... Anyway, I was digging in an old trunk when I found photographs of my father with a series of attractive women." Rory pushed her hair back with one hand. Her eyes looked bleak. "It didn't take me long to realize those photos were the reason why my dad moved out of the house for months at a time."

Mac winced.

"He betrayed my mother with so many women," Rory continued. "I've always felt—and I know Shay does too—that he betrayed us, his family. He cheated on my mom and he cheated us of his time and his love, of being home when we needed him. He always put these other women before us, before me. Yet my mother took him back, still takes him back."

Okay, now a lot of Shay's crazy behavior made sense. "Hell, baby."

"He said one thing but his actions taught me the opposite."

"What do you mean?"

Rory shrugged. "He'd tell me that he was going on a work trip but a friend would tell me that she saw him at the mall with another woman. Or he'd say that he was going hunting or fishing but he never shot a damn thing. Or ever caught a fish.

"And my mother's misery was a pretty big clue that he was a-huntin' and a-fishin' for something outside the animal kingdom."

Underneath the bitterness he heard sadness and the echo of a little girl who'd lost her innocence at far too young an age.

"I thought the world of him, loved him dearly and a part of me still does. But the grown-up me doesn't like him much and, after a lifetime of lies, I can't believe a word he says. I question everything he does. As a result, trust is a difficult concept for me and has always been in short supply." Rory dredged up a smile.

Mac swallowed his rage and stopped himself from voicing his opinion about her father. Telling Rory that he thought her father was a waste of skin wouldn't make her feel better. Rory was bright and loving and giving and her father's selfishness had caused her to shrink in on herself, to limit herself to standing on the outside of love and life, looking in. She deserved to be loved and cherished and protected—by someone, not by Mac but by someone who would make her happy.

God, he wanted to thump the man for ripping that away from her.

"Tell me about your childhood, Mac," Rory softly asked, dropping her head to rest it against the back of the couch. "Dear God, that wind sounds like a banshee on crack."

"Ignore it. We're safe," Mac told her, slipping his hand between her knees. He never spoke about his blue-collar upbringing in that industrial, cold town at the back end of the world. It was firmly in his past.

But there was something about sitting in the semidark with Rory, safe from the wind and rain, that made him want to open up. "Low income, young, uneducated single mother. She had few of her own resources, either financial or emotional. She relied on a steady stream of men to provide both."

He waited to see disgust on Rory's face or, worse, pity. There was neither, she just looked at him and waited. Her lack of reaction gave him the courage to continue. "I was encouraged *not* to go to school, *not* to go to practice, not to aim for anything higher than a dead-end job at the canning factory or on one of the fishing boats. When I achieved anything, I was punished. And badly."

Rory sat up, and in the faint glow of the lamp, he could see her horrified expression. "What?"

Mac shrugged. "Crabs in a bucket."

"What are you talking about?" Rory demanded.

"You put a bunch of crabs in a bucket, one will try to climb out. The other crabs won't let that happen. They pull at the crab who's trying to escape until he falls back down. My mother was the perfect example of crab mentality. She refused to allow me to achieve anything more than what she achieved, which was pretty much nothing."

"How did you escape?"

"Stubbornness and orneriness...and my skill with a stick. I waited her out and as soon as I finished school I left. I simply refused to live her life. There was only one person in life I could rely on and that was myself. I was the only one who could make my dreams come true…"

"And you did."

Mac looked at her. Yeah, he had. The wind emitted a high, sustained shriek and Rory grabbed his hand and squeezed. He couldn't blame her; it sounded like a woman screaming for her life, and the house responded with creaks and groans.

Through the screaming wind he heard the thump of something large and he looked into the impenetrable darkness to see what had landed on the veranda. A tree branch? A plastic chair his guys had left behind? Maybe it wasn't such a good idea to stay in the living room next to the floor-to-ceiling windows, even though they were covered with boards. He stood up and hauled Rory to her feet.

It was also the perfect time to end this conversation… Looking back changed nothing and there was nothing there he wanted to remember.

"Where are we going?" she asked as he picked up the lamp.

"Bathroom."

"Why?"

"It's enclosed and probably the safest place to wait out the storm," Mac said, pulling her down the passage.

"Are we in danger?" Rory squeaked, gripping his un-injured biceps with both hands as they walked into the solidly dark house.

"No." At least, he didn't think so, but while he was prepared to take his chances with the storm, he wasn't prepared to risk Rory. Mac pulled a heavy comforter from the top shelf in the walk-in closet and handed Rory the pillows from the bed. In the bathroom, Rory helped him put a makeshift bed between the bathtub and the sink. He sat with his back to the tiled wall and Rory lay down, her head on his thigh. Touching her hair, he listened to the sounds of the storm.

Rory yawned and tipped her head back to look at him. "I'm so tired."

Mac touched her cheek with the tips of his fingers. "Go to sleep…if you can."

"Can I put my head on your shoulder?" Rory asked. "At least then, if the roof blows off, I'll have you to hold on to."

"The roof isn't going to lift, oh, dramatic one." But he shifted down, placed a pillow beneath his head and wrapped his good arm around her slim back when she placed her head on his shoulder. Her leg draped over his and her knee was achingly close to his happy place. It would be so easy, a touch here, a stroke there…

Mac kissed her forehead and pulled her closer to him. "Go to sleep, Rorks. You're safe with me."

"Tonight's conversation didn't seem that light and fluffy, Mac," Rory murmured in a sleepy voice.

It hadn't been, Mac admitted. They'd have to watch out for that. It was his last thought before exhaustion claimed him.

Eight

There was nothing like the aftermath of a hurricane to decimate a romantic atmosphere, Rory thought, standing on the debris-filled veranda and looking out toward the devastated cove. The sea had settled and broken tree branches covered the beach. A kayak had landed in the pool and there were broken chairs on the beach path. The fence surrounding the property was bent and buckled and the power lines sagged.

Mac had gone to town at first light to call someone about cleaning up the property and to check on how the small fishing village north of the cove had fared. Rory's cell phone wasn't working and she felt cut off from the world. Taking a sip from her bottle of water, she felt sweat roll down her back. It was barely 7:00 a.m. but it was very hot and horribly humid.

The scope of the damage was awful but Rory was glad

to have some time to herself, away from Mac. Yesterday had been a watershed day—the sex was explosively wonderful and the storm had scared her into opening up to Mac, and that frightened her more than the wind.

Why had she shared her past with him? She never did that! Had she been that seduced by their wonderful lovemaking? Was it the romantic atmosphere and him being all protective that prompted her to emotionally erupt? They'd agreed to keep it light but last night's conversation had been anything but! Deep and soulful conversations led to thoughts of permanence and commitment, and they'd agreed they weren't going there. She was an emotional scaredy-cat and he was incapable of commitment.

Mac, she reminded herself, didn't want a relationship anymore than she did. He'd taught himself to be his own champion and she admired the hell out of him. But he didn't need her. Anyone who could fight his way out of the enveloping negativity of Mac's childhood didn't need anyone. He'd learned to survive and then to flourish. He was emotionally self-sufficient, and a woman would never be more than an accessory and a convenience to him.

What did it matter, anyway? Rory gripped the plastic bottle so hard that it buckled in her hand, the water overflowing to trickle onto her wrist. Men always disappointed and love never lasted and the fairy tales the world fed women about happily-ever-afters were a load of hooey. No, she'd stay emotionally detached, and by doing that, she'd never feel hurt or as out of control as she had when she was a child.

Rory straightened her spine. Mac was a nice guy, a sexy guy, but he wasn't *her* guy. It would be sensible for her to remember that because if she didn't and she did something imbecilic, like fall in love with him, she was just asking for big, messy trouble.

Maybe she should stop sleeping with him…

But look at him, Rory thought, watching as Mac walked up the path from the beach. How was she supposed to resist? He was shirtless and wearing a ball cap and board shorts, his chest glistening with perspiration.

Rory leaned on the railing, and as if he sensed her watching him, he turned and looked up at her, pulling his sunglasses from his face. "Hey. You okay?"

"Fine," Rory replied. "Was the village damaged?"

"Not too bad. Trees, some missing tiles…it could've been worse. Is the power back on?"

Rory shook her head. "No. And it's so damn hot. I'm desperate for a shower."

Mac gestured to the sea behind him. "Big bathtub on our doorstep. Come on down, we'll have a swim."

Rory pulled her sticky shirt off her body. "Good idea. Do you want some water?"

Mac nodded. "And a couple of energy bars. I'm starving."

"Five minutes," Rory replied. Instead of heading inside she just stared down at him, unable to get her feet to move.

It would be so easy to love him, she thought. She was already halfway there.

Yeah, but she couldn't trust him. And what was love without trust? An empty shell that would shatter at the first knock.

Don't be stupid, Rory, she thought as she turned away. *Just don't.*

By sundown there was still no power. They gathered up a beach blanket, a lamp and a makeshift supper and headed for the beach. In the golden rays of the sunset, they cleared sticks and leaves from a patch of sand, spread out the blanket and looked at the docile sea and the sky free of all but a few small clouds.

"If it wasn't for the mess you'd think nothing had happened," Mac said, echoing her thoughts. It was scary how often he did that. Scary and a little nice.

"Fickle nature," Rory agreed, pulling her tank top over her head and dropping the shirt to the sand. She shimmied out of her shorts and stood in her plain black bikini, desperate to feel the water against her skin. She turned to Mac and found him looking at her with a strange expression on his face. "Are you okay?"

"Yeah…just thinking how gorgeous you look."

Rory flushed and lifted her hand in dismissal. "I'm already sleeping with you, McCaskill, there's no need to go overboard."

Rory turned away and walked toward the sea, foolishly hurt by his compliment. She wasn't stupid. She'd seen the pictures of him in the papers, normally accompanied by a skinny, long-legged giraffe who could grace any catwalk anywhere in the world. Shay had been his first supermodel-gorgeous girlfriend, and every girlfriend since had been slinky and sexy. Tall, dammit.

Mac's hand on her shoulder spun her around. She swallowed when she saw the irritation in his eyes. "Don't do that!"

She widened her eyes to look innocent. "Do what?"

"Dismiss me. I never say things I don't mean and if I say you look gorgeous then I mean to say that you look freakin' amazing and I can't wait to get my hands on you."

Warmth blossomed in her stomach at his backhanded compliment. Freaking amazing? Did he really think so?

"I see doubt on your face again." Mac cradled her cheek in his hand. "Why?"

Oh, jeez, he would think she was stupidly insecure and horribly lacking in confidence. Which she was, but she didn't want him to *know* that. "Uh—"

"Why, Rory?"

Rory kicked her bare foot into the sand. "Um, maybe because all the girls you normally…uh, date…are about a hundred feet tall and stacked and I'm a munchkin with a flat chest and a complex."

Mac stared at her before releasing a long, rolling laugh. Rory narrowed her eyes at him while he tried to control himself, wiping at the tears in his eyes.

"Glad I amuse you," she said, her tone frosty.

"Oh, you really do." Mac took her hand and pulled her to the sea. Thoroughly irritated with him she yanked her hand from his and dived into an oncoming wave. She started to swim, only to be jerked back by a hand on her ankle. She rolled onto her back and scowled as she tried to pull her ankle from Mac's grip.

"Let me go." She tried, unsuccessfully, to kick him.

"Pipe down…*shrimp*."

Oh, that was fighting talk. She swiped her arm down and sprayed a stream of water into his face. Mac dropped her ankle and she launched herself at him, throwing a punch at his uninjured arm. "You jerk!"

Mac easily captured both her wrists in one hand and held them behind her back. Then he inched up two fingers to pull the strings that held her bikini top closed. He let her wrists go so he could pull the triangles over her head and toss the top onto the sand behind them before stepping back to look down at her breasts.

Moving them back into the shallows until they were standing in ankle deep water Mac placed his hands on her hips, keeping an arm's length between them. His gaze traveled from the tips of her head to where her feet disappeared into the water. Rory bit her lip and looked at the beach behind him, but Mac's fingers on her chin brought her eyes back to his face.

"I refuse to let you spend one more second thinking you are second-rate." Mac's voice was low and imbued with honesty. His fingers drifted down her neck, across her collarbone and down the swell of her breast. His thumb rubbed across her nipple and it puckered under his touch. "Yeah, you're small but perfect. So responsive, so sweet."

He bent his head and sucked her nipple into his mouth, causing her to whimper and arch her back. He licked and nibbled and then moved on to the other breast before sinking to his knees, his hands on her hips. He looked up at her, the gold and oranges of the sunset in his hair and on his face. "You are small but perfect."

He repeated the words, his thumbs tunneling under the sides of her bikini bottoms. "I lose myself in your eyes, drown in your laugh and feel at peace in your arms." His thumb skimmed over her sex and she whimpered when he touched her sweet spot. "I find myself when I'm deep inside you."

"Mac." She whimpered, needing him to…to…do something. More. Touch her, taste her. Complete her.

Rory thought she heard Mac say something like, "You are the fulfillment of every fantasy I've ever had," but all her attention was focused on his fingers, now deep inside her. He could've been proposing and she wouldn't have cared as her bikini bottoms dropped to the sand and his hot, hot mouth enveloped her.

He licked and she screamed. He repeated the motion and her knees buckled. He sucked and she fell apart, her orgasm hot and spectacular. When she sank to her knees in front of him, he tipped her flushed face upward and dropped a hot, openmouthed kiss on her lips. "As I said, you are utterly perfect. Let's swim naked," he suggested, picking up her bikini bottoms and throwing them in the same direction as her top.

Impossible man, Rory thought when her brain cells started firing again. Sexy, crazy, *impossible* man.

In the same restaurant they'd visited two weeks ago—a pink-and-yellow sunset tonight and no hurricane on the way—Mac tucked his credit card back into his wallet and gave Rory a crooked grin. "Eaten enough?"

Rory leaned back and patted her stomach. "Sorry, I'm a real girl who eats real food." *Not like those models you normally date*, she silently added.

"You ate fish stew, two empanadas and you still had pumpkin pudding." Mac shook his head. "I know every slim inch of you and I have no idea where all that food goes."

Rory picked up her drink, put the vividly green straw between her lips and sucked up some piña colada. Instead of responding, she fluttered her eyebrows at Mac, who smiled. God, she loved it when he smiled. It made her heart smile every single time.

Mac stood up and held out his hand. Rory put her hand in his and allowed him to pull her up from her chair. "Oof. You weigh a ton."

Rory slapped his shoulder. "Jerk."

"Well, you're going to work that food off."

Oh, she couldn't wait. Making love with Mac was fun, fantastic, toe-curling and, yes, it was athletic. Win win.

"What I have in mind is a bit more adventurous... Are you game?"

"Maybe," Rory carefully replied, doubt in her voice. "If it's not too kinky or too weird..."

His laughter, spontaneous and deep, rumbled across her skin and she shivered. Mac had a great laugh and, like smiling, he definitely didn't do enough of it.

"It's a surprise. A surprise that you have to work for but I promise it will be amazing." Mac brushed his lips across the top of her head. Then his arm snaked around her waist and he kissed her properly, crazily, tongues going wild. She melted against him, into him, swept up in her desire for him.

As usual, Mac was the first to pull back. He jerked back, looked down the beach and back to her mouth.

"What?" Rory pushed her hair off her face.

"Deciding whether to scrap my plans and hurry you home." Rory huffed her frustration when he stepped back and distanced himself from her. "Nope, I really want you to see this."

Mac glanced at the sunset, then at his watch and Rory noticed it was nearly dark. "Okay, it's dark enough, let's go."

"Go where?" Rory asked as he took her hand and led her down the restaurant steps toward the beach. She kicked off her sandals and sighed when her feet dipped into the still-warm sand. She picked up her shoes, slid her hand back into Mac's and followed his leisurely pace down the beach. What was he up to? And really, did it matter? It was a stunning summer's evening on the island, the air was perfumed and Mac was holding her hand, occasionally looking at her with the promise of passion in his eyes...

They walked in silence for another five minutes and then Mac angled right, walking toward the ocean until they saw a kayak and a young, hot surfer guy holding life jackets over his arm. Mac called a greeting and Surfer Boy grinned. Rory felt like a spare wheel when he bounded over the sand to pump Mac's hand, ask him how his arm was, to thank him for some tickets Mac had procured for him. Surfer Boy was about to launch into a play-by-play description when Mac interrupted him. "Marty, this is Rory. Are we all set to go?"

Marty realized he'd all but ignored her and blushed. "Sorry, hi, I didn't mean to be rude." He smiled ruefully. "I'm hockey obsessed, as you can tell. My folks have a place here so I spend my time between Vancouver and the island and I'm a huge Mavericks fan."

Rory's lips twitched in amusement. "Hi." She looked past him to the kayak at the water's edge before lifting an eyebrow in Mac's direction. "Are we're going paddling? At night?"

Mac grinned. "Yep."

"Sorry to point out the obvious, but we're not going to see much because it's dark," Rory responded. "And you definitely can't paddle with that arm."

Mac scowled. "I know and I hate it. But that's why you're paddling and I'm riding shotgun."

Rory looked at him, tall and built and strong. "Uh, Mac? I'm half your size."

"It's as flat as a mirror and it's not far. You'll be fine."

"Okay...but why?"

Mac took her hand, lifted it to his mouth and placed a hot, openedmouthed kiss on her knuckles. It was an old-fashioned, sexy gesture and Rory felt her womb quiver. "Trust me," he murmured, his eyes as deep a blue and as mysterious as the ocean beyond them. "It'll be worth it."

It was an intense moment, and Rory heard that sensible voice in her head. *Whatever is between us is about sex, not romance. Don't fall for it. Don't expect hearts and flowers along with the heat. Disappointment always follows expectations.*

She wouldn't be seduced by the island and the sunset and the heat in Mac's eyes. She would take this minute by minute, experience by experience, and she was not going to ruin it by letting her mind be seduced along with her body.

"Earth to Rory…?"

Rory saw Mac looking at her quizzically, waiting for a reply. What had he said?

"There are one or two other things I could think of that I'd rather do in the dark—" she gave Mac a mischievous look "—but what the hell. Okay."

The corners of Mac's lips kicked up and a laugh rumbled in the back of his throat.

"Funny girl," he replied in his coated-with-sin voice as Marty pretended to ignore their banter. Dropping her hand, Mac took a step back and gestured to Marty. "Right. You'll be here when we get back?"

"I'll be here," Marty promised. "You need life jackets but put on bug repellent first. And lots of it."

Marty pulled out a container from his back pocket and handed it to Rory. "If you don't slap it on everywhere, the mosquitoes will carry you away."

Rory wrinkled her nose. Where on earth were they

going? Knowing she would just have to wait and see, she rubbed the cream on her face, over her arms and down her legs. Then she pulled on a life jacket, tightened the clasps and went over to the double kayak.

She kicked off her shoes and pushed the kayak into the water before hopping into the seat. While she waited for Mac to get ready, she pulled her hair back from her face and secured it into a ponytail with the band she'd found in the back pocket of her cotton shorts. The stars were magnificent, she thought, a trillion fairy lights starting at the horizon and continuing ad infinitum.

She trailed her hand through the warm water, now impatient to get wherever they were going. Mac took the front seat after helping Marty push the kayak into deeper water, still looking irritated that he wasn't paddling—the man hated relinquishing control. Within a couple of strokes Rory found her rhythm and she followed Mac's directions across the small fisherman's harbor to what seemed to be an entrance to a coastal reserve. Mac unerringly directed her toward a channel between huge mangrove trees. Only the light of his strong flashlight penetrated the darkness. It really was an easy paddle despite Mac's bulk. She listened to the sounds coming from deep within the forest, birds and frogs, she presumed, as she navigated the low-hanging branches of a tree.

"Not far now." Mac's deep voice drifted past her ear as they leaned backward to skim under another branch. "Are you okay?"

"Sure."

"Not scared?"

"Please." She snorted her disdain. "I survived a life-threatening hurricane. Though I wouldn't mind if I was the one lounging around while you did the work."

"I wish I was. I feel like I've surrendered my man card," Mac grumbled, but she heard the grin in his voice.

"I'll reinstate it later," Rory replied in her sultriest voice.

Mac laughed and she cursed as the bow of her kayak bounced off another branch. "Dammit. How far do we have left?"

"We're almost there," Mac replied as she moved backward and around the branch with the aid of the flashlight Mac held. Rory paddled for a minute more and then the channel opened and they entered a small bay. Mac told her to head for the middle of the bay.

When she stopped, she looked at the shadows of the mangrove forest that surrounded them. The moon hung heavy in the sky and the air caressed her skin. Gorgeous.

"Look at your oar, babe," Mac softly told her. Rory glanced down and gasped with delight. Every paddle stroke left a starburst in the water, a bright streak of bioluminescence that was breathtakingly beautiful.

"Oh, my God," Rory said, pulling her hand through the water, hoping to catch a star. "That's amazing. What is it?"

"Dinoflagellates," Mac replied. "Prehistoric one-celled organisms, half animal, half plant. When they are disturbed, they respond by glowing like fireflies."

"They are marvelous. So incredibly beautiful."

"Worth the effort?" Mac asked, lazily turning around to look at her.

Rory leaned forward to rest her temple on his shoulder. "So worth it. Thank you." A fish approached the kayak and darted underneath, leaving a blue streak to mark his route.

Mac reached for her hand. Their fingers linked but

cupped, they lowered them into the water. When they lifted them out it looked like they held sparkling glitter. The water dropped back into the lagoon, and when the initial glow subsided, the glitter still danced in the water.

"The mangroves feed the organisms, releasing vitamin B12 into the water. This, with sunlight, keeps them alive," Mac told her.

Her heart thumped erratically, her fingers, in his, trembled. With want. And need. With the sheer delight of being utterly alone with him in this bay, playing in Mother Nature's jewelry box. She wanted more experiences like this with Mac. She wanted to experience the big and small of life with him. The big, like seeing the bay sparkle, the small, like sharing a Sunday-morning cup of coffee.

She wanted more than she should. She wanted it all.

Rory dipped her paddle into the water and looked at the sparkling outline…spectacular. She knew Mac was watching her profile, his gaze all coiled grace and ferocious intent.

This was beautiful. He was beautiful, too, Rory thought. But like the bioluminescent streaks, he was fleeting.

She could enjoy him, marvel over him, admire him, but he was so very, very temporary.

Nine

There was too much resistance in his arm, Rory thought, frowning. On day twenty-one of physio, a month after his injury she stood behind Mac, gently massaging his bicep and trying to figure out why he was having a buildup of lactic acid in his muscle. The resistance exercises she'd given him shouldn't have made this much of an impact. She'd been very careful to keep the exercises low-key, making sure the muscle wasn't stressed more than it needed to be.

Unless…she stiffened as a thought slapped her. Hell, no, he couldn't be that stupid, could he?

Rory held his arm, her hand perfectly still as she turned that thought over in her mind. He wouldn't be sneaky enough to go behind her back and push himself, would he?

Oh, yeah, he would.

"Problem?" Mac tipped his head back and she looked into those gorgeous, inky eyes. Look at him, all innocent. Rory whipped around the bed and stood next to him, her hands gripping her hips and her mouth tight with anger.

"Did you really think I wouldn't notice?" she demanded, making an effort to keep her anger in control.

Mac sat up slowly, and she saw he was deciding whether to bluff his way out of the situation. It would be interesting to see which way he swung, Rory thought. Would he be a grown-up and come clean, or would he act like he had no idea what she was talking about?

"I knew that I could push a little harder," Mac replied in a cool, even tone.

Points to him that he didn't try to duck the subject. Or lie.

"Did you get a physiotherapy degree in the last month or so, smarty-pants?"

Mac ignored her sarcasm. "I know my body, Rory. I know what I can handle."

"And I have a master's degree in physiotherapy specializing in sports injuries, you moron! I know what can go wrong if you push too hard too fast!" Rory yelled, deeply angry. "Are you so arrogant you think you know better than I do? That my degrees mean nothing because you know your body?"

"I utterly respect what you do," Mac calmly stated, linking his hands on his stomach, "but you don't seem to understand that this body is my tool, my machine. I know it inside out and I need you to trust me to know how far I can push myself."

"You *need* to *trust* me to know what's best for you in this situation," Rory shouted. "This is a career-threatening injury, Mac!"

"I know that!" Mac raised his voice as well, swinging his legs over the edge of the bed. "Do you not think I don't lie awake every night wondering if I'm going to regain full movement, whether I'll be able to compete again? The scenarios run over and over in my head, but I've got to keep moving forward. That means working it."

"That means resting it," Rory retorted. "You're pushing too hard."

"You're not pushing me enough!" Mac yelled as he stood up. "I can do this, Rory."

Rory looked at him and shook her head. *Look at him, all muscle and hardheadedness*, she thought. Beautiful but so incredibly flawed. He had to go full tilt, had to push the envelope. But he refused to accept that this envelope was made of tissue paper and could rip at a moment's notice.

Would rip at a moment's notice.

She couldn't stop him, she realized. He'd ignore her advice and go his own way.

Rory lifted her hands, palms out. "I can't talk to you right now."

"Rorks—"

"I'm not discussing this right now." Rory walked toward the door.

Mac's arm shot out to block her way. When she tried to duck underneath it, he wrapped his arm around her waist and held her, far too easily, against his chest. "No, you're not just walking out. We're going to finish this argument. We're adults. That's what adults do."

"Let me go, Mac." Rory pushed against his arm. She struggled against him, desperate to get away.

"God, you smell so good." Mac dropped his mouth to her shoulder and nuzzled her. His teeth scraped over her skin and Rory shuddered, feeling heat pool low in her abdomen. She shouldn't be doing this, she thought. She should be walking away, but Mac's hand cupping her breast, his thumb gliding over her nipple, shoved that thought away.

Stupid, stupid, stupid, she thought as she arched her back and pushed her breast into his palm. Mac pulled her nipple through the cotton fabric as he pushed the straps of her shirt and bra down her shoulder with his teeth. His breath was warm on her skin and she reached back to place her hand on the hair-roughened skin of his thigh, just below the edge of his shorts. Hard muscle tensed beneath her hand and he groaned as he pushed his erection into her lower back.

Ooh, nice. Rory twisted her head up and back, and Mac met her lips with his, his tongue invading her mouth to tangle lazily with hers. Damn, he kissed like a dream. His kisses could charm birds from trees, move mountains, persuade a nun to drop her habit…

Persuade. The word lodged in her head and she couldn't jog it loose. She tensed in his arms as she pulled her head away from his. Persuade. Coax. Cajole.

Seduce.

Rory closed her eyes and slumped against him. God, she was such a sap, so damn stupid. Mac was distracting her from the argument, hoping she'd forget he'd gone behind her back. He used her attraction to him against her, thinking that if he gave her a good time, she'd forgive him for being a colossal jerk!

She pushed his arm and stumbled away from him, shoving her hair from her face with both hands. God, she finally understood how being in a man's arms could make you go against your principles.

This is how it would be with him; she'd object, he'd seduce her into changing her mind. I get it, Mom, I do. But unlike you, I'm going to listen to my head and not my hormones.

Rory locked her knees to keep herself upright and took a deep breath, looking for control. She pulled down the hem of her T-shirt, wishing she were in her tunic and track pants, her uniform. She'd feel far more in control, professional.

"Did you really think I'd fall for your little let's-seduce-her-to-get-me-out-of-trouble routine? I'm not that shallow or that stupid. And you're not that good." Rory slapped her fists on her hips, ignoring the flash of angry surprise she saw in his eyes. "You went behind my back to exercise your arm. That was devious and manipulative. I don't like dishonesty, Mac, in any form. Because of that and because you obviously don't trust me, I think it's best that I leave."

She could see from the expression on his face that he thought she was overreacting. Maybe she was, but he'd given her the perfect excuse to run. To get out of this quicksand relationship before she was in over her head and unable to leave.

"Our contract will become null and void," Mac said, his voice devoid of anger or any emotion at all.

"I don't care." Rory told him. She wanted her clinic, but not at the cost of living in quicksand. "I'm going upstairs to pack. I'll be out of your hair in a couple of hours."

Mac swore and swiped his hand across his face. "God, Rory…running away is not the solution!"

"No, the solution is you being honest with me, listening to me, but you won't do that, so we have nothing to talk about," Rory snapped before walking out the door. Yes, she was scared, but she couldn't forget that he'd been dishonest with her. That was unacceptable.

She'd forgotten, she thought as she ran up the stairs to her room. *You can't trust him; you can't trust anyone. Disappointment comes easily to those who expect too much. Don't expect. Don't trust.*

She wouldn't do it again. She wouldn't be that much of a fool. Mac would do his own thing, always had and always would. It was how he operated. He'd charm with his sincerity, his kisses. He'd say all the right things but nothing would change, not really.

The best predictor of future behavior was past behavior, she reminded herself.

"I'm sorry I went behind your back, but I was trying to avoid an argument," Mac said from the doorway to her bedroom.

"Well, you got one anyway." Rory picked up a pile of T-shirts and carefully placed them in her suitcase, her back to him.

Mac leaned his shoulder into the door frame and felt like he'd been catapulted back ten years. The argument was different but her method of dealing with conflict was exactly the same as her sister's.

The difference between the two sisters was that he *wanted* to apologize to Rory, *needed* to sort this out. He didn't want her to run.

"I didn't touch you to distract you or to get out of trouble. You're right, I'm not that good."

Rory's narrowed eyes told him he had a way to go before he dug himself out of this hole. But that particular point was an argument for another day. He sighed. "And yes, I should've been upfront with you about doing the exercises. Though, in my defense, it's been a very long time since I asked anybody for permission to do anything."

Like, never.

"The lie bothers me, but it's the insult to my intelligence that I find truly offensive. That you would think I wouldn't realize…"

Ouch. Mac winced. "Yeah, I get that."

Rory sighed. "That being said, I can't take lies, Mac. Or evasions or half-truths."

Rory tossed a pair of flip-flops onto the pile of shirts in her suitcase. Mac cursed himself for being an idiot. She'd told him about her father and his deceit, and if he'd thought about it, he would've realized keeping secrets from her was a very bad idea.

He sucked at relationships and that was why he avoided them. So if he was avoiding relationships, why the hell was he determined to get her to stay?

"Don't go, Rorks. It isn't necessary. I need you. I can't do this without you."

He could, but he didn't want to. A subtle but stunning difference.

He needed her. For something other than her skill as a physio and the way she made him feel in bed. It was more than that…his need for her went beyond the surface of sex and skill.

Dammit, he hated the concept of needing anyone for anything. It made him feel…weak. He was a grown man who'd worked damn hard to make sure he never felt that way again.

Yet he was prepared to beg if he had to. "Please? Stay."

Rory turned slowly. "Will you listen to me?"

"I'll try," he conceded, and lifted his hand at her

frown. He wasn't about to make promises he couldn't keep, not even for her. "Will you try to accept that I know my body, know what I can do with it?"

"It's such a huge risk, Mac." Rory bit her lip. "You're playing Russian roulette and you might not win."

"But what if I do?" Mac replied. "If I do, I place myself and my team and my friends in a lot stronger position than we are currently in. It's a risk I'm willing to take."

"I'm not sure that I am." Rory sat down on the edge of the bed. "I have a professional responsibility to do what's best for you, and this isn't it."

"I'll sign any waiver you want me to," Mac quickly said.

Rory waved his offer away. "It's more than playing a game of covering the legalities, McCaskill. This is your career, your livelihood at stake."

"But it's *my* career, *my* livelihood." Mac held her eye. "My decision, Rory, and I'm asking you this *one time* to trust me. I can't live with negativity, I just can't."

"I'm not being negative, I'm being realistic," Rory retorted.

"Your perception of reality isn't mine." Mac sat down next to her on the bed and looked down at the cotton rug below his feet. "I really believe that part of the reason why I've been successful at what I try is that I don't entertain negativity. At all. If I can think it, I can do it, and I don't allow doubt. I need you to think the same."

"Look, I believe in the power of the mind, but everything I've ever been taught tells me you need time, you need to nurse this… It will be a miracle if you regain full strength in that arm."

He couldn't force her to believe, Mac thought in frustration. He wished he could. He blew air into his cheeks and rolled his head to release the tension in his neck.

"Okay. But if you can't be positive then I need you to be quiet." She started to blast him with a retort but he spoke over her. "I'm asking you—on bended knee if I must—to stay and to trust me when I tell you that I know my body. I won't push myself beyond what I can do." Here came the compromise. It sucked but he knew he didn't have a chance of her staying without it. "I won't do anything behind your back and I will listen, and re-spect, your opinion. I still need your help, if only to keep my crazy in check."

Rory stared at the floor, considering his words, and he knew she was wavering.

"You told me about your clinic, how much having your own place means to you. Don't give up on your dreams for your own practice because I'm a stubborn ass who doesn't know the meaning of the word *quit*."

Rory lifted her head to glare at him. "Low blow, Mc-Caskill, using my dreams to get me to do what you want me to do."

He shrugged as Rory glared at him. He didn't want her to leave and he would use any method he could to keep her on this island with him. He was that desperate.

"So, you'll stay?"

"For now." She pointed a finger at him. "You dodged a bullet, Mac. Don't make me shoot you for real next time."

On the private jet hired for the trip home, Rory watched as Mac stashed his laptop back in a storage space above his head. Looking at him, no one would realize Mac had gone through major surgery nearly eight weeks ago. She listened to him bantering with the flight attendant and couldn't help wondering if Mac was doing exercises on the side, working that arm in ways she didn't approve of.

Maybe. Possibly. His recovery was remarkable.

Rory thought back to their argument, still a little angry that he'd deceived her. Maybe it wasn't deliberate, maybe he'd just been thoughtless, but it had hurt. On the positive side, the argument had opened her eyes. It had been her wake-up call. From that moment on she'd stopped entertaining, even on the smallest scale, thoughts about a happy-ever-after with Mac.

He'd never be a hundred percent honest with her and she could never fully trust him.

There couldn't be love or any type of a relationship without trust, and she had to be able to trust a man with everything she had. She couldn't trust Mac so she couldn't love him. She'd decided that…hadn't she?

Okay, it was a work in progress.

The flight attendant moved away and Mac stretched out his legs, looking past Rory out the window by her head. Below them the island of Puerto Rico was a verdant dot in an aqua sea and their magical time together was over.

Back to reality.

Mac sipped his beer and placed his ankle on his knee. "This plane can't fly fast enough. Kade sounded stressed."

"He didn't say why he wanted you back in the city?" Rory asked. Mac had announced at breakfast that Kade needed him in Vancouver and by mid-morning they were on their way home.

Mac shook his head. "No, and that worries me." A frown pulled his eyebrows together and his eyes were bleak. He looked down at his injured arm and traced the red scar that was a memento of his operation. "What if it doesn't heal correctly? What will I do?"

She'd never heard that note in his voice before—part fear, part insecurity. "You go to plan B, Mac. There is always another plan to be made, isn't there?"

Mac picked up her hand and wound his fingers in hers. "But hockey is what I do, who I am. It's my dream, my destiny, the reason I get up in the morning."

Is that what he really thought? She stared down at his long, lean body. It was a revelation to realize she wasn't the only one in this plane with demons. She felt relieved, and sad, at the thought. "Yeah, you're a great hockey player, supposedly one of the best."

Mac mock-glared at her and she smiled. "Okay, you *are* the best...does that satisfy your monstrous ego?"

Mac's lips twitched but he lowered his face so she couldn't look into his eyes. That was okay. It would be easier to say this without the distraction of his fabulous eyes. "You aren't what you do, Mac. You're so much more than that."

"I play hockey, Rory, that's it."

Rory shook her head in disagreement. "You are an amazing businessperson, someone who has many business interests besides hockey. You are a spokesperson for various charities, you play golf and you do triathlons in the off-season. Hockey is not who you are or all that you do."

"But it's what I love best and if I can't do it...if I can't save the team by keeping it out of Chenko's clutches, I will have failed. It would be the biggest failure of my life." Mac sat up, pulled his hand from hers and gripped the armrests. *"I don't like to fail."*

"None of us do, Mac. You're not alone in that," Rory responded, her voice tart. "So, the future of the Mavericks is all resting on your shoulders? Kade and Quinn have no part to play?"

"Yes—no… I'm the one who was injured," Mac protested.

"Here's a news flash, dude, hockey players get hurt. They sustain injuries all the time. Kade and Quinn, if I remember correctly, are both out of the game because of their injuries. You getting injured was just a matter of time. You couldn't keep ducking that bullet forever! It's part of the deal and you can't whine about it."

"I am not whining!" Mac protested, his eyes hot.

Rory smiled. "Okay, you weren't whining. But your thinking is flawed. You are not a superhero and you are not invincible and you are not solely responsible for the future of the Mavericks. If you can't play again, you will find something else to do, and I have no doubt you will be successful at it. You are not a crab and there is no bucket."

Mac stared at her for a long time and eventually the smallest smile touched his lips, his eyes. He released a long sigh and sent her a frustrated look. "You might be perfectly gorgeous but you are also a perfect pain in my ass. Especially when you're being wise."

The mischievous grin that followed his words suggested their heart-to-heart was over. "Want to join the Mile High Club?"

Rory grinned. "What's that word I'm looking for? No? *No* would be it."

Mac turned in his seat and nuzzled her neck with his lips. "Bet I could change your mind."

"You're good, but not that good, McCaskill." Rory

tipped her head to allow him to kiss that sensitive spot under her ear. "But you're welcome to try."

Note to self: Mac McCaskill cannot walk away from a challenge.

Kade met them at the airport and kissed Rory's cheek before pulling Mac into that handshake/half hug they did so well. "Sorry to pull you back from the island sooner than expected, but I need you here."

Mac frowned. "What's happened?"

Kade looked around, saw that they were garnering attention and shook his head. "Not here. We'll get into it in the car. No, Rory, don't worry about your luggage, I've sent an intern to pick it up."

Nice, Rory thought. She could get used to this first-class life. She pulled her large tote bag over her shoulder, saw fans lifting their cell phones in their direction and wished she'd worn something other than a pair of faded jeans and a loose cotton shirt for the journey home. They'd both showered on the jet but Mac had changed from his cargo shorts and flip-flops into a pistachio-green jacket, a gray T-shirt and khaki pants. He looked like the celebrity he was and she looked like a back-packer.

Sigh.

Rory stepped away, distancing herself as fans approached Mac and Kade for their autographs. After signing a few, Mac jerked his head in her direction and the three of them started walking—Rory at a half jog. In the VIP parking lot, Kade finally stopped at a low silver sports car and opened the back door for Rory to slide in. Mac took the passenger seat next to Kade and within minutes they were on the highway heading back to the city.

"Talk." Mac half twisted in his seat to look at Kade, pulling his designer cap off his head and running his hand through his hair. "What's up? Why did we have to get home so quickly?"

Rory heard the note of irritation in Mac's voice. Funny, she would've thought he'd be happy to be returning home, to be getting back into the swing of things. Yet she couldn't deny they'd been enjoying the solitude of Cap de Mar, the long, lazy sun- and sea-filled days punctured by long, intense bouts of making love.

"How's your arm?" Kade replied.

"Fine."

Rory rolled her eyes. "Fine" was boy-speak for "I don't want to talk about it."

"Improving," Rory chimed in half a beat behind him. She ignored Mac's narrowed eyes and continued to speak. "It's a lot better but he's definitely not ready to play yet. If that's what you are thinking, then you can forget about it."

"I could play," Mac said, his tone resolute.

"Do it and die," Rory stated in a flat, don't-test-me voice. Hadn't they had this argument? Had he heard anything she'd said?

Kade swore, ducked around a pickup truck and a station wagon and floored the accelerator. Rory prayed they would arrive at their destination—wherever that was—in one piece.

Where was her destination? Mavericks' headquarters? Mac's house? Her apartment? She and Mac had been living together, sleeping together, for a little more than a month. But now they were back to normal and island rules didn't necessarily apply to Vancouver. Right, this was another reason why she avoided relationships; she hated walking through the minefield of what was socially acceptable.

"Slow down, bud. Not everyone craves your need for speed."

Kade slowed down from the speed of light to pretty damn fast. She'd take it, Rory decided, and loosened her hold on her seat belt.

"Right," Mac continued. "What's going on?"

Rory saw Kade's broad shoulder lift and drop, taut with tension. "God, so much. First, the press, especially the sports writers, are speculating that your injury is a lot worse than we've been admitting to and they are looking for the angles. Speculation has been running wild."

Rory saw a muscle jump in Mac's cheek and she wondered what it was like to live life under a microscope.

"Widow Hasselback is also asking how you are and I heard she met with the suits from the Chenko Corporation last week. She told me they've increased their offer."

Mac closed his eyes and gripped the bridge of his nose with his thumb and forefinger. His curse bounced around the car. "That's not all," he said.

"I wish it was," Kade agreed. "Bayliss, our new investor, would like to watch a practice match before making a commitment."

Mac frowned. "That wouldn't normally be a problem. We often have people coming to watch practice, but so many of the team are still on vacation."

"Between us, Quinn and I have reached them all. They understand what's at stake and they'll be there," Kade reassured him.

Mac pulled out his cell phone and swiped his thumb across the screen. "Scheduled for when?"

Kade's worried glance bounced off hers in the rear-view mirror. "The day after tomorrow. At four." He looked apologetic. "According to Bayliss, it's a take-it-or-leave-it deal."

The day. After. Tomorrow.

Rory shook her head. "Well, that's all fine and good but you can count Mac out of that match."

"I'm playing," Mac said, and she immediately recognized his don't-argue-with-me voice.

Well, this time she would out-stubborn him. Rory pulled in a breath and reminded herself to keep calm. Yelling at Mac would achieve nothing. If she wanted to win this argument she would have to sound reasonable and in control. And professional. "I admit that your arm is vastly improved and that no one, looking at you, would suspect how serious your injury actually is. But it's not mended, and one wrong move or twist would undo all the healing you've done and possibly, probably, aggravate the injury further."

"I'm fine, babe."

"You are not fine!" Rory heard her voice rise and she deliberately toned it down. "You are not fully recovered and you certainly don't have all your strength back. I strongly suggest, as your physiotherapist, that you sit this one out."

Mac ignored her to nod at Kade. "I'll be there."

"Did you hear anything I said?" Rory demanded from the backseat, her face flushed with anger. "Do you know what you are risking? One slap shot, one bump and that's it, career over, McCaskill!"

"Stop being dramatic, Rory," Mac said in a hard, flat voice. "I keep telling you that I know what I am capable of and you've got to trust me. I know what I'm doing."

"I know that you are being a friggin' idiot!" Rory shouted.

Mac turned around and looked her in the eye. His direct gaze locked on hers and she immediately realized that nothing she could say or do would change his mind. He was playing, nearly two months after surgery. He was risking his career, all the work they'd done... Rory felt like he was tossing away all her hard work too.

"I took my vacation time to help you heal. I've spent hours working on you, working on getting you to where you are right now. You play and you've wasted my time and your money," Rory said, her voice rising along with her anger.

"I don't have a choice, dammit! Why can't you understand that?" Mac yelled back. "This is about my family, my team, securing something that means more to me than anything else!"

Of course it did, Rory realized. To Mac, the Mavericks were everything. He wouldn't change his mind or see reason. Kade and Quinn and the team would always be his top priorities. Her opinion, as his lover or his physiotherapist, didn't really count.

She was done fighting him, done fighting this. Why did she care anyway? This was a temporary affair, a fling. He was a client. At the end of the day it was his choice whether to mess up his life or not; she had no say in it. It was his arm, his career, his future, his stupidity.

But she didn't have to be part of it. Rory sucked in air, found none and pushed the button to open her window a crack. Cool, rain-tinged air swirled around her head and she lifted her face to cool her temper. "You do this and I'm out of here. Professionally and personally."

"Are you serious?" Mac demanded, his tone hard and, maybe she was being a bit fanciful, tinged with hurt.

"Hell, Rory," Kade murmured.

"It's my professional opinion that your arm is insufficiently healed to play competitive hockey. I am not going to watch you undo all the hard work we've done and I am certainly not going to watch you injure yourself further."

Mac rubbed the back of his neck and he darted a scowl at Kade. "Pretend you're not here," he told him.

"Done," Kade promptly replied.

Mac turned his attention to her and she pushed her back into her seat, not sure what he was about to say. She just knew it would be important. "Rory, listen to me."

She dropped her gaze and closed her eyes. When he looked at her like that, all open and exposed, she found it hard to concentrate.

"No, look at me…"

Rory forced her eyes open.

"I know that asking you to trust me is difficult for you. It's not something you do easily. And I know I'm asking you to put aside your learning and your experience. You think that I believe I'm invincible or a superhero. I'm not. I know I'm not… I'm just someone who knows what he is capable of, what his body is capable of. This isn't just a practice match. It's the most important practice match of my life, of Kade's life, of Quinn's. If I sit it out I'm risking this team, my friends' futures, my brothers' futures. This isn't about me and my ego."

"It will be about you if you do more damage to your arm. Then neither you nor your team will have a future… or the future you want." Couldn't he see she was trying to protect him from himself? She was trying to be the voice of reason here?

"Trust me, Rory. Please, just this once. Trust me to know what I'm doing. Stand by me, support me. Do that by coming to the practice, make sure that my arm is taped correctly. It'll be fine. I'll be fine. Be positive."

"And if I don't?" Rory demanded.

Mac just shrugged before quietly telling her that he'd play anyway.

"So, really, this entire argument has been a waste of time." Rory turned away so he didn't see the burning tears in her eyes. With blurry vision she noticed that Kade was turning down Mac's street, and within a minute he stopped the car.

The silence was as heavy as the freighter that was making its way across the bay as Mac unclipped his seatbelt and opened his door.

"One of the interns will be along shortly with your luggage," Kade told him, giving him a fist bump. Mac gripped his shoulder and squeezed before leaving the car. In the open doorway Mac bent his knees to look over his seat at Rory. "You joining me, Rory?"

No. She wanted to go home, pull on her pajamas, grab a glass of wine and cry. "I don't think so."

Mac gave her a sharp nod and his lips tightened with annoyance. "As you wish. I'm certainly not going to beg."

"Like you would know how," Rory muttered, and his eyes flashed as he slammed the door shut on her words.

Rory folded her arms across her chest and hoped Kade didn't notice that her hands were shaking. "Can you take me home, Kade?"

"Yep. Can do. Come and sit up here with me."

Ten

Was she just being stubborn, Rory wondered as Kade capably, and silently, maneuvered his very fancy sports car through the city streets? She'd always been the type of therapist who encouraged her patients to listen to their bodies, to tune in to how they were feeling. She generally listened. If they said they felt better, she trusted they were telling the truth. Why couldn't she do that with Mac? Why was she balking?

Because there was so much at stake. This one decision could have far-reaching and potentially devastating consequences. Mac loved hockey above everything else and he was risking his entire career on a still fragile tendon and a practice match. She didn't want him to lose all that he'd worked for. He might be willing to risk it, but she wasn't prepared to sanction that risk. He was thinking of the team, she was thinking about him—only him.

There had to be another way. There was always another way. They just hadn't thought about it yet.

"Would it be such a bad idea to let this corporation buy the Mavericks?" she abruptly asked Kade.

Kade considered his response. "It would definitely be different. They have a history of clearing the deck and changing all the management, the leadership. That would mean Quinn, Mac and I would be figuratively on the streets."

"Other teams would snap you up," Rory argued.

Kade nodded as he stopped at a traffic light. "Sure, but we wouldn't be on the *same* team. We've been together for nearly fifteen years, Rory. We fight and argue and irritate each other to death but we know each other. We *trust* each other."

"There's that damn word again," Rory muttered.

"One you seem to have a problem with," Kade observed, sending her a smile. He really was a very good-looking man, Rory noticed. Not Mac hot, but still…phew!

"Am I being unreasonable?" she demanded, slapping her hand repeatedly against the dashboard. "The man has been injured! It was serious. I'm trying to protect him."

"Yeah. And he's asking you to trust him to know what he's doing," Kade responded, gently removing her hand from his dashboard and dropping it back into her lap. "It's too expensive a car to be used as a punching bag, honey."

Rory winced. "Sorry." She shoved her hands under her thighs to keep them from touching something she shouldn't and sighed heavily. "He makes me nuts."

Kade laughed. "I suspect he feels the same way about you." He tapped his finger against the steering wheel before turning his head to look at her. "Mac never asks anyone for anything."

Rory looked puzzled, not sure where he was going with this.

"He injured his arm because he tried to move a fridge on his own, something either Quinn or I or any of his teammates, coaching staff, support crew, maintenance guys or office staff would've helped him with...*had he asked.*"

"Try living with him for nearly two months," Rory muttered, reminded of all the arguments she'd had with Mac. "I think it has something to do with the fact that his mother was emotionally, probably physically, neglectful of him. He learned not to ask because his needs were never met," she mused.

Kade switched lanes and sent her an astonished look. "He told you about his mother?"

"Not much. A little." Rory shrugged.

"Holy crap."

Rory shrugged again, brushing off his astonishment. "Not asking for help is stupid. Everyone needs someone at some time in their lives."

"I agree. I've been trying to tell him that for years," Kade said, turning into her street. He pulled up behind a battered pickup and switched off the growling engine. Pushing his sunglasses up into his hair, he half turned in his seat. "So, we agree that we are talking about a man who is ridiculously independent and stupidly self-sufficient and hates asking for a damn thing?"

"Precisely," Rory agreed, reaching for her bag, which sat on the floor by her feet. She dug around for her house keys and pulled out the bunch with a flourish. "Found them! Yay."

Kade's hand on her arm stopped her exit from the car. When she looked back at him, his expression was serious. "Interesting then that our self-sufficient, hate-to-ask-for-anything friend asked you to be there at the practice game, asked you to trust him. Practically begged you…"

Rory sucked in a breath and scowled at him. "Oh, you're good," she muttered as she stepped out of the car.

"So I'm frequently told," Kade smugly replied. Rory shook her head as she climbed out of the low seat, charmed and amused despite the fact that he'd backed her into a corner. She turned back to look at him and he grinned at her through her open window. "Frequently followed by…*can we do that again?*"

Rory slapped a hand across her eyes.

"I'll leave your name with security. Day after tomorrow. Four p.m."

Rory managed, using an enormous amount of self-control, not to kick his very expensive tires as he pulled away.

Mac couldn't help glancing around the empty arena as he hit the rink, as at home on the ice as he was on his own two feet. Stupid to hope that she'd be here. Intensely stupid to feel disappointed. There was nothing between them except some hot sex and a couple of conversations.

He was happy the way he was, happy to have the odd affair with a beautiful woman, happy with his lone-wolf lifestyle. Wasn't he?

Not so much.

Mac glanced at the empty seats and banged his stick on the ice in frustration. One thing. He'd asked her one damn thing and she'd refused. Talk about history repeating itself… It served him right for putting himself out there. He'd learned the lesson hard and he'd learned the lesson well that when it came to personal relationships, when he asked, he didn't always receive. With his mother he'd never received anything he needed.

His childhood was over, he reminded himself.

Besides, it didn't matter, he had an investor to impress, a team to save, Vernon's legacy to protect. Mac glanced over toward the coach's area and immediately saw Quinn and Kade standing, like two mammoth sentries, on either side of a slim woman and an elderly man who bore a vague resemblance to Yoda. The woman wore jeans and a felt hat and the older man was dressed in corduroy pants and a parka. These were their investors? Where were the suits, the heels, the briefcases?

Hope you have what we need, old man, Mac thought, as the rest of the team followed him onto the ice. Hellfire, his arm was already throbbing and he'd yet to smack a puck.

Maybe Rory was right and playing wasn't such a great idea. He swung his injured arm and only sheer force of will kept him from grimacing. The team physio had strapped his arm to give it extra support but the straps were misaligned and, he was afraid, doing more harm than good.

Crapdammithell!

"McCaskill!"

Mac spun on his skates and there she stood, a resigned look on her face. His heart bumped and settled as he skated toward her. She stood next to a large man who looked familiar, and it took Mac a minute to place him. His nurse from The Annex...what was his name? Troy? Unlike Rory, Troy was wearing a huge smile and his gaze bounced from player to player in the manner of a true fan.

Mac stopped at the boards in front of Rory and sent her a slow smile. Damn, he'd missed her.

"Thanks for coming," he said, wishing he could take her into his arms, kiss her senseless. He wanted, just for a moment, to step out of these skates, out of the arena and into the heat of her mouth, to feel her pliant, slim, sexy body beneath his hands. Huh. That had never happened before. Skating, hockey, the ice…nothing could normally top that.

Mac looked at Rory, arms folded across her chest, her expression disapproving. That didn't worry him; he'd learned to look for the emotion in her eyes. Those gray depths told him everything he needed to know about how she was feeling. Yeah, she was worried, but resigned. A little scared, but he could see that she was trying to trust him, trying to push aside her intellect to give him the benefit of the doubt.

Rory narrowed her amazing eyes at him. "I'm not for one moment condoning this, and if you do any more damage I will personally kick your ass."

Deeply moved—he understood how hard this was for her—he sent her a crooked grin, silently thanking her for taking this chance on him, on them.

Rory, stubborn as always, tried to look stern but her eyes lightened with self-deprecating humor. And, as always, there was a hint of desire. For the first time, he easily recognized tenderness in her steady gaze.

And concern. She was so damned worried about him. When last had someone cared this much? Never? Mac felt his heart thump, unaccustomed to feeling saturated with emotion.

"Noted," Mac gruffly said, needing a moment to regroup. Or ten. Pulling in a deep breath he pulled off his glove with his teeth and held out his hand for Troy to shake. "Good to see you."

Troy pumped his hand with an enthusiasm that had Mac holding back a wince. "You play?" he asked Troy.

Troy nodded. "College."

"When we're finished with the practice match, maybe you'd like to borrow some skates and join us on the ice?" Mac asked.

Troy looked delighted. "Awesome. My gear is in the car so I don't need to borrow a thing. Wow. Awe. Some."

Rory rolled her eyes and looked at Mac again. "You okay?"

"Pretty much. Better now that you are here." Mac looked over the ice to the other side of the rink, where Kade and Quinn were still in deep conversation with the investor. Quinn didn't look like he was about to call the team to order anytime soon. "Speaking of, can I borrow you for a sec?"

Rory nodded and he pushed open the hinge board and stepped off the ice. He sat on a chair and looked up at Troy. "It's great that you are so damn big, dude."

Troy grinned and made a production of fluttering his eyes at him. "I didn't think you noticed."

"Cut it out, Troy," Rory muttered.

Mac laughed and jerked his thumb toward Rory. "She's more my type. But I do need you to stand in front of me so Quinn and Kade, and especially that small old guy, can't see me."

Troy, smart guy, immediately moved into position. "Like this?"

"That works." Mac pulled off his jersey and leaned down and grabbed Rory's bag, holding it out to her. "I need you to re-tape my arm. The team physio did it but he's done something wrong, it's hurting like a bitch."

Rory looked like she was about to say "I told you so," and he appreciated her effort to swallow the words. While he ripped the stabilizing tape off his arm with his other hand, taking quite a bit of arm hair with it, Rory pulled out another roll of tape. He groaned when he saw that it was bright pink. "You're kidding me, right?"

"Consider it my silent protest," Rory said, a smile touching her mouth. She was still worried about him. He could see it in her eyes, in her tight smile. But she cut the tape into strips and carefully ran the tape over his biceps and elbow, her eyes narrowed in concentration.

"Quinn's getting ready to move," Troy told them.

"Nearly there," Rory muttered, smoothing the end of the last piece of tape across the other two. She nodded. "That should give you more support, especially when you extend."

Mac did a biceps curl and he sighed with relief. He took the jersey Rory held out to him and pulled it over his head. When he was dressed, he stood up and dropped a hot, openmouthed kiss on her lips. "You are brilliant."

"Do *not* hurt yourself."

"Don't nag." Mac kissed her again, still in awe that she was here, that she was helping him, standing by him, doing this. She'd shoved aside her training, had placed her trust in him, something she so rarely gave…

Quinn's impatient whistle broke into his thoughts and his voice drifted across the ice calling them to order. Mac turned back to Rory. "Kade has invited the team and some suits to a cocktail party tonight at Siba's. You know—the bar in the Forrester Hotel? Meet me there at seven?"

Rory scowled at him but her eyes were soft and still scared. "Maybe, if you're not back in the hospital."

Mac grinned at Troy. "Such a sarcastic little ray of sunshine. Thanks for your help. I'll see you in a bit."

"She'll be there," Troy told him.

"You'll damn well go," Mac heard Troy telling Rory as he skated, slowly it had to be said, away from them. "That man is nuts about you."

He really was, he reluctantly admitted.

"You are so in love with him," Troy crowed as he flung his hockey bag into the trunk of his battered SUV. Rory eyed his piece of rusty metal; she hated driving anywhere with Troy because she was quite certain her chances of, well, dying were increased a thousand percent whenever its tires met the road.

Rory, her hand on the passenger-door handle, looked down at the front wheel and sighed her relief. The tires had been changed and Troy had promised her it had just had its biyearly service. Rory had replied that it needed a funeral service but she'd eventually abandoned her idea of taking a taxi to the arena and allowed Troy to drive her in his chariot of death.

Rory tugged at the handle and cursed when it refused to open. Troy, already behind the wheel, reached across and thumped the panel and the door sprung open, just missing hitting Rory in the face. "I hate this car," she muttered, climbing in.

Troy nodded his head. "Yeah, me too. But it's paid for, thereby freeing up money for the nursing home."

Rory, grateful that they'd left the subject of Mac and her feelings, sent him a concerned look. "How is your mom? Any more walkabouts?"

Troy momentarily closed his eyes. "No, she's fine. Well, as fine as she can be." He stared at the luxury car parked next to them. "I've found a home just outside the city, a place that looks fantastic. They have space for her, could take her tomorrow, but I just can't afford it."

"I could…" She had to offer to loan him the money. He wouldn't take it, but she wished he would. He was her best friend, an almost-brother…why didn't he realize that she'd move mountains for him if she could?

Troy sighed. "I love you for offering but…no. I can't." Troy turned the key and the car spluttered and died. He cursed, cranked it again and Rory held her breath. It rumbled, jerked and eventually put-putted to life. "You wouldn't think that I'd just had it serviced, would you?"

"Nope. Then again, I think trying to service this car is like putting a Band-Aid on a slit throat."

"Nice," Troy said as they pulled out of the arena parking lot. "Let's get back to the interesting stuff. When did you fall in love with Mac?"

"Ten years ago," Rory replied without thinking. She jerked up and scowled at her friend. "I didn't just say that out loud, did I?"

Troy grinned. "You so did."

"Dammit." She didn't want to be in love with Mac. That meant she had to give him up, she'd have to retreat, do what she did best to protect herself and fade away. Loving Mac carried too many risks, too much potential heartache.

"So, are you going to keep Mac around or are you going to dump him when he gets too close?"

Lord, Troy knew her well. She had to make a token protest. "I don't do that."

Troy snorted. "Honey, you *always* do that. You meet a guy, you go on a couple of dates and when you think something might have a chance of developing, you find an excuse to dump him. You have massive trust issues."

"So does Mac. He also has abandonment issues!" she added.

"It's not a competition, Rory! Jeez," Troy snapped as they approached the first set of traffic lights. "Man, these brakes are soft. Didn't they check them?" They stopped and Troy looked at her. "Okay…continue."

Rory stared at the drops of rain running down the windshield. She might as well tell him, she thought, he knew everything else about her. "You know how Shay loves to tease me about stealing her boyfriends?"

"Yeah, and you get all huffy and defensive and embarrassed."

"She was dating Mac when she walked in on us…we were about to kiss," Rory quietly stated. "How would she feel if I started dating him, started a relationship with him?"

"I bet she'd be fine with it." Tory rolled his eyes, and without taking his eyes off the road instructed his cell phone to call Shay.

"What are you doing?" Rory demanded.

"Calling Shay," Troy replied, as if she were the biggest idiot in the world. Which she was, because she was talking to him about Mac.

"Troyks!" Shay's bubbly voice filled the car.

"Hey, oh gorgeous one. I'm in the car with Rory and we have a question for you."

"Shoot," Shay replied.

"It's not important—" Rory stated, leaning sideways to talk into the phone.

"Back off, sister." Troy growled. "Rory's using you as an excuse not to date Mac McCaskill. So how would you feel about them getting it on? You know, even though you're married to the hunkiest homicide detective in the city," Troy added, his tone wry.

"My Mac?" Shay asked.

Her Mac, Rory scowled. And didn't that just answer her question right away?

Shay was quiet for a minute. "Well, judging from the way they were eyeing each other way back when, I'd say it's about ten years overdue. A part of me is still slightly jealous that he never looked at me like that."

Like what? "Nothing happened!" Rory protested.

"Maybe, but you both wanted it to," Shay responded. "I think he'd be really good for you."

"He almost cheated on you, with me!" Rory half yelled. Okay, the straws she was grabbing were elusive but she was giving it her best shot.

"He was twenty-four, we were having problems and whenever the two of you were in the same room you created an electrical storm. Besides, as you said, nothing happened. It's not that big a deal."

Shay must've forgotten that being kissed by Mac was a very big deal.

"Go for it, Rorks."

Okay, who was this woman and what had she done with Rory's insecure, neurotic sister? "Are you high?" Rory demanded. "He's a commitment-phobic man-slut! He changes women like he changes socks!"

"I don't think that's true. Not so much and not anymore." Shay laughed. "I liked Mac. I still like Mac. He was a good egg and he put up with an enormous amount of drama from me. You should date him, Rorks, give this relationship thing a spin. Who knows, you might end up being... I don't know...*happy*?"

Troy looked triumphant and Rory placed her hands over her face. "You are high. It's the only explanation..."

"Or that my hot detective husband came home for lunch and, well, let's just say food wasn't a priority," Shay smugly stated.

Troy groaned and Rory let out a strangled *ewww*. Shay disconnected the call on a happy laugh. Rory stared out the window for a long time before turning to Troy. "Do you agree?" she quietly asked him. "Do you think I should take a chance, see where this goes?"

"Do you really love him?"

Rory thought about his question, not wanting to give a glib answer. "I'm worried that it's temporary craziness, that when the fire dies down, I'll run...or he'll run...and someone will get hurt. I'm scared to get hurt."

"Aren't we all?" Troy reached across the seats to grip her fingers in his. "Yeah, it might fail. It might burn out. You might get hurt."

"So encouraging," Rory murmured.

Troy sent her a sweet, sweet smile. "But, honey, what if it doesn't? What if this is the amazing love story you've been waiting for? What if he is the big *it*? What if it works?"

Rory looked at him and slumped in her seat. "Humpf."

Troy laughed, pulled his hand back and then his face turned serious. "Don't run, honey, not this time. Stand still and see what happens. Will you?"

Rory smiled at him and, liking the connection, reached across the seat to link her fingers back into his. "Yeah. I think I will. If—"

Troy groaned. "Oh, God."

Rory ignored his protest "—you will consider borrowing some money from me to move your mom into that home."

Troy sighed. "Diabolical."

Rory's smile was smug. "I try."

Eleven

Mac ran a hand through his hair and unbuttoned the jacket to his gray suit. He took a sip of his whiskey and looked at his watch; Rory was late but that was okay. He needed a moment to himself, to think, even if he had to take that moment while standing in a crowded cocktail bar, surrounded by his friends and colleagues. He sipped again and ignored the pain in his arm—thanks to his session on the ice—and the noise around him, ignored the insults, jokes and crude comments flying over his head. The pain wasn't as bad as he'd thought it would be but he definitely didn't have the power and strength in the limb that he was used to. His teammates had tried to cover for him and he was grateful for their efforts. Hopefully they'd done a good enough job to fool Bayliss.

On the plus side, Mac thought, Rory *had* arrived at the practice. He'd been surprised at the relief he felt, astonished that as soon as he saw her, his heart rate accelerated but his soul settled down.

She was there. Everything was all right in his world. When had that happened? When had she become so important to his emotional well-being that she could calm him with one look, with one sarcastic comment?

If you do any more damage I will personally kick your ass.

It wasn't an "I love you" or "I will support you no matter what," but it was Rory's version of "Okay, this one time, I'll trust you." He could work with that.

God, he *wanted* to work through whatever this was with her. Was it love? He didn't know, but he knew it was *something*. Many women had caught his eye over the years, and he'd slept with quite a few of them—probably more than he should have—but Rory was still the only person who'd come close to capturing his heart.

But…and, hell, there was always a *but*, Mac thought, staring down at the floor between his feet. *But* he didn't know if he could spend the rest of his life reassuring her that he wouldn't cheat, that he wouldn't let her down. He *wouldn't* cheat, but there would come a time when he disappointed her, when he wouldn't be there for her, when things went wrong. Would she bail at the first hint of trouble or would she cut him some slack?

He was a man, one with little experience of this thing called a relationship or how to be in it, and he knew, for sure, that he'd mess up. When he did, and it was a *when* and not an *if*, would she talk it out or would she walk? If she walked, would he be able to stand it? The rational side of him suggested it might be better not to take the chance, to call it quits now before anyone—him—got hurt. That would be the clever, the practical, the smart thing to do.

Except that would mean not having Rory in his life, and he didn't think he could go back to his empty life, hopping from one feminine bed to another. Nor did he think he could become a monk. Both options sucked. Mac scrubbed his hand over his face...

Relationships were so damn complicated and exhausting.

"Mac."

Quinn nudged his elbow into Mac's ribs and Mac turned to look down into the weathered face of Kade's investor. He'd changed into an ugly brown suit and combed his thin hair but he still didn't look like someone who could provide what they needed. *Don't judge a book by its cover*, Mac reminded himself. The granddaughter looked spectacular, Mac noticed, because he was a man and that was what men did. Her bright red hair was pulled back into a low ponytail and her wide eyes darted between him, Kade and Quinn.

Kade cleared his throat. "Mr. Bayliss, meet Mac Mc-Caskill. Mac, Mr. Bayliss and his granddaughter, Wren."

Mac shook the man's hand with its surprisingly strong grip and made the appropriate comments. After they exchanged the usual pleasantries, Kade and Quinn drew Wren into another conversation and Mac tried not to squirm when Bayliss regarded him with a steady, penetrating look. "You've definitely lost power in your arm. Your slap shot was weak and ineffectual."

Hell, Mac had hoped he wouldn't notice. The old man was sharper than he looked. Mac pasted a nothing-to-worry-about expression on his face and shrugged. "I pulled a muscle a while back and this was my first practice. It'll be fine soon. I'm regaining power every day."

"We'll see. I'm not sure if you will ever regain your form."

Mac felt like the old man had sucker-punched him. "That's not something you need to worry about." He forced himself to keep his voice even. "I *will* be back to full strength soon and I *will* lead this team next season."

"We'll see," Bayliss repeated, and Mac wanted to scream. "Luckily, I see enough talent in this team to want to invest whether you are part of it or not, whether you play or not. It was nice meeting you, Mr. McCaskill. We'll talk again."

Mac stared at Bayliss's back as he and Kade walked away, then he forced himself to sip his drink, to look as though he hadn't been slapped.

Whether he played or not? Hell, if he didn't play, what could he do for the team? Kade was the management guy. Despite his youth, Quinn was a damn excellent coach… what did Mac bring to the party apart from his skill on the ice? If playing wasn't an option, there was no way he was going to float around the Mavericks on the outside looking in, making a nuisance of himself. He was either a full partner or not. A full contributor or not.

God, *not*. Was that a possibility?

"Want to dance, Mac?"

He blinked at the perfectly made-up face to his right and couldn't put a name to the gorgeous blonde. He looked toward the entrance, still didn't see Rory and decided what the hell. Dancing was better than standing there like an idiot freaking out over his future. He nodded, handed his glass to a passing waiter and allowed the blonde to lead him to the dance floor. When they reached the small circle, he placed his hands on her hips and wished she was Rory. He could talk to Rory about the bombshell he'd just experienced, about the fear holding him in its icy grip.

She'd help him make sense of it, Mac thought as his dance partner moved closer, her breasts brushing his chest. He felt nothing, no corresponding flash of desire and no interest down south. Huh, so if things didn't work out with Rory it looked like he'd be going the monk route.

He tried to put some distance between them but the dance floor was crowded and there was little room to move. Mac sighed when she laid her head on his shoulder. She didn't feel right, smell right; she was too tall, too buxom, too curvy…where the hell was Rory?

Over the heads of most of his fellow dancers he looked toward the door and there she was, dressed in a scarlet cocktail dress he wanted to rip off with his teeth. She had a small bag clutched under her arm and she was holding her cell phone… She was here, *finally*, and all was well with his world.

Then he lifted his eyes back up to hers and his heart plummeted at the expression on her face. Her eyes were huge and wide, her skin pale and she looked like she'd been slapped. Even from a distance he could tell her eyes were full of tears and her bottom lip trembled. *Oh, crap…*

He wanted to yell that her addition sucked. Two plus two did not equal seventeen! He was just dancing with the woman, not doing her on the dance floor. He hadn't given his dance partner one thought; in fact, he'd been desperately waiting for Rory to arrive to rescue him…

One dance and the accusations, as sure as sugar, were flying, silent and deadly. He could read her thoughts as clearly as if she'd bellowed them across the room. *I can't trust you. You've let me down. You've disappointed me.*

The voices in his head mocked him. Hell, even his mother's voice came to join the suck-fest.

You'll never be quite good enough. This is why you should keep your distance. This hurt is gonna be your constant companion for the rest of your life. You don't deserve normal and you sure as hell don't deserve love... She doesn't trust you. She never will. You always manage to mess it up...

The expression on Rory's face put it all into perspective. They'd been back together for a day, sort of, and with one dance with a complete stranger, he'd been unfairly fouled. And if that wasn't life telling him this would never work then he didn't know what was.

Rory looked down at her phone, lifted it to her ear and bit her lip. She sent him another look, one he couldn't quite interpret, spun on her heel and left the room. She was running as hard and as fast as she could. Mentally, emotionally and, dammit, literally.

That was that, Mac thought, walking off the dance floor toward the bar. He felt like he was carrying a fifty-pound anvil around in his chest instead of a heart. Since he wasn't about to have sex in the near future and he might be saying goodbye to his career with the Mavericks, he might as well have a drink.

Or many.

Rory sat next to Troy's bed, holding his hand and willing him to wake up. She'd been at his bedside for twelve hours straight and he was still unconscious. Rory looked at his medical chart at the end of his bed and told herself there was no point in reading it again, it wouldn't change the facts.

Troy, on his way to start his evening shift at The

Annex next door, had failed to stop at a traffic light
and plowed his rust bucket into the side of a truck. He'd
smacked his head on the steering wheel and had swelling on the brain. When the swelling subsided they would
reevaluate his condition.

That damn car, Rory thought, placing her forehead
on his cold wrist. Guess the car service hadn't included
checking the brakes. The car was a write-off, Rory had
been told by the paramedics; it was their opinion that
he'd been lucky to escape alive.

Rory shuddered. Troy was her best friend and she
couldn't imagine her life without him. And speaking of
people who were important to her, where the hell was
Mac? She'd risked using her cell in the ICU and left two
brief, urgent, *desperate* messages on his cell for him to
call her but he'd yet to respond. Why not? Why was he
ignoring her? What had changed?

Sure she'd seen him dancing with that blonde but
that didn't worry her. Anyone with a brain in her head
would've noticed that it had been the blonde making all
the moves. Mac had been supremely disinterested. In fact,
despite the devastating news she'd just received about
Troy—one of the nurses in the ER had texted her as soon
as he was rushed in—she'd immediately noticed Mac
looked distracted, worried. His eyes were bleak and that
telltale muscle in his jaw was jumping.

Was this what their life would be like going forward,
Rory wondered? Her being pushed down his priority
list because there was something more important he
needed to do, somewhere more interesting he needed
to be? Could she cope with playing second fiddle to his
career, his friends, his teammates? She'd done that with
her father and she'd hated every moment.

She couldn't do that, not again. She loved Mac with everything she had but she wouldn't sacrifice herself for him, for any man. She didn't expect him to jump hurdles when she asked for any little thing, but Troy's critical condition was pretty mammoth. She had a right to ask Mac for his emotional support, to be there for her. At the very least, he could reply to her damn messages!

Damn, life had been so uncomplicated when she'd been unattached. Boring, but simple.

Mac, sitting on the couch in Kade's office, propped his feet onto the coffee table and stared at the massive photograph on Kade's wall. It was of the team, naturally, minutes after the final whistle of the Stanley Cup Final. He and Quinn and Kade had their arms around each other, all of them wearing face-splitting grins. Would he ever be that happy again, Mac wondered?

"How long are you going to sit over there and stare moodily at my wall?" Kade asked, replacing the handset of his desk phone into its cradle. "'Cause I've got to tell you, it's getting old."

Mac lifted a lazy middle finger and kept staring at the photograph. "That was a really good day at the office."

Kade's eyes flicked to the photograph. "It was. Now are you going to sit here and reminisce about the past or are you going to tell me what's got your lacy panties in a twist?"

Mac pulled a face. Over the past four days he'd been avoiding his friends to spend his days on his balcony staring out at the view, and he was, frankly, tired of himself and his woe-is-me attitude.

Rory and he were kaput. Admittedly, she had left two messages on his voice mail the night she bolted from the bar, which he'd ignored. Really, what was there to say? She either trusted him or she didn't, and it was clear that she didn't.

There was no point in discussing the issue.

Game over. Move on.

"Anymore news from the Bayliss camp?" Mac asked, dropping his feet to the floor and reaching for the bottle of water he'd placed on the coffee table.

Kade leaned back in his chair. "I'm expecting to see the first draft of an agreement today."

Even if Mac wasn't part of the day-to-day equation he'd be a part owner, and he was glad to see progress. At least with Kade and Quinn at the helm the Mavericks would have a good chance of keeping their identity. "That's good news."

Kade shrugged. "We'll see what the document contains. I know that Wren, the granddaughter and a PR specialist, has some strong ideas about what she wants to happen with the franchise."

Mac rubbed his jaw, thick with stubble. "Yeah, I don't think I'm part of those franchise plans."

Kade frowned at him. "What do you mean?"

"Didn't you hear what Bayliss said the other night?" When Kade shook his head, Mac explained, "He noticed that my arm was weak and expressed doubts as to whether I would still have a place on the Mavericks next season."

Kade narrowed his eyes. "That will never be his decision to make." His eyes radiated hot frustration even though his voice was calm. "He's providing marketing and merchandising opportunities, access to bigger sponsorship deals, connections. He will not be allowed to interfere with the team and its selection."

"Yeah, I don't think he got that memo," Mac replied in his driest voice. He took a deep breath and bit his lip. "If I, and my injury, become a point of contention, I'll back off. If it means keeping the team out of the clutches of that soul-sucking corporation then I'll be a silent partner."

Kade rolled his eyes. "Shut the hell up, McCaskill, you suck as a martyr. You will be back, at full strength, by the time the season starts or I will kick your ass. And I can still do it," Kade warned him.

"You can try." Mac stood up and crossed to the floor-to-ceiling windows. When he turned back to Kade his expression was serious. "We should think of a plan B, just in case I'm not."

"Rory told me you've made excellent progress."

Mac shrugged. He had, but it would take a lot more work, and he'd keep at it. He'd keep pushing himself but Rory wouldn't be there to monitor his progress, to keep him in check. The chances were high that he'd push himself too hard and do some serious damage. Or, because he was scared to make the situation worse, he wouldn't do enough.

Funny how he'd work his ass off for his arm but not for his heart.

Mac jerked at the thought and felt like a million lightbulbs had switched on in his head. Where had that thought come from? Did it really matter? The truth was the truth…and what he was thinking about his arm should apply to his life, as well. He and Rory had started something ten years ago, and because they were young, and dumb, they'd walked away from it not recognizing what it actually was.

A connection, a future, safety. She'd always been what he'd needed, what his soul needed.

Either way, without her, he was screwed. He was screwed anyway; his arm ached, his heart ached. He was thoroughly miserable. He wanted to see her. He needed to see her. He needed to see if she also thought they had something worthwhile, a connection worth working *on*. There was a good possibility she'd say no but he was willing to take the risk, to do the work. Nothing worth achieving came easy and if he failed, yeah it would suck but he refused to live with regret. He knew what he wanted and was prepared to work his ass off to get it.

He wanted Rory.

And if he failed to win her, he'd survive. He always did.

But he had no intention of failing. Because anything was better than this Rory-shaped emptiness inside him.

He belted toward the door, tossing a "Later" over his shoulder and ignoring the deeply sarcastic "Good chat" that drifted out of Kade's office.

Five days after his accident Troy finally opened his eyes. Three hours after that, when he started arguing with his nurse, Rory realized she could leave him. She could go home to her own bed and have a decent night's sleep. She could spend more than a couple of hours in her apartment, eat something other than fast food, cut down on her coffee.

Leaving Troy and the nurse to bicker, she walked out of his room. Once she was in the hallway, she placed her forearm against the nearest wall and buried her face in the crook of her elbow. Troy was going to be fine. She could stop worrying and start thinking about something other than planning his funeral. Rory felt the tears track down her face and thought how ridiculous it was that she was crying now, when he was finally out of danger, when it was all but over.

Intellectually she knew her reaction was because she could finally relax. She could stop the continuous praying, the bargaining with God. Stupid, but human nature, she thought. Saints alive, she was so tired.

Rory recognized the big hands on her hips and sighed when Mac gently turned her around. Through her tears she noticed his gentle, compassionate expression, the tenderness in his eyes. Even though she was mad at him—he'd certainly taken his time getting here!—she was still ridiculously glad to see him. Her throat tightened as the strength of her tears increased. She felt like she would shatter from the effort it took to not fling herself against his chest and burrow into his warmth.

He took the decision from her by sliding his big hand around the back of her neck and pulling her to his chest. Her arms, shaky with exhaustion, slid around his waist. His other arm held her as her knees buckled.

"It's okay, honey. I've got you," he said in her ear. "I've got you and I'm not letting you go."

She wished she could believe him but she was so fatigued, so emotionally drained she couldn't think. All she knew was that Mac was finally here and she could rest. So she did. Rory wasn't sure how long she stood in his arms. All she knew was that he was strong and solid and *there*. She wasn't alone.

When she'd regained some of her equilibrium, she stepped back, dashed a hand against her wet cheeks and stared at his hard chest. "How did you know I was here?" she asked in a brittle voice. Her tears, it seemed, were still very close to the surface.

Mac pushed her hair off her forehead. "Well, since

your phone has been off and you weren't at your apartment, I started to get worried. So I called Shay and asked about you."

"And she told you I was here?"

"Mmm, after coercing season tickets out of me," Mac said on a small smile that quickly died. "You should've told me about Troy. Why didn't you?"

Rory wasn't so tired that she couldn't react to that. "I thought my rushing from that bar was a good enough hint that something was drastically wrong! And you could've returned my messages!"

"I thought you were running from me because you saw me dancing with that blonde."

"She wasn't worth worrying about. No, I'd just heard about Troy."

Mac closed his eyes in obvious frustration. "I am such an idiot."

"No arguments from me," Rory said, stepping out of his reach. She gestured to Troy's door. "Troy had an accident. It was touch and go for a while."

"I know. Shay told me. She also told me you've spent every minute of the day with him since it happened."

Rory rubbed the back of her neck. "Not every minute. I went home to shower."

"He doesn't have any family?" Mac closed the distance between them.

"Only a mother who has dementia. That's why Troy was driving a crappy car, all his spare cash goes to her nursing home fees."

Mac's hand drew circles on her back and she had to restrain herself from purring like a cat. Rory, knowing how his touch could relax her and tempt her to forgive him too easily, snapped her spine straight. "Anyway, why are you here? I suppose you've been worried about your physio sessions." She tried to sound breezy but it didn't come out that way. "Sorry about that."

Mac's smile was one she'd never seen before, a combination of tenderness, protectiveness and love. It scared the hell out of her.

"Look, I'd appreciate it if you gave me a day to get some rest and then we can get back on track and schedule some sessions. Have you been doing your exercises?" she demanded.

Mac shook his head and bent his knees so they were eye to eye. "Rory?"

"Yes?"

"Shut up for a sec, okay?" Mac waited to see whether she would talk again, and when she didn't, he nodded his satisfaction. "So this is what is going to happen—I'm taking you back to my place and you're going to stand, or sit, in my shower until you are pink and boneless. Then you are going to eat something, soup maybe, and then we are going to climb into bed where you will sleep in my arms. Got it?"

"Uh…" She was beyond tired. She couldn't even find the energy to respond, let alone argue.

"Just say yes."

Rory nodded as tears welled again. "Excellent." Mac wound his arm around her shoulders and walked her down the passage toward the exit. "I like it when I get to boss you around," he teased.

Rory wasn't too tired to allow him to get away with that comment. "Don't get used to it, McCaskill. It's only because I'm exhausted."

Rory opened her lids and squinted in the bright sunlight stabbing her eyes. She placed her arm in front of her face to cut out the glare, looking out from under her arm across the pale floorboards to the partially open doors that led to a balcony.

A pair of very large sneakers were on the floor and a T-shirt, one she didn't recognize, was draped over the back of a black bucket chair. Through the open doors she saw a pair of bare feet up on a wrought-iron table, perilously close to a carafe of coffee.

Coffee. She'd kill for some. Rory sat up, looked down and couldn't help noticing she was naked. Casting her mind back, she remembered Mac carrying her up the stairs to his bedroom, stripping her down and pushing her into bed. She had a vague recollection of a warm body wrapped around hers as she fell asleep. Clasping the sheet to her chest, she sat up and pushed her hair out of her eyes, running her tongue over her teeth.

Coffee or a toothbrush? Either would do nicely right now.

"You look good in my bed."

Rory turned her head to see Mac standing in the doorway leading in from the balcony wearing a pair of straight-legged track pants and a black T-shirt. His hair was messed and his beard was about three days past stubble and she thought he was the sexiest creature she'd ever laid eyes on.

"Hi," she said, self-conscious.

"Hi back," Mac replied on a smile. "You're looking better, thank God. You scared me...you were totally out of it."

"I felt shell-shocked," Rory admitted, looking around. "Can you pass me something to wear?"

"Why? I rather like you naked," Mac replied, teasing. He picked up the black T-shirt that lay across his chair and held it up. "I did a load of laundry earlier and I tossed your clothes in too. Will this do?"

"You can do laundry?" Rory asked, amused as she caught the T-shirt he tossed her way.

"I can do lots of things," Mac replied, his voice quieter. "Would you like some coffee?"

Rory nodded and watched as he walked back out onto the balcony and returned with a cup of coffee, which he handed over. Rory took a sip and quickly realized it was barely warm but strong enough to put scales on her chest. Okay, so Mac wasn't as together as he sounded, she thought. Very good to know that she wasn't the only one in the room wondering what she was doing here.

What *was* she doing here?

Mac sat on the edge of the bed, his bended knee touching her thigh. He stared down at the floor, and when he spoke, his voice vibrated with emotion. "I once told you that hockey is everything to me, that it was the highest priority in my life."

"Mmm-hmm?"

"It has been my life for the past fifteen years. It's afforded me this amazing lifestyle and I've loved every moment I've spent on and off the ice."

Okay, he wasn't telling her anything new here.

"I love you more."

Rory's mouth fell open. Had he really said what she thought he'd said? She needed to make sure. "Say that again?"

"You are the highest priority in my life. You make it better, brighter and more fun." Mac sent her an uncertain look and his hand gripped her thigh covered by the sheet. "Look, I know I screwed up. I know you needed me, and I let my insecurities get the best of me. I hate that I let you down. I want to do better. I *will* do better. And I know you have trust issues too. You say you don't do relationships but I'd like us to try.

"Before you say no let me say this—I will never cheat on you, I promise. Actually, the closest I've ever come to cheating was that kiss we shared. I've never been involved with anyone deeply enough for this to be an issue but, in my defense, I've always ended one affair before I started another."

"Um…okay?"

"But you aren't an affair. You are the only person I can be real with. Someone I can really talk to… You are my best friend. I'm sorry I wasn't there for you. I want to make it up to you. I'll spend my whole life making it up to you, if you'll let me."

Rory placed her hand over her heart, her lower lip trembling as she listened to this innately masculine man humble himself before her.

"Give me a shot, Rory. Give *us* a shot," Mac pleaded, emotion radiating from his eyes.

"What if we fail, Mac?" she asked in a quiet voice.

"Aw, baby…" Mac blew out a breath and shrugged. "I don't fail and you're too important to me to let that happen. But if we do, then we'll go down knowing we gave it our best, knowing we loved rather than living a half-life, guarding our hearts and thoughts and emotions."

"You make it sound so easy," Rory whispered.

"It'll be anything but easy," Mac replied. "It'll be tough, and we'll fight and we'll sometimes wonder what the hell we were thinking. But through it all we'll love each other." Mac pushed an agitated hand through his hair. "We'll have to spend time apart when I'm on the road. But you'll have your own practice to keep you busy and we'll talk every night and text every hour. We'll spend every minute we can together and we'll work at it, dammit, because the one thing we are both good at is hard work, Rorks. If we work at loving each other as hard as we do at everything else, we can't do anything but succeed."

It was a compelling argument, Rory thought, wishing she could throw her fear aside and launch herself into his arms, into their future. "I'm scared, Mac."

"So am I." Mac leaned forward and rested his forehead against hers. "We can be scared together. Do you think you can love me, Rorks? Some day and at some stage?"

Rory pulled her head back, astounded at his comment. She placed a hand on his chest. "You think I don't love you?"

"Well, you haven't exactly uttered the words," Mac said conversationally, but she could feel his galloping heartbeat under her hand.

Rory linked her arms around his neck and looked into his eyes. "I do love you. I think I fell in love with you the first time you almost kissed me." Rory placed her forehead against his temple. "I thought I was going to be alone forever but I can't be. It's no longer who I am, who I've become by knowing you. Who I am now is someone who loves you—now, tomorrow, forever. I might have had a hand in rehabilitating your arm but you rehabilitated my heart."

Mac's hand on her neck tightened in response. "Oh, Rorks, you slay me. So, we agree that we love each other and this is it?"

"I so agree to that."

"Excellent." Mac grinned. "Now, let's move on to another important issue…"

Rory lifted her eyebrows as he pulled his T-shirt over his head. "I think we've covered the high points."

Mac dropped a hard, openmouthed kiss on her lips before lifting her shirt up and over her head. "Getting you naked is always going to be very high on my agenda."

Rory curled her hand around his neck as he pushed her back into the pillows. His eyes were soft as they connected with hers. He swallowed, started to speak, cleared his throat and tried again. "Everything that is most important to me is here, right now. I'm holding my world in my arms," Mac said, his tone low and soaked with tenderness. "It feels good."

"It feels amazing," Rory replied, her voice cracking with emotion. Blinking her tears away, she lifted her hips and wiggled. Her smile turned naughty as her hand drifted down his back to rest on one very fine butt cheek. "*You* feel amazing. So, McCaskill, are you going to kiss me or what?"

Mac grinned. "Oh, yeah. Anytime, anywhere—*everywhere*—for the rest of your life. Starting right now…"

* * * * *

PREGNANT BY THE MAVERICK MILLIONAIRE

JOSS WOOD

One

Funny.
Built.
Sexy.
Smart. So, so, smart.
Courteous, hot, confident.

He was the entire package, a gorgeous combination of everything any woman would ever want or need for a flash-in-the-pan encounter. That being said, Brodie Stewart knew there were at least a billion women in the world who would slap her senseless for what she was about to do and she didn't blame them.

"Brodie? Did you hear me? I asked if you want to come upstairs," Kade whispered into her ear, his hand on her rib cage, his thumb rubbing the underside of her right breast.

She licked her lips and tasted him on her tongue, inhaled the citrus and spice of his soap-scented skin and tipped her head sideways to allow his lips to explore the cords of her neck. Man, he was good at this, Brodie thought.

She should step away, she *should stop this*…

She'd been saying the same thing for three weeks. She shouldn't have waited for Kade every early morning on the running trail, shouldn't have felt the butterflies in her stomach when he loped toward her, a six-foot-plus slab of celebrity muscle. She shouldn't have laughed at his jokes, responded to his gentle flirting. And she certainly shouldn't have accepted his offer to return to his place for a lazy cup of Saturday morning coffee/sex after their seven-mile loop around Stanley Park.

As much as she wanted to know what that cocky, mobile mouth could do, she definitely should *not* have kissed him.

She'd thought she had it all worked out, had convinced herself she could handle this, him. It wasn't like she hadn't had sex since Jay. There had been a few guys—okay, two—since the accident a decade ago. On paper, Kade was perfect. The ex-professional ice hockey player, now second in charge of the Vancouver Mavericks, was resolutely single. Proudly unavailable and, unlike most females of a certain age, Brodie had no desire to change him. In fact, one of the reasons she'd said yes to his offer for coffee was because she knew exactly what he wanted and it wasn't a happily-ever-after with her.

Okay, it had been a while and she was out of practice, but why, oh, dear Lord why, couldn't she get past her hang-ups and have a quick tumble with the gorgeous, very practiced Kade Webb?

Maybe it was because something about him resonated with her, because he was more than a pretty package. Because his kisses were deep and compelling and made her quiver with more than a quick physical connection. He reminded her of love, of intimacy, of emotional connections.

She really didn't want the reminder.

Brodie peeled herself off Kade's wide chest and dropped a quick so-sorry kiss on his chin, her lips brushing the golden stubble on his jaw. She rolled off the leather couch, stood up and walked over to the floor-to-ceiling folding doors leading to an expansive balcony. Brodie placed her hand on the cool glass. From this penthouse loft downtown he had the most amazing view of False Creek and the Granville and Burrard bridges. It was a big-bucks view and absolutely fabulous. She took it in…and gave herself time to form a response to his question.

Reluctantly Brodie turned and placed her hands behind her butt, leaning against the glass. Her heart and libido wanted to return to his embrace, trace those long, hard muscles, taste his naturally olive-shaded skin, shove her hands into his loose, surfer-boy blond hair, watch those brown eyes deepen to black as passion swept him away. But her brain was firmly in charge and it was telling her to run, as far and as fast as she could, before she found herself in a situation that was out of her control.

God, he was going to think she was a tease, that she was playing him. She wasn't, not really. She was just protecting herself.

Emotionally. Psychically. In all the ways she could.

Brodie felt his eyes on her but stared down at her sneakers, wishing she was wearing more than a tight hoodie and running tights. She knew he was waiting for an explanation for her blowing hot and cold, for kissing him senseless and then backing away. She couldn't tell him—this man she'd jogged with, who knew nothing more about her than her name and that she liked to run—that even though she was crazy horny, the idea of sex, *with him*, reminded her of intimacy and intimacy scared the skin off her.

He was supposed to be a fun time, a quick thing but, dammit, Kade Webb had stirred up emotions she thought were long dead. Of all the men in Vancouver, why him? He was such a cliché—handsome, wealthy, charming, successful. In Jane Austen's world he would've been called a rake and three hundred years later the moniker still suited him well.

Brodie sighed, wishing she'd played this differently. Everyone knew what a fitness fanatic he was, how fast he ran, and it was common knowledge that he ran most mornings in Stanley Park. She'd wanted to see if she could, in any way, keep up with him. Instead of keeping pace with him at the crack of dawn, she should've hung back and kept her distance. At first he'd been amused with her idea that she could match his long-legged stride, but she'd run track in college. She had speed and stamina on her side. When he realized he couldn't shake her he started bantering with her. Many runs and many conversations led to this morning's invitation for coffee/sex.

She'd enjoyed those random conversations so much she'd frequently forgotten she was jogging with the city's most elusive bachelor. To her, he was just a guy with a wicked sense of humor, a sharp brain and, admittedly, a very sexy body. Running alongside him had certainly not been a hardship. She'd actually taken pleasure in his appreciation of her.

So much so that she'd thought she was strong enough, brave enough, to have a casual encounter on a Saturday morning as any other confident, sophisticated, modern woman would. Yeah. Right.

"You've changed your mind, haven't you?" His voice was as rich as the sunbeams dancing across the wooden floor. Her eyes flew up to meet his and, to her relief, she didn't see any anger in his expression, just regret.

"I'm so sorry. I thought I could." Brodie lifted her hands in an I-don't-know-what-happened gesture.

"Was it me? Did I do something you didn't like?"

Aw...

Brodie blushed. "No, you're fabulous. God, you must know you kiss really well and I'm sure..." Her blush deepened. "I'm sure you do everything well."

Kade pushed himself into a sitting position on the couch and placed his ankle on his knee. He leaned back and the muscles in his big arms flexed as he linked his hands behind his head, his expensive running shirt pulling tight across his broad chest. She could see the ridges of his stomach and knew the fabric covered a perfect six-pack of sexy-as-sin muscles.

Stop thinking about his body, his stomach, about those hard thighs...

"Maybe you'd feel more at ease if I tell you you're in control here. You say no—to anything, at any point—and I'll back off," Kade quietly stated.

This was a prime example of why she was attracted to him. Beyond the charm, beneath the sexy face and the scorching body, was the man she suspected the public never saw; someone who was thoughtful enough to put her at ease. Someone who could quiet her fears, who could make her consider casting off a protective layer or two.

Thoughtful Kade reminded her of Jay, which reminded her of the person she'd been before her life had been turned inside out. The open, happy, sunny girl who'd loved life with a vengeance. A young woman who had the world at her feet.

That was what scared her most about being with him. He made her remember who she'd been before she wasn't that person anymore.

Sex she could handle, but she was terrified of feeling good, contented. She couldn't deal with happiness.

Not when she knew how quickly it could be ripped away.

Brodie bit her lip and lifted her hands in the air. She saw a hint of frustration pass across Kade's face.

"Okay, then I really don't understand. You seemed to be as into me as I am into you."

Brodie scratched the back of her neck. "Yeah, I'm a mess. It's difficult to explain but trust me when I tell you it's all me and not you."

Kade nodded. "Oh, I know it's all you 'cause if I had anything to do with it then you'd be naked and panting right now."

Well, there wasn't a hell of a lot to say to that. She should just go. "This was a very bad decision on my part." Brodie moved away from the window and clasped her hands behind her back. "I'm really sorry to blow hot and cold."

Kade stood up and raked his fingers through his hair. "No worries. It's not the end of the world."

She was sure it wasn't, not for him. He'd had a variety of woman hanging off his arm since he was eighteen years old and new to the Mavericks. In sixteen years, that was a lot of women and a lot of hanging. With one call, one text message, he could have Brodie's replacement here in ten minutes.

So, there was an upside to this stupid scenario; she would never be one of "Webb's Women."

As she walked toward the door, Kade's phone buzzed and he picked it up off the coffee table. He swiped the screen with his thumb and frowned as he read the text message.

"Quinn and Mac are on their way up," he said.

Quinn Rayne and Mac McCaskill, Kade's best friends, his ex-teammates and current business partners. Yeah, she wasn't proud to admit that, like every other obsessed Mavericks fan, she read about their exploits in the papers and online. The women, although Kade wasn't quite as much a player as Quinn and Mac, the crazy stunts—mostly Quinn—the scandals... Quinn again. Actually, these days, it was mostly Quinn who gave the press grist for the mill.

Brodie glanced at her wristwatch. It was 7:36 a.m. on a Saturday morning. "So early?"

"Yeah, weird." Kade stood up and walked across the expansive loft to the kitchen area. He opened a huge fridge and pulled out two bottles of water. He waved one in her direction. "Want one?"

Brodie nodded and easily caught the bottle he lobbed in her direction. "Thanks." She gestured to the door. "So, I think I should go."

Kade nodded his agreement, saw she was struggling to crack the top and walked toward her. He took the bottle, opened the lid and handed it back to her. "There you go."

"Thanks," Brodie said and gestured to the couch. "Sorry, you know...about that."

Kade's expression was pure speculation. "Maybe one day you'll tell me why." They heard a clatter of footsteps outside the door. "My boys are here."

"I'll get out of your way."

Kade moved past her and opened the door to his friends. Brodie opened her mouth to say a quick hello, but her words died at the looks on their faces. They pushed past her to flank Kade, looking pale. Their eyes were rimmed with red.

"What's wrong?" Kade demanded, his voice harsh.

Brodie watched as they each put a hand on Kade's shoulders. Her stomach plummeted to the floor at their expressions; she recognized them instantly. They were the bearers of bad news, the harbingers of doom. They were going to tell him his life was about to do a 180.

She'd seen the same expression on her aunt's face when Poppy had told her that her parents, her best friend, Chelsea, and her old friend but new boyfriend Jay were dead, along with six other people, in a nightmarish accident. They'd been on their way to a dinner to celebrate her twentieth birthday and apparently life had thought being the lone survivor of a multivehicle crash was a suitable gift.

Why was I left behind?

"Tell. Me." Kade's snap brought her back to his hall, to the three men looking like the ground was shifting under their feet.

"Kade, Vernon had a heart attack this morning," Quinn said, his words stilted. "He didn't make it, bud."

She saw the flash of denial on Kade's face, the disbelief, and she quietly slipped out the door. Grief was an intensely personal and private emotion and the last thing he needed was a stranger in his space, in his home. Besides, she was still dealing with her own sorrow, still working through losing her own family, her closest friend and the man whom she'd thought she'd marry.

Sorry, Kade, she thought. *So, so sorry*. A long time

ago she'd had a brave heart and a free spirit and she hoped the news of his friend's death wouldn't change the core of who he was, like the same kind of news had changed her.

But life *had* changed her and she wasn't that free-spirited girl anymore. She walked back into her real life knowing she certainly wasn't the type of woman who could handle sexy, bachelor millionaires tempting her to walk on the wild side.

Six months later

Brodie typed her client's answer into her tablet, hit Enter and looked up. Dammit, she thought, instantly recognizing the interest in his eyes. This appointment was already running overtime and she really didn't want to fend off his advances.

This was one downside to dealing with male clients in her matchmaking business. Because she was reasonably attractive they thought they would skip the sometimes tedious process of finding a mate and go straight for her.

"What type of woman are you looking for?" she asked, deliberately playing with the massive-but-fake emerald-and-diamond monstrosity on the ring finger of her left hand.

"Actually, I was going to say a tiny blonde with a nice figure but I'm open to other possibilities. Maybe someone who looks like you…who *is* you. I have tickets for the opera. Do you like opera?"

Ack. She hated opera and she didn't date her clients. Ever. She didn't date at all. Brodie sent him a tight smile and lifted her hand to show him her ring. "I'm flattered but I'm engaged. Tom is a special ops soldier, currently overseas."

Last week Tom had been Mike and he'd been an ace detective. The week before he'd been Jace and a white-water adventurer. What could she say? She liked variety in her fake fiancés.

Brodie took down the rest of his information, ignored his smooth attempts to flirt with her despite her engagement to Tom and insisted on paying for coffee. She watched as he left the café and climbed into a low-slung Japanese sports car. When she was certain he was out of view, she dropped her head to the table and gently banged her forehead.

"Another one asking for a date?" Jan, the owner of the coffee shop, dropped into the chair across from Brodie and patted her head. Despite Brodie trying to keep her distance from the ebullient older woman, Jan had, somehow, become her friend. She rarely confided in anybody—talking about stuff and discussing the past changed nothing, so what was the point?—but Jan didn't let it bother her. Like her great-aunt Poppy, Jan nagged Brodie to open up on a fairly regular basis.

Funny, Brodie had talked more to Kade in three weeks than she had to anybody—Jan and Poppy included—for the last decade.

Well, that thought had barreled in from nowhere. Brodie rarely, if ever, thought about Kade Webb during daylight hours. Memories of him, his kiss, his hard body under her hands, were little gifts she gave to herself at night, in the comfort of the dark.

"Being asked out on dates is an occupational hazard." Brodie stretched out her spine and rolled her head on her shoulders in an effort to work out the kinks.

Jan pushed a pretty pink plate holding a chocolate chip cookie across the table. "Maybe this will make you feel better."

It would, but Brodie knew there was something other than sympathy behind Jan's fat-and-sugar-laden gesture. "What do you want?"

"My cousin is in her thirties and is open to using a matchmaker. I suggested you."

Brodie scowled at her friend, but she couldn't stop herself from breaking off the corner of the cookie and lifting it to her mouth. Flavors exploded on her tongue and she closed her eyes in ecstasy. "Better than sex, I swear."

"Honey, if my cookies are better than sex, then you ain't doing it right," Jan replied, her voice tart. She leaned forward, her bright blue eyes inquisitive. "You having sex you haven't told me about, Brodie?"

She wished. The closest she'd come to sex was Kade Webb's hot kiss six months ago, but sex itself? She thought back. Three or so years?

She was pathetic.

After taking another bite of the cookie, Brodie pulled her thoughts from her brief encounter with the CEO of the Mavericks professional ice hockey team and narrowed her eyes at her friend. "You know I only take men as my clients, Jan."

"Which is a stupid idea. You are halving your market," Jan said, her business sense offended. But Brodie's business model worked; Brodie dealt with men, while her associate Colin only had women clients. They pooled their databases and office resources. As a result, they were doing okay. In the hectic twenty-first century— the age of the internet, icky diseases and idiots—singles wanted help wading through the dating cesspool.

"Women are too emotional, too picky and too needy. Too much drama," Brodie told Jan. Again.

Brodie snapped off another piece of cookie and wrinkled her nose when she realized she'd eaten most of it. She was a sucker for chocolate. And cookies. Thank the Lord she had a fast metabolism. She still ran every day, but never in the morning.

"The men don't really want to date me. They just like the attention I pay them. They tend to forget they are paying *me* to pay attention. And I know far too much about them too soon."

An alert on her tablet told her she'd received a new email. Jan pushed herself to her feet. "I'll let you get back to work. Do you want another cup of coffee?"

Brodie already had caffeine-filled veins but why should that matter? "Please."

She swiped her finger across her tablet and accessed her inbox. She'd received quite a few messages when she'd been dealing with Mr. Suave but only one made her pulse accelerate.

Your donation to the auction at the Mavericks' Charity Ball filled the subject line and all the moisture in her mouth disappeared. Jeez, she'd had a brief encounter with Kade months ago, shouldn't she have forgotten about him by now?

Unfortunately Kade wasn't the type of man who was easily forgotten. And, if she had to be truthful, she still missed those early-morning runs when it seemed like they had the park to themselves. She missed the way her heart kicked up when she saw him, missed the way he pushed her to run faster, train harder. She'd enjoyed him, enjoyed that time with him, more than she should have.

Brodie rubbed her hands over her face and gave herself a mental slap. She was almost thirty, a successful business owner and matchmaker to some of the sharpest, richest, most successful bachelors in the city. She should not be thinking about *the* sharpest, richest, best-looking bachelor in the city.

Pathetic squared. Brodie shook her head at her ridiculousness and opened the email.

Dear Ms. Stewart,

On behalf of the Chief Executive Officer of the Vancouver Mavericks, Kade Webb, may I extend our heartfelt gratitude for your donation to the Mavericks' auction to be held on June 19.

Attached is your invitation to a luncheon my department is hosting for our valued sponsors earlier on the day. You are most welcome to attend the ball and charity auction; the cost and details are attached.

We look forward to your presence at lunch on the 19 of June. Please see the attached document for the venue and time.

Yours,

Wren Bayliss

Public Relations Director

Vancouver Mavericks

Thanks but, no thanks. She wouldn't be attending. Donating to the charity auction had been Colin's idea and he could attend the luncheon and ball on their behalf. She wasn't even sure donating their services to the charity auction would raise any money... What bachelor or bachelorette would admit to wanting to use a matchmaker in a room full of their friends and colleagues? Their business was based on discretion and her clients came to her, mostly, via word of mouth. But Wren, and Colin, had dismissed Brodie's concerns. They seemed to think sisters, brothers and friends would bid on their siblings' or friends' behalf. Besides, the guest could bid silently via cell phone as well, so anonymity, if it was required, would be assured.

Thanks to the competition of online matchmaking Colin was convinced they needed to cement their position as matchmakers to the elite of Vancouver society and they needed to network more and foster relationships. Being part of the Mavericks' silent auction was a huge coup and would be excellent direct advertising to their target group. Since marketing and PR was Colin's forte, she'd told him he could represent them at the luncheon.

Yes, a part of her reluctance was the fact there was a chance Kade would be at the function. Months might've passed but she was still embarrassed down to her two-inch designer heels. She'd acted like a ditzy virgin who said yes but meant no. God! How could she be in the same room with him without wanting to jump him—the man still fueled her sexual fantasies—but also wanting to hide under the table?

Her computer dinged again and she looked at the new message that popped into her inbox.

Hey, Brodes,
I presume you received an invite to attend the sponsor's lunch hosted by the Mavericks? I can't attend. Kay and I are seeing a fertility specialist that day. Can you go and do the thing for us both?
Thanks,
Col

Brodie groaned.
Please let Kade not be there, she prayed.

Two

"Whose stupid idea was this?"

Kade Webb scowled at his two best friends and rolled his shoulders under his suit jacket, wishing he was anywhere but in the crowded, over-perfumed bar area of Taste, one of the best restaurants in Vancouver. He'd spent most of last night reading P&L statements and had spent a long, tedious morning with Josh Logan's hardass agent negotiating a deal to buy the hotshot wing, and all he wanted was to plant himself behind his messy desk and make a dent in his paperwork. He was trying to finalize their—his, Mac's and Quinn's—partnership with old man Bayliss, Wren's grandfather, so the four of them could make a solid counteroffer to buy the Mavericks franchise before Vernon's widow sold it to Boris Chenko, a Russian billionaire who owned a string of now generic sports franchises.

Kade didn't have the time to socialize. To play nice.

What he really wanted, despite it only being noon, was a cold beer, a long shower and some hot sex. Or, to save time, some long, hot sex in a shower. Since he hadn't had time to date lately the hot sex would have to be a solo act later—how sad, too bad—but really, he'd give it all up, sex included, for a solid eight hours of sleep.

He was burning the candle at both ends and somewhere in the middle, as well.

"Will you please take that scowl off your face?"

Kade looked down into the face of his newly appointed director of public relations and wondered, for the hundredth time, why there was no sexual attraction between him and Wren. She was gorgeous, slim, vivacious and smart, but she didn't rock his boat. He didn't rock hers, either. They were friends, just like he was with Mac's new fiancée, Rory, and for the first time in Kade's life he was enjoying uncomplicated female relationships.

That being said, he still wouldn't say no to some uncomplicated sex.

"Kade, concentrate!" Wren slammed her elbow into his side and he pulled his attention back to business.

"Your guests of honor, the main sponsors, should be arriving any minute and you need to pay them some special attention," Wren insisted, a tiny foot tapping her only indication of nervousness.

"Who are they again?"

Frustration flashed in Wren's blue eyes and Kade held up his hands in apology. "Wren, I've been dealing with player negotiations and your grandfather as our new partner, and fending off Myra's demands for us to make a counteroffer. Sponsors for this ball haven't been high on my priority list."

"Did you read *any* of the memos I sent you?"

Kade shrugged. "Sorry, no. But you can tell me now and I'll remember."

He had a phenomenal memory. It was a skill he acquired as a child hopping from town to town and school to school following the whims of his artist father. Within a day of arriving in a new place, he'd find a map and memorize the street names so he'd know exactly where he was at all times. He'd felt emotionally lost so often that being physically lost was going a step too far. His memory helped him catch up with schoolwork and remember the names of teachers and potential friends, so he could ease his way through another set of new experiences.

Wren ran through the list of the bigger donations and then said, "The Forde Gallery donated one of your father's paintings, a small watercolor but pretty."

Jeez, he remembered when his father had to swap paintings for food or gas or rent money. Even his small paintings now went for ten grand or more… It was a hell of a donation.

"We have dinners on yachts, holidays, jewelry, the usual bits and pieces businesses donate. The item that will be the most fun and will get the crowd buzzing is the matchmaking service…"

"The what?"

"Brodie Stewart and Colin Jones are providing their matchmaking services. The winners, one girl and one guy, will be matched up and sent on three dates to find a potential mate. Sounds like fun, doesn't it?"

Brodie Stewart? His Brodie? The girl who'd kissed like a dream but who'd bailed on him before they got to the bedroom?

"It sounds like hell." Kade managed to utter the response even though his mind was filled with memories of Brodie, dark hair spilling over her shoulders as she lay against his chest, bright green eyes languid and dreamy after one spectacular hot, wet kiss. He dimly recalled her saying something about her having her own business but why did he think she was in consulting?

"Is she attending this lunch?" Kade asked and hoped Wren, or his friends, didn't hear the note of excitement in his voice.

"You know this Brodie person?" Quinn demanded. And there was the problem with being friends with someone for so damn long. There was little you could get past them.

"Not really," Kade replied, sounding bored.

"Let me give you a hint about your boss, Wren," Mac stated, his arm around Rory's waist. "When he lies he always sounds disinterested, faraway, detached."

Unfortunately, being in love hadn't affected Mac's observational skills and he was as sharp as ever. "Shut the hell up, McCaskill, you have no idea what you are talking about. I met Brodie once, a while ago."

"Why didn't you tell us about her?" Quinn demanded, unsatisfied.

"Do you tell me about the women you meet?" Kade responded.

Quinn thought for a moment before grinning. "Pretty much, yeah. And if I don't tell you, then the press will."

Kade pulled a face. The society pages of their local papers and many internet sites devoted far too much time speculating about their love lives. Mac had provided a break for Kade and Quinn as the media devoured the news that he was settling down with the lovely Rory, but recently they'd restarted their probing inquiries about the state of his and Quinn's love lives. Many of the papers hinted, or outright demanded, it was time the other two "Maverick-teers" followed Mac's example.

Kade felt that he would rather kiss an Amazonian dart frog.

Only Mac and Quinn knew his past, knew about his unconventional upbringing as the son of a mostly itinerant artist who dragged him from place to place and town to town on a whim. They understood his need to feel financially secure and because they worked together, invested together and always stuck together, the three of them, along with Wren's grandfather, were in the position to buy their beloved hockey team, the Vancouver Mavericks.

Yeah, he might be, along with Quinn, a wealthy, eligible and elusive bachelor, but he had every intention of staying that way. Legalities and partnership agreements and a million miles of red tape—and his belief in the loyalty of his friends—had allowed him to commit to his career with the Mavericks, formerly as a player and now as the CEO and, hopefully, as a future co-owner. But a personal commitment? Hell no.

He'd learned that hard lesson as a child. As soon as he found someone to love—a dog, a friend, a teacher, a coach—his father would rip it away by packing up their lives and moving them along. Emotional involvement sent Kade backward to his powerless childhood.

He'd hated that feeling then and he loathed it now. His theory was if you didn't play in a rainstorm, then you wouldn't get hit by lightning. He made damn sure the women he dated had no expectations, that they thoroughly understood he was a here-now-gone-tomorrow type of guy. That they shouldn't expect anything from him.

Despite his up-front attitude, there were always women who thought they could change his mind so he'd still had to ease himself out of situations. Sometimes he managed it with charm, sometimes he had to be blunt, but when he sensed his lovers were becoming emotionally invested, he backed off. Way, way off.

Brodie Stewart was the only woman who'd ever turned the tables on him, who'd backed away before he could. Backed away before he'd even gotten her into bed.

"...she had all the emotional depth of a puddle!"

Kade pulled his attention back to the conversation and caught the tail end of Rory's comment. She was scowling at Quinn and he looked unrepentant, being his bad-boy self.

"Honey, I wasn't dating her for her conversational skills," Quinn stated.

Rory shook her head and rested her chin on Mac's shoulder. "One day you are going to meet someone who you can't resist and I hope she gives you hell," Rory said, her tone and expression fierce.

"Rorks, unfortunately butt-face here claimed you before I did so I am destined to be a free spirit." Quinn put his hand on his heart, his eyes laughing.

Rory, smart girl that she was, didn't fall for Quinn's BS. Instead, she poked Quinn's stomach. "You will meet her and I will not only laugh while I watch you run around her like a headless chicken, I will encourage her to give you as much trouble as possible." She stretched past Quinn to jab Kade in the stomach. "That goes for you, too, Kade. The female population of Vancouver has spoiled you two rotten."

"I'm not complaining." Kade smiled, taking a sip of his lime-flavored water.

"Me neither," Quinn quickly agreed. He stuck his tongue in his cheek as he continued to tease Rory. "And I don't think we've been spoiled—we've been treated as per our elevated status as hockey gods."

"That just shows how moronic some women can be," Rory muttered. She looked up at Mac and narrowed her eyes. "You're very quiet, McCaskill. Got anything to say?"

Mac dropped a kiss on her forehead and another on her mouth. "Hell no! This is your argument with my friends. But, since I am taking you home and hoping to get lucky, I'll just agree with everything you say."

Quinn made the sound of a cracking whip and Kade rolled his eyes before he said, "Wimp."

"You might wear the trousers but Rory picks them out," Quinn added and immediately stepped back to lessen the impact of Mac's big fist smacking his shoulder. "May I point out that before Rory snagged you, you were—"

"No, you absolutely may not." Wren's cool voice interrupted their smack talk. "Can you three please act like the responsible, smart businessmen that people—mistakenly I might add—think you are and behave yourselves? The first sponsor has arrived."

Kade didn't need Wren's nod toward the ballroom to tell him Brodie had arrived. He'd felt the prickle of anticipation between his shoulder blades, felt the energy in the room change. He was super aware of her. As he slowly turned, he felt the world fade away.

She hadn't changed, yet…she had. It had only been six months, but somehow she was a great deal more attractive than he remembered. Her dress hugged a toned body and her long black hair was now a short, feathery cap against her head. What definitely hadn't changed was her ability to send all his blood rocketing south to a very obvious and inconvenient place.

"Well, well, well…isn't this interesting?" Mac drawled in Kade's ear.

"First time I've seen our boy gobsmacked, dude," Quinn added. "Shut your mouth, boyo, you're drooling."

Kade ignored his friends. Life had unexpectedly dropped Brodie back into his realm again and he wanted what he'd always wanted every time he'd laid eyes on her: Brodie in his bed, under him, naked and legs around him…eyes begging for him to come on in.

Her perfume reached him before she did and he realized it was the same scent he remembered. It took him straight back to those early-morning runs in the park, to crisp air and the hesitant smile of the black-haired girl who waited for him by the running store and kept up with his fast pace along the seawall. He hadn't run in the park since the morning he'd heard about Vernon's death.

And kissed Brodie.

It had been an incredible kiss and the one highlight of a couple of really tough, horrible months. If only he had the memory of taking her to bed, too…

So it turned out he didn't want long, hot sex with any random woman. He wanted to make love to Brodie. Interesting.

Crazy.

And pretty damn dangerous. He wouldn't—couldn't—allow her to know the effect she had on him, how he instantly craved her and the crazy chemical reaction he was experiencing. It wasn't clever to admit she was the only woman he'd ever encountered who could thoroughly disconcert him, who could wipe every rational thought from his brain.

Okay, he was officially losing it. Maybe it was time, as Wren had suggested, he started acting like the CEO he was supposed to be.

With anyone else, he could do it with his eyes closed. Around Brodie, he might have to put his back into it.

So here goes...

Brodie held out her hand to Kade and hoped her smile wasn't as shaky as she felt. "Kade, it's been a while."

"Brodie." Kade took her hand and she held his eyes even though her pulse skittered up her arm and straight to her belly. She met his eyes and felt her heart roll over, as it always did. She knew his eyes were a deep brown but today, against his olive complexion and dark blond hair, they glinted black.

Oh, this wasn't good. He was a sexy man. They'd kissed but that wasn't enough of a reason for her hormones to start doing their crazy dance. She looked down at their intertwined hands and could easily remember what his tanned fingers felt like on her back, his wide hand sliding over her butt, his lips on hers...

Dammit, Brodie!

Kade touched her elbow and gestured to his friends. Hot, hot and *steamin'*. Brodie wanted to fan herself. Quinn Rayne was the ultimate sexy bad boy, Mac McCaskill was even better looking—if that was possible—after falling in love with the attractive woman tucked into his side, and Kade...? Why, with him looking as fantastic as he did, the urge to jump him and do him on the nearest table was nearly overwhelming.

This was the problem with Kade Webb, Brodie reminded herself. He had the ability to turn her from a woman who considered all the angles into a wild child who acted first and regretted later. She hadn't made an impulsive decision for nearly a decade and yet, around him, that was all she seemed to do! For weeks she'd met him in the park as the sun rose. Then she'd accompanied him home, kissed him senseless and been so tempted to make love to him. Around him, *impulsive* was her new middle name.

Stewart, start acting like the adult you are! Immediately!

Pulling herself together, Brodie greeted Kade's friends, kissed Wren hello and looked, and sounded, like the professional she normally was.

Quinn smiled at her. Whoo boy, it was a potent grin and she could easily imagine girls falling like flies at his feet. That smile should be registered as a weapon of mass destruction, but Brodie caught the wariness in his eyes and the intelligence he hid behind his charm. "So, you're Brodie."

"I am."

"And you're a matchmaker."

"I am." Brodie tipped her head, assessing him. "Would you like me to find you someone?"

She had to smile when Quinn flushed and sent a help-me look at his friends. Since Quinn's exploits, mostly in love, kept Vancouver entertained on a weekly basis, she knew he had no problem finding a date. Finding a *partner* was a very different story.

"You know, most of my clients don't have any problems meeting women and they often date a variety of women."

Quinn frowned. "So why do they need you?"

"Because they are dating the wrong type of women. They want to be in a relationship," Brodie patiently explained. "Do you want to be in a relationship, Mr. Rayne?"

She was taking the circuitous route to find out what she desperately wanted to know: would Kade be bidding for her matchmaking services? The thought of matching him to any of Colin's clients made her stomach roil. Colin's clients were wonderful women, but Brodie thought the *ick* factor was a bit too high to match her fantasy man with a flesh-and-bone woman.

She'd rather pick her eyes out with a cake fork.

"Hell no! And why am I the focus of attention?" Quinn complained. "Kade is as much of a lone wolf as me!"

Brodie lifted an eyebrow in Kade's direction, as if to say "Are you?" He immediately read her question and responded with an inscrutable smile.

Brodie looked around, her eyes falling on the honey blonde surgically attached to Mac's side. Rory's look was speculative, bouncing from Quinn to Kade and back again. Brodie recognized her assessing, mischievous look. This was a woman wanting to cause trouble...

Mac's deep voice broke her train of thought. "Your hands are empty, Brodie. What would you like to drink? Wine? A soda?"

A small glass of wine couldn't hurt, could it? "I'd love a glass of Tangled Vine Chardonnay."

Rory tipped her head and looked at Quinn. "Is that the wine you brought over the other night? It was seriously yummy."

Quinn nodded. "I'll bring a case over tonight. What's for supper?"

"Risotto. Troy is joining us tonight," Rory replied.

Mac looked appalled. "We're having them for supper again? Troy I don't mind, but these two? Babe, they are like rats, if you keep feeding them, we are never going to get rid of them."

"Kade and I are the rats," Quinn told Brodie, smiling. He lifted a huge shoulder. "What can I say? She's a good cook."

Brodie looked into Mac's eyes and noticed the amusement under his fake scowl. Yeah, he looked hardass and a bit scary—they all did—but she could see these men shared a bond that went beyond love. It was too easy to say they loved each other, but it was more than that; there was loyalty here and support, a deep and profound desire to make sure their "brothers" were happy. She couldn't help feeling envious of their bond despite knowing she'd chosen her solitary state. She'd had friendships like that; bonds with Jay and Chels that couldn't be broken by anything except death.

She still missed them, every day. She missed the people who could finish her sentences, who got her jokes. She missed the I-know-it's-after-midnight-but-I-brought-you-pizza conversations. She missed Chelsea, missed those crazy antics—"I'm outside your window and I have a date. Toss down your lucky belt/new shoes/red lipstick/flirty dress."

She missed Jay, the boy who knew her inside out, the man she'd just been getting to know. His sweet kisses, his endless support, his newly acquired fascination with her body. She still missed the man she thought she'd spend the rest of her life with…

She hadn't been able to reconnect with people on that level again. She wasn't prepared to risk heartbreak. Having her heart dented by loss and being left behind without any emotional support sucked. It stung. It burned. It made her cautious and wary. Scared.

She was very okay with being scared. "And I'm sending you a bill for the food we buy," Mac grumbled. "Spongers."

"Rory's a great cook and she likes having us around. Maybe she needs a break from you," Quinn told Mac as he took the glass of wine Kade had ordered for her off the waiter's tray and handed it to Brodie, ignoring Kade's scowl. "I'll bring the wine."

Rory grinned. "Excellent. I love that wine."

"Might I remind you that you won't be able to drink it for a year or so?" Mac muttered.

Rory frowned and then her expression cleared and a small, tender smile drifted across her face. She touched her stomach and Brodie immediately caught on. It took Mac's friends seconds longer to catch up. And, judging by Quinn's and Kade's stunned faces, that wasn't news they'd been expecting. But once they realized what Mac had revealed, they swept Rory into their arms for a long, emotional hug. Kade hugged Mac, as did Quinn, and Brodie felt tears prick her eyes at their joy for their friend. She stepped back, feeling she shouldn't be here, sharing this precious, intimate moment. She half smiled when she noticed Wren doing the same thing.

Weird that Brodie seemed to be present for some of the big, personal Maverick moments. Vernon's death, Mac's baby... She was an outsider, on the wrong side of this magical circle, so it didn't make sense that she was again in the position to hear something deeply personal. This time, at least, it was good news.

"This wasn't how we planned on telling you," Rory said, jamming her elbow into Mac's side.

Brodie looked at Rory, who had her back to Mac's chest, his big hands on her still very flat stomach. "Congratulations," she murmured.

"Yeah, huge congratulations," Kade said, before slanting a sly look at Mac. "Now you're going to have two children under your feet, Rorks."

"Ha-ha." Mac scowled.

"I know, right?" Rory replied, her voice wobbly. "I'm going to be a mommy, Kade."

"You'll be great at it," Kade assured her and tipped his head at Mac. "But he'll need some training."

"I'm not old enough to have friends who are about to be parents." Quinn clapped Mac on the shoulder and nodded to the bar. "We definitely need champagne. I'll get some."

Wren shook her head and stepped forward. "As much as I hate to break up the party we have work to do and a lunch to host."

Quinn wrinkled his nose. "Our head girl has spoken."

Wren threaded a hand through his arm and pulled him toward the dining area. "C'mon, brat. I've put you at a table where you can't misbehave."

Brodie felt Kade's hand on her back and she immediately, subconsciously moved closer to him, her fingers accidentally brushing the outside of his hard thigh.

Kade tipped his head and dropped his voice so only she could hear his words. "It hasn't gone away, has it?"

Brodie wished she could deny it, dismiss his comment, but she couldn't lie to him. Or herself. She forced herself to look him in the eye. "No."

His fingers pushed into her back at her reluctant admission. "So, just to be clear, we're saying this crazy attraction is still happening?"

"Yep." One-syllable answers were all she could manage.

"So are we going to do anything about it this time?"

Wren's efficient voice interrupted their low, intense conversation. "Kade, you're at the main table up front. Brodie, I'll show you to your seat."

Brodie gave Kade a little shrug and followed Wren into the private dining room of Taste. When she tossed a look over her shoulder, she flushed when she noticed Kade was still watching her.

And he didn't stop looking at her for the next ninety minutes.

He wanted her. The heated looks they'd exchanged over the three tables that separated them left her in no doubt of that. Jeez, it was a minor miracle the room hadn't spontaneously combusted from the sparks they were throwing at each other.

He wanted her as much as he had six months ago, possibly more. It was insane; it was exciting.

What *was* she going to do about it?

She knew what he wanted, to take up where they'd left off in his loft. In the ladies' room Brodie pulled a face at her reflection in the mirror above the bathroom sink and ran her wet fingers over the back of her neck, hoping to cool herself down but knowing it was a futile gesture. She was hot from the inside out and it was all Kade Webb's fault.

Every look he'd sent her, every small smile, had told her he wanted her in the most basic, biblical way possible.

She was pretty sure she'd returned his message. With interest.

Brodie sighed. Having a fling with Kade wouldn't hurt anyone. Unlike an affair with a married man it wasn't icky, immoral or dishonest. It wouldn't be embarrassing or hurtful. It wouldn't—unless she did something really stupid, like fall for the guy—be painful.

She hadn't had an affair, or sex, for a long, long time; she hadn't been naked with a man since Jared the IT guy and he was around three, or was it four, years ago? She was nearly thirty and she was tired of dating herself.

Could she do it? Could she have a one-night stand with Kade? Was she okay with being another puck he shot into his sexual net? Brodie grimaced at her bad analogy. But could she be another of Webb's Women?

If she was looking for a relationship, and she wasn't because she was relationship-phobic, Kade would be the last person she'd be interested in. Brodie gripped the vanity and stared at the basin, thinking hard.

He was famous and she'd matched enough semifamous guys to know how much time and effort it took to date a celebrity. She couldn't think of anything worse than having your life dissected on social media platforms or in the society columns, but some women got off on it.

She hadn't considered any of this that long-ago morning when she'd agreed to coffee. Everything had moved so quickly and she'd only been thinking in terms of a couple of hours spent with him. But she had noticed that over the last six months the spotlight on Kade had become even bigger and brighter. His life was routinely dissected; his dates scrutinized. The press was relentless and easily turned a movie into a marriage proposal, a dinner into destiny.

Brodie shuddered. Yuck.

That being said, she still wanted him.

If she could go through with it this time—and that was a big if—she couldn't ignore the fact that a quick fling with Vancouver's most eligible, slippery bachelor could have consequences. If they did do the deed and it became public knowledge, as these things tended to do with the Mavericks, it would affect her business. She had a database of clients who trusted her, who confided in her. Quite a few of them thought she was engaged, and a liaison with Kade would not inspire her clients to trust her judgment.

Men, she'd realized, were frequently a lot more romantic—or traditional—than most woman gave them credit for. They could have affairs, play the field and have one-night stands, but they wouldn't appreciate their matchmaker doing the same.

No, it was smarter and so much more sensible to ignore Kade's suggestion that they continue what they'd started. Sleeping with him probably wouldn't be as good as she imagined; she'd probably romanticized exactly how good Webb's kissing was to excuse her crazy, uninhibited behaviour when she was alone with him. No, best to keep her distance…

Good decision, Brodie thought, eyeing her reflection in the mirror. Sensible decision.

Adult decision.

Safe decision.

So why did it feel so damn *wrong*?

Three

The ladies' room was on a short flight of stairs above the men's restroom and when she stepped into the passage, she looked down and saw the blond head and muscular shoulders that could only belong to Kade.

She flicked off a piece of fluff from her shocking pink blouson dress, belted at the waist and ending midthigh. Nude heels, scalpel-thin, made her legs look like they went on for miles. Back in her apartment it had seemed very suitable for a business lunch, but when Kade looked up and his eyes darkened from a deep brown to a shade just off black, she knew he wanted to rip off her clothing with his teeth. Keeping her hand on the banister, biting the inside of her lip, her heart galloping, she walked down the three steps to the marble floor, a scant couple of inches from his broad chest.

He didn't give her any warning or ask for her permission, his mouth simply slammed into hers. Brodie had to grab his biceps to keep from falling off her shoes. Those amazing hands covered a great deal of her back and she was sure her dress would sport scorch marks from the heat. She was intensely aware of him and could feel the ridges of his fingers, the strength in his wrists.

Brodie wound her arms around his neck and pressed her mouth against his. He tasted like coffee and Kade and breath mints and his lips seemed to feel like old friends. Warm, firm, dry. Confident. That word again. His hands bumped up her spine, kneading as he worked his way to her shoulders, moving around to catch her face. His thumbs skated over her cheekbones as he deepened the kiss, his tongue sliding into her mouth.

Loneliness—the slight dissatisfaction that hovered like a fine mist around her, the ever-present sorrow— dissipated as he took command of the kiss, pushing her back against the wall and pushing his knee between her thighs. This was kissing—raw, raunchy, flat-out sexy. Brodie felt heat and warmth and moisture gather and felt an unfamiliar pull of fulfillment, a desire to lose herself in the heat and strength and sexiness of this man.

Kade's hand skimmed the side of her chest, down her waist and around to her butt, his fingers strong and sure, experienced. He cupped a cheek, pulled her up and into him, and she sighed as his erection pushed into her stomach. He yanked his mouth off hers and she tumbled into his sinfully dark eyes. "Same old, same old."

Brodie placed her hands on his pecs and tried to regulate her breathing. Where was an oxygen tank when she needed one? She felt Kade's fingers on her cheekbone, tracing her jaw. "Brodie? You okay?"

Fine. Just trying to get my brain to restart. Brodie placed her forehead on his sternum and pulled in some much needed air.

"Dammit, Kade," she eventually muttered.

"Yep, we're a fire hazard," Kade agreed, resting his chin on the top of her head. "What are we going to do about it?"

"Nothing?" Brodie suggested.

"Yeah…not an option." She heard the determination in his voice. She knew he would do what it took to get what he wanted.

What *she* wanted. He wouldn't need to do much persuading—she was halfway to following him to hell and back for an orgasm or two.

She was allowed to share some amazing sex with someone who knew what he was doing, her usually quiet wild child insisted. She was twenty-nine, mostly normal but terribly sexually frustrated.

You had this argument with yourself earlier. He's single. You're single. You don't need anyone's permission…

Kade didn't need to use charm, or to say anything at all. She was doing a fine job of talking herself into his bed all on her own.

"Brodie?" Kade stepped back and bent his knees so he could look her in the eye. "What do you say? Do you want to take this to its very natural conclusion?"

Brodie gripped his big biceps, or as much of it as she could get into her hand. He felt harder, more muscular than she remembered. How was that possible? She wanted to undo the buttons on his shirt, push aside the fabric and see what other wonders lay under his expensive clothes. Was his chest bigger? His shoulders broader? His thighs stronger?

"Are you going to put me out of my misery sometime soon?" Kade asked. He sounded like sleeping with her was neither here nor there. Then she took another look at his expression, read the emotion in his eyes.

There was frustration, a whole lot of desire and a hint of panic. Because he thought she might say no? He looked a little off-kilter and not as suave and as confident as she'd first suspected. His hint of insecurity made her feel steadier. That their chemistry had rocked him allowed her to regain her mental and emotional balance.

"God, woman, you're killing me."

She knew if she said yes, there would be no going back. She couldn't get cold feet, couldn't retreat this time.

She was a little scared—and she should be. She'd laid out all the arguments in the ladies' room. But she could no more stop a freight train than miss this second chance to find out if he was as good as her imagination insisted.

Time to put them both out of their misery. Brodie slowly nodded. "Yeah, let's revisit the past. One night, not a big deal?"

"You sure?"

She knew he was asking for some reassurance she wouldn't change her mind midway through, so she placed her hand on his cheek and nodded. "Very sure. On the understanding this is a one-time thing and it stays between us."

Relief flashed across Kade's face and she felt his fingers flexing on her back. "I never kiss and tell. But are you sure we'll be able to stop after one night?"

Brodie shrugged. Probably not. "We can give it our best shot."

Kade stepped back and ran a hand around the back of his neck. "Interesting," he said.

Brodie frowned. "What is?"

"You have a very…businesslike approach to life. And sex."

She supposed she did, but life had taught her to put emotion away from daily life. If she allowed emotion to rule, she would've crawled into a cave after the accident and never come out. She turned her back on her feelings because they were so big, so overwhelming. Before the tragedy, she'd loved hard...wildly, uninhibitedly. She'd engaged every one of her senses and she'd been the most emotional creature imaginable.

A car accident had taken her family, but emotion had hung around and nearly killed her, too. To survive she'd had to box it up and push it away...because she couldn't feel happy without feeling sad. No joy without pain. No love without heartbreak.

It was easier just to skate.

Brodie lifted her chin and sent Kade a cool smile. Time to get the conversation back on track. "So, when and where?"

Kade lifted his eyebrows in surprise and Brodie sent him a look, daring him to make another comment about her frankness. He looked like he wanted to and Brodie prayed he wouldn't. Kade seemed to have the ability to look beyond her shell to the mess inside...

She didn't need anyone upsetting her mental apple cart.

Kade looked at his watch and thought for a minute. "I have meetings this afternoon or else I'd whisk you back to my place right now."

That was something her old self would've done, Brodie mused. Breakfast at midnight, dancing in the rain, unplanned road trips and afternoon sex. The Brodie she was today didn't do wild anymore.

"And tonight is the ball. Are you coming?" Kade placed his hand flat on the wall behind her head and she had to resist the urge to rest her temple on his forearm.

Brodie shook her head. "No. Besides the tickets are sold out."

The corners of Kade's mouth tipped up. "I'm sure I know someone who can slip you inside."

It was tempting, Brodie thought, but no. Attending the ball with Kade would make it seem like a date and she didn't *date*.

"Why don't you give me a call in a day or two?" she suggested.

"I don't know if I can last that long," Kade said, his tone rueful. He jammed his hands into his suit pockets and Brodie couldn't help her urge to straighten his tie. "But...okay."

"Lipstick on my face?" he asked.

"No, you're fine."

Kade nodded. "Give me your cell number. And your address."

Brodie put the info in his phone. Kade nodded his thanks.

Kade's eyes warmed to the color of rough cocoa. "Do you work from home?"

"No, I share an office with my friend and associate downtown. He's also a matchmaker."

Kade scratched his chin. "I am still wrapping my head around the fact you set people up and they pay you for it. It's...weird."

She couldn't take offense. Frequently she thought it was a very odd way to earn money—especially for someone who'd once specialized in international banking and who intended to remain single for the rest of her life. But she was curious as to why he thought her business was weird so she asked him.

Kade rubbed the back of his neck. "I guess it's because I've never had a problem finding dates.'

It was such a common misconception. "Neither do most of my clients. They aren't looking to date, they are looking to settle down." She saw him wince and she had to smile. "So I guess you're not going to be a client anytime soon?"

"Or ever."

Kade pushed all thoughts of her career out of her head when he lifted his hands to cradle her face. She shivered with a mixture of lust and longing. Her hands drifted across his chest and skimmed his flat, ridged belly.

"I can't wait to spend some time with you." He bent to kiss the sensitive spot between her shoulder and neck. He lifted his head and gave her a hard stare. "Soon, I promise."

Brodie swallowed in an attempt to put some saliva back into her mouth.

Keeping his hands on her face, Kade twisted his wrist to check the time and softly cursed. "I've got to get back to the office, I am so late." The pad of his thumb brushed her bottom lip. "Please don't talk yourself out of this, Brodie."

She wanted to protest, wanted to reassure him, but she didn't. "See you."

Kade nodded abruptly, dropped a hard, openmouthed kiss on her lips, then whipped around and headed back to the restaurant.

"You'd better make it very soon, Kade Webb."

She'd run ten kilometers and had a cold shower, and despite it being four hours later, she could still taste Kade on her lips. Her lady parts were buzzing; her heart was still thumping. Her heart rate had actually *dropped* when she'd all but sprinted around Stanley Park. How was she going to function for the next couple of days if this heightened state of awareness didn't dissipate?

It had to dissipate—she couldn't live like this.

God, this was why she ran from entanglements. It was so much easier to slide on the surface of life. She didn't like feeling this way. It felt too much like she was...

Well, *living*. Living meant anticipation, excitement, lust, passion. She wasn't good at any of it anymore and she didn't deserve to feel all that, not when her entire family, practically everyone she had ever loved, was no longer around to do the same.

Why didn't I get hurt?

Why did I live when other people died?

Survivor's guilt. She was the poster child for the condition. Brodie walked across her living room, hands on her hips, her brow furrowed. She'd seen the psychologists, read the literature. She knew guilt was common and part of the healing process. Her healing process was taking a damn long time. She knew she isolated herself. Living a half life wasn't healthy—it certainly couldn't bring her loved ones back. But she couldn't stop thinking she didn't deserve to be happy.

Love was impossible.

The sound of her intercom buzzing broke into her thoughts. Brodie pushed back her hair, frowning. She wasn't expecting anybody—her great-aunt Poppy, who lived on the floor below, was out of town—so she couldn't imagine who could be leaning on her doorbell.

Brodie walked to her front door and pressed the switch. "Can I help you?"

"I have ninety minutes, can I come up?"

Kade. Holy freakin'... Because her mouth was instantly bone-dry, she found it difficult to form words.

"C'mon, babe, don't make me beg," Kade cajoled.

This was madness. This was crazy. She should tell him to leave, tell him that she didn't want him to come up. But that would be a big, fat lie… She did want to see him, preferably naked.

So Brodie pressed the button to open the door downstairs and wrenched open her apartment door to watch him run up. He was still dressed in his suit from earlier. His tie was pulled down and he carried a small gym bag and a tuxedo covered in plastic over his shoulder.

Hunky, sexy, determined man, Brodie thought, leaning against the door frame. Kade reached her and flashed a quick smile but didn't say a word. He just grabbed her hand, yanked her inside, kicked her door closed and threw his stuff on the nearest chair. Then two strong hands gripped her hips and swept her up and into him, her feet leaving the floor. Then his mouth was on hers, warm and demanding, and his tongue swept inside, allowing her to taste his frustration-coated passion.

Whoo-boy!

After a minute had passed—or a millennium, who could tell?—Kade gently lowered Brodie to her feet, but he kept his lips on hers, his tongue delving and dancing. She responded, awed by the pent-up longing she felt in the intensity of his kiss. Her response must have seemed just as demanding, as urgent. Brodie moved her hands to his shirt, tugging it out of his pants. Desperate to feel his skin on hers, she moaned her frustration and then resented the brief separation from Kade's body as he stepped away to unbutton and remove his shirt.

Brodie moved forward and ran her lips across his bare chest, stopping to flicker her tongue over his nipple, to rub her cheek on his chest hair. He was such a man. From the hardness of his muscles to the slightly rough texture of his skin and the smell that called to her senses, he awakened every cell in her body. She could no more stop this than she could stop a freight train. Neither did she want to, she realized.

She needed him, right now. She had to have him— in her, around her, sharing this with her.

"Bed," Kade muttered against her jawline.

"Too far." Brodie managed to lift a hand and wave to the right. "Desk, over there."

"That'll work."

Running his hands over her bottom, Kade lifted Brodie onto the edge of the desk and pushed the files and papers off the table. They slid and tumbled to the floor. She didn't care. Part of her knew this was a mistake, but she didn't care about that, either. Nothing mattered but having him in her arms, allowing him to make indescribably delicious love to her.

Kade quickly stripped her of her clothing, while Brodie watched him through heavy, half-closed eyes. Keeping one hand on her breast, he reached into his suit pants and yanked his wallet out of a pocket. Scattering cards and cash, he found a condom and ripped it open with his teeth. He shed the rest of his clothes, and slipped the condom on. Brodie was not shocked when Kade grabbed the flimsy material of her panties and ripped them off her. His erection was hard and proud as he rubbed himself against her most secret places, seeking her permission to enter.

His lips followed his erection, and Brodie thought she would turn to liquid. Just when she could tolerate no more, Kade lifted his head to worship her breasts with his mouth, tongue and lips. Brodie closed her fingers around him and relished the sound of his breathing, heavy in the quiet of the early evening. Brown eyes met green as she tugged him toward her. Kade's one hand slid under her hip and the other cradled her head, both encouraging her to ride with him.

The desk felt like a soft bed. The cold coffee she'd left there earlier could have been the finest champagne, the mixed-up papers rose petals. They were locked together. Finally. Kade moved within her and Brodie followed. Kade demanded and she replied. Deeper, longer, higher, faster. She met him stroke for stroke, matching his passion, uninhibited, free.

On that thought Brodie fractured on a yell and a sob. Then Kade bucked and arched and collapsed against her, his body hot.

"Brodie?" he muttered against her shoulder. "You alive?"

"Uh-huh."

"Desk survived?"

Brodie's mouth curved into a smile. She patted the wood next to her hip. "Looks like it. You?"

Kade kissed her neck before reluctantly pulling out of her. He straightened and turned away. "Yeah, I'm fine—"

Brodie sat up and frowned at his stream of curses. "What on earth…?"

Kade grimaced at the condom in his hand and then back to her. "The condom split. Dammit, it was brand-new."

Brodie hopped down from the desk and looked around for her shirt, which had landed on the back of her couch. Well, that was a big bucket of freezing water. Dressing quickly, she thought about what to say, how to act. Expressing anger or disappointment was sort of like bolting the stable door after the horse had fled. It wouldn't help. So she decided to be practical.

"If you want to, uh…clean up, my bedroom has an en suite bathroom, second door on the right."

Kade, utterly unconcerned with his nudity, stalked away. Brodie folded his suit pants, hung his shirt over the back of a chair and tucked his socks into his shoes. Picking up her ruined panties, she balled them in her hands before walking into her kitchen and throwing them into the trash can.

Putting her hands on her hips, she considered the angles. What were the chances of her becoming pregnant? She was on a contraceptive, which she took religiously. Was it even the right time of the month for her to be ovulating? Walking toward the calendar she kept on the side of her fridge, she tried to remember when last she'd had her period. Brodie counted back and pursed her lips. She'd be okay, she decided. There was no need to panic.

"And?"

Brodie turned to look at Kade standing in the square doorway, still naked, still hot. "It'll be fine. No need to stress, I'm on the pill."

Relief, hot and sure, flooded Kade's face, his eyes. "Good."

Brodie bit her lip, wondering how to phrase her next question. She didn't want to offend him, but… "Do I need to get myself tested for anything, well, yucky?"

Kade shook his head. "I had a medical three weeks ago and I always use a condom. This is the first time one has broken, I promise."

Well, that was a relief and a less awkward conversation than she'd thought it would be. When Kade grabbed her shirt and pulled her toward him all thoughts of pregnancy and STDs evaporated. He kissed her, long and slow. "You have too many clothes on."

Man, how was she supposed to resist when he made her feel all squirmy and hot? "You don't have any condoms left."

"You do. I saw some in your bathroom cabinet."

Brodie pulled a face. She'd bought them years ago, during her sleeping-with-the-IT-guy phase. "They've been in there for years."

"I checked the expiration date, we're good to go." Kade's lips nibbled her jaw. "You good to go?"

"Bed this time?" Brodie asked.

"And in the shower the next."

Brodie glanced at the clock on her kitchen wall. Twice more in an hour and fifteen minutes?

Well, she'd heard about Kade Webb's ambition, but she'd never thought she'd see it in action.

Kade walked out of her bathroom dressed in his tuxedo pants, his white dress shirt hanging loose. While he was showering she'd run a brush through her hair, pulled on a loose cotton sweater and a pair of yoga pants and was now sitting cross-legged on her bed, trying to act like it was an everyday occurrence for Kade to be in her apartment, showering in her bathroom.

"Why aren't you going to the ball? Surely it's a good place to promote your business?" Kade asked as he sat down next to her to pull on his black socks. "After all, you came to the lunch."

"I came as a sponsor, not to tout for business." Brodie placed her elbows on her knees and her face in her hands. "I've got to be careful how I network. It's not like I can work the room, handing out business cards. My business is based on discretion and most of my clients come to me via word of mouth. Our website and contact numbers are on the program—if someone wants to talk to us they'll call. I only match guys and I can practically guarantee no man there will talk business to me at the ball, not when they can be overheard."

"Would I know any of your clients?"

"More than a couple." Brodie held up her hand. "And no, I'll never tell so don't bother asking."

Kade sent her a quick, assessing look. "I bet a lot of the guys hit on you."

Brodie cocked her head at him. "Why would you think that?"

"So they do, I can see it in your eyes. As for how I know…?" He shrugged. "Say I'm a guy and I'm looking for someone. Then I meet you and think; hey, she's gorgeous and nice, I don't need to look any further. Men are lazy."

"It happens," Brodie admitted.

"How do you deal with them?" Kade pulled on his dress shoes—hand-tooled black leather, Brodie noticed as she scooted off the bed and walked over to her dressing table. She picked up her diamond-and-emerald ring and threw it in his direction.

"Nice ring," he commented and threw it back at her. "Except it's fake."

"As fake as the fiancés I invent every week so I have a good excuse not to date," Brodie replied.

"Ah." Kade bent over to tie his laces and turned his head to look at her. "You've never been tempted?"

Brodie took a moment to consider his question. She was surprised when Kade's eyes narrowed. With jealousy? Not possible.

"My clients are successful, frequently really nice, quite rich men. They drive expensive cars, have gorgeous homes and are intelligent. All very eligible."

Kade scowled.

"But they are also men who are looking to settle down and I am not." Brodie placed her ring back in the shallow bowl holding the jewelry she most often wore. "Besides, becoming involved with a client, in any way, is very unprofessional."

"Good thing I'm not your client, nor will I ever be." Kade sat up and reached for the two sides of his shirt. "I'd rather shoot myself than allow a matchmaker, you or anyone else, to set me up."

Brodie silently admitted she'd rather walk on molten lava than have him as a client.

Kade cocked his head. "So why don't you date?"

Brodie flushed. "Because there are two types of dating. People either date for sex or date for a relationship. I don't do relationships, as a rule. And I very rarely do—" she waved her hand at her bed "—this. I'm as virulently anticommitment as you think you are."

"As I *think* I am?"

Brodie shrugged. She'd seen him with his friends, seen how much he enjoyed his connection with them. He'd be a great husband, a stunning father—if he ever moved out of his party-hearty lifestyle.

Kade held her eyes for a long moment before making a production of looking at his watch. He sent her a crooked grin. "I'm only in it for the hot sex, thanks."

Brodie smiled back. "Then don't win the bid on my auction."

Kade reached into his bag for his bow tie and draped it around his neck, quickly tying it without the use of a mirror. "I very definitely won't," he promised her. "I've got to move or else Wren will have my head."

"Have fun."

Kade picked up his bag and jacket and walked over

to her. He dropped a kiss on her temple, then her mouth. "I'd much rather be having fun with you."

Brodie made herself smile. She was pretty sure he said that to all the girls. "'Bye. See you."

"See you," Kade said, walking out of her bedroom. Within seconds she heard her front door open and close and two minutes later, heard the roar of his sports car.

So that was that. She'd had the fantastic sex she'd been craving. But she'd forgotten how much she enjoyed talking to Kade, how easily they slid into intimate conversation. It was as if there were no barriers and it felt way more intimate than post-sex conversation should be. So why on earth was she craving more?

Four

Kade reached for his glass and took a long sip of whiskey. How much longer could this damn ball last?

It was eleven now. If Quinn would move the auction along, Kade could be out of here by midnight. Was it too late to phone Brodie? Was she exhausted? Would he come across as desperate if he called her again so soon? If she was in bed, what was she wearing? A slinky negligee or a tank top and boxer shorts or just her golden skin?

He loved her skin. He loved everything about her body and when he'd held her earlier he'd felt... How had he felt?

Kade cursed the action in his pants. He needed more than a whiskey on ice, he needed a plunge into an ice-fishing hole. At this rate, when he got Brodie where he wanted her—under him—he'd last about two seconds. His reaction to her was ridiculous, insane... There had to be some sort of scientific explanation for why they wanted to rip each other's clothes off at the drop of a hat. Shouldn't the amazing sex they'd shared earlier have taken the edge off? Was it pheromones? Biological instinct? But why her and not one of the many, many good-looking women—many of them Mavericks groupies—scattered throughout the ballroom? None of this made sense.

All he was certain of was that he wanted Brodie again. Urgently. Immediately. Tonight.

Move the hell on, Rayne!

"And now, one of our more interesting donations," Quinn announced. Kade turned his attention back to the stage. "Ms. Brodie Stewart, one of the city's best matchmakers, is offering the opportunity to bid on her matchmaking services. So if you are a guy and are looking for a good woman, Brodie can find one for you." Quinn looked at the Mavericks who occupied the back tables and nodded. "I know one or two, or ten, of my men who should bid."

"I'll bid on a date with Ms. Stewart!" someone shouted from the back. Kade looked down at the photograph of Brodie on the program and couldn't blame the guy for trying his luck. She was gorgeous…

But, for the immediate future, she was *his*.

"She's too smart to date you, Higgins," Quinn warned. "A reminder, this is a matchmaking service for men looking for their perfect woman. So, who is going to give me a hundred dollars?"

Immediately a couple of hands shot up and Kade watched, astounded, as the bids flew up to a thousand dollars, then two. Bids were still bouncing around the room when a cool female voice cut across the hubbub. "Three thousand dollars."

Quinn spun around and his genial smile turned to a scowl. Rory had her paddle raised and was holding his intense stare.

"On whose behalf are you bidding, Rory?" Quinn asked, his frown clearly stating her bidding had better not have anything to do with him.

Kade leaned back in his chair and grinned. Oh, this was going to be fun. Rory had been nagging Quinn about his ability to jump from woman to woman and hobby to hobby—skydiving, white-water rafting, and his obsession with superfast motorcycles—and was determined to nag him into settling down with a wife and two-point-four kids.

She didn't have a hope in hell of changing Quinn. He was even more entrenched in his bachelor lifestyle than Kade. But Kade would enjoy watching her try. He was also damn grateful she was nagging Quinn and not him...

He liked Rory, loved her even, but he wouldn't tolerate her interfering in his life.

Rory's smile was stolen straight from an imp. "Are you taking my bid or not, Rayne?"

Quinn held up two fingers, turned them to his eyes and flipped them around in her direction. "I'm watching you. McCaskill, make sure your woman behaves."

"Yeah, right." Mac leaned back and folded his arms against his chest. "This has nothing to do with me."

"Three-five." A voice from the back got the auction back on track.

"Three-seven," Rory countered.

"Three-eight," Wren calmly stated. She was bidding on behalf of the silent bidders, those who didn't want the room to know they wanted to use a matchmaker.

"Four." Rory waved her paddle in the air.

Four grand? Wow, not bad. The audience obviously loved the notion of being professionally set up.

The bids climbed and Rory matched every one. As the bids went higher, Quinn's face darkened. Oh, yeah, he knew exactly what she was up to. She was buying Brodie's services to find Quinn a woman who would stick around for more than a nanosecond. She was playing with fire, Kade thought, but he couldn't help admiring her moxie.

"Rory," Quinn warned after her bid topped five thousand dollars.

"Quinn," Rory drawled and added another hundred dollars onto her bid.

"You can't bid against yourself," Quinn snapped.

"I just did." Rory's face was alight with laughter. "Oh, I am so going to enjoy this, Rayne. And so will you. So, be a darling. Bang your gavel and tell me I've won."

Quinn looked at Mac. "Doesn't she drive you crazy?"

Mac dropped a kiss on Rory's temple and smiled. "All the time."

Quinn smacked the gavel and told her she'd won the bid before pointing the gavel in her direction. "I won't use it. You can't blackmail me into doing this, Rory."

Rory placed her hand on her heart and batted her eyelashes in his direction. "Quinn, you wound me. I would never dare to set you up." Kade, along with the rest of the guests, leaned forward in their chairs, eager to hear more. "You keep telling me you're not ready for a relationship and I respect that. I do. Besides, wait your turn."

Huh? If this wasn't for Quinn who was she setting up?

"It won't be my turn. *Ever*." Quinn looked relieved

and perplexed at the same time. "So then, pray tell, who is the sacrificial lamb to be led to slaughter?"

Kade smiled at his description as Rory stood up and walked around the table to his side. Oh, crap, oh double crap, he thought as she placed a hand on his shoulder. Kade felt his teeth slam together.

She wouldn't dare. She wasn't that brave.

"Why, who else but one of my favorite people in the whole world? I bought this for my very good friend, Kade Webb." Rory sent Kade a huge smile. As if she could charm him into changing his mind about tossing her from the nearest balcony.

"I just know Brodie will find Kade a stunning woman. I'm counting on her to find someone who'll make him supremely happy."

Dammit, hell, crap.

The room erupted into hoots of laughter and excited chatter. Dammit, hell, crap multiplied.

Kade met Mac's eyes and scowled when his friend raised his glass in a mocking toast. "Welcome to my crazy world, dude."

Kade really liked his best friend's fiancée and thought it wonderful they were having a baby, but his anger over her stunt hadn't disappeared.

What the hell was she thinking? Had she been thinking at all? He didn't need anyone to find him a woman! And he certainly didn't need his current lover to find him a new love!

If he could get past Mac, he had very strong words for Rory. He didn't allow anyone to play fast and loose with his life and he allowed no interference when it came to his sex life. Rory hadn't just stepped over the line, she'd eradicated it.

From his seat in his low-slung German sports car Kade stared at the still dark windows of Brodie's apartment and ran a hand over his jaw. It had taken all his acting skills to breeze through the rest of the evening, to bat away the wisecracks, to laugh at the admittedly good-hearted banter. Well, everyone's banter except his partners' had been good-natured. Mac and Quinn had teased him mercilessly.

For that they would pay...

Kade was perfectly capable of finding his own woman and he didn't want to be in a relationship. Damned women and their meddling. He refused to have anything to do with Rory's scheme and he refused to feel guilty about her wasting her money. She shouldn't have pulled such an asinine trick in the first place!

And if he found out Mac had anything to do with this, then he and McCaskill would go a couple of rounds in the ring, no holds barred.

Kade massaged his temples. It was past 6:00 a.m. He'd had no sleep. He hadn't changed out of his tux. His head was pounding and he wanted nothing more than to climb into bed with Brodie and lose himself in her. He'd done that last night, he remembered. With Brodie the world had disappeared, and for the few hours they were together, he'd relaxed and forgotten. Forgotten about his responsibilities, his past. He'd stopped worrying about his future. With her he'd lived in the moment, something he usually couldn't do.

He wouldn't start to rely on her to feel like that, wouldn't enjoy what they had more than he should. He'd keep it light, he promised himself. This was a one-time, short-term thing. He wasn't looking for long term and neither was she.

All well and good, he thought, but how was he going

to handle this stupid situation Rory had placed him in? He had to tell Brodie. That was why he was sitting in front of her apartment complex at the butt crack of dawn.

Brodie had said this—whatever it was between them—would probably be just be one night. And she'd also said something about sleeping with clients being unprofessional.

But if he didn't take up Rory's offer and didn't allow Brodie to set him up, then he wouldn't be her client. He knew their chemistry was combustible enough for more than one night. So everything would be fine. Either way, he had to tell her.

Rory Kydd, if you weren't a woman and if my best friend didn't love you so much, I would kick your very nice ass all over Vancouver.

Maybe he was overthinking this. Brodie was sensible. Kade felt a bit of his panic recede. There was no way she'd accept the challenge to match him. She'd just laugh off Rory's bid and the money would go to charity…no harm, no foul.

He'd call Brodie later, he thought, when he was rested and clearheaded. He lifted his hand to touch the ignition button. His finger hovered there but instead of allowing the powerful engine to roar to life, he instructed his onboard computer to call Brodie.

What are you doing, idiot?

Yet he allowed the cell to ring and eventually he heard Brodie's sleep roughened, sexy voice. "'Lo."

"I'm outside. Let me come up."

"Kade? What time is it?"

"Early." Kade opened the door and climbed out of his expensive car.

He started walking to the front door and his heart

jumped when a light snapped on in a corner room on the top floor. She was awake.

Kade flew up the stairs. As he reached her apartment the door opened and Brodie stood in the dark hall, her hair mussed, wearing nothing more than a hockey jersey. His number. Lust and warmth and relief pumped through him. Rory and her machinations were instantly forgotten; his world was comprised of this woman and how desperately he wanted her.

"What's wron—"

Kade cut off Brodie's words by covering her mouth with his. Without ending the kiss, he picked her up, kicked the door shut with his foot and carried her to her bedroom.

They were being perfectly adult about this, Brodie decided as she poured coffee into two mugs. Civilized. So far they'd managed to avoid the awkwardness that normally accompanied the morning after the night before.

He hadn't faked any emotion he didn't feel and she hadn't felt like she was being used. They'd made love, slept a little, made love again and then Kade asked if he could use her shower. She offered to make him breakfast. He declined but said he'd take a cup of coffee.

As extended one-night stands went, it was practically perfect. Then why did she feel like she didn't want it to end?

She was just being silly; she was tired and not thinking straight. After she'd had a solid eight hours of sleep, she'd be grateful Kade was so good at this. Brodie frowned. He'd obviously had a lot of practice.

"Are you going to drink it or just stare at it?"

Brodie turned slowly and sucked in her breath. Kade

naked was a revelation, but Kade in a wrinkled tuxedo wasn't too shabby, either. Too shabby as in freakin' damn hot. "Uh…"

Kade walked over to her, lifted the cup to her mouth and tipped it. "Coffee, a magical substance that turns 'uh' into 'good morning, honey.'"

Brodie rolled her eyes as he took her cup and sipped from it. "I'd forgotten you were a morning person. It's okay to kill happy, cheerful morning people, I checked."

Kade handed her cup back and walked over to the pot and poured his own. He leaned his butt against her counter and sipped. "You need a shower and six hours of sleep."

"Eight." Brodie pulled out a wooden chair from the table and dropped into it. "And you're the one who woke me up so early so it's your fault."

Kade grinned. "I didn't see you fighting me off. Sorry about your panties, by the way."

"You owe me a new pair," Brodie told him, both hands wrapped around her cup. Such a nice tuxedo… and it fitted him beautifully. The bow tie was gone and his face was shaded with blond stubble. Then she sat up straighter, remembering why Kade was wearing a tuxedo. "The ball! I'd forgotten… How did it go? Did you manage to raise any money from my donation?"

"Uh, yeah. It sold."

"You don't sound too enthusiastic." Brodie cocked her head. "Didn't it make any money at all? I'm *so* sorry."

"It made quite a bit of money. That's not the problem."

"There's a problem? How can there be a problem with my gift? The guy comes to me, I set him up on three dates and hopefully there's a happily-ever-after."

"It all depends on who the guy is."

Right, now she was confused. "So who is the guy?"

"Me."

She knew it was early and she wasn't a 100 percent awake, but she thought, maybe, Kade had said *he* was the one she would be working with.

"Please tell me you are joking?" Brodie begged. She knew instinctively that Kade hadn't had anything to do with her donation. So whose stupid idea was this? "Mac? Quinn?"

"Rory."

So Brodie hadn't misinterpreted Rory's mischievous look after all. Rory was very brave, or very stupid, and obviously very determined to get Kade hitched. Pity she hadn't a clue that Brodie and Kade could spark a wildfire from one kiss.

Damn. She'd just had earth-scorching sex with her client. She'd unwittingly and unknowingly broken her number-one rule. Brodie took a sip of coffee and pushed past the surge of jealousy to work out how, exactly, she was going to do this. Unfortunately there wasn't a manual dealing with the pesky problem of how to match your one-night stand.

God, this was far too confusing for someone whose blood didn't start to circulate until she'd had three cups of coffee. Think this through… Sex, ball for him and sleep for her, sex, client.

Brodie lifted her head to glare at him. Kade had come over to her house and seduced her again, knowing her views about dating her clients. Brodie stood up, anger obliterating the last of her sleepiness.

"How dare you! Why didn't you tell me right away that Rory had bid on my services for you! What the hell,

Kade? Did you not think that might have had an impact on my decision to sleep with you again?"

"Whoa, hold on…" Kade lifted his hands.

"You should've told me! I had a right to know, you manipulative jerk!"

"That's not fair."

Brodie brushed past him and tossed her coffee into the sink. "The hell it's not. You knew about this and you knew I'd back off from sleeping with you if you told me. So you didn't say a damn word!"

"I thought about telling you." Kade jammed his hands into the pockets of his pants and scowled.

"*Thought* about it?"

"Yeah! I was going to explain what she'd done, tell you I wasn't going to do it. I was hoping we'd have a laugh about it."

"I'm not finding anything vaguely funny in this."

Kade shoved his hands into his hair, linked his fingers behind his head and stared at her with hot eyes. "I didn't mean to make you feel used, or bad. The truth is that when you opened the door the only thing I could think about was the fact you were nearly naked. I had to have you. Again. Being set up was the last thing on my mind."

She wanted to tell him she didn't believe him, but she saw the truth in his eyes. He'd wanted her like she'd wanted him. Impulsively. Wildly. Crazily. Their need for each other didn't stop to, well, *think*. And, damn, it was hot.

And deeply, utterly problematic. She couldn't control her attraction to him and it seemed Kade was having a similar problem. Such need wasn't healthy, nor was it easy to resist. She needed to step back, to create some distance between them, but every time they were in the same room all they wanted to do was rip off each other's clothes.

They had to stop the madness—this was supposed to be a one-night fling. They were already on day two—sort of—and Kade was like any other man: he wasn't going to walk away from fabulous sex.

She didn't want to walk away from it, either, but for her, being with him felt like it was about more than just the sex. With him she felt alive and vibrant and animated and she couldn't afford to feel like that, even if it only happened in the bedroom. She might come to like it and, worse, get used to it. How would she get that genie back in its bottle?

So this had to stop now. She liked her life exactly as it was. Bland, safe, predictable.

She needed to walk away, far, far away. But Kade just needed to kiss her and she'd be all *yes, please, take me now.*

So she was going to match him.

"You're making too big a deal of this, Brodie," Kade stated. "Just tell Rory we are seeing each other, that there's a conflict of interest. Tell her to let you match Quinn."

Ha! Right. Kade would get out of the matchmaking, keep sleeping with Brodie and annoy Quinn in the process. For Kade, it would be a trifecta win.

But that wasn't going to happen. Brodie shoved aside the heat and the lust and ordered herself to use her brain.

"That would be rude and disrespectful. No, Rory's bid was for you so I will match you."

If she hadn't been feeling so miserable she would've laughed at his horrified face. "What? No!"

Her thinking hat firmly in place, Brodie paced the free area in her small kitchen. "Wren is a smart cookie and I bet she's already thinking of ways to spin this to generate PR for you. Mavericks fans will lap it up. They need a feel-good story, what with the owner's recent death and the future of the team still up in the air. And you released one of their favorite players last month. They are not happy with *you*."

"You seem to know a lot about my business."

Brodie waved away his comment, not feeling the need to tell him that after he left last night she jumped online to read about him and the Mavericks.

"I had solid reasons for releasing him," Kade argued. "It didn't matter that he was the best rookie in the league, a BC native and one of the first graduates from the Mavericks Ice Hockey Academy. He was photographed snorting coke, he was underperforming as a player and he was undisciplined. He had more chances than most, not that the fans care about that." Kade's tone was flat, his eyes bleak.

It had been a joint decision to boot the player, but as CEO, Kade took the flak. He led from the front, Brodie realized, and she had to admire him for that.

Quickly, she returned to the topic at hand. She couldn't afford to get sidetracked *admiring* him. "Matching you would be good publicity, for the Mavericks and for me."

"Not happening."

"Go to the office, see what Wren's working on. I guarantee it's something similar to what I've been thinking."

A muscle jumped in Kade's jaw and he tipped his head back to look at the ceiling. "I'm going to kill Rory, I really am. Want to help me bury her body?"

At his rueful words the rest of Brodie's anger dissipated. "I'll dig the grave."

Brodie raked her hair back from her face, then grabbed her mug from the sink and poured coffee back into the cup. She took a couple of sips. "I'm sure this is the most interesting conversation after a one-night stand in the history of one-night stands."

Kade rolled his head and Brodie assumed he was trying to work out the tension in his neck. "It's not exactly the conversation I planned on having."

Brodie's heart bounced off her ribs. She shouldn't voice the words on her lips but she had to—it would drive her nuts if she didn't. "What would you have said?"

Kade stepped closer and curled his hand around her neck. "I would've said that I had a great time and I would've asked if we could do this again."

Yeah, that's what she'd thought and that's exactly what she couldn't do. She'd liked it too much, liked having him around. She needed distance and a lot of it. Matching him would give her that.

"We can't," Brodie whispered. "It's too complicated. And, if I'm going to be setting you up...too weird."

"That's not confirmed yet. I'll try my damnedest to get out of it."

He'd come around, Brodie realized. It was too good a story to pass up, too good an opportunity to give the fans something to smile about. And Kade always, always put the Mavericks first.

Kade pulled her forward so her cheek lay against his chest. "If I do this, and I'm not saying I will, when it's done, can we...?"

Brodie knew she should just kill this...thing between them but she simply couldn't. "Let's just play it by ear." She pulled back and looked up at him, forcing her lips to curve into a smile. "You never know, one of those women might be the love of your life and another one-night stand with me will be the last thing on your mind."

"Not freakin' likely," Kade retorted.

Brodie stepped away and folded her arms, trying to remove herself from him mentally and physically. She had to stop *feeling* and keep *thinking*. "We will have to meet professionally, though. I need information from you to find out what you are looking for."

Kade glared at her. "You're talking like this is a done deal! If this happens, be very clear, I'm not looking for *anything*, with anybody! Find me three women who are marginally intelligent, someone who I can talk to for two hours over dinner."

"This is my business, Kade. If we do this, we will do it properly…"

Kade swore and started to roll back his sleeves, revealing the muscles and raised veins in his forearms. Brodie imagined those hands on another woman's skin and felt sick. Now she was adding jealousy to her messy heap of tangled emotions? Wasn't there enough crazy on that pile?

She took a breath. Seeing him with someone else would be good for her. It would put even more distance between them. And that was what she was trying to do here.

"That's the way I work, Kade. It's not up for negotiation."

"Dammit, crap, hell," Kade muttered another string of swearwords under his breath as he finished rolling up his other sleeve. When he was done, he placed his hands on either side of Brodie's face, gave her a hard kiss and picked up his jacket. "We'll talk about this again."

Brodie touched her lips as he walked out of her kitchen, leaving as quickly as he'd arrived.

So that was that. Well, then.

She was now Kade's matchmaker.

Five

Three weeks later Brodie sat in her usual seat at Jan's waiting for Kade, her trusty tablet on the table in front of her. How was she supposed to ask Kade all these intensely personal questions knowing he'd touched, caressed and kissed every inch of her body?

What had she done to piss off the karma fairy?

Brodie placed her cheek in her hand and swallowed down her nausea. Her stomach roiled and she tasted bile in the back of her throat every time she thought about this upcoming interview. She'd had twenty-one days, thanks to Kade's insane schedule and Wren wanting maximum publicity, to feel this way. Three weeks of restless sleep, of feeling on edge, miserable.

Angry.

Once you've done this interview and you've entered the relevant data into the program, you can find his three dates and get on with your life.

Her donation to the auction only included three matches. She wouldn't have to set him up again if none of those woman suited. One batch, she decided, was enough.

And then, when it was done, she'd walk away for good and Kade Webb would be a memory of the best sex she'd ever experienced.

As she'd predicted, Wren had made a charming PR story of Rory's matchmaking gift. Every few weeks, depending on Kade's schedule, a new "date" for Kade would be introduced to the public. Their likes and dislikes would be posted on the Mavericks' website with their photos. Pictures and short video clips of their date would be uploaded and the public could comment. Once all three women had been on a date with Kade, the public would vote on their favorite match.

Such fun and games, Brodie thought. Brodie slipped out of her lightweight cardigan and draped it over her bag. It was hot in the coffee shop, something she'd never experienced before. Usually the air-conditioning made her feel chilly. She also had a headache; damn, she hoped she wasn't getting sick again. That was all she needed.

Brodie heard the tinkle of the chimes announcing a new arrival into the coffee shop. She looked toward the door and immediately sighed. Kade embodied business casual in his dark gold chinos, steel-gray jacket and checked shirt under a sweater the color of berries. Successful and urbane. Too sexy for words.

And she wasn't the only one reacting to his arrival. She felt the collective intake of female breath and knew many sets of ovaries were shivering in delight. Kade pushed his sunglasses onto the top of his head and looked around. He smiled when he saw her and her heart stumbled. Stupid organ.

Kade bent down and brushed his lips across her cheek, and she inhaled his cologne. Sandalwood and spice and something all Kade. She felt her nipples prickle and cursed. Yep, the attraction hadn't lessened one damn bit.

Annoyed she couldn't control her reaction to this man, she frowned at him. "You're late."

"Two minutes and hello to you, too," Kade replied as he sat down. He leaned forward and gripped her chin. "Why are you looking tired? And pale?"

So nice to know she was looking her best, Brodie thought. "I'm fine."

"You sure?"

"I had a chest infection shortly before the auction, maybe it's coming back."

"Are you coughing? Short of breath? Should you see a doctor?"

"I'm fine, Webb. Jeez, stop fussing." She pulled her tablet toward her, hitting the power button. "Shall we get started?"

"Tired and pale and *grumpy*. Can I order some coffee first?" Kade tapped her hand with his finger and waited until she met his eyes. "This situation is crazy enough without us snapping at each other."

She heard the rebuke in his voice and blushed. She was acting like a child. Okay, it wasn't the ideal situation, but she shouldn't be taking her bad mood out on him. He didn't want to be set up any more than she wanted to set him up and he was right, it would be a lot easier if she acted like an adult, even better if she could be friendly.

Pull yourself together, Stewart.

Brodie straightened her shoulders and sent him an apologetic smile. "Sorry. Hi...how are you?"

Kade nodded. "Good. Sorry we haven't been able to meet before this but I've been swamped."

Brodie had realized that. If the papers weren't talking about his upcoming dates, then they were discussing the Mavericks' purchase of Josh Logan, superstar wing, the negotiations to buy the franchise and the legal action against the Mavericks for unfair dismissal by the former star rookie. "What do your lawyers say?"

"About the dismissal?" Kade asked to clarify. He shrugged. "He's wasting his time, and mine, but we all know that. He doesn't have a leg to stand on. It's just a pain in my ass, to be frank." Kade scowled at her tablet. "As are these stupid dates. Seriously, Brodie, I don't want to answer your questions...just choose three women and let's get it over with. Nobody will know but us."

She wished she could but it went against her nature to cut corners. Besides, her questionnaire revealed a lot about her clients and she was curious about Kade.

Not professional, but what the hell? They'd never date and this was the only way she'd be able to assuage her curiosity. "I can't enter the data until I have the answers and I can't match you until I have the data."

"How long does it take?" Kade demanded as Jan approached their table.

"An hour for the long version, half hour if you only answer the compulsory questions." Brodie looked at Jan. "Kade, this is my friend Jan. Jan, Kade Webb."

"I figured." Jan shook his hand. "What can I get you, Kade? Brodie here usually has a coffee milk shake."

Brodie shuddered. She couldn't stomach it today. Too rich...

"Not today, Jan. I'll just have a glass of water."

Jan frowned at her. "You okay?"

"I'm feeling a little flu-ey," Brodie reluctantly admitted. "Hot, a little dizzy and I have a headache." Jan put her hand on her forehead and Brodie slapped it away. "I don't have a temperature and I'll see a doctor if I start coughing, okay?"

"When did you last eat?" Jan demanded.

Maybe that was what was wrong with her. She'd had soup for supper last night and she'd skipped breakfast. She was, she realized, starving. A hamburger would chase away her malaise. "I am hungry." She turned to Kade. "Jan's hamburgers can cure anything from depression to smallpox. Do you want one?"

Kade nodded. "I can eat."

Brodie ordered two cheeseburgers with everything and when Jan left, Brodie smiled at Kade. "Her burgers are really good." She reached into her bag, pulled out her reading glasses and slid them onto her face. "Shall we get started?"

Kade had never considered glasses to be sexy but Brodie's black-rimmed frames turned her green eyes, already mesmerizing, to a deep emerald. He loved her eyes, he thought as he answered questions about his date of birth, his height, his weight. Then again, he also loved her high cheekbones, her stubborn chin, her small but very firm breasts and those long, slim legs.

He liked everything about her and he wished he could blow off lunch and take her to bed. When this stupidity was over, he promised himself. When it was done, he'd kidnap Brodie for the weekend, take her somewhere private and keep her naked in his bed until he'd burned this craving for her out of his system.

He was hardly sleeping and when he did, his dreams were erotic, with Brodie taking the starring role. He thought about her at the most inappropriate times. Memories from the night they shared obliterated his concentration. It was torture trying to negotiate when he recalled the way Brodie fell apart under his touch.

Brodie pinching his wrist pulled him back to their conversation. "What?"

"I asked…siblings?"

"None." He'd always wanted a brother, someone to take the edge off the loneliness growing up. Someone to stand by his side as he entered the hallway of a new school or joined a new team. Someone who could help him recall the towns they'd lived in and in what order.

"Parents?"

"My father lives in the city, my mother died when I was ten." He snapped the words out. He rubbed a hand over his jaw. God, he didn't want to do this. He never discussed his childhood, his past, his on-off relationship with his socially inept, now reclusive father. "You don't need information about my past so move along."

He saw the furrow appear between Brodie's eyebrows. Well, tough. His childhood was over. He finally had his brothers in Mac and Quinn and he was content. Sometimes he was even happy.

Kade leaned back in his seat. If he had to answer personal questions, then so did she. "And your parents? Where are they?"

"Dead." Brodie didn't lift her head. "I was twenty."

"I'm sorry, Brodes."

"Thanks. Moving on…what characteristic in a woman is most important to you? Looks, empathy, humor, intelligence?"

"All of them," Kade flippantly answered, wishing

he could ask how her parents died, but he could tell the subject was firmly off-limits. "Do you have siblings?"

"No." Brodie tapped her fingernail against the screen of her tablet. "I'm asking the questions, Webb, not you."

"Quid pro quo," Kade replied. "Were you close to your parents?"

He saw the answer in her eyes. Sadness, regret, sheer, unrelenting pain. A glimmer suggesting tears was ruthlessly blinked away. Oh, yeah…they might've passed many years ago, but Brodie was still dealing with losing them.

He was fascinated by this softer, emotional Brodie. She was fiercely intelligent, sexy and independent, but beneath her tough shell she made his protective instincts stand up and pay attention. He wanted to dig deeper, uncover more of those hidden depths.

"Tell me about them, Brodie."

"Where is our food?" Brodie demanded, looking around. "I could eat a horse."

"Why won't you talk about them?" Kade persisted. And why couldn't he move off the topic? He never pushed this hard, was normally not this interested. Maybe he was getting sick? He was definitely sick of this matchmaking crap and he hadn't even started with the dates yet. He just wanted to take Brodie home and make love to her again. Was that too much to ask?

Apparently it was.

Brodie finally, finally looked at him and when she did, her face was pale and bleak. "Because it hurts too damn much! Satisfied?"

Dammit, he hadn't meant to hurt her. Brodie flung herself backward and stared out the window to watch the busy traffic.

"Sorry, sweetheart," he murmured.

"Me, too." Brodie, reluctantly, met his eyes. "Please don't pry, Kade. I don't talk about my past."

Maybe she should. Someone, he realized, needed to hear her story and she definitely needed to tell it. It was a shock to realize he wanted to be the one to hear her tale. He wanted to be her friend, to offer comfort. To find out what made her tick.

Jan approached them with two loaded plates. She set the first one down on the table in front of Brodie and then put a plate in front of him. If the burger tasted as good as it smelled, then he was in for a treat, he thought, as he snagged a crispy fry and shoved it into his mouth.

He reached for the salt and frowned when he saw Brodie's now white face. She stared at her plate and, using one finger, pushed it away.

"What's wrong?" he demanded. "I thought you said you were hungry?"

"I was, not anymore." Brodie swallowed and reached for her water. "I think I am definitely getting sick. I'm hot and feeling light-headed."

Jan narrowed her eyes at her, then silently, and without argument, picked up Brodie's plate. Kade didn't understand the long, knowing look Jan sent Brodie and he didn't give her another thought after she walked away.

He frowned when Brodie picked up her tablet and swiped her finger across the screen. "Just choose three women, Brodie, I'm begging you. Any three."

Brodie, who, he was discovering, could give lessons in stubbornness to mules, just shook her head. "Not happening. So here we go…"

Do you base your life decisions more on feelings or rational thinking?

Are you more extroverted or introverted?

Is your bedroom, right now, messy or neat?

Are you more driven or laid-back in your approach to life?

After twenty-five minutes, Kade had a headache to match hers.

A week later Brodie tucked her wallet back into her tote bag and stuffed her phone into the back pocket of her oldest, most comfortable Levi's. Slinging her tote over her shoulder, she took a long sip of the bottled water she'd just purchased and ignored the craziness of the airport. Brodie looked up at the arrivals board, thankful Poppy's flight had landed fifteen minutes ago. Brodie really didn't want to spend her Saturday morning hanging around waiting.

As per usual, there were no empty seats.

Brodie shook her head and headed for a small piece of wall next to a bank of phone booths. Propping her tote behind her back, she placed her booted foot up on the wall, leaned her head back and closed her eyes. God, she couldn't remember when last she'd felt this overwhelming tiredness.

She was overworked, run-down, stressed out. Maybe she was flirting with burnout. She'd been working fourteen-and sixteen-hour days for the last few weeks, partly to keep up with her ever increasing client list. The publicity around Kade had resulted in a surge of business. Work was also an excellent way to stop thinking—obsessing—about Kade.

She really didn't like the amount of space he was renting in her brain. And she wished she could just make a decision on who was going to be his first date. She knew she was being ultra picky but she couldn't help it. She wanted pretty but not blow-your-socks-off attractive. She wanted a good conversationalist but not someone who was intriguing. She wanted smart but not too smart.

She didn't want him to date anyone at all.

Which was ludicrous—she had no claim on the man and hadn't she decided they needed some distance? God, maybe she was the source of her own exhaustion. Donating to the charity auction had not been one of her smarter ideas. Sure, it was a good cause, but following up her one-night stand with finding her said ONS someone else to have a one-night stand with left a sour taste in her mouth.

Brodie silently urged her great-aunt to hurry up. Poppy had the energy and enthusiasm of a ten-year-old with a tendency to talk to everyone she encountered. Brodie wondered how long Poppy would be staying in town before the travel bug bit again. She'd visited more countries in three years than most people did in a lifetime and Brodie couldn't help but admire her great-aunt's sense of adventure. It took courage to travel on her own and to make friends along the way.

Just hurry yourself up, Poppy. I really am feeling, well, like hell. And the sooner we get out of here, the happier I'll be.

A cramping stomach accompanied Brodie's nausea. She clenched her jaw and clutched her stomach, frantically thinking about what she had recently eaten that could have given her food poisoning. Cornflakes? Last night's boiled egg?

Brodie took a series of deep breaths, sucked on some more water and felt the nausea recede. When she opened her eyes again she saw Poppy, one hand on her travel case and the other on her hip, a speculative look on her face.

Brodie managed a wan smile. "Hey, you're here. That

was quick." She kissed Poppy's cheek and gave her a long hug. "How was Bali?"

"Loved it," Poppy replied. "I was considering staying another month but then I was invited to join a cruise to Alaska leaving in the next month."

"You're leaving again?"

Poppy dropped into a recently vacated empty seat. "You look dreadful. Are you sick?"

"Yeah, so nauseous. I must've eaten something bad last night.

Poppy grinned. "Unless you've discovered sex in the last six weeks and someone has dropped a bun in your oven. But that's not likely since you have the world's most boring sex life."

Brodie stared at her great-aunt while Poppy's words sank in.

No, no... God, *no*!

"I'm not pregnant." Brodie ground out the words, pushing back her hair. She wasn't even going to consider such a ridiculous scenario. She was on the pill! Brodie scrabbled in her bag for another bottle of water and after trying to open it with a shaking hand, passed it over to Poppy for help twisting off the cap. Brodie felt her body ice up with every drop she swallowed.

"Pregnancy would explain how you are feeling and is a result of sex. So, have you had any lately?"

Admitting to sex made the possibility of her being pregnant terribly real. "One time, weeks ago. The condom split."

"Ah, that would explain it."

"It explains nothing! I'm on the pill!"

"Even the pill can fail sometimes."

Brodie lowered the bottle and started to shake. Could she possibly be pregnant with Kade's baby?

From a universe far away Brodie felt Poppy's hand on her back. "Come on, Mata Hari, let's find you a pregnancy test and you can tell me who, what, where and when."

Three pregnancy tests could not be wrong. Unfortunately.

It had taken a week of Poppy's nagging for Brodie to find her courage to do a pregnancy test and now she desperately wished she hadn't.

Brodie stared at the three sticks lined up on the edge of her bathroom counter and hoped her Jedi mind trick would turn the positive signs to negative. After five minutes her brain felt like it was about to explode so she sat down on the toilet seat and placed her head in her hands.

She was pregnant. Tears ran down her face as she admitted that Poppy had called it—the girl who had the sex life of a nun was pregnant because Kade Webb carried around a faulty condom.

Jerk. Dipstick. Moron.

Brodie bit her lip. What was the moron/jerk/dipstick doing tonight? It was Saturday. He might be on a date with one of her suggestions for his first date. Which one? The redhead with the engineering degree? The blonde teacher? The Brazilian doctor? Brodie pulled her hair. If she thought about Kade dating, she'd go crazy.

Maybe, instead of feeling jealous of those women, it would be sensible to consider the much bigger problem growing inside her. The exploding bundle of cells that would, in a couple of weeks, become a fetus and then a little human, a perfect mixture of Kade and her.

She wasn't ready to be a mommy. Hell, she wasn't ready—possibly wouldn't ever be ready—for a relationship. And motherhood was the biggest relationship of them all. It never ended. Until death…

Brodie felt the room spin and knew she was close to panicking. She couldn't be responsible for another life. She couldn't even emotionally connect to anyone else. How would she raise a well-balanced, well-adjusted kid with all her trust and loss and abandonment issues?

How could she raise a kid at all? She couldn't do this. She didn't have to do this. It was the twenty-first century and if she wanted, she could un-pregnant herself. Her life could go back to what it was before… She could be back in control. She wouldn't have to confront Kade. She wouldn't have to change her life. By tomorrow, or the day after, she'd be back to normal.

Brodie stood up and looked at her pale face in the mirror. Back to normal. She wanted normal… Didn't she? She wanted smooth, unemotional, uncluttered. She wasn't the type who wanted to sail her ship through stormy seas. She'd experienced the tempests and vagaries and sheer brutality of life and she didn't want to be on another rocking boat.

Right. Sorted. She had a plan. So why wasn't she feeling at peace with the decision? Why did she feel at odds with herself and the universe?

"You can't hide in there forever." Poppy's voice drifted under the door. Brodie reached over and flipped the lock. Within ten seconds Poppy's keen eyes saw the tests and the results. Poppy, being Poppy, just raised her eyebrows. "What are you going to do?"

Brodie lifted her shoulders and let them hover somewhere around her ears. It would help to talk this through with someone and since Poppy was here Brodie figured she was a good candidate. "I'm thinking about—" she couldn't articulate the process,"—becoming un-pregnant."

If she couldn't *say* it, how was she going to *do* it?

Poppy, unmarried by choice, didn't react to that statement. "That's one option," she stated, crossing her arms over her chest, her bright blue eyes shrewd.

"Raising a child by myself is not much of an option," Brodie snapped.

"Depends on your point of view," Poppy replied, her voice easy. "Your parents thought you were the best thing to hit this planet and they had you in far more difficult circumstances than you are in now."

Brodie frowned. "I'll be a single mother, Poppy. My parents were together."

"They were married, yes, but your father was in the army, stationed overseas. Your mom was alone for six, eight months at a time and she coped. Money was tight for them." Poppy looked at Brodie's designer jeans and pointed to her expensive toiletries. "Money is not an object for you. You are your own boss and you can juggle your time. You could take your child to work or you could start working more from home. This is not the disaster you think it is."

Brodie tried to find an argument to counter Poppy's, but she came up blank. Before she could speak, Poppy continued. "Your parents were practically broke and always apart and yet they never once regretted having you. They were so excited when you came along."

Brodie's mom had loved kids and had wanted a houseful but, because she'd had complications while she was pregnant with Brodie, she'd had to forgo that dream. "I can't wait until you have kids," she'd tell Brodie. "I hope you have lots and I'll help you look after them."

Except you are not here when I need you most. You won't be here to help and I'll have to do it...alone.

Poppy wouldn't give up her traveling to become a nanny. Besides, knowing Poppy, she'd probably leave the baby at the supermarket or something.

"What about the man who impregnated you?"

"You make me sound like a broodmare, Pops," Brodie complained, pushing her hand into her hair. She looked around and noticed they were having this life-changing discussion in her too-small bathroom. "And why are we talking in here?"

"Because I'm standing in the doorway and you can't run away when the topic gets heated."

"I don't run away!" Brodie protested. Though, in her heart, she knew she did.

Poppy rolled her eyes at the blatant lie. "So, about the father."

"What about him?" Brodie demanded.

"Are you going to tell him?"

Brodie groaned. "I don't know what the hell I am going to do, Poppy!"

Poppy crossed one ankle over the other and Brodie saw she'd acquired a new tattoo in Bali, this one on her wrist. "I think you should talk to him. The decision lies with you but he was there. He helped create the situation and he has a right to be part of the solution."

"He doesn't have to know, either way."

"Legally? No. Morally? You sure?" Poppy asked.

Brodie tipped her head up to look at the ceiling. "I was at the point of making a decision," Brodie complained. "Thank you for complicating the situation for me, Great-aunt."

"Someone needs to," Poppy muttered, looking exasperated. She pointed a long finger at Brodie's face.

"Your problem is that since your parents and friends died, you always take the easy route, Brodie."

"I do not!"

"Pfft. Of course you do! Not having this baby is the easy way. Not telling the father is the easy way. Living in this house and burying yourself in your work—finding other people love but not yourself!—is taking the easy route. You need to be braver!"

"I survived a multicar pileup that wiped out my parents and best friends!" Brodie shouted.

"But it didn't kill *you*!" Poppy responded, her voice rising, too. "You are so damn scared to risk being hurt that you don't live! You satisfy your need for love by setting up other people. You keep busy to stop yourself from feeling lonely, and you don't do anything exciting or fun. Do you know how thrilled I am to find out that you've had a one-night stand? I think it's brilliant because someone finally jolted you out of your safety bubble. And, dammit, I hope you are brave enough to talk to the father, to have this kid, because I think it will be the making of you."

Through Brodie's shock and anger she saw Poppy blink back tears. Poppy was the strongest person she knew and not given to showing emotion. "I want you to be brave, Brodie. I want you to start living."

Brodie felt her anger fade. "I don't know how," she whispered. "I've forgotten."

Poppy walked toward her and pulled her to her slight frame. "You start by taking one step at a time, my darling. Go talk to the father…" Poppy pulled back to frown at Brodie. "Who is the father?"

"Kade Webb."

"My baby has taste." Poppy grinned. "Well, at the risk of sounding shallow, at the very least the baby will be one good-looking little human." Poppy grabbed Brodie's hand and pulled her from the bathroom. "Now come and tell me how you met and, crucially, how you ended up in bed."

Six

Date one of three and he was officially off the publicity wagon until he had to do this again next month.

Well, he would be done as soon as she left his apartment. He wouldn't offer her any more wine, Kade decided. He wasn't going to extend the date any longer than he absolutely had to. He'd wanted to have supper at a restaurant but Wren had insisted he cook Rachel dinner in his expansive loft apartment. Cooking her dinner would show the public his caring, domestic side.

The public, thanks to the photographers who'd hovered around, would also see his residence in downtown Vancouver and Simon, his mutt. Kade stroked his hand over Si's head, which lay heavy on his thigh. Simon, whom he'd found in an alley on one of his early-morning runs, considered Kade his personal property and any woman would have to fight his dog for a place in his life.

Kade stifled his sigh and resisted the urge to look at his watch. When he'd received the portfolios of his potential dates from Brodie, he'd flipped through the three candidates and opted to eat with the doctor. Then he'd contacted Wren and instructed her to arrange his first date for as soon as possible. Breakfast, lunch and supper...whenever, she just had to get it done. Wren, efficient as always, had done exactly that. One down, two to go.

"And then I spent three months working in the Sudan with Médecins Sans Frontières."

His buzzer signaled someone was downstairs wanting to come up. Kade smiled at his guest, hoping Wren had read his mind and come to rescue him.

You're a big boy, he heard Wren's amused voice in his head. *If you can talk them into bed, then you sure as hell don't need my help to talk them out of your apartment.*

Or maybe it was Quinn downstairs. The doctor was his type—brainy and built. Quinn would, if Kade asked him, take Rachel off his hands. Kade stood up and walked across the open space to his front door and intercom. He pressed the button, called out a greeting and shrugged when no one answered.

It had to be Mac or Quinn. They both usually hit the buzzer to signal they were on their way up.

Kade turned to walk back to his guest. It was definitely time to maneuver her out the door. Please let Quinn be thundering up the steps, he thought. *Please.*

A tentative knock told him it wasn't Quinn, or Mac, and Kade frowned. Who else would be visiting him at 9:45 p.m. on a Saturday night? Then again, whoever it was would be a distraction and he'd take what he could get.

Sending a fake smile of apology in Rachel's direction, he walked back to the door and opened it. As per usual when he saw Brodie, his mouth dried up and his heart flipped once, then twice.

What was it about this woman that turned his brain to mush? If he compared her to Rachel, Brodie came up short. She was wearing ratty jeans and a tight T-shirt in pale gray, a perfect match to her complexion. Pale gray tinged with green. Her eyes were a flat, dark, mossy green and accessorized by huge black rings. Her hair was raked off her face and she looked like a spring ready to explode.

"We need to talk… Can I come in?"

Kade tossed a look over his shoulder and sighed when he saw Rachel walking in their direction, a puzzled look on her face. "Hi, there." Rachel appeared at his shoulder and he watched Brodie's eyes widen as she gave the buxom doctor a good up-and-down look.

"Doctor Martinez." Brodie's voice cooled.

Brodie stepped to the side and looked across his apartment to the small dining table at the far end of the room. Kade sighed. Fat candles, muted light, wineglasses, her heels next to her chair. It looked like everything it really wasn't, a romantic dinner for two.

Kade heard the click of Si's nails against the wooden floor and waited for the dog to take his customary place at Kade's side. Si, to Kade's surprise, walked straight past him and up to Brodie. Kade waited for the growl and cocked his head when Simon nuzzled his snout into Brodie's hand. Brodie immediately, and instinctively, dropped to her haunches and rubbed her hands over Si's ears and down his neck.

Delight flickered in her tired eyes. "Oh, he's gorgeous, Kade. I didn't know you had a dog."

"We haven't exactly had a lot of time to talk," Kade

pointed out and Brodie flushed. "Meet Simon, part Alsatian, part malamute, all sappy. I've had him about two months."

"He's a lovely dog," Rachel said, her tone bright and chirpy. Oh, hell, he'd forgotten she was there.

Kade watched as Brodie stood up slowly, a blush creeping up her neck. Kade could see she was ready to bolt. He wanted to hustle Rachel out, pull Brodie in, pick her up and cradle her in his arms and find out, in between kisses, what was making her so very miserable.

Because she was—he knew it like his own name.

Brodie darted a look at Rachel and he saw her suck in a breath. He watched how she added two and two and somehow ended up with sixty-five.

Brodie lifted her hands and stepped back. "I am being inexcusably rude, I'm so sorry." She gave them a smile as fake as this date.

"But you said you needed to talk," Kade reminded her. "I'm sure Rachel will excuse us."

"Please… It's really not important," Brodie insisted and jammed her hands into the back pockets of her jeans. "I'm so sorry to have disturbed your evening. Good night."

"Brodie." Kade didn't want her to leave.

"Good night!" Rachel called, turning and walking back to the table. He watched, irritated, as she picked up his full glass of wine to take a healthy sip. She cradled the glass between her ample breasts and sent him a speculative look.

Kade stopped by the coatrack and pulled her bag and jacket from a hook and held them out to her.

Rachel put down her wine and cocked her head. A small, regretful smile tilted her wide mouth upward.

"Well, that sucks," she cheerfully stated, suddenly

looking a lot warmer. Kade scratched his forehead in confusion. But before he could ask for an explanation, Rachel spoke again. "Want to tell me why you are doing the dating thing when you are completely besotted with your matchmaker?"

"I am not besotted with her!" Kade responded, thoroughly disconcerted by the observation.

"Well, something is happening between you two." Rachel slipped into her shoes, then walked over to him and took her jacket and purse from his hands. "Pity, because I rather like you."

Kade rubbed his hand across his forehead. "Look, I enjoyed our evening…"

Rachel laughed. "Oh, you big, fat liar! I've never worked so hard in all my life to impress someone and most men are easily impressed!"

He had to smile and was so damn thankful he wasn't dealing with the drama queen he'd expected her to be. "I'm so sorry. I'm really not besotted with her but it *is* complicated. And these dates are…" Could he trust her not to spill the beans?

"A publicity stunt?" Rachel had guessed before he could say more. "I figured that out as soon as I saw the look on your face when you opened the door. Don't worry, I won't say anything."

Kade let out a relieved sigh. "Thank you." He bent down and placed a kiss on her cheek. "I really appreciate it. I'll take you home."

Rachel patted his biceps. "I'll call a cab and you can go and find your girl so that you can sort out your complications."

Kade watched her walk out of his loft, resisting the urge to deny there was anything between him and Brodie besides some great sex and a couple of laughs.

There was nothing to sort out, nothing to worry about. If that was the case, then he shouldn't be desperate to find out exactly what it was Brodie wanted to say.

He was just curious, he told himself. It didn't mean he had feelings for her. He wasn't besotted with her.

Besotted? What a ridiculous word! He wasn't… He couldn't be. He didn't *do* besotted. But he would admit to being curious, that wasn't a crime.

Brodie left the rain forest and the Willowbrae Trail and walked onto one of the vast, sandy beaches characterizing this part of the west coast of Vancouver Island. She stared at the huge waves rolling in from Japan and slipped out of her sneakers, digging her toes into the cool sand.

This place—Poppy's cabin—with its magnificent sea views, was her hideout, the place she ran to every time her life fell apart. She and her family had spent many holidays here, in winter and summer and the seasons in between. This was where she felt closest to them. After the accident, she'd spent six weeks up here, to recuperate. Her body healed quickly but her heart never had.

Despite the memories, she still wanted to run up here when life threw her curveballs. Here, if she didn't think too much, her soul felt occasionally satisfied. This was her special place, her thinking place.

Two days had passed since she'd left Vancouver and she'd spent all that time thinking of Kade, and trying *not* to obsess about what happened between him and Doctor Delicious after Brodie left.

The thought of him and another woman so soon—was six weeks soon?

And she still had to tell him about the pregnancy. Brodie placed her hands on her stomach and sucked in a breath. She also needed to tell him she intended to keep this child, to raise it on her own.

Poppy was right. Keeping the baby would take courage and sacrifice and…well, balls. Brodie also knew her parents would have wanted her to keep the child, to care for the next generation of Stewarts as they'd planned to do.

So she'd decided to be a mommy. She needed to tell Kade he was going to be a daddy. There was no rush, Brodie thought, as she picked up a piece of driftwood and tossed it toward a bubbling wave. She had eight or so months.

Or, hell, maybe not.

Brodie recognized his stride first, long and loose. His blond hair and most of his face was covered by a black cap. Simon, Kade's huge, sloppy mutt, galloped between him and the waves, barking with joy. Then Simon recognized her and let out a yelp of elated welcome. Brodie was glad that he, at least, looked happy to see her.

Kade did not. He stopped in front of her, tipped back the rim of his cap and scowled. "Sixteen missed calls. Six messages, Stewart. Seriously?"

"I needed some time alone," Brodie replied, rubbing Simon's ears. She looked up into Kade's frustrated eyes. "Why are you here?"

The wind blew Kade's cotton shirt up and revealed the ridges of his stomach. Brodie had to stop herself from whimpering. "I'm here because you came to my loft, looking like hell on wheels, saying we needed to talk. I've spent the last two days looking for you."

Brodie picked up a small stick and threw it for Simon, who ran straight past it into a wave. "I suppose Poppy told you where I was."

"When I managed to find her," Kade muttered.

Brodie frowned. "She's not difficult to find. She lives below me."

"Not for the last two nights. She finally came home, on a Harley, with a guy who was at least fifteen years younger than her."

Brodie grinned. "Good for Poppy." At least one of them was having fun.

Brodie felt her throat tighten. She had to tell him, now.

"Kade..." Brodie met his eyes, dug deep and found a little bit of courage. "The night we were together... Do you remember how we brushed off the issue of the split condom?"

Kade frowned and his face darkened. She didn't need to say any more, she could see he'd immediately connected the dots. "You're...?" He rubbed his hands over his face.

"Pregnant," Brodie confirmed.

"But you said you were on the pill," Kade stuttered and the color drained from his face.

"I was on the pill, but apparently it fails sometimes."

Kade linked his hands behind his head. He looked shaken and, understandably, mad as hell. Brodie couldn't blame him; she'd experienced those emotions herself.

"Might I remind you," she added, "the condom *you brought* was faulty."

"So you're saying this is my fault?" Kade shouted, dropping his hands. Simon whined and Kade patted his head to reassure him everything was okay. Brodie wished he'd reassure her, too.

Brodie made an effort to hold on to her own slipping temper. "I'm not blaming you, I'm explaining what happened."

Kade dropped a couple of F-bombs. "I'm not ready to be a father. I don't want to be a father!"

"Being a mother wasn't in my five-year plan, either, Webb."

Kade folded his arms across his chest and glared at her. "You don't seem particularly upset about this."

Where was he the last couple of nights when she'd cried herself to sleep? The same nights she'd paced the floor? "I'm pregnant and it's not something that's going away. I have to deal with it. You, however, do not."

"What the *hell* do you mean?"

Brodie tucked a strand of hair behind her ear and shrugged. "If you want I'll sign a release absolving you of all responsibility for this child."

Kade stared down at the sand and Brodie noticed his hands, in the pockets of his khakis shorts, were now fists. He was hanging on to his temper by a thread. "Is that my only option?"

"What else do you want? You just said you don't want to be this baby's father. Have you changed your mind? That would mean paying child support and sorting out custody arrangements. Is that what you want?"

"For crap's sake, I don't know! I'm still trying to deal with the idea you're saying you're pregnant!" Kade yelled.

"I'm *saying* I am pregnant?" Brodie frowned. Did he think she was making this up for kicks and giggles? "Do you doubt me?" she asked, her voice low and bitter.

"We slept together several weeks ago, how can you be sure?" Kade retorted. "Have you done a blood test? How can I be sure you're not jerking my chain?"

Brodie's mouth fell open. How could he, for one moment, think she would lie about this? Didn't he know her at all? Actually, he didn't, Brodie admitted. They'd shared their bodies but nothing of their thoughts or feelings. And now they were going to have a baby together... No, judging by his lack of enthusiasm, she was going to be walking this road solo.

Brodie slapped her hand on his chest and pushed. He didn't shift a millimeter and her temper bubbled. "I am not lying, exaggerating or jerking your chain! This isn't fun for me, either, Webb, but I'm going to be an adult and deal with it!" Her chest felt tight and her face was on fire. "I've done my part. I've informed you. I'll get my lawyer to draw up a document releasing you from your parental rights."

Brodie spun around and started toward the path leading back to the cabin. God, she was tired. Tired of stressing, tired of arguing. Just plain exhausted. Tired of dealing with the emotions Webb yanked to the surface whenever she was around him. She just wanted some peace, to retreat, to shut down.

"I don't know what I want!" Kade hurled the words and Brodie felt them bounce off the back of her head.

Brodie slowly turned and shrugged. "I can't help you with that. But accusing me of lying certainly doesn't help make sense of the situation."

Embarrassment flashed across Kade's face. He stared at the sand and then out to sea. She could see the tension on his face. "It's happened before...with two other women. They said I made them pregnant."

Brodie tipped her head. "Did you?"

His look was hot and tight and supremely pissed off. "Hell no! When my lawyers asked for DNA proof they backed down."

Of course they did. Brodie sighed and tried to ignore the growing hurt enveloping her heart. "So, naturally, I'm just another one-night stand, another woman you slept with who wants to trap you." She released a small, bitter laugh and lifted her hands in a what-was-I-thinking? gesture. "That's an example of how extraordinarily stupid I can be on occasion. Goodbye, Kade."

Brodie took a couple of steps before turning around once more. "My lawyer will contact yours. I really don't think we have much more to say to one another."

Brodie walked away and Kade didn't call her back, didn't say another word. When she hit the trail to the cottage, Brodie patted her stomach.

So it'll be you and me, babe. We'll be fine.

Of course she would. She always was.

So that wasn't what he'd been expecting, Kade thought as he sank to the sand and stared at the wild waves slapping the beach.

Brodie was pregnant? With *his* child? What the hell…? He scrubbed his face with his hands. What were the chances? And why was fate screwing with him?

Kade stroked Si's head and rubbed his ears. With his busy schedule, just remembering to feed and walk Si was problematic. And life was expecting him to deal with a child?

This was karma, Kade thought. Life coming back to bite him in the ass because he'd been so rude about Mac becoming a father. But Mac had Rory—patient, calm and thinking—to guide him through the process.

Kade didn't have Brodie and, judging by the final sentence she'd flung at him, he didn't need to worry about her or his child. She was prepared to go it alone.

He shouldn't have accused her of lying. Brodie wasn't another bimbo trying to drag a commitment out of him. Brodie didn't want a relationship. She didn't need a man in her life. She was independent and self-sufficient and

she was strong enough to raise her child—their child—
on her own.

If he wanted to he could walk away, forget about this
conversation and forget he had a baby on the way. According to Brodie all he needed to do was sign a piece
of paper and his life would go back to normal.

No child.

No Brodie.

Pain bloomed in the area below his sternum and he
pushed his fist into the spot to relieve the burn. Could
he do it? Could he walk away and not think about her,
them, anymore?

Probably.

Definitely.

Not.

He couldn't keep Brodie off his mind as it was. There
was something about her that was different from any
other woman he'd ever known. He was, on a cellular
level, attracted to her, but despite her I-can-handle-
whatever-life-throws-at-me attitude, he sensed a vul-
nerability in her that jerked his protective instincts to
life. She also had more secrets than the CIA, secrets he
wanted to discover. Oh, he wasn't thinking of her with
respect to the long term or a commitment. He hadn't
turned *that* mushy and sentimental, but he couldn't dismiss her.

It would be easier if he could.

As for her carrying his child…

He'd always been ambivalent about having children.
As a child, his family situation had been dysfunctional
at best, screwed up at worst. He'd been an afterthought
to his parents and when his mom died, he'd been nothing more than a burden to his head-in-the-clouds father. Practicality had never been his dad's strong suit

and, teamed with a wildly impulsive nature, having a ten-year-old was a drag. A kid required food, clothes and schooling, and sometimes his dad hadn't managed any of those. To his father, Kade had been a distraction from his art, a responsibility he'd never signed on for.

Kade felt his jaw lock as the realization smacked him in the face: his child would be a distraction from his own career and a responsibility he'd never signed on for.

Like father, like son.

Except he wasn't his father and he refused to follow in the man's footsteps. It was *his* condom that broke; Kade was as responsible for the pregnancy as Brodie. He took responsibility for his actions, both in his business and in his personal life. He faced life like a man, not like the spoiled child he'd frequently thought his father to be.

And, for some reason, he couldn't get the image of Brodie, soft and round with pregnancy, out of his head. He could see a child sleeping on her chest; he wanted to watch her nursing. Dammit, he could even imagine himself changing a diaper, running after his toddler on a beach, teaching the boy to skate.

For the first time ever, Kade could imagine being part of a family, working for and protecting *his* family. Having his own little tribe.

It wouldn't be like that, really. Of course it wouldn't. Nothing ever worked out like a fairy tale, but it was a nice daydream. He and Brodie weren't going to have the dream but they could have something…different.

He could share the responsibility of raising their child. Taking responsibility meant paying all the bills their child incurred. From pregnancy to college and beyond, he'd supply the cash. Kade hauled in some much-needed air. Cash was the easy part. He had enough to financially support hundreds of kids. The notion of being a *father* had him gasping for air. Being a dad. Because there was a difference; he knew that as well as he knew his own body.

He couldn't be like his father...

Kade never half-assed anything. He didn't cut corners or skimp on the details. He worked. And then he worked some more. He worked at his friendships; he worked at his career. He gave 110 percent, every time.

And he'd give being a dad 110 percent, as well. His child would not grow up feeling like a failure, like an afterthought, like a burden. He wasn't going to perpetuate that stupid cycle.

And if Brodie didn't like that, then she'd better get with the program because that was the way it was going to be. He wasn't going to be a husband or a long-term lover, but he'd be a damn good father and, more importantly, he'd be there every step of the way...

Seven

Brodie placed her heels on the edge of the Adirondack chair and rested her chin on her knees, the expansive view of the Florencia Bay blurry from the tears she refused to let fall. She was used to being alone. She'd made a point of it. But for the first time in nearly a decade she felt like she could do with some help. Just a shoulder to lean on, someone to tell her she could do this, that she was strong enough, brave enough.

She wanted a pair of arms to hold her, someone else's strength to lift her, a little encouragement. This was the downside of being alone, Brodie realized. When you'd consistently kept yourself apart there was no one you could call on. She'd made this bed and now she had to sleep in it.

Alone.

Well, this sucked. Brodie shoved the heels of her hands into her eye sockets and pushed, hoping the pressure would stop the burning in her eyes. That she wanted to cry was utter madness. She was pregnant, not dying. She was financially able to raise this child and give it everything it needed—she had to stop calling it an *it*!—and this situation didn't warrant tears. If memories didn't make her cry, then her pregnancy had no right to. She was stronger than that.

Brodie straightened her shoulders. So she was going to be a single mother, big deal. Millions of women all over the world did it on a daily basis, a lot of them with fewer resources than she had. *Stop being a wuss and get on with it. Rework those plans; write a list. Do something instead of just moping!*

She needed to see a doctor and she needed to contact her lawyer. She needed to stop thinking about stupid Kade Webb and the fact he'd accused her of scamming him.

The jerk! Oh, she so wasn't going to think about him again. From this moment on he was her baby's sperm donor and nothing else.

She simply wasn't going to think about him again.

"Brodie."

Brodie looked up at the clear blue sky and shook her head. "Seriously?"

No one, not God, the universe or that bitch karma, answered her. Brodie reluctantly turned her head and watched Kade walk across the patio toward the other Adirondack chair. Without saying a word, he sat down, rested his forearms on his thighs and dropped his hands between his knees. Simon sat near the edge of the stairs and barked at a seagull flying over his head.

Kade had come straight from the beach, Brodie realized. Sand clung to his feet, which were shoved into expensive flips-flops, and clung to the hair on his bare calves. He had nice feet. Big feet. He was a big guy, *everywhere*.

And it was his *everywhere* that had put her into this situation. She scowled. "What now, Kade?"

Kade turned and looked at her. "I don't want to fight."

"That's fine." Brodie dropped her legs and pointed to the stairs. "So just leave."

"That's not happening, either." Kade calmly leaned back and put one ankle onto his opposite knee. He rolled his shoulders and looked around, taking in the wood, steel and glass cabin and the incredible view. "This place is amazing. Do you own it?"

She had some money but not enough to own a property like this. "Poppy's."

Why was he here? Why was he back? Was he going to take more shots at her? She didn't think she could tolerate any more this morning. She felt nauseous and slightly dizzy and, dammit, she wanted to crawl into his arms and rest awhile.

Huh. So she hadn't wanted just anyone to hold her, she'd wanted Kade's arms around her. And she'd called *him* a moron? She took the prize.

"What do you want, Kade?" she asked, weary.

"Are you okay?" Kade waved in the direction of her stomach, his brown eyes dark with—dare she think it?—concern. "I mean, apart from the whole being-pregnant issue?"

"Why?"

"You just look, well, awful. You're like a pale green color. You've lost weight and you look like you haven't slept properly in a month."

Nice to know she was looking like a wreck. Especially when the description came from a man who graced the front covers of sports magazines.

"Do you need to see a doctor? Maybe they could run some tests to check if there is something else wrong."

"I'm fine, Webb. I'm pregnant. I puke, a lot. I don't sleep much because I've been stressed out of my head!"

"Stressed about telling me?" Kade asked, linking his hands across his flat stomach.

Brodie stood up and went to the balustrade. "Partly. But that's done so…feel free to leave."

Kade didn't look like he was going anywhere anytime soon. He just held her hot gaze. "I'm sorry I reacted badly." His smile was self-deprecating and very attractive. "Not my best moment."

"Yeah, accusing me of trying to trap you was a high point," Brodie said, looking toward the beach. "Apology accepted. You can—"

"Go now? Why are you trying to get rid of me?"

"Because I have stuff to do! I need to call my lawyer, see a doctor, plan mine and the baby's future!" Brodie cried.

Kade stood up, walked over to her and touched her cheek with his fingers. "It's not going to be like that, Brodie."

"Like what?" Brodie whispered.

"I know you think you are going to do this alone—because, hell, you like being self-reliant—but I'm in it for the long haul."

"What?" Brodie demanded, thrown off-kilter. What was he talking about?

"I am going to be this baby's father in every way that counts."

Brodie looked at him, aghast. What was happening here? "Wha-at?"

"You're going to have to learn to be part of a team, Brodie, because that's what we are, from this point on." Kade tapped her nose and stood back, his stance casual. But his eyes, dark and serious and oh, so determined, told another story.

"I don't understand."

"I am not going anywhere. We're in this. *Together*."

What? No! She didn't play nicely with others. She had no idea how to work within a team. She was a lone wolf; she didn't function within a pack. And really, what the hell did he think he was doing, acting all reasonable and concerned?

That wasn't going to work for her. She made her own decisions and she didn't like it that with Kade, she wasn't in charge. He might sound laid-back but beneath his charm the man was driven and ambitious and bossy.

But even as she protested his change of heart, she had the warm fuzzies and felt a certain relief she wouldn't be carrying this burden alone.

Even so, she shook her head. "There is no *we*. This baby is my problem, my responsibility."

"This baby is *our* problem, *our* responsibility. Mine as much as yours," Kade replied, not budging an inch. "Quit arguing, honey, because you're not going to win."

Behind her back Brodie gripped the balustrade with both hands. "What does that mean? Are you going to change diapers and do midnight feeds? Are you going to drive around the city trying to get the kid to sleep? Or are you just going to fling some money at me?"

Anger flickered in Kade's eyes. "I'll do whatever I need to do to make your life easier, to be a father. I will support you, and the baby, with money, but more importantly, with my time and my effort. I'm repeating this in an effort to get it to sink into that stubborn head of yours, you are not in this alone."

"I want to be," Brodie stated honestly. It would be so much easier.

His fingers touched her jaw, trailed down her neck. "I know you do, but that's not happening. Not this time."

Panic flooded her system and closed her throat. Wanting to protest, Brodie could only look at him with wide, scared eyes. She needed to push him away, to end the emotion swirling between them. "You just want to get into my pants again."

The only hint of Kade's frustration was the slight tightening of his fingers. She waited for him to retaliate but he just brushed his amused mouth in a hot kiss across her lips.

"So cynical, Brodie." He rubbed the cord in her neck with his thumb and Brodie couldn't miss the determination on his face and in the words that followed. "I want you, Brodie, you know that. But that is a completely separate matter to us raising a child together. One is about want and heat and crazy need, the other is about being your friend, a support structure, about raising this child together as best as we can."

"We can't be both friends and lovers, Kade!"

"We can be anything we damn well want," Kade replied. "But for now, why don't we try to be friends first and figure out how we're going to be parents and not complicate it with sex?"

He confused and bedazzled her, Brodie admitted. She couldn't keep up with him. She felt like she was being maneuvered into a corner, pushed there by the force of his will. "I don't know! I need to think."

Kade smiled, stepped back and placed his hands in the pockets of his khaki shorts. "You can think all you want, Brodie, but it isn't going to change a damn thing. I'm going to be around whether you like it or not." He ducked his head and dropped a kiss on her temple."You might as well get used to it," he murmured into her ear.

Before Brodie got her wits together to respond, Kade walked across the patio to the outside stairs. He snapped his fingers. Simon lumbered to his feet and they both jogged down the stairs. Brodie looked over the balustrade as they hit the ground below.

"And get some sleep, Stewart! You look like hell," Kade called.

Yeah, just what a girl needed to hear, Brodie thought. Then she yawned and agreed it was a very good suggestion.

Kade glanced down at his phone, the red flashing light indicating he had a message. He looked across the table to his friends and partners and saw they were still reading a condensed version of Logan's contract. He slid his finger across the screen and his breath hitched when he saw Brodie's name.

He hadn't spoken to her for two days but he kept seeing her in his mind's eye, looking down at him from the patio of the cabin—bemused, befuddled, so very tired. He had deliberately left her alone, wanting to give her time to get used to the idea of them co-parenting.

Back in the city. Thought that you might want to know.

Kade smiled at her caustic message. Not exactly gracious but coming from the independent Brodie, who'd rather cut off her right arm than ask for help, it was progress.

He quickly typed a reply.

Feeling rested?

A bit.

Any other symptoms?

Do you really want to know? He grimaced at the green, vomiting emoji tacked onto the end of the message.

Ugh. Will bring dinner. Around 7?

Tired. Going to bed early.

Oh, no. When was she going to learn that if she retreated he would follow? You have to eat. I'm bringing food. Be there.

Suit yourself.

That was Brodie speak for "see you later." Kade tapped the screen and smiled. The trick with Brodie, he was learning, was to out-stubborn her.

"Kade, do you agree?"

"Sure," he murmured, looking straight through Quinn. He'd have to tell his friends at some point but there were reasons why he didn't want to, not yet. He was still wrapping his head around the situation and he wasn't ready for his friends to rag him about it. He still felt raw. The situation was uncertain and, consequently, his temper was quick to the boil.

Besides, it was one of those things he needed to discuss with Brodie… Was she ready for the pregnancy to become public knowledge?

He didn't think either of them was ready for the press. Especially since Brodie was supposed to be finding his dream woman. His next date. She was, after all, his damned matchmaker.

No, he definitely wasn't ready for the news to be splashed across the papers and social media. It was too new and too precious. Too fragile. Kade half turned and put his hand into the pocket of his suit jacket, which was hanging off the back of his chair. Pulling out a container of aspirin, he flipped back the lid and swallowed three, ignoring the bitter powder coating his mouth.

He'd had a low-grade headache since he'd left Brodie and he'd been popping aspirin like an addict. It was a small price to pay for a very large oops.

Kade looked up when he heard a knock on the glass door. Two seconds later his personal assistant leaned into the room. "What's up, Joy?"

"There's someone here to see you and she's not budging," Joy told him after tossing a quick greeting to Quinn and Mac. Joy snapped her fingers. "Someone Stewart."

Kade frowned. Brodie? Was something wrong? She'd just been texting him. He stood up abruptly and his chair skittered backward. Crap! Something must be wrong. Brodie would never come to his office without calling first. He started toward the door and stopped when he saw the slight, stylish figure of Poppy Stewart walking toward them.

"Poppy? Is she okay?" He winced at the panic in his voice.

Poppy frowned. "Why wouldn't she be?" she said when she reached him. Kade placed a hand on his heart and sucked in a deep breath while Poppy graciously, but very firmly, sent Joy on her way. "We need to talk."

"You sure she's okay?"

"When I left she was eating an apple and drinking ginger tea. She has a slew of appointments today and was heading downtown later." Poppy walked into the conference room and Mac and Quinn rose to their feet.

"My, my, my," she crooned, holding out a delicate hand for them to shake, her mouth curved in a still sexy smile. "You boys certainly pack a punch."

Kade rubbed his forehead. God, he wasn't up to dealing with a geriatric flirt. And why the hell wasn't the aspirin working?

"Poppy, why are you here?" he asked, dropping back into his chair.

Quinn pulled out a chair for Poppy and gestured for her to sit. "Can I offer you something to drink? Coffee? Tea?"

"I'm fine, thank you," Poppy replied.

Mac frowned at Kade. "I'm Mac McCaskill and this is Quinn Rayne."

God, he was losing his mind along with his manners. "Sorry, Poppy. Guys, this is Poppy Stewart."

"Stewart?" Quinn asked. "Any relation to Brodie Stewart, the matchmaker?"

"Great-aunt," Kade briefly explained. He caught his friends' eyes and jerked his head in the direction of the door.

Mac just sat down again and Quinn sat on the edge of the conference table. It would take a bomb to move them, Kade realized, so he stood up. "Let's go to my office, Poppy. We'll have some privacy there."

"You need privacy from your best friends?" Poppy asked.

Mac lifted an eyebrow. "Yeah, do you?"

"Right now, yeah!" Kade snapped. He rubbed his

jaw before gripping the bridge of his nose with his finger and thumb.

"You haven't told them," Poppy said and he heard the amusement in her voice. Glad she was finding this funny because he sure as hell wasn't.

"Told us what?" Quinn asked, his eyes alight with curiosity.

Poppy's open hand drifted through the air, silently telling him it was his call whether to answer his friends or not. They had to know sometime. If he told them now, then he'd avoid them nagging him to distraction.

Kade looked toward the open door and crossed the floor, slamming it shut. They all knew the signal: closed door meant what was said in the room stayed in the room. Both Mac and Quinn nodded their agreement.

"Brodie is pregnant," Kade quietly said. He handed Mac a rueful smile. "I'm right behind you in the new-dads line."

Kade was grateful that beyond quietly congratulating him, Mac and Quinn didn't make a big song and dance over his announcement. Instead they just left the room, still looking shocked. All their lives were changing at a rapid pace. Just a few months ago they had been the most eligible bachelors in the city. Now Mac was getting married and he and Kade were both going to be fathers.

Then again, none of them ever eased their way into a situation, Kade thought as Mac shut the door behind him. They always jumped into the deep end and swam hard. "They took it rather well," Poppy said, linking her hands around her knee.

"They were behaving themselves in front of you," Kade explained. "Trust me, when they get me alone, they'll rip into me."

Kade dropped his head and rubbed the back of his neck. White-hot pain shot up his spine and bounced off the back of his skull. Hell, he hadn't had a migraine for years and, he recalled, they always started like this. It had been so long since an attack he'd stopped the habit of carrying medicine with him to take the edge off the pain.

"Are you unhappy about this baby, Kade?"

Kade had to concentrate hard for her words to make sense. "Not unhappy. Surprised, getting used to the idea. Wondering how we're going to make it work."

"You will," Poppy told him, sounding convinced. "And Brodie being pregnant is the reason I am here.

"I am scheduled to go on a cruise in a week or so. Ordinarily I would cancel the cruise and stay home with Brodie. I'm worried about her. But I am one of the tour leaders and they need me."

Kade held up a hand and silently cursed when he saw his vision was starting to double. Dammit, he had about fifteen minutes, a half hour at most, before he fell to the floor. "Do you want her to move in with me?"

"Not necessarily, but I am worried about her, Kade. She's sick and stressed and she's not sleeping, not eating. If no one keeps an eye on her, I worry I'll come back to a skeleton that swallowed a pea."

"How long are you away for?" God, it was getting difficult to concentrate.

"Two months. Are you okay? You look awfully pale."

That would be a negative. "I'll look after her... I'll keep an eye on her," Kade muttered, slurring his words.

"Oh, my God, you really don't look well. Can I call someone for you?"

He wanted to shrug off the pain, to act like nothing

was wrong, but it felt like there were pickaxes penetrating his skull. "Call Mac, Quinn. Tell them…migraine."

"I'm on it." Poppy jumped up so fast the foot of her chair scraped along the floor and the sound sliced through Kade's head as he dropped his head to the desk.

When Brodie arrived at Kade's loft, Quinn opened the door to let her in. Brodie was surprised when he bent down and dropped a friendly kiss on her cheek. "Hey, pretty girl."

She couldn't feel offended. Quinn was so damn good-looking he could charm a fence post out of concrete. "Hey, Quinn." Brodie dropped her bag on the hall table and saw Mac standing by the floor-to-ceiling windows looking out at the incredible views of the city. "Hi, Mac."

"Hi, Brodie." He walked over to her and, equally surprisingly, dropped a kiss on her cheek.

"How is he?" she asked, biting her bottom lip.

"He's over the worst of it and this one was bad." Mac ran a hand through his hair.

"Does he get them often?" Brodie asked.

Quinn shook his head. "No, not anymore. He used to when he first joined the Mavericks but he hasn't had one for years."

"We think it's stress-induced," Mac quietly added. He looked at her stomach and back up to her eyes again and Brodie flushed. "He's got quite a bit to be stressed about at the moment."

"I told him he doesn't have to be! This is my problem. I can deal with it." Brodie felt sick and sad. It wasn't her fault Kade had endured two days of pain, that he'd been restricted to a darkened room, all because she'd told him she didn't need him.

She didn't need him.

"You don't know Kade at all if you think he'd just walk away from you and his child," Mac replied, ignoring her flash of temper. "And it's not only your situation causing his stress. He's dealing with a hell of a lot, work-wise, at the moment."

Brodie folded her arms across her chest and sucked in a calming breath. Mac was right; she didn't really know anything about Kade and she knew even less about what he dealt with on a daily basis.

Brodie looked down at the container of soup in her arms. She'd had a friend in college who suffered from migraines and she knew she battled to eat anything solid for days afterward. Chicken soup had been all her friend could stand. So, Brodie had whipped up a batch and decided to bring it over.

A little get-better-soon gesture from her baby's mommy to her baby's daddy. That was all that this visit was. All it could be. "Is he awake? Would he like something to eat?"

Quinn took the container from her and walked toward the kitchen. "He's still sleeping and likely to be asleep for another hour or two." Quinn exchanged a look with Mac and spoke again. "Hey, can you do us a favor?"

"Maybe," Brodie cautiously answered.

Quinn put down the container and placed his hands on the center island separating the dining area from the kitchen. "Can you hang out here for an hour or two and then wake Kade up and try to get him to eat?"

Mac nodded his agreement. "Our new player arrived in the city earlier this afternoon and the three of us were supposed to take him out to dinner. Quinn and I can still do that if you hang around here and feed Kade."

"Sure."

"We'll call you later and see how he's doing. If you think he's okay, then we'll go back to our own places."

"You've been here for two days?" Brodie asked, surprised.

Mac flushed. "We've taken shifts. He's a friggin' miserable patient and we could do with a break."

Kade had good friends, Brodie realized. Very good friends. There for each other through thick and thin. Brodie ignored her envy and nodded. "Go, I'll be fine."

"We know you will." Quinn walked up to her, placed his big hands on her shoulders. He gave her a slow, sweet, genuine smile. "Congratulations on the baby, Brodie. We can't wait to meet him...or her."

Brodie felt her throat tighten. "Thank you."

Quinn turned away and Mac bent down to give her a small hug. "Yeah, from me, too, Brodie. I don't know how you two are going to make this work but we're rooting for you. And Rory wants to have lunch. She says the two of you are reasonably smart people and you can figure out the pregnancy thing together."

"I'd like that," Brodie murmured.

Quinn pointed at the container. "Make him eat. He'll feel better for it."

Mac clapped Quinn on the shoulder and steered him to the door. "Stop fussing. Brodie can handle it."

"I know but he gets all depressed and mopey after a migraine," Quinn complained.

"Brodie. Will. Handle. It." With a last eye-roll at Brodie, Mac steered Quinn through the doors. He looked back and flashed Brodie a grin. "I swear after raising these two, having a kid is going to be a breeze."

Eight

"Go away, Quinn."

"Sorry, not Quinn." Brodie pushed open the door to Kade's bedroom and walked into the darkness to stand at the end of his bed. Her eyes adjusted and she took in his broad back, the yummy butt covered in a pair of loose boxers, the muscled thighs and calves. He was in great shape—long, lean and muscular. Powerful.

"Brodie?" Kade rolled over and leaned on one elbow. He pushed his hair back from his forehead and squinted at her. "What are you doing here?"

Brodie clasped her hands behind her back. "I brought you some chicken soup and your buds asked me to check on you to see if you're not, well, dead."

"They'd be so lucky," Kade growled, sitting up and resting his elbows on his bent knees.

"How are you feeling?"

"Horrible."

"That good, huh?"

Kade lifted a muscular shoulder. "It's a combination of relief that the pain is gone and mental exhaustion. My head is sore."

"Do you still have headache?"

"Not a migraine…" Kade tried to explain. "It's more like my brain is tired. For a day afterward I feel exhausted, like I have a mental hangover."

"Are you sure you're not pregnant? Add nausea and vomiting and that's how I feel all the time."

"Sorry, babe." Kade patted the mattress next to him. "What are you doing over there? Come here."

She really shouldn't. If she sat down next to him she wouldn't be able to keep her hands to herself and then she'd get naked and he had a headache. And he needed to date other women—women she'd found for him!—and she was supposed to be keeping a mental and emotional distance so there were like, a hundred reasons why she shouldn't sit down, why she shouldn't even be here…

Despite all that, Brodie walked around the bed to sit on its edge. Kade immediately wound an arm around her waist, pulled her backward and spooned her from behind. His hand covered her breast and she sighed. "Kade…"

"Shhh." Kade touched his lips to her neck and thumbed her nipple. It bloomed under his touch and she felt heat rushing down, creating a fireball between her legs.

"I need you," Kade whispered in her ear. "I need to be inside you, touching you, being with you. Say yes, Brodes."

Brodie rolled over to face him and touched his jaw, his lips. She opened her mouth to speak but Kade placed his fingers over her lips. "I don't want to hear that this is a bad idea, that we shouldn't, that this is madness. I know it is and, right now, *I don't care*."

Oh, in all honesty, she didn't, either. Wasn't she allowed to step away from the complications and just enjoy his touch, take pleasure in the way he made her feel? Making love to Kade was sheer bliss and, after the weeks she'd endured, wasn't she entitled to some fun? To escape for a little while? It didn't have to mean anything. She wanted him, needed him—in her, filling her, completing her.

"You have too many clothes on, babe." Kade covered her breast with one hand. She arched into his hand, frustrated at the barriers between him and her skin.

"I'm happy for you to take them off as quickly as you can," Brodie whispered, curling her hand around the back of his neck.

"Then again, I rather like you like this. All flushed and hot and horny."

Brodie whimpered when Kade's hard mouth dropped over hers and his tongue tangled with hers. He used his arm to yank her on top of him and her thighs slid over his hips so she was flush against his erection, the heat of which she felt through her loose cotton trousers. His mouth teased and tormented hers—one minute his kisses were demanding and dominating, then he'd ease away. Lust whipped through her as she angled her head to allow him deeper access. His kisses seemed different from anything they'd shared before…there was more heat, more desire, more…of something indefinable.

Unsettled but still incredibly eager, Brodie gripped his shoulders as he undid the buttons on her shirt and exposed her lace-covered breasts to his intense gaze. Kade used one finger to pull down the lace cup and expose her puckered nipple. Then his tongue licked her and sensations swamped her. She moaned when he flicked open the tiny clasp holding her bra together and revealed her torso to his exploring hand. He pulled aside the pale yellow fabric of her bra and swiped his thumb across her peaked nipple. She arched her back, silently asking for more. Kade lowered his head and took one puckered nipple into his mouth, his tongue sliding over her, hot and wet. Kade heard her silent plea for him to touch her and his hand moved to her hip, pushing underneath the waist of her trousers.

"Lift up," he muttered and Brodie lifted her hips and straightened her legs, allowing him to push the fabric down her thighs.

Kade tapped her bottom. "Move off for a sec."

She rolled away and he whipped off his boxers. He put his hands on her knees and pulled them apart before dragging his finger over her mound, slipping under the fabric to find her wet and wanting.

"I want you so much."

"Then *take* me." Really, did the man need a gilded invitation?

Kade sent her a wicked smile. "Yeah, in a minute."

"How's your head?"

Kade looked down and lifted an eyebrow. "Just fine and eager to say hi."

Brodie laughed and slapped his shoulder. "Your other head!"

"Also fine."

Brodie rubbed her thumb against the two grooves between his eyebrows. "Liar. Do you want to stop?"

Brodie hissed as two fingers slipped into her passage.

"Do I look like I want to stop?"

"Kade!" She reached for him, fumbling in her eagerness to get him inside her. "Please, just…I want you."

"I want you this way first. I want to watch you come, with my fingers inside you and my mouth kissing yours." Kade lifted his head and looked into her eyes. "You look good like this, Brodie. You look good anywhere, anyhow."

She was so close, teetering on the edge. *"Kade!"*

"You take my breath away when you lose yourself in me, in the way I make you feel. How do I make you feel, Brodie?"

He was expecting her to speak, to think? How could she answer when she felt like she was surfing a white-hot band of pure, crazy sensation?

"Tell me, Brodie."

"Free," Brodie gasped. "Safe. Sexy."

Cherished, Brodie silently added as her climax rocked her. All those wonderful, loved-up, fuzzy emotions she had no business experiencing. Brodie cried out, partly in reckless abandon and partly in pain as her heart swelled and cracked the plaster she'd cast around it.

She was being wild but she didn't care. She'd deal with the consequences, and the pain, later. Right now she just wanted to feel.

She wanted to feel alive. Just for a little while.

Brodie had to open various cupboard doors before she found soup bowls and three drawers before she found a ladle. She placed a bowl of soup in the microwave to heat and while it did its thing, she scratched around until she found place mats and flatware.

Brodie looked up as Kade entered the kitchen and her breath caught in the back of her throat. Kade looked shattered but somehow, just dressed in a pair of straight-legged track pants and a plain red T-shirt, hot. His hair was damp from his shower and his stubble glinted in the bright light of the kitchen.

Kade frowned and walked over to a panel on the wall and dimmed the lights. "Better," he muttered. He walked back to the island and pulled out a bar stool and sat down.

The microwave dinged. Brodie grabbed a dish towel and pulled out the hot bowl of soup. She put it onto the place mat and pushed the mat, a spoon and the bowl in Kade's direction.

He wrinkled his nose. "I appreciate the offer but I don't think I can eat."

"Listen, Quinn—who, surprisingly, is a fusser—will call and I need to tell him you ate or else he is going to come over here and make you eat." Brodie dished some soup for herself. "And frankly, tonight I think he could make you. You look about as tough as over-boiled noodles."

"Thanks."

"At least I didn't say you look like hell." Brodie pointed her spoon at him.

Kade winced. "Sorry, but you did. You are looking better. Still tired, but better."

"I've been living on chicken soup." Brodie sat down and nodded at his bowl. "It's good, try it."

Kade dipped his spoon, lifted it to his mouth and Brodie waited. When he smiled slowly and nodded she knew he approved. "It's my mom's recipe. A cure for all ailments." And, years later, still doing its job.

They ate in comfortable silence until Brodie looked around the loft and sighed. "My dad was a builder. He would've loved this place."

"You sound uncomfortable when you talk about your parents," he said. "Why?"

Because she was, because she felt guilt that they'd died and she didn't. Because she still missed them with every breath she took. Kade waited for her explanation and, despite her tight throat, she told him what she was thinking. "It's just hard," she concluded.

"You're lucky you experienced such love, such acceptance. They sound like they were incredibly good parents."

Brodie pushed away her plate, looking for an excuse not to talk. But she couldn't keep doing that, not if they were going to co-parent. She needed to learn to open up, just a little. "They were. I was the center of their universe, the reason the sun came up for them every morning." She rested her chin in the palm of her hand. "That makes me sound like I was spoiled, but I wasn't, not really. They gave me more experiences than things. They gave me attention and time, and, most importantly, roots and wings. I felt…lost when they died. I still feel lost," Brodie admitted. "And so damn scared."

Kade took one more sip of soup before standing up. He picked up the bowls and carried them to the sink, leaving them there. On his return trip, he stopped at Brodie's chair and held out his hand. "Let's go sit."

Brodie put her hand in his and followed him across the room to the mammoth sofa. Kade sat down and pulled Brodie next to him, placing his hand on her knee to keep her there. They looked at the city lights and Brodie finally allowed her head to drop so her temple rested on Kade's shoulder.

"What scares you, Brodie?"

Brodie heard his quiet question and sighed. "Love scares me. Feeling attached and running the risk of losing the person I am attached to scares me. Being a mommy scares the pants off me."

"Why?"

"I know how quickly life can change. One day I was bright, happy and invincible. The next I'd lost everyone that mattered to me." She had to continue; she couldn't stop now. "I not only lost my parents in a single swoop, but my two best friends, too. I survived the accident with minor physical injuries and major emotional ones."

He didn't mutter meaningless words of sympathy. He just put her onto his lap, his arms holding her against his broad chest.

Him holding her was all she needed.

"Tell me about your childhood," she asked, desperate to change the subject.

Kade stared out the window at the breathtaking views of False Creek and the city. Brodie wondered if he ever got used to it. Kade, reading her mind, gestured to the window. "I do my best thinking here, looking out of this window. It's never the same, always different depending on the time of day, the month, the season. It's a reminder that nothing stays the same. As a kid my life was nothing *but* change."

Brodie half turned so she could watch his face as he talked. This was the first time they'd dropped some of their barriers and it was frightening. This was something she'd done with her friends, with Chels and Jay. She was out of practice.

"After my mom died, my dad packed up our house, sold everything and hit the road. He wanted to see the country. He wanted to paint. He couldn't leave me behind and he wouldn't stay so I went along. I went to many, many different schools. Some for months, some for only weeks. In some places I didn't even get to school. My education was—" Kade hesitated "—sporadic."

Brodie knew if she spoke she'd lose him so she just waited for him to continue talking.

"But while I hated school, I loved to play hockey and I could always make friends on the ice. Especially since I was good and everyone wanted me on their team. But invariably I'd find a team, make some friends, start to feel settled and he'd yank me off to someplace new."

"I'm sorry."

"So in a way we're the same, Brodie."

Brodie frowned, unsure of where he was going with this. "How?"

"You're scared to become emotionally involved because you're scared to lose again. I'm scared for the same reason." Kade dropped his hand to pat her stomach. "We're going to have to find a way to deal with those fears because this little guy—"

"It could be a girl."

Kade's smile was soft and sweet. "This baby is going to need us, what we can give her. Or him. Individually or together."

His words were low and convincing and Brodie finally accepted he wasn't going to change his mind about the baby. He was determined to play his part parenting their child. Okay then, that was something she would have to get used to.

So, how did they deal with their attraction while they learned to navigate the parenting landscape?

"Problem?"

Brodie wiggled her butt against his long length and heard his tortured hiss. "The fact that we are stupidly attracted to each other is a problem."

"It is?"

"I am not falling into a relationship with you just because we are going to be co-parents, Kade."

A small frown pulled his strong eyebrows together. "Were we talking about a relationship?"

"I just… We just…" Dammit, he made her sound like a blithering idiot.

"Relax, Brodie." He touched her lips, her jaw. "I want you, just like I wanted you forty-five minutes ago, last week, six weeks ago. Not because of the baby but because you drain the blood from my brain. It's a totally separate issue from us being parents. We can do it."

"I don't see how."

"That's because you could complicate a three-piece jigsaw puzzle," Kade teased. "So we slept together again…"

"Yeah, we weren't supposed to do that."

The corners of Kade's mouth tipped up in amusement. "On, the plus side, at least we know you won't fall pregnant."

"Ha-ha." Brodie stared at his broad chest. "I still think we should try to be friends. Our lives are complicated enough already without dealing with sex."

"Why can't we be friends who make love?"

"Because it never works. What if you meet someone you like, someone you desire more than me? I still have to find you two more dates. What if you fall head over heels in love with one of them?"

Kade's hand on her thigh tightened and then relaxed. "What if the sky fell down in the morning?" he drawled. "Do you always borrow trouble like this?"

Her sky had fallen down and trouble had landed on her door. She just wanted to protect herself from it happening again. Was that so wrong? Talking to him, opening up, was dangerous. If she wasn't careful she could love him. She couldn't—wouldn't—allow herself to do that.

Brodie started to move away, to climb off his lap, to find some physical and emotional distance, but his arms held her close.

"No, don't go, Brodes. Just rest that brain of yours, take some time to regroup. Stop thinking."

It was such a huge temptation to rest a while in his embrace. Surrounded by him she felt like nothing could hurt her, that the world and her life weren't quite as scary as she imagined them to be.

"Just rest, sweetheart. We'll figure it out, I promise." Kade's deep voice sounded almost tender. Brodie curled into him and placed her cheek on his chest, her ear directly over his heart. If she closed her eyes she would just drift off…

Brodie rolled over onto her stomach and looked across the coffee table. It was a beautiful day and the sky was a bright, clear blue. Beyond False Creek the Pacific Ocean looked grumpy and the wind teased the water, creating white horses on its surface. If she ignored the morning sickness, she felt better than she had for days, maybe weeks.

Last night, instead of thinking, planning, shoring up her defenses, instead of arguing, she'd allowed Kade to pull her head back to his chest and loop his arms around her. His hand, drawing lazy circles on her back, had lulled her to sleep. She had a vague memory of him picking her up and placing her on the large couch and wrapping his long body around hers as she slept. He'd kept her restless dreams at bay and the feeling of being protected, cared for, had allowed her to drop into a deep, rejuvenating sleep.

Brodie sat up and pushed her hair out of her eyes. She looked over her shoulder and saw Kade standing at the center island, watching her. Something deep, hot and indefinable sparked between them and Brodie bit her bottom lip. Sexy, rumpled man, she thought. How was she supposed to resist him?

"Come here, Brodie," Kade said, his voice as deep and dark as his gaze, the order in it unmistakable.

She knew what would follow if she stood up. She heard it in his voice, saw it in the desire flashing in his eyes, in the way he gripped the counter, tension rippling through his arms. He wanted her...

Brodie knew she shouldn't, knew this was a mistake but she stood up anyway. On shaky legs, she crossed the space to the kitchen, walked around the island and stopped a foot away from him. Seeing a half-empty glass of orange juice, she picked it up and took a long sip. Excitement and desire caused her hand to shake and orange juice ran down her chin.

Kade wiped the droplets off with his thumb. "I have to kiss you."

Brodie started to speak but Kade shook his head. "No, don't say it's a mistake, that we shouldn't be doing this. Just forget about everything else. This is just about you and me... There are no other complications right now. They'll be back later, but right now...? There's nothing but you...and me."

"I was just going to tell you to hurry up," Brodie whispered, lifting her face. "Hurry up and kiss me, Kade."

Kade leaned forward, cupped the side of her face in his hand and lowered his mouth to hers. Part of her thought that if Kade did nothing else but kiss her for the rest of her life, she could die happy. Another sec-tion of her brain just squawked warnings: they had to be friends only. She still had to be his matchmaker. They shouldn't be doing this. If the media found out they would go nuts. Then Kade took control of her mouth, her brain shut down and she felt energized, revitalized, as if he'd plugged her in to recharge.

"Take me to bed, Kade," she muttered against his lips as her arms looped around his neck and her fingers played with the taut skin there.

Kade groaned. "Yeah, that was my intention. Except that my bed is too far." Kade used his forearm to push everything standing on the center island to the far edge of the block before bending his knees and wrapping one arm around her hips. In one easy, fluid movement he had her sitting on the island, their hands and mouths now perfectly aligned. Brodie placed her palms on Kade's shoulders and tipped her head to give him better access so he could brush his lips against her neck, her jaw, her cheekbones.

"You are so beautiful."

She wasn't, not really, but right now she believed him. Feeling sexy and confident, she dropped her hands and gripped his T-shirt, slowly pulling it up and over his chest, wanting to get her hands on those muscles. Kade used one hand to finish pulling the T-shirt over his head and toss it to the floor. Brodie sucked in her breath. His track pants were low on his hips, displaying his ripped abdomen, those long obliques over his hips. Those sexy muscles made her feel squirmy and stupid and so, so wanton.

Brodie's fingers drifted over his abdomen and hips, the side of her hand brushing his erection. She heard Kade suck in a breath. Liking the fact that she could make him breathe faster, that she could make his eyes glaze over, she pushed her hands inside his pants and pushed them over his hips to fall into a black puddle on the wooden floor.

"Whoops." She smiled against his mouth.

"Since the urge to strip is all I ever think about when you are in the room, I'm not complaining," Kade said, his mouth curling into a delighted smile.

His smile could melt ice cream, make women walk into poles and stop traffic. It heated up every one of Brodie's internal organs and made them smile, too.

He had a hell of a smile, Brodie thought, especially when she felt it on her skin.

Nine

A few days later, Brodie parked her car next to Kade's and ran an appreciative hand over the sleek hood. Had Kade realized this car was something he'd have to give up or, at the very least, that he'd need to buy a new one to transport the baby? There was no room for a car seat and she doubted a stroller would fit in the trunk.

So much was changing, Brodie thought as she headed to the entrance of his apartment building, quickly keying in the code to open the front doors. She and Kade were sort of lovers, kind of friends, about to be parents. The parenting bit was the only thing she was certain of, she thought as she walked into the private elevator that opened into Kade's hallway.

Kade could rocket her from zero to turned-on in two seconds flat. And he was funny and smart… She was crazy about him.

Brodie rested her head against the panel of the elevator, petrified she was building castles in the air. She was pregnant and it was so natural to look to the father of her baby for sex, for comfort. It made complete sense. Who wanted to be a single parent, who wanted to go through this frightening, exhausting, terrifying process alone? But castles built on fantastic sex and thin air and wishes could collapse at a moment's notice. Kade wasn't going to be her happily-ever-after guy. She didn't believe in happily-ever-after. She believed in getting through, doing the best she could, building a safe and secure life. There was only one person she could rely on 100 percent and that was herself.

Brodie hit the emergency stop button and rested her forehead against the elevator door. She had to pull back from him, had to put some distance between them. She was being seduced by what-ifs and how-it-might-be's. She couldn't afford to think of Kade as anything more than the father of her child. He was her temporary lover but he wasn't her partner or her significant other.

He *definitely* would never be her husband.

The last time she'd planned her future she'd had it ripped from her. She'd lost everyone she'd loved in one fell swoop and she refused to take that risk again.

She couldn't taste love, hold love and lose love again. That was too big a risk to take.

She smacked the emergency button and the elevator lurched upward.

No, she'd had her fun...too much fun. It was time to back the hell away and get a handle on this relationship. She needed to dial it back to a cordial friendship. She could do that. And she *would* do that before the story broke in the press. Presently the press saw her as nothing more than his matchmaker but they'd soon sniff out the truth. With her spending nights at his place, they'd been lucky to keep it a secret this long.

Luck, as she knew, always ran out.

Kade walked into his loft, ignored Mac and Rory and Quinn, and walked straight over to Brodie. He picked her up and turned her upside down so her head was facing the floor. She gurgled with laughter and placed her hands on the floor to steady herself.

"Kade, she's pregnant!" Quinn grabbed his arm. "What are you doing?"

"I'm getting blood to her head, something that was obviously missing when she chose my date," Kade replied, easily restoring Brodie to her feet. "She's lucky I didn't hang her over the balcony."

Brodie wiped her hands on the seat of her pants and sent him a cocky smile. She hadn't been remotely scared at being tossed around like a doll, Kade mused. Her eyes were bright and full of mischief. "Really, Stewart?"

Brodie attempted an innocent shrug. "What? She's a biokinetics engineer and a part-time entertainer."

"And a full-time loony. She wants to be a freakin' mermaid." Kade pointed an accusing finger at Brodie.

"What are we talking about?" Mac asked, mystified.

"The latest date Brodie and Wren sent him on. He had lunch with her today," Quinn explained. He turned to Kade. "You do know it's weird that you're going on these dates while Brodie is pregnant with your child?"

No, the thought hadn't occurred to him, he sarcastically, silently replied. Brodie and he had an understanding—basically, they both understood they had no idea what they were doing. "Blame Wren. Besides, the dating is done."

"When did you do date number two?" Mac asked.

"A couple of weeks back. Teacher, triathlete. We had lunch," Kade answered him. "I am now off the dating hook."

"Anyway, getting back to today and this date—" he pointed a finger at Brodie "—revenge will be sweet."

Brodie didn't seem particularly concerned, so Kade left her to talk to his friends and headed for the kitchen. On the plus side, he'd fulfilled his duties to Wren's publicity campaign. The public could vote, speculate and talk about his love life until the damn cows came home but the only woman who interested him, on any level, was standing on his balcony, carrying his child.

He opened the fridge, yanked out a beer, saw Quinn behind him and reached for another. Kade handed Quinn a bottle and closed the fridge door with a nudge of his knee. He cracked open the beer and took a long swallow. He looked across the loft to the balcony where Brodie stood. It was a nice evening, his friends were here and he'd ordered Thai for dinner. He'd had a busy, drama-free day and then he'd joined Quinn and Mac on the ice for a workout. While the news had been unexpected, he was going to be a father and he was starting to become excited at the prospect.

Life *should* be good.

So what was the problem? In a nutshell, it was this half on, half off, up-in-the-air arrangement he had with Brodie. Half friends, sometimes lovers, future parents, both of them wanting, on some level, to run. He was jogging in place but Brodie had her sneakers on and was about to sprint, as hard and as fast as she could.

As soon as she could.

Kade felt he was living the same life he'd lived with his father, not sure how the next move would affect him.

Every day was new territory for him and he felt as unsettled as he had when he was a child.

Quinn's fist smacking into Kade's biceps rocked him back to the here and now. "What the hell was that for?"

"I talk to both you and Mac but neither of you listen! It's like talking to a blow-up doll."

"You should know," Kade grumbled, rubbing his arm.

Quinn's fist shot out again but Kade stepped back and the fist plowed through air. Kade sent Quinn a mocking glance. "Too slow, bro."

Quinn picked up his beer bottle, sipped and after lowering it he spoke again. "You concentrating, dude?"

"Yeah." Kade leaned against the kitchen counter and crossed his legs. "Speak."

"Your dad is having an exhibition in a couple of weeks, downtown."

So? His father was a well-respected artist and frequently held exhibitions in the city. James didn't invite him to any and Kade didn't attend. It worked for both of them. "Not interested."

"The exhibition is called 'Retrospective Regrets.'"

Kade didn't give a crap. His father wasn't part of his life, hadn't been part of his life for a long, long time. And he liked it that way.

"I just thought you might like to tell him he's going to be a grandfather."

He hadn't wanted a son so Kade doubted he'd be interested in a grandchild. But maybe he should give James the benefit of the doubt? Maybe he'd changed. Kade cursed at the hope that flickered.

"I'll think about it."

Quinn knew better than to push. He just shrugged

and lifted his beer bottle in Brodie's direction. "What are you going to do about her? Are you going to marry her, live with her, demand joint custody?"

Kade wished he knew. "I definitely want joint custody, everything else is up in the air." He rested his beer bottle against his forehead and sighed. "It's all craziness."

"Well, I suggest you figure out what you are before the news of your impending fatherhood hits the papers. If you don't know they'll decide for you."

Because the media's focus had been on his dates and the future of the team, so far he and Brodie had managed to dodge that bullet, but Kade wasn't under any illusions they'd keep the baby a secret indefinitely.

Quinn grinned. "On the plus side, my BASE jumping and having to talk myself out of being arrested aren't quite so bad when you measure them against the fact that another Maverick-teer is going to become a father, barely a month after Mac."

Kade would cross that burning bridge when he came to it. And talking about daredevil stunts... "Talking of, are you insane? You could've been killed!"

"Only if my chute didn't open," Quinn cheerfully agreed. "Then I would've made a dent in the concrete. *Splat!*"

Kade sent Brodie an anxious look, grateful she hadn't heard Quinn's cavalier attitude toward death. "Not funny, Rayne." Kade stopped, whirled around and slapped his hand on Quinn's hard chest. He scowled at his best friend. "Brodie lost everyone she loved in one accident. Don't you dare be glib about death, yours or anyone else's, around her! Got it?"

Quinn rubbed the spot on his chest. "Jeez, okay! Got it."

Kade walked away and Quinn scowled at the ceiling. "I'm running out of friends to play with," he muttered.

Later in the week, after a night long on pleasure and short on sleep, Brodie stood at the center island in Kade's kitchen, and scowled at her daily calendar on her tablet screen. Her schedule was utterly insane and she would be rushing from one appointment to another, all with men looking for a happily-ever-after. Didn't they realize the closer and the more perfect the relationship, the more pain they could expect to feel if the relationship went south? The end always hurt the most when the connection felt the best. Argh...she normally never thought about how her clients progressed after she matched them. Damn this situation with Kade for making her so introspective!

Kade, on his way up from the gym, walked past her to the sink and filled a glass with water. He whistled when he caught a glimpse of her schedule. "And I thought I had a hectic day ahead."

"Crazy, isn't it?" Brodie sipped her coffee and scowled at the screen. "I won't take all these men on as clients, some I'll be able to help and some I'll discard because, well, they'll be idiots."

Kade rested the glass on his folded arm. "Why matchmaking, Brodie? Why earn your living from something you don't believe in?"

Why would he think that? "But I do believe in it. I do believe people function best when they are in healthy, stable, supportive relationships. Being alone sucks."

"But you avoid relationships. You are alone," Kade pointed out.

"Yeah, but that's the choice I've made." Brodie

picked up a banana from the fruit bowl and slowly peeled it. "I know it's ironic that I, commitment-phobic as I am, own a matchmaking service."

Kade put his hands behind him and gripped the counter. "Okay, so why do you?"

Brodie looked across the loft to the rainy day outside. She took a bite of the banana, chewed it slowly and then placed it on the side plate next to her half-eaten toast. Should she tell Kade? Was she brave enough to open up a little more? She rarely—okay, never—spoke about Jay. She had trained herself not to think about him. But Kade was the father of her baby and she almost trusted him. Well, as much as she could.

"In the car crash, I didn't only lose my parents, I lost my best friends, as well. Chelsea and Jay. We were all in the car. I survived, and they didn't. We were like you and Mac and Quinn—inseparable." Brodie swiped her finger across the program to close her calendar. "Jay and I always knew that, one day, we'd move on from being best friends. Three weeks before the crash, we finally admitted we loved each other. We started sleeping together, everything was new and bright and wonderful." Her voice cracked and Brodie cleared her throat.

Kade took a step forward but Brodie held up her hand to stop him. If he touched her she would start to cry and she had clients to see. "I lost my world in the space of three minutes. But I was so loved, Kade. So damn much."

"And you don't want that again?"

"I can't *lose* that again. I'll have this child and that'll be enough. This child arrived by sheer fluke and I've accepted that the baby is life's way of forcing me to love again. To love in a different way."

"And will that be enough?"

Brodie lifted one shoulder in a tiny shrug. "It has to be. It's all I'm prepared to risk." Her smile felt a little shaky. "I am going to be the best mother I can be. I am going to be your friend, your lover, for as long as that works or until you meet the woman you can't live without." Brodie rubbed her hands across her eyes. "I hope you find her, Kade. I'd like you to. I think you deserve her."

"And I think you deserve the same."

"I wouldn't be that lucky, not twice. Life doesn't work that way." Brodie pushed her tablet into its case and sighed. "I have to go. Busy day."

"It's barely seven, Brodie, and I need to talk to you about something else."

Brodie frowned at his tone. Being bossed around so early in the morning really didn't work for her. "Okay, what?"

"So gracious." Kade walked across the kitchen to take a mug from a shelf. He jammed it under the spout of his coffee machine and pushed a button. Brodie tapped her fingers against the counter, listening to the sounds of the beans grinding. She was feeling exposed and hot, like her skin was a size too small for her body. That's why she didn't usually talk, she reminded herself. It made her feel sad and funny and…weird.

"I'm going to need to tell the press something about us and soon."

"Why?"

Kade looked at her over the rim of his mug. "We spend a lot of time together and someone is going to realize that. And when you start showing, they'll go into overdrive. Wren suggests we hit them with a press release and cut off the speculation. So what do you want to be called? My girlfriend, my partner, my common-law wife?"

Brodie grimaced as he said the word *wife* and Kade scratched his head. "Okay, so not wife. What?"

This was far too much to deal with so early in the morning. "I don't like titles. I don't believe in them. We are what we are..."

"I'll just tell the press that. It'll work," Kade said, sounding sarcastic.

"I don't know, Kade!" Brodie cried. "Tell them we are friends, that we intend to remain friends, that we are having a baby together! That's all the information they are entitled to. That's all the information we have."

"They'll make it up if we don't give them more. Or they'll dig and dig until they find more," Kade warned.

She couldn't control their actions, Brodie thought. She could only control her own. And right now she had to get to work or else she'd be late for her breakfast appointment. Besides, she really didn't want to talk about this anymore. With Kade or the world. "I'm not ready to say anything yet. And I've got to go."

"Dammit, Brodie! We have to deal with this at some point."

Yeah, but not now.

"Think about it," Kade told her, obviously frustrated. "Are you coming back here tonight?"

Brodie slung her bag over her shoulder and walked toward the front door feeling hemmed in. "Maybe."

That one word was, right now, all she could commit to.

Brodie looked up when Colin tapped on the frame of her door and ambled into her office.

"Hey, Col." Brodie rested her forearms on her desk and sent him a fond smile.

"How are you feeling?"

"I'm well. The morning sickness has passed, as has the tiredness." Brodie bit her bottom lip. "Did you tell Kayla?"

A shadow passed through Colin's eyes as he nodded. Colin and Kayla had been trying to get pregnant for more than five years and were now trying IVF. Hearing Brodie had become pregnant via a one-night stand had probably rocked Kayla.

"She took it rather well, considering. She said to tell you she wants to meet the baby's daddy."

Yeah, about that. Brodie still hadn't told Colin, or anyone else, about Kade.

"Maybe," Brodie hedged.

Colin sighed. "You're going to keep us guessing, aren't you?"

Brodie rubbed her forehead with her fingertips. "It's complicated. We're trying to work through it and until we have a plan, I'd rather just keep his identity quiet." She wrinkled her nose. "I might end up parenting on my own and he won't be a factor."

Not that there was a snowball's chance in hell of that happening. This was, after all, Kade she was talking about.

"Understood," Colin said, before straightening. "So, business..."

Business talk she could do. Mostly because it stopped her thinking about Kade and their future. Business wasn't complicated or demanding and it didn't mess with her head. Or her libido. "What's up?"

"I don't know about you but I am overwhelmed. My schedule is crazy."

Brodie looked at her screen and the thirty unopened emails from prospective clients. Ironically, the publicity generated from being Kade's matchmaker had generated almost too much business. "It's crazy."

"I was approached by a couple out of Los Angeles who want to relocate to Vancouver. They have a matchmaking business in the city." Colin passed her a black-and-pink business card.

"I know the Hendersons," Brodie said, flicking her nail against the card. "I investigated their business model when I was starting this business. They are reputable, smart and sensitive."

"Well, they have just sold their business and they are moving here."

Brodie immediately connected the dots. "Are they going to start up here?"

"They want to semi-retire. They want to work but they don't want the responsibility of running an office or staff."

"Are you thinking about bringing them on board… with you?"

Colin picked up her pen and tapped it against his knee, leaving tiny blue dots on his khaki pants. "And with you, if you are as overwhelmed as I am. It's a win-win situation. We feed them clients, take a commission and we manage how big a bite they take."

Brodie looked at the pile of folders on her desk and realized it might be the answer to her crazy workload. And she'd find it easier to juggle her career and being a new mother if she had some help. "Are they keen?"

"They are keen to talk," Colin replied. "They'll fly out here if we ask them to."

Her phone chirped and Brodie looked down at the screen.

Will be home late. Will you be okay?

God, she'd been okay for the past three months and for nine years before that. She'd managed to feed herself, dress herself, get herself to work, establish a career. Why did Kade and Poppy think she had dropped sixty IQ points just because she was now pregnant?

Arrrgh.

Brodie ignored Kade's message, pushed back her chair and stood up. She gripped the back of the chair.

"Or we could go to them." God, a trip out of the city would be an unexpected blessing, Brodie thought. She could get some distance from Kade, have some time alone to think.

You just don't want to deal with the emotions Kade pulls to the surface.

I just want some time to think! Is that too much to ask?

You've got to stop lying to yourself...

Oh, shut up.

Brodie looked at Colin. "What do you think? You up for a trip?"

"Sure. Are you allowed to fly?"

Brodie tamped down her irritation. "I am only a few months pregnant. The baby is the size of pea so yes, I can fly. Jeez!"

Her phone beeped again. I can cancel dinner if you want me to.

Kade! Really? She tipped her head at Colin and sent him an I-dare-you look. "Let's fly out tonight, see the Hendersons in the morning? I might stay in Cali for the weekend, do some sightseeing, some shopping."

Colin jumped to his feet, nodding enthusiastically. He was always up for an adventure and was, thank goodness, impulsive. "That sounds like an excellent idea. I'll call the Hendersons. Can you book flights?"

She could and she would, she thought, glancing down at the screen of her phone. Because she *definitely* needed to put a border and a couple of cities between her and Kade Webb.

Ten

Kade couldn't remember when he'd been this angry. Angry, disappointed…hurt, dammit. And the fact he was hurt pissed him off even more.

Gone away. Will be back in a few days.

A few days had turned into a week and he still didn't know where the hell Brodie was and, crucially, whether she was all right. She was ducking his calls and not returning his increasingly irate text messages. His… whatever the hell she was…was AWOL and he was not amused. Not amused as in ready to slam his fist into the wall. He'd do it but he recalled, from previous experience, it hurt like a bitch.

Kade stood on the balcony off his master suite and gripped the edge of the balustrade, peering past the trees to the street below, hoping to see Brodie's car. He wanted to make sure she was okay, to make love to her, to put her over his knee and spank her silly for driving him out of his mind with worry.

What if she never came back? What if she'd just packed up and left town, heading for…wherever? What would he do? How would he find her? Would he make the effort to track her down?

Of course he would. Apart from the fact she drove him insane, she was the mother of his child. For that reason alone he'd follow her to the ends of the earth…

Jesus, Brodie, where the hell are you?

Kade heard the subdued chime signaling someone had accessed his private elevator and since Quinn was out of town and Mac was home with Rory, it had to be Brodie. *Thank God.* She was the only other person who had the code.

Kade waited for the elevator doors to open and his heart both stumbled and settled when she stepped into his loft. He did a quick scan, confirmed she was physically in one piece and told himself not to lose his temper.

Yeah, that wasn't going to happen.

Brodie only needed one look to see Kade was pissed and exceptionally so. His eyes were the color of bittersweet chocolate and flat with anger and residual worry. She'd needed time away but she'd been wrong to avoid his calls, to avoid talking to him.

She'd done him a disservice; Kade was a fully functioning adult and he would've understood her need for some time alone to think. But she'd been unable to pick up the phone and tell him that—due to embarrassment and pride. Instead she'd let him worry and, judging by the increasingly irate messages he'd left her, stew. She deserved the verbal slap she was about to get and she braced herself to take it.

She'd created this situation and she wasn't going to whine about the consequences. She'd acted like a child because she'd felt smothered, and she deserved to be treated like a child now that she'd returned. He'd yell and she'd apologize and hopefully it would all be over soon.

"Hey."

Kade frowned and started to walk in her direction. Ah, hell, he was even angrier than she realized. Brodie lifted up her hands in apology. "I'm so—"

Her words were cut off by his hot mouth on hers and she could taste his frustration. His fingers dug into her hips and he yanked her into him, slamming her against his hard frame and his even harder erection. She couldn't help it; she encircled her arms around his neck and poured her own frustrations into the kiss…

I want you but I don't want to rely on you. I like feeling protected and cared for but it scares me spitless. I'm so close to falling in love with you but I can't let myself be that vulnerable again.

Brodie felt Kade tugging her shirt from her jeans and sighed when his warm hands spanned her back. His thigh pushed between hers and suddenly she was straddling his hard leg. Her body responded immediately by rocking against those hard muscles, moaning when the friction caught her in exactly the right place. Kade immediately responded by slipping his hand down the back of her jeans and he growled when her tight pants stopped his progress.

"Get them off."

This was too intense, too urgent, and Brodie knew they should back off, but she didn't want to. She wanted him out of control and reckless, demanding and insistent. He was feeling raw and so was she. It added an edge of excitement she'd never experienced before. It was primitive sex—hot, urgent—and she wanted to ride this maelstrom with him.

If they worked off enough frustration they'd be able to talk calmly and she'd be forgiven sooner. Besides, there was nothing wrong with channeling their anger into something that afforded them a great deal of pleasure…

Kade's fingers working the zipper of her jeans pulled her back into pleasure. He pushed her pants and her thong down to her ankles. Brodie stepped out of her backless wedges and kicked her feet free as Kade placed one hand behind her butt and lifted her up and into him. His tongue invaded her mouth again and she knew this would be hot and fast and crazy.

Bring it on!

Matching his urgency, she pulled his shirt up his back and over his head, forcing him to let her go so she could pull it off his arms. She ran her hands down his torso—she'd missed his body, missed *him*, more than she should. Far more than was healthy.

She hated that but she loved this. Loved his hot, masculine, hair-roughened skin. She placed her mouth on his chest to taste him as her hands dropped to his shorts, pulling his belt open with unsteady hands. She needed to feel him in her grasp, needed to taste him on her tongue, to fill her, to complete her.

She needed him.

She both loved and hated the need he stirred inside her.

Kade pushed her hands aside and quickly stripped. She reached down to touch him but he grabbed her wrists to stop her. He encircled them with one hand; easily restraining her while his other hand gripped her jaw and tipped her face up so her eyes collided with his.

Anger and desire were both still there. "We probably shouldn't do this."

"I know." Brodie licked her lips. "But I want to anyway."

"You sure?" Kade demanded, his voice rough. "Because it's not going to be pretty. I'm going to ride you, hard."

Brodie lifted her chin. "I can take everything you hand out, Webb. I'm not a hothouse flower."

The fingers on her jaw loosened and his touch turned tender. "Dammit, Brodie." He rested his forehead against hers.

It was her turn to touch his jaw, to allow her fingers to walk over his face. "You won't hurt me and I need you. I need you so damn much."

Those amazing eyes hardened, just a fraction. There was hurt beneath the anger and she was sorry for it. "You could've fooled me."

Brodie gave him what she could. "Right now, I need you as much as you need me. Give me that, Kade. The rest we can fight about later."

"And we will fight."

"I know." But that was for later so Brodie stood up on her tiptoes to align her mouth with his.

"How are we going to do this?" she whispered against his lips. "Where are we going to do this? Bedroom? Couch?"

Kade's eyes darted around the room. "Too far. Too civilized."

He spun her around and placed her hands on the hall table. Standing behind her, he put his palm on her stomach and pulled up her butt. Brodie swallowed, ferociously excited. So this was…new.

Kade's hand stroked her spine and her lower back, kneaded her butt before sliding between her cheeks to find the damp, moisture between her legs. She heard him sigh and then he was sliding inside her, the position filling her more deeply than he ever had before.

She felt exposed and dominated, but thrilled to her core, which he happened to be touching. His arms encompassed her, crisscrossing her from chest to thigh, and she felt protected and enveloped as her climax built. He was so deep inside he hardly needed to move and his thrusts turned gentle. Bright white lights sparked in her head as the warm, rushing wave pummeled her.

She screamed; he groaned. He pumped against her, once, twice, and then he exploded inside her, his arms tightening as a shudder ran through his body. Slowly coming back to herself, Brodie realized her fingernails were digging into Kade's forearms. The only thing keeping her from doing a face-plant on the floor was Kade's python-like grip. She sucked in a shallow breath and felt his lips on her neck. She was still half-dressed, her bra and shirt still on.

Whoa, Nelly.

Kade's arms loosened and he pulled her upright, sliding out as he did so. He dropped one arm but kept the other around her waist, anchoring her to his side. Brodie stared at the oil painting above the hall table and wondered if she could ever look at it again without remembering the hot sex they'd had beneath it.

"You okay?" Kade asked, his voice low, rough.

Brodie cleared her throat and nodded. "Yeah."

"I didn't hurt you?"

Brodie looked down at his arms and saw the deep grooves her nails had left in his skin. She traced her fingertip over the marks. "I should be asking you that."

"I'm good." Kade's arm tightened once and his hands flexed on her hips before he let her go. He picked up her jeans and handed them to her. "Go on up. I'll get clean downstairs."

Normally they'd shower together after sex and frequently showering would lead to round two. Brodie sighed. Guess that wasn't going to happen today.

He was still mad. Well, he'd warned her. Brodie nodded and walked toward the stairs, embarrassed he would watch her bare butt the whole way.

But when she turned around at the top of the stairs he'd disappeared to the lower level and his solitary shower.

Wishing she could run away again, Brodie headed into his bedroom and the en suite bathroom. She wouldn't get away with running again.

Brodie found Kade on the balcony, dressed in a faded pair of jeans and a pale blue T-shirt. He sat close to the edge, his bare feet resting on the railings, a beer in his hand. Brodie, dressed in the clothes she'd arrived in, saw there was a diet cola and a glass on the table so she sat down and perched on the cushion.

Kade poured her cola into the ice-filled glass and handed her the cold drink. He sat back and linked his hands behind his head looking like the urban, relaxed businessman he was. Except she also saw the tension in his jaw, the banked anger in his glittering eyes.

"You missed your doctor's appointment and the first ultrasound."

"I called and rescheduled."

"Thanks for letting me know," Kade said, his tone bitter.

Brodie frowned. She'd briefly mentioned the appointment to him and he'd never indicated his intention to go with her. "I didn't know you were planning to go with me."

Kade cut her a look. "Of course I was, Brodie."

Wow…okay. "I thought you'd only take an interest in the baby once it was born."

"I. Take. An. Interest. In. You." Kade spat out the words.

"Oh."

After a couple of minutes, Kade broke the silence. "I was worried about you. I thought something had happened to you, to our baby. I couldn't find you. I didn't know where to start looking."

Brodie closed her eyes at the note of desolation in his voice, the hurt he was trying so hard to hide. Brodie turned her head and looked at his hard profile, the way the evening breeze picked up his hair and blew it over his forehead.

"My dad did that once."

Oh, God, no.

"Did what?" she asked, not really wanting to know the answer because she knew it would make her feel ten times worse than she already did.

"Disappeared. I was about ten and I came home from school and he wasn't around. By eight that night I was worried, by midnight I was terrified. Three days later I was out of food and out of my mind with worry. Ten years old and I had cramps in my stomach from hunger. The morning of the fourth day I decided to skip school and go to the police. I was leaving the house when he pulled into the driveway, looking like he'd rather be anywhere rather than back in whatever town that was, with me."

Brodie gripped the arms of her chair and closed her eyes, silently cursing Kade's waste-of-space parent. She heard Kade stand up and felt the brief kiss on the top of her head. "I was terrified then but that had nothing on what I felt this past week." Kade's voice sounded like it had been roughened with sandpaper. "Everything is up in the air with us and I get that. I don't want to take over your life or control it or you. But if—when—you go, keep in contact, okay?"

Brodie nodded once, sharply, and forced the words past the tears in her throat. "I don't know what you want from me, Kade."

Kade walked around the chair and stood between her and the railing, the dim lights on the balcony casting shadows over his taut face. "I have no idea, either. I'm as confused about where to go, what to do as you are. But the one thing I do know for sure is that running away doesn't help. My father ran from town to town, from creditor to creditor, nothing ever changed. Because wherever you go, there you are."

Kade's fingers raked through his hair. "But maybe you could talk to me before you run. And I need you to come to grips with having me in your life. Because, even if we aren't going to be together, I am still going to be part of your life because—" he pointed to her midsection "—that is my kid, as well. We're in this together. So, on some level, I need you to trust me, to believe I won't let you down."

But he would. Everyone did.

Before she could respond, he continued, "But, Brodie, you only get this one chance. You run again and that's it. That's you telling me you don't want me in your life, in any capacity."

Brodie bit her bottom lip. "And the baby?"

"I will not abandon my child." Kade rubbed the back of his neck. "Lawyers, supervised visits until the baby is old enough and formal arrangements for custody. We'll be handing over the baby in parking lots. We'll be apart and separate, co-parenting but not communicating."

God, that sounded…awful. Dismal. Depressing.

"Don't do that to us, Brodie. Don't make it like that," Kade said, his voice soft. "I'm not asking for anything other than for you to let me in. To share something of yourself, to trust a little, or even a lot."

Kade's hand drifted over her hair and he bent down to kiss her temple. "I'm going to bed. Feel free to join me. Let me know if you decide to leave."

Brodie nodded.

"And Brodie?"

"Yes?"

"Don't ever ignore my calls again, okay?"

Brodie tied the laces on her running shoes, brimming with energy. Her morning sickness was all but gone and she felt energized and healthy and ready to resume exercising. She wasn't going to hurtle around Stanley Park like she normally did but she'd get her heart rate up and her blood flowing. Surely that had to be good for the baby?

Brodie left her apartment and skipped down the stairs, thinking she still missed her early-morning runs with Kade. So much had changed since they'd first met. She was carrying Kade's baby, they were having hot sex, sometimes at his apartment and, like last night, sometimes at hers. After their fight last week, she was doing her best to be more open, to communicate better.

She loved spending time with him and she couldn't help wondering whether he felt the same, if he missed her at all when she wasn't around? Oh, she knew he liked her, he adored making love with her, but was that the sum total of his feelings? Was he feeling more, wanting more?

Because, dammit, *she* was starting to want more.

Brodie nibbled the inside of her lip. She'd promised herself she wouldn't do this again, with any man, but she was sliding further and further down this slippery slope that might be love. With every smile, every conversation with Kade, she felt another one of her walls dissolving. Soon she'd be stripped bare and at the mercy of the vagaries of life and love. It would hurt.

And how would she ever know if Kade truly loved her and not the idea of her as the mother of his child? What if they became too swept up in playing the happy family and when the novelty wore off he decided this wasn't what he'd signed up for and bolted? How would she cope then?

No, teetering on the edge of love or not, she couldn't risk relying on him and being let down. People always thought they wanted one thing and then it turned out they wanted another. Sure, everyone had a right to change their minds, but she'd prefer it wasn't her heart Kade practiced on.

She'd rather be his friend and his part-time lover for as long as that lasted. When it ended, she'd still be his friend. And he'd be hers. She could do that…

Possibly.

Brodie pulled open the front door, ran down the pathway and bumped smack into a bunch of men standing on the curb. Cameras flashed and she lifted a hand to shield her eyes. What the hell?

"How long have you being seeing Kade?"

"When are you due?"

"Is it a boy or a girl?

"When did you and Kade hook up? Before you matched him?"

"Are you getting married?"

She didn't need to be a rocket scientist to realize the press knew Kade was the father of her baby and she wasn't going for a run this morning.

"You owe us a statement, Ms. Stewart."

"She owes you nothing, Johnson." Kade's deep voice broke through the shouting. Brodie looked up and there he was, holding out a hand. His car was idling behind the reporters and it represented safety and quiet, both of which she needed right now. Brodie grabbed his hand and allowed him to pull her through the throng of reporters.

"Aw, come on, Kade. We need something."

"I can give you a swift kick if that would help." Kade opened the passenger door for Brodie and she slipped inside. Kade shut her door but she could still hear the questions, the demands. Then the crowd quieted and Brodie looked out the window to see that Kade, his back to her and blocking the cameras, had quieted the crowd. "You guys can take potshots at me, ask me anything, but Brodie is off-limits."

"How long have you been together?"

"Are you getting married? Are you living together?"

"Was her matchmaking you just a publicity stunt? Did you lead those women on?"

"Has Myra accepted your offer to buy the franchise? We hear that the rookie is going to sue you personally."

Kade didn't say another word but walked around the car to the driver's seat. He opened his door and dropped inside. He slammed the door shut but rolled down his window.

"You said we can ask you anything. Not fair, Webb!"

Kade grinned. "I said you can ask me anything, I never said I would answer." Kade started the car, floored the accelerator and drove off. Brodie turned around in her seat to look at the agitated crowd behind them.

"They do not look happy."

"Screw them." Kade veered the car around the corner.

Brodie grabbed her seat belt and pulled it over her chest, clicking it into place. She looked at the creeping speedometer and bit her lip, tasting fear in the back of her throat. "Slow down, please?"

Kade sent her a quick look, then immediately slowed down and placed his hand on her knee. "Sorry. You okay?"

"Fine," Brodie replied, looking at his annoyed profile. "So, how did they find out? Did Wren do a press release?"

"No." Kade shook his head. "We were trying to delay it as long as possible, to put some distance between you becoming pregnant and arranging those stupid dates for me."

"So how did they find out?"

"Someone recognized us when we went to see the ob-gyn."

Brodie twisted her lips. "Anyone in the waiting room could've leaked the story, could've taken a photograph of us."

"And they did. They sold the story to the tabloids and

the paper that broke the news has had a photographer following us for at least two weeks. We're a double-page spread," Kade told her, driving in the direction of his apartment.

"Dammit." Brodie sighed. "Guess I am now, officially, one of Webb's Women."

"You are Webb's only woman." He glanced down at her stomach. "Unless there's a girl in there, then you'll have to share the spotlight."

He was using a jokey, upbeat tone and she didn't know whether he was being serious or not. He placed his free hand on her tummy but kept his eyes on the road. "Twenty-six weeks, Brodes, and we'll know."

Kade glided to a smooth stop in front of a traffic light and turned his head to look at her.

"God, the press will eat you up and spit you out."

"I am tougher than I look, Webb." The light turned green and Kade accelerated away.

"Just keep saying 'no comment.' Maybe you should move in with me—my place is a lot more secure than yours."

That wasn't going to happen. Brodie noticed Kade's eyes were dark with worry and his jaw was rock-hard with tension. She knew he cared for her, that he loved making love with her, but even after her trip to California and their fight, she hadn't been sure of how much until this moment. He was genuinely worried for her. Did that mean he loved her?

Stop jumping to conclusions. You're getting way ahead of yourself.

If she moved into the loft, then there was no way she'd be able to keep any emotional distance from him. Whenever they were together she found herself leaning into his shoulder, almost grabbing his hand, and she spent far too much time staring at his mouth.

"Nothing is going to happen to me. I'm healthy, the baby is healthy. And I can deal with the press."

Kade tapped his finger against his steering wheel. "Tell me again in two weeks when they are still shouting questions at you every time you step outside," he muttered.

"I'll be fine." Really, how bad could it be?

Eleven

"I feel like I've answered a million questions about me, what about you?"

Brodie clicked Save on her tablet and watched her database update before her eyes. She recognized the flirtation in the man's voice, the barely disguised interest. She glanced down at her bare ring finger and wished she was wearing her fake engagement ring. It had been a brilliant way to deflect unwanted male attention.

Thanks to the media that wasn't going to work anymore.

Ross Kimball was new to Vancouver, a marine biologist, and he knew no one in the city. During her hour-long interview she'd ascertained he was wealthy, judging by his nice suit, expensive watch and designer shoes. He'd only been in the city a month, he knew nothing about ice hockey, which was brilliant since she was tired of being gossip-column fodder and if she heard the words *Kade's baby-mama* bandied about again she'd stab someone with a fork.

For this moment in time she was Brodie again, matchmaker and businesswoman, and not the woman Kade impregnated. Win.

"As soon as I receive your background report and after I receive your first payment, I'll start the process."

Ross smiled. "Great. Would you like another cup of tea? Juice? Coffee?"

Brodie started to refuse but then she saw loneliness flicker in his eyes. What would it hurt to spend ten minutes talking to this guy? And it would be refreshing to talk to someone who did not want to discuss her and Kade and the baby she was expecting. Instead of refusing she nodded and leaned back in her chair. "Okay. I'll have an orange juice."

They spoke of the weather and the city and Ross's impressions of her hometown. "So, how did you become a matchmaker?" Ross asked.

Brodie gave him the standard spiel and when she was finished, added softly, "I hope I find you someone you can connect with."

"Are you...connected with anyone?"

She'd opened the door to these questions so she'd give him a little leeway. "It's complicated."

"It usually is."

"I'm seeing a guy. We're friends. Good friends."

"You're not in love with him?"

How could she answer when she wasn't sure what the answer was? How could she be in love with Kade when what they had was so different from what she had before? Jay had been sunshine and light, easygoing and happy-go-lucky. Kade was powerful, frequently sarcastic and reticent. The two men were galaxies apart. How could she possibly love such wildly differing men?

Was it love or was it just lust?

"What are you thinking about?" Ross asked.

"The difference between love and lust," Brodie replied.

"Tell me."

"Love is an intense affection for each other. It takes times to grow." Like fifteen years. "Lust is based on physical attraction." Lust was wanting to jump Kade every time he walked into the room. "It can transform into love over time. Love is about how interconnected two people are."

She and Kade were having a baby together. How much more interconnected could they be? He knew about Jay and her parents. Her great-aunt regularly called his cell for a chat. His friends had become hers, she was far more comfortable in his loft than she was in her own apartment and he'd taken her car to be serviced. She picked up his laundry.

They were interconnected.

Maybe she loved him. But that thought made her feel intensely guilty because this bubbling mess of feelings she had for Kade was deeper and darker and harder and crazier than she'd ever felt for Jay. She had survived his death. She knew without qualification she could not live in a world that did not have Kade in it.

God, this was crazy! What had happened to her? Why was she doing this? She knew what it felt like to love and lose, and what if she allowed herself to delve into this emotion and all he wanted to be was her friend with brilliant benefits? What if he, tomorrow or the next day or the year after that, met the love of his life and decided to move on from her, from them? How would she stand it? How would she cope seeing him and talking to him and co-parenting with him while knowing he left her to sleep in another woman's bed? That he was holding another woman, loving her, laughing with her?

Brodie was such a fool. This had to stop. She had to pull herself back from the brink, to keep control. Yes, withdrawing from Kade would hurt but it would be nothing compared to what could happen down the line.

She could do this; she had to do this.

"Wow. That was one hell of a trip you took," Ross said, his expression speculative.

"Sorry." Brodie picked up her juice and took a long swallow. "What were we talking about?"

"Your fellow and whether you were in love with him."

"I don't believe in love." The words flew out of Brodie's mouth. Seeing his startled expression, she wished she could take them back. But then, suddenly, it was more important someone listen to what she was *saying*. Because if she could convince him, then maybe she could convince herself.

"At least not for me. I believe in sex. I believe in friendships, in being independent, in standing on my own two feet. I believe in my career, in forging my own path, in keeping an emotional distance."

"He's not the one?"

Brodie made herself meet his eyes, trying to talk herself off the ledge. "I'm having his baby and, admittedly, he's stuck around but I don't expect he'll stay for much longer. Having a baby is a novelty, a whim, and he'll lose interest. He has a low boredom threshold."

Oh, God, nothing was further from the truth, and verbalizing those lies didn't change how she felt about him. They just made her feel nasty and bitchy and guilty, dammit!

Under the table she patted her tummy and silently spoke to her child. "Ignore that, kiddo, your dad is not like that. In fact, the problem is that he is utterly wonderful. I just don't know how to handle him."

Kade stood in front of the six-by-eight-foot oil painting dominating one wall of the gallery and reluctantly admitted his father was a ridiculously talented artist.

He recognized the scene—it was the view from the rickety back porch of a cabin in Pleasant, a town north of Whitehorse. He hadn't seen the snow-covered mountains, the icy beauty of the scene, he just remembered his skates had been too small and he'd had holes in his parka. And the cupboards had held little more than bread and cereal. His father had just spent the last of his money on more oil paints, a canvas and brushes.

Kade looked at the familiar signature in the bottom corner and waited for the flood of resentment and the bite of pain that usually accompanied it. When neither arrived, he took a step back and cocked his head, wondering what had changed. His father was his father and his childhood hadn't been a barrel of laughs, but it was, thank God, long over. Being his father's son had taught him resilience, how to be tough, that nothing came to people who didn't work their asses off. James's success was proof of that. He'd been consumed by his art and had thrown everything he had into it and, judging by the fact that this painting was on sale for seventy-five thousand dollars, sacrificing a relationship with his son had been worth it.

Kade blew out his breath, finding it strange not to feel bitter. He really didn't, not anymore. His father was his father, selfish and obsessive. Nothing was important to his father but his art. That there was no hint of the child who explored the country with him in any of the paintings exhibited was a pretty big clue he wouldn't care that he was about to become a grandfather.

Art was all that mattered.

Kade had felt like that about his career until Brodie dropped back into his life. Suddenly he had to—wanted to—think about someone else. He couldn't work fourteen-or sixteen-hour days anymore. He needed to find a balance between work and home, especially when the baby arrived. Besides, he didn't want to spend so much time at work. He enjoyed Brodie's company and he wanted to spend time with his child. He would not be his father's son.

Kade turned away from the painting, finally at peace with the fact that he would never have a relationship with James. He'd lost his father a long time ago, if he'd ever really had him. Kade could finally put these particular demons to rest.

With a considerably lighter heart Kade left the gallery. As he stepped onto the sidewalk, he felt his cell vibrate. He read the incoming message from Wren and clicked on the link she provided.

A reporter had gotten Brodie to open up—through subterfuge, but still. Worse, he'd gotten her to talk about how she was feeling, something Kade had difficulty doing. Strange that it should hurt so much. She could talk to strangers but not to him?

And then there was what she'd said to the blogger, scumbag that he was. Her words had Kade feeling like a clawed hand was ripping his heart apart. She didn't believe in love, didn't want it in her life and didn't believe Kade could provide it.

Despite everything they'd gone through, she still thought he was playing games, that he would bail. He might no longer think he was his father's son but Brodie certainly did, judging by the fact that she'd publicly stated she was expecting him to leave.

Man, that hurt. Even more painful than the hunger, the fear, the uncertainty he'd experienced as a kid. To have the woman in his life thinking so little of him…it felt as if she'd used his heart as a hockey puck.

Why? Kade stared down at his screen, unable to get his feet to move. Why did he care so damn much?

Because he loved her.

Crap, dammit, hell.

Because, like he'd always been with his father, Kade was desperate for her to love him. Because, again like his father had been, Brodie was Kade's world. And, like James, Kade wasn't hers.

How the hell had he let this happen?

Kade started to walk. He needed to move or else he would scream. He was in love with her, she didn't love him. What did he do now? He could walk away, break it off. In a couple of months he could sic his lawyers on her, demanding custody rights, and they could communicate that way. He didn't have to talk to her again if he didn't want to.

He didn't want to; he felt too raw.

Or he could go to her, give her a chance to explain. See if there was anything they could salvage out of this train wreck of a relationship. No, not a relationship; Brodie didn't believe in those… He should just let the lawyers deal with it, with her, but his feet didn't agree. They just kept walking in the direction of Brodie's office.

They might, if he was really lucky, let him walk right on past her building.

* * *

It was after eight in the evening and Brodie was exhausted. She couldn't wait to go home, maybe sink into the spa bath, preferably naked, with Kade. Pushing her chair back from her desk, she stood up and winced when the button of her black pants pushed into her stomach. She was going to have to buy some bigger clothes. Her tummy was growing at an alarming rate and, unfortunately, she suspected her bottom was following the trend.

Maybe Kade could show her some exercises she could safely do to keep her butt from spreading. Her tummy was on its own.

Brodie opened her lower drawer to pull out her bag and sighed when her computer signaled the arrival of a new email. She'd never been able to ignore a ringing phone or a new message so she clicked the mouse.

What?

It took a moment for her to make sense of the words on the screen. It was from the company she and Colin used to run background reports. It was fairly important their clients were who they said they were. That they weren't broke, had a criminal record...

Because she was swamped with clients this week, she'd done the interview with Kimball before she received the background checks, something she didn't like to do. If she had waited, she would've known Ross Kimball was not who he said he was. He wasn't living at the address he stated; there were no marine biologists working in the area, or in the country, under that name and his contact numbers were bogus.

Brodie pulled out her chair and sat down. She'd been played and played well. Who was Kimball and why had he used such an elaborate ruse to meet her?

It didn't take her long to come up with an answer. Kade. And her relationship with him.

Since the world found out she was carrying Kade's baby—*a new generation of Mavericks!*—she'd been bombarded with requests for interviews and she'd refused every offer. Her standard response was a consistent and, she guessed, infuriating "no comment."

As Kade had said, the press had gone looking for a story and Ross had sneaked in via the back door. He'd played the role well, she thought. She hadn't once suspected he wasn't who he said he was.

So, who did he work for and what had he penned? And how could she find out, preferably before Wren and Kade did?

What had she told the man? They'd discussed the city and how lonely it could be, he'd flirted with her and she'd shut him down...

Shut him down by telling him she didn't believe in love...

"'Brodie Stewart is a walking contradiction, someone who earns a very healthy living matching people in that eternal quest for true love while discounting the notion for herself.'"

Brodie jerked her head up and winced when she saw Kade standing in the doorway to her office, reading from his phone. Well, guess she didn't have to go looking for the article. Kade—via the annoyingly efficient Wren, she presumed—had accessed it on his smartphone. And, judging by his furious expression, he was less than thrilled by its contents.

Brodie leaned her head against the back of her chair. "Who is he?"

"Ross Bennett. A blogger with an enormous following. Quite well-known for his ability to twist the truth,"

Kade replied, looking back down at the screen. Then he started to read, his tone flat and terrifyingly devoid of all emotion.

"In an interview with Ms. Stewart, she candidly admitted she didn't believe in love. 'I believe in sex. I believe in being independent, of standing on my own two feet. I believe in my career, in forging my own path, in keeping an emotional distance.'

"She doesn't seem to have much faith in Kade Webb, either. Webb, according to Ms. Stewart, won't stick around for the long haul. To Kade, having a baby is a novelty and she expects him to lose interest."

Brodie gripped the arms of her chair. Oh, this was bad. This was very bad.

"Luckily for the Mavericks, Bennett is regarded as a trash-talking, sensation-seeking journalist. He is best to be ignored. Wren thought he was sucking the story out of thin air, but I heard your voice in those words. What happened?"

"He posed as a client and he fooled me," Brodie reluctantly admitted.

Kade leaned a shoulder into the wall, his face a blank mask. His eyes were flat and emotionless and his mouth was a hard line. Kade was, she knew, incandescently angry. Maybe this was the final straw; she'd pushed him away so many times…maybe this time she'd pushed him too far. She'd tested his commitment to sticking by her and their child and he'd passed every test. But this was no longer a game, she realized; she'd pushed too hard and too far.

She didn't need him to verbalize his intentions; he

was done. The moment she'd both dreaded and welcomed was here and the pain would follow. She would deal with it and then she would go back to her safe, emotion-free life.

The life she wanted, she reminded herself. The life she felt comfortable in. The lonely, color-free, safe, boring life.

"Did I ever give you reason to think I would fade away?"

"No."

"That I was playing at being a father?"

Brodie shook her head.

"I read that blog while standing outside the gallery exhibiting my father's latest work. It struck me you could've been describing my father—that's the way he was, the way he acted."

God, she hadn't thought of that. Hadn't meant him to think that. He was *nothing* like the man who sired him. "I'm sorry."

"Being sorry doesn't help, neither does how I feel about you." Kade shook his head. "I can't keep doing this, Brodie. I can't fight your fear anymore, you've got to do that yourself. I told you I'll be here for you but you don't want to believe it and I can't force you to."

Kade shoved a hand into his hair. "For you to think that, verbalize it, means you either believe it or you want to believe it. It doesn't matter which. Either way it tells me you are intolerant of intimacy and you deliberately cut yourself off. And this—" Kade showed her the screen "—this is you running. I'm not going to be the sap who runs after you, begging you to give me another chance. I did that with my father, I will not do it again. I've given you enough chances. I'm worth more than that and, frankly, so are you."

Brodie felt the kick in her stomach, in her heart, in her head. "Okay."

"Okay? That's it? That's all you have to say?"

She wouldn't throw herself at his knees and beg him not to leave her. It was better this way; it had to be. "What do you want to do about the baby?"

"The baby? God!" Kade looked like he wanted to put his fist through a wall. "Right now I'm so damn mad at you I can't think! Do you not understand you are throwing away something pretty amazing to hide behind those walls you've built up? I'm scared, too, Brodie. Raising kids, being together, is meant to be scary!"

"There are no guarantees, Kade."

"Of course there aren't! You just take what happiness you can and run with it. You just feel damn grateful for it." Kade rubbed his hands over his face. "I'm talking to a freaking brick wall. Have fun hiding out, Brodie. As I said, I'm done."

Brodie nodded once and bit her bottom lip, everything in her trying to keep the tears at bay. "Okay."

"Okay? That's all you have? For God's sake…" Kade slapped his hand against the door frame as he whipped around. "Talking to a friggin' wall."

Brodie waited until she heard the door to the outer office slam closed before she finally allowed herself to cry. Hunched over and hurting, she watched from a place far away as tears ran off her face and dropped to the carpet below.

Yeah, the pain was here, accompanied by desolation and despair. It was okay, she'd been here before and she'd handled it.

She could do it again.

But right now she just wanted to cry, for herself, for

her child, for the butterflies in her stomach that were dying a slow and excruciating death.

Kade was convinced he held the record for the fastest heartbreak in the history of the world. Within the space of the afternoon he'd realized he loved Brodie and that nothing would ever come of it. His mind wanted to stop loving her but he knew his heart always would.

Kade loosened his tight grip on the stem of his wineglass and stared at False Creek, for the first time not seeing the beauty below him. It had been twilight when he returned home from work tonight, three weeks since he'd walked out of Brodie's office and her life. And while he could remember the exact date and time his life turned dark, he had no idea what time it was now.

Brodie had done what he'd expected, maintained radio silence. They hadn't spoken, messaged, emailed or texted each other and he felt adrift. Before Brodie hurtled her way into his life he'd felt content with his lot, generally happy. He hadn't wanted a relationship and had been content to have an affair here, a one-night stand there. No promises, no hassle.

Brodie had been nothing but a hassle and an all-around pain in his ass, but when she wasn't annoying him, she brought light and laughter to his life. Kade placed his forearm over his eyes and cursed his burning eyes.

He finally loved someone with everything he had and she wanted jack from him. Life was laughing at him.

He wanted to go to Brodie, wanted to beg her to allow him to be part of her life, but he knew that was a road heading straight to a deeper level of hell. He'd be seeing her again in five months or so anyway, and maybe by then he would've stopped thinking about what they could've had.

Growing up with his father had taught Kade that chasing rainbows led to disappointment. You couldn't force someone to love you. Love wasn't something to be demanded; it either was or it…wasn't.

He loved Brodie and while he suspected she could love him, she didn't. She wouldn't allow herself to love him and he wasn't going to beg. He wanted everything and he wouldn't settle for anything less. He couldn't; the resentment would kill him and, worse, it would kill his love for her.

So he'd love her from a distance for the rest of his life. That was the way it had to be so the sooner he got used to feeling like crap, the better.

Kade sat up, rested his forearms on his thighs and dangled the glass between his knees. He could wallow or he could distract himself. He could call Quinn and they could go clubbing. He could go to Mac and Rory's for dinner. He could do some work or a gym session.

What he wasn't going to do was to sit on this couch in the dark and feel sorry for himself. Yet it was another fifteen minutes before he got up and another ten before he crossed the room to flick on some lights.

He just needed time, he told himself. A millennium or two might be long enough to get over her.

Twelve

The summer holidays were almost over and the vast beaches on the west side of Vancouver Island had been, for all intents and purposes, returned to the birds and the crabs that were the year-round residents of the island. Soon the leaves would start to turn, winter would drop the temperature and the storms would roll in.

But for now, Brodie and Poppy walked the empty beach, bare feet digging into the sand, watching the rolling waves kiss the shore. The stiff breeze pushed Brodie's thin hoodie against her round tummy and kicked sand up against her bright blue yoga pants. She loved this place, Brodie realized. Away from Vancouver, away from the city, she could breathe and think.

"When are you going to stop punishing yourself for living?" Poppy asked as she took Brodie's arm.

Brodie pushed a hunk of hair out of her eyes and squinted at Poppy. "I'm not punishing myself."

"Really? Well, the way I see it there is a man on the

mainland who wants to be part of your life, who wants to raise this baby with you, but you are determined to take the hard road and do it all by your little lonesome. Is that not punishing yourself?"

"That's me protecting myself," Brodie retorted.

"From what? Pain?" Poppy asked. "From loneliness?"

Brodie stared out to sea and focused her attention on a ship on the horizon and ignored Poppy's probing questions. She didn't want to think about Kade, though there was little else she thought about these days. She definitely didn't want to talk about him.

But Poppy wasn't intimidated by Brodie's scowling face or her frown. "News flash, you are so damn lonely you don't know what to do with yourself."

"Pops, please."

Poppy dropped her arm and they stood side by side, looking out to sea. Poppy released a long breath. "Do you see that ship?"

She'd only been staring at it for the past half hour. Brodie nodded, glad Poppy had dropped the subject of Kade. "It's a container ship, probably headed for Japan."

Poppy nodded, her expression contemplative. "There's a saying about ships and leaving the harbor… do you know it?"

Brodie shook her head.

"It goes something like this—'a ship in the harbor is safe, but that's not what ships are built for.'"

Brodie wrinkled her nose. How silly she'd been to think Poppy had dropped the subject; Poppy only stopped when she'd brought you around to her way of thinking.

"Ships aren't built for safety but neither are humans.

We should take risks. We *have* to take risks. You and Kade? Well, that's a risk worth taking."

"I'm scared. Of loving him too much, scared it won't last forever. Scared he thinks he loves me but only loves me because of this baby. So scared he might—"

"Die?" Poppy interrupted. "What if you die? What if a freak tsunami washes you off the beach right now? What then? What if you die giving birth? What then?"

"That would suck," Brodie admitted.

"It really would. But would you want Kade to be alone for the rest of his life, to—metaphorically speaking—wear black widower's weeds, too scared to love again, laugh again? To live again?"

Dammit. She knew where Poppy was going with this but she couldn't find anything to say to get out of this quandary. All she could think of was that it was easier for Poppy to say it than for Brodie to do it.

"Well?" Poppy demanded.

"But—"

"There are no buts. Jay would hate to see you like this. Your parents would be so disappointed in you." Poppy grabbed Brodie's chin and forced her to meet faded blue eyes. Poppy's body might be old but her eyes were alive and fierce and determined.

"Do you love him?"

Brodie couldn't lie, wouldn't lie. "Yes."

"These are your choices and you need to think them through. You can wallow and live a miserable half life until you die. You can keep punishing yourself, keep disappointing yourself because you don't have the balls to choose differently."

"God, Poppy."

Poppy ignored Brodie's desperate laugh. "Or you can take your butt back to the city, throw yourself at his feet and apologize for being an ass. Find out if he loves you, if this is a forever thing. Face your fears."

"That's a hard decision to make, even harder to do," Brodie protested.

"Do it anyway," Poppy suggested. "Be brave enough to be happy, Brodie. Don't let your fear win. You are stronger than that, more courageous than you think. Just do it, my darling. Reach out and grab the future you've always wanted."

"But what if I'm too late?" Brodie asked, unsure why she was asking this question because she wasn't going to go to Kade, wasn't going to ask for another chance. That was crazy talk…wasn't it?

Poppy's sweet smile held more than a trace of satisfaction. And triumph. "What if you're not?" She placed a wrinkled hand on Brodie's face. "Don't make me get tough with you, Brodie."

"This isn't you being tough?" Brodie demanded with a sarcastic laugh.

"Honey, I haven't even warmed up yet. I can go on for hours," Poppy stated prosaically. "You might as well just give in now and save us both the time and energy."

Brodie put her arms around Poppy's waist and rested her head on her great-aunt's shoulder. "Well, when you put it like that…"

Brodie used her shaking index finger to key in the code that would take her straight up to Kade's apartment. She hoped he hadn't changed the code. That would be mortifying. She entered the last number and waited for the elevator doors to slide open. When they did she had to force herself to step inside.

She could do this. She had to do this.

If she didn't speak to Kade tonight, she never would.

She would talk herself out of being brave. She'd allow herself to backslide, to rationalize why she would be better off alone.

Talk the truth, even if your voice shakes.

Poppy's words stuck with Brodie and she repeated them to herself as the elevator took her higher, and closer, to the love of her life.

And he was that. Jay, dear Jay, had been marvelous, but her feelings for Kade were deeper, harder and stronger. Maybe that's why she'd been fighting this so hard. Loving Kade wouldn't be easy but he'd be worth it.

She had to tell him, had to see if he felt the same.

As the elevator stopped at the top floor she touched her stomach in that age-old protective gesture women had been using through the centuries.

Wish me luck, baby. Here's hoping we get to be a family.

Brodie stepped into the dark loft, the lights from downtown Vancouver dancing in the floor-to-ceiling windows. The apartment was ridiculously quiet and she bit her lip, feeling like an idiot. She hadn't considered the notion that Kade might not be here. He could be anywhere—with his friends, out of town, on a date. The only thing worse than Kade coming home with a date would be finding Kade upstairs in bed with another woman. With the doors closed, she wouldn't be able to hear a thing.

It had only been three weeks. He wouldn't have moved on so soon, would he? Then again, she'd kept pushing him away, telling him that what they had was only sex. Maybe he was upstairs, doing all those fabulous things he did to her...

Brodie threw her bag onto the couch and stormed toward the staircase. If she'd been bawling her eyes out

while he slept his way through the pack of puck bunnies, Brodie might be forced to do something drastic.

What, she wasn't sure, but it would hurt. A lot.

Brodie flung open the door to his bedroom and hurtled over the threshold, stopping when she realized his
enormous bed was neatly made and, crucially, empty.
Brodie closed her eyes and hauled in a deep breath.

"You're acting like a crazy woman, Stewart," she
muttered.

"Can't say that I disagree."

Brodie whirled around and saw Kade standing in
the doorway to his en suite bathroom, a towel wrapped
around his narrow hips. Man, he was gorgeous. How
could she have walked away from that?

He was sexy and hot but he was also a good man.
Someone who was loyal and kind and considerate and...
hers.

"What are you doing here, Brodie?" Kade asked, his
expression forbidding.

"Uh..." Okay, she was being silly but she just had to
make sure. "Is there anyone in there with you?"

Kade turned his head to look back into the bathroom.
"Busted. Come on out, honey," he called.

Brodie's heart ker-plunked. She placed a hand on her
sternum and tried to find something to say.

"God, Brodie, don't be an idiot," Kade snapped.
"There's no one here. I was just messing with you."

Brodie scowled. "Don't do that, okay?"

"I think I've got a right," Kade retorted. He pushed
his hand through his wet hair. "I can't stand here, almost naked, with you in the room. Why don't you go
downstairs and keep walking across the apartment until
you hit the elevator. I doubt there's anything you have
to say that I want to hear."

"No." Brodie lifted her chin.

"*No?*"

"No, I'm not going to do that."

Kade shrugged, sent her a sarcastic smile and walked to his closet. Dropping the towel to the floor, Brodie watched him go into the small room, bare-ass naked. Man, he was so messing with her.

"So why are you here? Missing the sex?" Kade asked as he reached for a pair of sweats.

"Yes," Brodie replied, thinking honesty was the best policy. "Of course I am. We are fabulous together and I love making love with you."

Kade pulled on the sweats and turned, gripping the top of the door frame with white fingers. "Is that what you're back for?" He took in her leggings and bohemian shirt. "Fine. But you're a bit overdressed. Strip."

"Stop being a jerk, Kade," Brodie snapped.

"Then again, if it's just sex you're back for, then I am not interested." Kade dropped his arms. He rubbed his hands over his face and when he looked at her again, those beautiful eyes were bleak. And his voice, when he spoke again, sounded desolate. "Just go, Brodie. Please."

She'd done this, Brodie thought, ashamed of herself. She'd hurt him. She'd wounded this powerful, smart man just because she'd been too scared to take a chance. To live. Well, that stopped now, right this minute. She needed to be better than that; her child—their child— and Kade deserved better. But how to tell him? What to say?

Brodie walked past the bed to the open balcony doors and thought about Vancouver Island. Remembering Poppy and their conversation, Brodie pushed her shoulders back and placed her hands behind her, anchoring herself to the door frame.

"When I was about eleven, I was a bridesmaid and I fell in love with the idea of love. I became slightly obsessed with weddings, with the idea of happily-ever-after. Jay was the boy from down the road and even then, I thought he might be the one."

Brodie risked looking at Kade, relieved to see he was interested in what she was saying. His expression was still remote and, to be honest, scarily forbidding, but he hadn't kicked her out. It was progress but she had a long way to go. "I made a scrapbook. What my dress would look like, the color scheme, my bridesmaids' dresses, the whole shebang."

"Is there a point to this?" Kade asked, impatient.

Brodie ignored him. "Strangely, I pretty much nailed what I wanted for a wedding at eleven. When I flipped open the scrapbook shortly before the accident, excited because Jay and I were moving on from being best friends to something more, there was little I wanted changed. But one aspect jumped out at me and it's been bugging me."

"Pray tell."

Still sarcastic, Brodie sighed. "Jay was dark-haired and blue-eyed, short and stocky," Brodie continued. "My eleven-year-old self didn't have him in mind when she was imagining her groom. Jay looked nothing like the tall, blond, sexy man in my scrapbook."

Kade didn't say anything but Brodie noticed his expression had turned from remote to speculative.

"Do you think my younger self knew something I didn't? Even then? Don't you think that's spooky?"

"I don't give a damn about your eleven-year-old self," Kade stated, his tone brisk. "I want to know what you want, right now."

Right, time to jump off this cliff. God, she hoped

he was going to catch her. "You." Her voice cracked
with emotion. "I just want you. Any way I can get you."

"Explain that," Kade demanded, his eyes locked on
hers.

Brodie wished he would come to her, initiate contact. "This has nothing to do with the fact we have
such incredible sexual chemistry, or that you're my
baby's father. Or that you are hot, which, I have to say,
is a bonus..." Brodie smiled but Kade didn't react. He
didn't say a damn thing, just continued to stare at her
with those hot, demanding eyes.

Oh, crap. He was going to make her say it. She
hauled in a breath and gathered her courage. "I love
you. I just want to be with you." Brodie bit her bottom
lip. "I'm so sorry about what I said, did. I was trying to
fall out of love with you. But I need you to know I believe you are nothing like your father, that I know you
will be a spectacular dad."

Kade rubbed his jaw and then the back of his neck.
"Jesus, Brodie."

"I'm sorry. For everything I said because I was so
damn scared." Brodie stared at her red ballet pumps.
She turned her head and looked at Kade. He seemed
gobsmacked and, she had to admit, not very damn
happy at her proclamation. She'd been too late. She'd
lost him.

Brodie forced her rubbery legs to walk toward the
door. She scooped up her bag as she walked past the
bed.

"What do you want from me, Brodie?" Kade intercepted her and placed both his hands on her upper arms.

Brodie shrugged. "Nothing you can't give me, openly
and honestly. I just want you in my life, any way I can
get you. With or without the baby, I love you. It's taken

me a while, but now it's suddenly simple. It's fine that you don't love me. I still want you to be my friend, to co-parent with you, to be our baby's dad."

Kade cupped the side of her face with his big hand and she finally saw the beginning of a smile. "For a bright woman, you can be incredibly dense on occasion."

What did that mean? What was he trying to say?

Kade's thumb drifted over her bottom lip, down her chin. "I can love you. I do love you."

Brodie felt her heart expand, fill with a warm, bright light. Before it could start dancing around her rib cage, she grabbed it in an iron fist. "In what way?"

"In every way that counts. " Kade kissed the corner of her mouth. "And more. A lot more."

She loosened the hold on her heart. "Meaning?"

"Meaning I love you, too. I will always love you. I never expected this to happen to me, not like this. We met again and I feel like I've been riding a hurricane and I've loved every minute. You drive me nuts, you turn me on. I think about you all the damn time." He swallowed some emotion and Brodie blinked back her tears.

"I imagine the family we can have, the fun we'll have," Kade continued, "I dream about the love that will color our lives."

Brodie smiled slowly, her heart dancing. She placed her hands on his pecs and rested her forehead on his chest. "Oh, God, I feel light-headed. I am so relieved." Kade's hand cupped the back of her head. "While I was running away, I realized I'd so rather be scared with you than be without you. I'd rather stand in an electrical storm with you than be safe by myself. You're my it, Kade—the blond, big man my eleven-year-old self recognized so long ago."

"Brodie." Kade's arms tightened around her and easily lifted her so her mouth aligned with his. "Welcome home, baby. Don't run away anymore."

"Thank you for giving me another chance," she murmured against his lips.

"I've missed you." A mischievous smile crossed his face as humor and relief chased the last residue of hurt and disappointment from his eyes. "So does this mean I have to get rid of the girl in the bathroom?"

Brodie tapped on the door to Kade's office and popped her head in. It was the end of the day and her man sat behind his desk, his fingers flying across his keyboard. He looked up and the frown on his face disappeared as his smile reached his eyes. They'd been back together for a month and the butterflies in her stomach were still going mad, occasionally accompanied by a tiny flutter that was all Baby Webb.

"Hey, gorgeous." Kade leaned back in his chair as she closed the door behind her. She walked over to his desk and plopped herself into his lap, lifting her face for a thorough, very sexy kiss. Kade pulled away and placed his hand on her round tummy. "How's my other girl?"

"Your *boy* has started to play ice hockey in my womb," Brodie replied. "We have a doctor's appointment next week."

"I haven't forgotten." Kade looked at his watch. "As much as I love the idea of you surprising me at work, I thought you had a late meeting."

"I did but I canceled." She was about to add she forgot to wear her fake engagement ring but she knew that might prompt Kade to suggest he buy her a real ring.

She knew a proposal was coming but she wanted to do something different...

Hence her visit to his office.

Brodie climbed off his lap and sat on the edge of his desk so she could see his face. "So, Wren called me and told me she's posted the final blog on our endeavor to find your happily-ever-after."

"You're my happily-ever-after." Kade placed a hand on her knee. "I told her to take that nonsense down. It's silly to have it on the site when everyone knows we are together, a couple, in love and that we are having a baby."

"Still—" Brodie tapped her finger on the screen of his laptop "—take a look."

"You've seen it?" Kade asked, sitting up.

"I approved it. I hope you do, too." She licked her lips and watched as he double-clicked the icon on the screen to bring up the Mavericks' website. He went to the relevant page and started to read. Brodie tucked her shaking hands under her thighs and read along with him.

There was a photo of them in the top right-hand corner with the words *Kade's future* as a title.

As a matchmaker, I have matched many couples and it gives me great pleasure to play a small part in helping people find happiness in love. I have, in the process of trying to find Kade's life partner, found the same happiness and nobody was more surprised than I was when I realized Kade was mine.

I never thought that love, permanence and commitment would be a part of my future again but I am honored and thrilled to have found it with Kade.

He and our child are my future, my joy, my
heart. So, sorry, ladies of Vancouver, but Kade
Webb is officially and permanently off the market.
Yours,
Brodie

Brodie found her courage and said the words she'd
been practicing for the past week. "So, my mom's engagement ring is very real and I'd like to wear it. Are
you game, Webb?"

Brodie watched as Kade slowly turned and sent her
his charming, emotional, full-blown smile. He leaned
back in his chair and linked his hands across his stomach. "You proposing, Stewart?"

Brodie lifted one shoulder. "It's a suggestion..."

"I like your suggestion," Kade softly answered her.

Warmth coursed through her, relaxing and rejuvenating her at the same time.

Kade gestured to the screen. "Why this, Brodes? It's
a pretty public declaration."

That was the point. Brodie attempted to explain. "I
know, it'll be the only time I'll ever do or say something
about us on social media, but I needed to. I've lived in
the shadows for so long. I've protected myself so well,
I wanted to show you exactly how committed I am to
you, to us. I wanted you to know I'm still scared but I'm
not going to run away." She stared at her shoes. "Maybe
it was just me breaking through my cocoon."

Kade stood and tipped up her face. "Thank you." He
placed his hands on the desk and dropped a sexy, sweet
kiss on her mouth. "I love you so damn much and I can't
wait to marry you. Hand the ring over and I'll do the
bended-knee thing."

Brodie grinned. "I can't wait to see you on bended knee and I love you back."

Kade smiled against her lips. "First and last time. Now that our future is sorted, let's talk about the important stuff."

"Where we're going to live—your loft—and when we're going to get married? I was thinking the sooner the better."

Kade's eyes glinted. "Actually, I was talking about the *really* important stuff, like how soon I can get you naked—"

The door burst open and they broke off their deep kiss and looked around to see Quinn standing in the doorway.

"Oh, for God's sake, do you two do anything other than grope each other?" he demanded, slapping his hand over his eyes.

"Not really, no." Kade scowled at his friend. "What do you want, jerkoid?"

"Rory's on her way to the hospital, she's in labor. We're going to have our first Maverick baby!"

Kade grabbed his jacket and Brodie's hand. "We're right behind you." At the door he kissed Brodie again and tucked her into his side. "The future looks good, babe."

Brodie sighed and placed a hand on her stomach. "It really does."

And this time, for the first time in far too long, she was convinced of it.

* * * * *

MARRIED TO
THE MAVERICK
MILLIONAIRE

JOSS WOOD

This book is dedicated to my own Cal,
the port I run to in any storm.

I am so grateful to have you in my life.

One

Quinn Rayne flew across the parking lot on the Coal Harbour promenade, his feet slapping an easy but fast rhythm as he dodged both tourists and residents taking a late afternoon stroll on the paved and pretty walking and biking path next to the marina. The earbuds in his ears and his dark sunglasses were an excellent excuse to ignore the calls of recognition, the pointed fingers.

Even after a decade of being in the spotlight, he still wasn't used to being an object of curious, sometimes disapproving, fascination. Surely the residents of Vancouver could find someone new to discuss? There had to be someone in the city who was a bigger badass than he was reputed to be.

As he approached the marina, he slowed his sprint to a jog and then to a walk, fingers against the pulse point in his neck and his eyes on his watch. After two minutes he nodded, satisfied. He might not be playing professional ice hockey anymore, but he was as fit as he'd ever been. He'd see whether his players, when they returned to practice next week, had also maintained their fitness. For their sakes, he hoped so.

Quinn walked to the access gate to his wharf. He punched in his code to open the gate and jogged down to where his yacht was berthed. Because he owned one of the prime sites, he had unobstructed views of Burrard Inlet, with Stanley Park to his left and Grouse Mountain in front of him. Living on the water was more adventurous than living in a house and God knew how much he craved adventure.

Quinn stepped onto the *Red Delicious* and quickly ran up the steps to the main deck, the quickest way to access the living area. He slid open the door, pulled his earbuds from his neck and tossed them, his cap and his sunglasses onto the sleek table to his right. He glanced at his watch and wondered if he had time for a shower before Mac and Kade arrived to report back on a meeting they'd attended earlier with Warren Bayliss, their partner and investor.

Bayliss was an essential part of the ongoing process to buy the Mavericks franchise from the current owner, Myra Hasselback, who was also considering selling out to a Russian billionaire who owned a string of boring sports franchises. Quinn didn't need his brother's string of degrees to know that when he, a full Mavericks partner, was excluded from the meeting Warren called, then there was trouble in paradise.

And that it had his name on it.

Quinn walked into the massive open-plan living area and immediately noticed the small form tucked into the corner of his oversized sofa, a cup of coffee in her hand, staring out of the floor-to-ceiling glass windows. One foot was tucked up under her butt; her other—long, slim and sexy—was bent. She'd been sitting like that on the beach at Sandy Cove the first day he'd met her, gap-toothed and grinning, a six-year-old dynamo. She was his girl-next-door or, to be technical, the girl from three houses down. His childhood companion and his teenage confidante.

Sensing his presence, she turned her head, deep-red curls bouncing. Freckles splattered across her nose and onto her cheeks, each one perfect. God, he loved her freckles, had missed those freckles, her face.

He slapped his hands on his hips, not sure if he was just imagining her or if she was really sitting there, bright hair and makeup-free but so damn real he could barely breathe.

"*Red*. What the hell are you doing here?"

Her smile slammed into his sternum and Quinn's heart bounced off his rib cage. Callahan's deep, dark eyes danced as she jumped to her feet and Quinn found himself smiling, properly smiling, for the first time that day. He reached out, grabbed her and swept her into his arms. She weighed less than a feather and he easily whirled her around. The scent of wildflowers hovered around her. It was in the hair he buried his face into, on the warm, smooth skin he could feel beneath the barrier of her shirt. Her laugh rumbled through her and instantly lightened his mood. She'd always had the naughtiest, dirtiest laugh.

Cal Adam was back and his world made a little more sense.

Her feet still off the ground, Cal placed her hands on his shoulders and pushed away from him, her eyes clashing with his. "Hi."

"Hi back."

"You always had the prettiest eyes," Cal said, the tips of her fingers coming to rest on his cheekbone. "Ice green with a ring of emerald." She patted his cheek and rubbed her hand through his too-long, overly full beard. "Not sure about this, though. You're hiding that sexy face."

Quinn tightened his arms, his lower body responding as she wound her legs around his waist. A picture of her wet and naked, in exactly this position, appeared on his internal big screen, but he brushed it away. This was Cal, his oldest friend, his best friend—having lascivious thoughts about her was weird. And wrong.

He patted her small, tight butt. "Glad to see that you've picked up a bit of weight since the last time I saw you." It had been nearly two years ago and she'd been in hospital with a stomach bug she'd caught in Panama. Cal had looked almost skeletal. Always petite, at least she now looked on the healthy side of slim.

Cal smiled again, dropped a quick kiss on his lips, a kiss that had Quinn wanting more, needing to find out whether her lips were as soft as they appeared, whether that mouth that looked like it had been made for sin could, actually, sin. What was his problem? Was he now such a player that it was a habit to take every encounter with every woman to the bedroom? Even Cal?

Cal wiggled, her feet dropped to the maple floor and Quinn released her. She stepped back and pushed a curl behind her ear.

"*Red Delicious*, Q? That's an odd name for a boat." Cal made a production of fluttering her eyelashes. "Or did you name it after me?"

He grinned. "You wish I did. Nope, it was pure co-incidence."

"Honestly, she's stunning," Cal stated, looking around.

Quinn followed her gaze. The sleek lines of the sixty-five-meter yacht were echoed in the minimalist furniture and cool white, grey and beige. Sometimes he thought it a little stark…

"It needs some color. Some bold prints, some bright cushions," Cal said, echoing his thoughts. Despite their long time apart, they still thought along the same lines.

"She's beautiful and bigger than your last yacht. How many does she sleep?"

"Ten on the lower deck. The master cabin is aft with a walk-in wardrobe and spa bath and there's another full cabin forward. Two small cabins midship There's another smaller, cozier lounge…that's where I watch TV, wind down. Two decks, one off the main bedroom and another entertainment deck with a Jacuzzi."

"Impressive. I want to see it all. When did you acquire her?"

"About a year back." Quinn ran a hand down Cal's hair and her curls wound around his knuckle. The smell of her shampoo wafted over to him and he wondered when Cal's hair had turned so soft and silky. So damned girly. Cal shoved her hands into the back pockets of her skinny jeans and arched her back. The white silk T-shirt pulled against her chest and Quinn noticed her small, perky breasts and that she was wearing a lacy, barely-there push-up bra.

He rolled his shoulders, uncomfortable. *Right. Enough with that, Rayne.*

Quinn rubbed the back of his neck as he walked across the living area to the kitchen. He opened the double-door fridge and peered inside, hoping that the icy air would cool his lascivious thoughts.

"Water?" he asked, his words muffled.

Cal shook her head. "No, thanks."

He slammed the fridge door closed and cracked the lid on the water bottle before lifting it to his lips.

"How is your dad?" he asked, remembering why she was back in the city, back home.

"Okay. The triple heart bypass was successful. I went straight from the airport to the hospital and spent some time with him. He was awake and making plans so I suppose that's a good sign."

"I'm glad he's okay."

"He'll be fine. Stressing about when he can get back to work." He saw the worry in her eyes, heard fear in her flat tone. "The doctors said he won't be able to return to work for a couple of months and that sent him into a tailspin."

"He had the operation a few days ago. Maybe he should relax a little. The foundation won't grind to a stop because he isn't there."

The Adam Foundation was the wealthiest charitable organization in Canada, funded by the accumulated wealth of generations of her Adam ancestors. Money from the Adam Foundation allowed an ever-changing group of volunteers, and Cal, to travel the world to assist communities who needed grassroots help.

Cal bit the inside of her lip and her arched eyebrows pulled together. "He'll need somebody to run it until he's back on his feet."

"Is that person you?" he asked, annoyed by the spurt of excitement he felt. God, he and Cal hadn't lived in the same city for ages and having her around would be a very nice change.

"Maybe," Cal replied, unenthusiastic. "We'll talk about it later."

Quinn frowned as he tried to work out why Cal felt so ambivalent toward the city they'd been raised in. It was beautiful, interesting and eclectic, but Cal only came home when she absolutely had to. Maybe it had something to do with the fact that her husband had been killed when the light aircraft he'd been piloting crashed into a mountain to the north of the city around four…no, it had to be five years ago now.

She'd married the same week she turned twenty-four and, thanks to their massive argument about her nuptials—Quinn had loudly and vociferously told her that she'd lost her mind—he'd missed both her birthday and her wedding that year.

"Does the press corps know you are home?" Quinn asked, changing the subject. Like him, Cal had a hate-hate affair with the press.

"Everyone knows. They were at the airport and at the hospital."

"Remind me again where you flew in from?" It had been a couple of months since they last spoke and, while they exchanged emails regularly, he couldn't recall where her last project had been. Then again, Cal—as the troubleshooter for her family's foundation—jumped from project to project, country to country, going where she was needed to ensure everything ran smoothly. She could be in Latin America one week and in the Far East the next. Cal collected frequent-flier miles like politicians collected votes.

"Africa. Lesotho, to be precise. I was working on a project to counter soil erosion." Cal nodded toward the center island of the kitchen, to his landline and cell phone. "Your cell rang and then your phone. Mac left a voicemail saying that he and Wren and Kade were on the way over to discuss today's train wreck." She tipped her head and narrowed her amazing, blue-black eyes. "What trouble have you landed yourself in now, Q?"

Quinn heard Mac's and Kade's heavy footsteps on

the outside stairs and lifted a shoulder. "You know what they say, Red—the trouble with trouble is that it starts off as fun."

After greeting his best friends—who were also his partners, his colleagues—and Wren, the Mavericks' PR guru, he gestured for them all to take a seat and offered drinks. While he made coffee, Cal was hugged and kissed by his friends and asked how she'd been. It didn't matter how infrequently they saw her, Quinn mused, she automatically slotted back into his life and was immediately accepted because Mac and Kade understood that, just like they did, Cal had his back.

Quinn delivered mugs of coffee and sighed at their doom-and-gloom faces. He could deal with their anxiety—Mac and Kade constantly worried that he'd kill himself chasing his need for adrenaline—but he didn't like their frustration and, yeah, their anger. His teammates and their head of publicity were pissed. Again. Not necessarily at him but at the situation he'd found himself in.

He tended to find himself in a lot of *situations*.

Hell, Quinn thought as he pushed his fingers through his sweat-dampened hair and gathered it into a knot at the back of his head, *here we go again*.

"Make yourself some coffee, bro. You're going to need it," Mac suggested, leaning back and placing his booted foot on his opposite knee.

"I'll do it," Cal offered.

Though he appreciated her offer, Quinn shook his head. "Thanks, Red, but I've got it."

Quinn ran his hand over his thick beard as he walked around the island into the kitchen to where his coffee machine stood. He picked up his favorite mug, placed it under the spout and pushed the button for a shot of espresso. The machine gurgled, dispensed the caffeine and Quinn hit the button again. He wanted whiskey, but he supposed that a double espresso would have to do.

"So how did the meeting with Warren go?" he asked as he turned around.

Mac, as forthright as ever, gestured to Cal. "Maybe we should do this in private."

Cal immediately stood up and Quinn shook his head. "You know that you can talk in front of Cal. What I know she can know. I trust her."

Mac nodded and rubbed his jaw as Cal sat down again. "Your choice."

"Warren is less than happy with you and he's considering pulling out of the deal."

Quinn gripped the granite island to keep his balance, feeling like a forty-foot wave had passed under the bow of the yacht. "*What?*"

"And why?" Cal demanded, his shock echoed on her face. "What has Quinn done?"

"Is this about the interview Storm gave?" Quinn asked.

"Partly," Kade replied.

Quinn took a sip of his coffee, planted his feet apart and looked out to the water. Earlier in the week he'd woken up to the news that his three-week stand had, a month after he ended it, decided to share the intimate, ugly details of their affair and final breakup. Storm tearfully told the world, on an extremely popular morning breakfast show, that Quinn was emotionally unavailable, that he constantly and consistently cheated on her. For those reasons, she now needed intensive therapy.

None of it was true, but she'd sounded damn convincing.

He'd been played; the world was still being played. He'd made it very clear to her that he wasn't looking for a relationship—and three weeks did not constitute a relationship!—but she'd turned their brief and, to be honest, forgettable affair into a drama. Storm's interview was a massive publicity stunt, the next installment in keeping her admittedly gorgeous face in the news.

"Come and sit down, Quinn," Kade said, gesturing to a chair with his foot. Quinn dropped his long frame into the chair and rested his head on the padded back. His eyes darted from Kade's and Mac's faces to Cal's. Her deep, dark eyes—the exact color of his midnight-blue superbike—reflected worry and concern.

"It's just the latest episode in a series of bad press you've received and Warren is concerned that this is an ongoing trend. He told us, flat out, the Mavericks can't afford any more bad press and that you are the source."

"Does he want me out of the partnership?" Quinn demanded, his heart in his throat.

"He's hinting at it."

Quinn muttered an obscenity. The Mavericks—being Mac and Kade's partner—was what he did and a large part of who he was. Coaching the team was his solace, his hobby and, yeah, his career. He freakin' loved what he did.

But to own and grow the franchise, they needed Bayliss. Bayliss was their link to bigger and better sponsorship deals. He had media connections they could only dream about, connections they needed to grow the Mavericks franchise. But their investor thought Quinn was the weak link.

Craphelldammit.

Quinn looked at Cal and she slid off the barstool to sit on his chair, her arm loosely draped around his shoulders. Damn, he was glad she was back in town, glad she was here. He rarely needed anyone, but right now he needed her.

Her unconditional support, her humor, her solidity.

He looked at Wren, their PR guru. "Is he right? Am I damaging the Mavericks' brand?" he asked, his normally deep voice extra raspy with stress.

Wren flicked her eyes toward the pile of newspapers beside her. "Well, you're certainly not enhancing it." She linked her hands together on the table and leaned forward, her expression intense. "Basically, all the reports about you lately have followed the same theme and, like a bunch of rabid wolves, the journos are ganging up on you."

Quinn frowned. "Brilliant."

"Unfortunately, they have no reason to treat you kindly. You did nearly run that photographer over a couple of weeks back," Wren said.

Quinn held up his hands. "That was an accident." Sort of.

"And you called the press a collective boil on the ass of humanity during that radio interview."

Well, they were.

Wren continued. "Basically, their theme is that it's time you grew up and that your—let's call them exploits—are getting old and, worse, tiresome. That seeing you with a different woman every month is boring and a cliché. Some journalists are taking this a step further, saying, since Kade and Mac have settled and started families, when are you going to do the same? That what was funny and interesting in your early twenties is now just self-indulgent."

Quinn grimaced. Ouch. Harsh.

Not as harsh as knowing that he'd never be able to have what they had, his own family, but still…

Seriously, Rayne, this *again? For the last five years, you've known about and accepted your infertility! A family is not what you want, remember? Stop thinking about it and move on!*

Kade picked up a paper and Quinn could see that someone, probably Wren, had highlighted some text.

Kade read the damaging words out loud. "Our sources tell us that the deal to buy the Mavericks franchise by Rayne, Kade Webb and Mac McCaskill, and their investor—the conservative billionaire industrialist Warren Bayliss—is about to be finalized. You would think that Rayne would make an effort to keep his nose clean. Maybe his partners should tell him that while he might be a brilliant and successful coach, he is a shocking example to his players and his personal life is a joke."

Kade and Mac held his gaze and he respected them for not dropping their eyes and looking away.

"Is that something you want to tell me?" he demanded, his voice rough.

Kade exchanged a look with Mac and Mac gestured for Kade to speak. "The last year has been stressful, for all of us. So much has happened—Vernon's death, our partnership with Bayliss, buying the franchise."

"Falling in love, becoming fathers," Wren added.

Kade nodded his agreement. "You generating bad publicity is complicating the situation. We, specifically the Mavericks, need you to clean up your act."

Quinn tipped his head back to look at the ceiling. He wanted to argue, wanted to rage against the unfair accusations, wanted to shout his denials. Instead, he dropped his head and looked at Cal, who still sat on the arm of the chair looking thoughtful.

"You've been very quiet, Red. What do you think?"

Cal bit her bottom lip, her eyes troubled. She dropped

her head to the side and released a long sigh. "I know how important buying the franchise is and I'd think that you'd want to do whatever you could to make sure that happens." She wrinkled her nose at him. "Maybe you do need to calm down, Q. Stop the serial dating, watch your mouth, stop dueling with death sports—"

The loud jangle of a cell phone interrupted her sentence and Cal hopped up. "Sorry, that's mine. It might be the hospital."

Quinn nodded. Cal bent over to pick up her bag and Quinn blinked as the denim fabric stretched across her perfect, heart-shaped ass. He wiped a hand over his face and swallowed, desperately trying to moisten his mouth. All the blood in his head travelled south to create some action in his pants.

Quinn rubbed the back of his neck. Instead of thinking about Red and her very nice butt, he should be directing his attention to his career. He needed to convince Bayliss he was a necessary and valuable component of the team and not a risk factor. To do that, he had to get the media off his back or, at the very least, get them to focus on something positive about him and his career with the Mavericks. Easy to think; not so easy to do.

As Cal slipped out the glass door onto the smaller deck, he acknowledged that his sudden attraction to Red was a complication that he definitely could do without.

"Callahan Adam-Carter? Please hold for Mr. Graeme Moore."

Cal frowned, wondered who Graeme Moore was and looked into the lounge behind her, thinking that the three Mavericks men were incredibly sexy. Fit, ripped, cosmopolitan. And since Quinn was the only one who was still single, she wasn't surprised that the press's attention was on him. Breakfast was not breakfast in the city without coffee and the latest gossip about the city's favorite sons.

Over the years his bright blond hair had deepened to the color of rich toffee, but those eyes—those brilliant, ice-green eyes—were exactly the same, edged by long, dark lashes and strong brows. She wasn't crazy about his too-long, dirty-blond beard and his shoulder-length hair, but she could understand why the female population of Vancouver liked his appearance. He looked hard and hot and, as always, very, very masculine. With an edge of danger that immediately had female ovaries twitching. After a lifetime of watching women making fools of themselves over him—tongues dropping, walking into poles, stuttering, stammering, offering to have his babies—she understood that he was a grade-A hottie.

When she was wrapped around him earlier she'd felt her heart rate climb and that special spot between her legs throb. Mmm, interesting. After five years of feeling numb, five years without feeling remotely attracted to anyone, her sexuality was finally creeping back. She'd started to notice men again and she supposed that her reaction to Quinn had everything to do with the fact that it had been a very long time since she'd been up close and personal with a hot man. With any man.

It didn't mean anything. He was Quinn, for God's sake! *Quinn!* This was the same guy who had tried to raise frogs in the family bath, who had teased her mercilessly and defended her from school-yard bullies. To her, he wasn't the youngest but best hockey coach in the NHL, the wild and woolly adrenaline junkie who provided grist for the tabloids, or the ripped bad boy who dated supermodels and publicity-seeking actresses.

He was just Quinn, her closest friend for the best part of twenty years.

Well, eighteen years, to be precise. They hadn't spoken to each other for six months before her wedding or at any time during her marriage. It was only after Toby's death that they'd reconnected.

"Mrs. Carter, I'm glad I've finally reached you."

Mrs. Carter? Cal's stomach contracted and her coffee made its way back up her throat. She swallowed and swallowed again.

"I've sent numerous messages to your email address at Carter International, but you have yet to respond," Moore continued. "I heard you were back in the country so I finally tracked down your cell number."

Cal shrugged. Her life had stopped the day Toby died and she seldom—okay, never—paid attention to messages sent to that address.

"I'm sorry. Who are you?"

"Toby Carter's lawyer and I'm calling about his estate."

"I don't understand why, since Toby's estate was settled years ago," Cal said, frowning.

Moore remained silent for a long time and he eventually spoke again. "I read his will after the funeral, Mrs. Carter. Do you remember that day?"

No, not really. Her memory of Toby's death and burial was shrouded in a mist she couldn't—didn't want to—penetrate.

"I handed you a folder, asked you to read the will again when you felt stronger," Moore continued when she failed to answer him. "You didn't do that, did you?"

Cal pushed away the nauseating emotions that swirled to the surface whenever she thought or talked about Toby and forced herself to think. And no, she hadn't read the will again. She didn't even remember the folder. It was probably where she left it, in the study at Toby's still-unoccupied house.

"Why are you calling me, Mr. Moore?"

"This is a reminder that Mr. Carter's estate has been in abeyance for the last five years. Mr. Carter wanted you to inherit, but he didn't want to share his wealth with your future spouse. His will states that if you have not remarried five years after his death, you inherit his estate."

"What?"

"His estate includes his numerous bank accounts, his properties—both here and overseas—and his shares in Carter International. Also included are his art, furniture and gemstone collections. The estate is valued in the region of $200 million."

"I don't want it. I don't want anything! Give it to his sons."

"The will cannot be changed and his assets cannot be transferred. If you remarry before the anniversary of his death, then you will no longer be a beneficiary of Mr. Carter's will and only then will his estate be split evenly between his two sons."

Toby, you scumbag. "So I have to marry within four months to make sure that his sons inherit what they are— morally and ethically—entitled to?" Cal demanded, feeling her heart thud against her rib cage.

"Exactly."

"Do you know how nuts this is?"

After begging her to read his emails, Moore ended the call. Cal closed her eyes and pulled in deep breaths, flooding her lungs with air in order to push back the panic. Everything Toby owned was tainted, covered with the same deep, dark, controlling and possessive energy that he'd concealed beneath the charming, urbane, kind personality he showed the world.

Cal scrunched her eyelids closed, trying not to remember the vicious taunting, her confusion, the desperation. He was five years dead and he could still make her panic, make her doubt herself, turn her hard-fought independence into insecurity. She couldn't be his heir. She didn't want to own anything of his. She never wanted to be linked to him again.

To remain mentally and emotionally free of her husband, she couldn't be tied to anything he owned. She'd marry the first man she could to rid herself of his contaminated legacy.

Cal turned as she heard the door to the lounge slide open and saw Quinn standing there. She pulled a smile onto her face and hoped that Quinn was too involved in his own drama to notice that she'd taken a starring role in one of her own.

Quinn frowned at her, obviously seeing something on her face or in her eyes to make him pause. "Everything okay?" he asked as he gestured her inside.

Cal nodded as she walked back into the lounge.

"Apart from the fact that I need a husband, I'm good." Cal saw the shocked expressions that followed and waved her comment away. "Bad joke. Ignore me. So, have you found a solution to your problem? Any ideas on how to get Quinn some good press?"

Wren leaned forward and crossed her legs, linking her hands over her knees, her expression thoughtful. "I wish you weren't joking, Cal. Quinn marrying you would be excellent PR for him."

Mac and Kade laughed, Quinn spluttered, but Cal just lifted her eyebrows in a tell-me-more expression.

"You're PR gold, Callahan. You are the only child of a fairy-tale romance between your superrich father and Rachel Thomas, the principal soloist with the Royal Canadian Ballet Company, who is considered one of the world's best ballerinas. You married Toby Carter, the most elusive and eligible of Vancouver's bachelors until these three knuckleheads came along. The public loves you to distraction, despite the fact that you are seldom in the city."

Could she? Did she dare? It would be a quick, convenient solution.

Cal gathered her courage, pulled on her brightest smile and turned to Quinn. "So, what do you think? Want to get married?"

Two

Cal called a final good-bye to Quinn's friends and closed the sliding door behind them. She walked through the main salon, passed the large dining table and hesitated at the steps that would take her belowdecks to the sleeping cabins below. Quinn had hurried down those stairs after she'd dropped her bombshell but not before telling her that her suggestion that they marry was deeply unamusing and wildly inappropriate.

She hadn't been joking and the urge to run downstairs and explain was strong. But Cal knew Quinn, knew that he needed some time alone to work through his temper, to gather his thoughts. She did too. To give them both a little time, she walked back into the kitchen and snagged a microbrew from his stash in the fridge. Twisting the top off, she took a swallow straight from the bottle. She'd been back in Vancouver for less than a day and she already felt like the city had a feather pillow over her face.

Being back in Vancouver always did that to her; the city she'd loved as a child, a teenager and a young woman now felt like it was trying to smother her.

Cal pulled a face. As pretty as Quinn's new yacht was, she didn't want to be here. A square inch of her heart— the inch that was pure bitch—resented having to come back here, resented leaving the anonymity of the life she'd created after Toby. But her father needed her here and since he was the only family she had left, she'd caught the first flight home.

Cal ran the cold bottle over her cheek and closed her eyes. When she was away from Vancouver, she was Cal Adam and she had little connection to Callahan Adam-Carter, Toby's young, socially connected, perfectly pedigreed bride. Despite the fact that she stood to inherit her father's wealth, she was as far removed from the wife she'd been as politicians were from the truth. The residents of her hometown would be shocked to realize that she was now as normal as any single, almost-thirty-year-old widowed woman who'd grown up in the public eye could be.

She'd worked hard to chase her freedom, to live independently, to find her individuality. It hadn't always been easy. She was the only child of one of the country's richest men, the widow of another rich, wildly popular man and the daughter of a beloved icon of the dance world. Her best friend was also the city's favorite bad boy.

To whom, on a spur-of-the-moment suggestion, she'd just proposed marriage. Crazy!

Yet…yet in a small, pure part of her brain, it made complete sense on a number of levels and in the last few years she'd learned to listen to that insistent voice.

First, and most important, marrying her would be a good move for Quinn. She was reasonably pretty, socially connected and the reporters and photographers loved her.

She was also so rarely in the city that whatever she did, or said, was guaranteed to garner coverage. In a nutshell, she sold newspapers, online or print. Being linked with her, being *married* to her, would send a very strong message that Quinn was turning his life around.

Because nobody—not even Quinn Rayne, legendary bad boy—would play games with Callahan Adam-Carter. And, as a bonus, her father and Warren Bayliss did a lot of business together, so Bayliss wouldn't dare try excluding Cauley's son-in-law from any deal involving the other two Mavericks.

Yeah, marrying her would be a very good move on Quinn's part.

As for her…

If she wanted no part of Toby's inheritance, then she needed to marry. That was nonnegotiable. And in order to protect herself, to protect her freedom and independence, she needed to marry a man who was safe, someone she could be honest with. She knew Quinn and trusted him. He lived life on his own terms and, since he hated restrictions, he was a live-and-let-live type of guy. Just the type of man—*the only type of man*—she could ever consider marrying.

Quinn wouldn't rock her emotional boat. She'd known him all her life, and never thought of him in any way but as her friend. The little spark she'd felt earlier was an aberration and not worth considering, so marrying him would be an easy way out of her sticky situation. No mess, no fuss.

And if she took over the management of the foundation for a while and found herself back in the social swirl, being Quinn's wife would assuage some highbrow curiosity about her change from an insecure, meek, jump-at-shadows girl to the stronger, assertive, more confident woman she now was. Nobody would expect Quinn—the Mavericks' Bad Boy—to have a mousy wife.

This marriage—presuming she could get Quinn to agree—would be in name only. Nothing between them would change. It would be a marriage of convenience, a way to help to free herself from Toby's tainted legacy.

It would be a ruse, a temporary solution to both their problems. It would be an illusion, a show, a production—but the heart of their friendship, of who they were, would stay the same.

It had to. Anything else would be unacceptable.

Provided, of course, that she could get Quinn to agree.

Was she out of her mind? Had she left the working part of her brain in... God, where had she been? Some tiny, landlocked African country he couldn't remember the name of. No matter—what the hell was Cal thinking?

Quinn had been so discombobulated by her prosaic, seemingly serious proposal that he'd shouted at her to stop joking around and told his mates that he was going to take a shower, hoping that some time alone under the powerful sprays of his double-head shower would calm him down.

It was the most relaxing shower system in the world, his architect had promised him. Well, relaxing, his ass.

He simply wasn't marriage and family material. God, he was barely part of the family he grew up within, and now Cal was suggesting that they make one together?

Cal had definitely taken her seat on the crazy train.

But if she was, if the notion was so alien to him, why did his stomach twitch with excitement at the thought? Why did he sometimes—when he felt tired or stressed—wish he had someone to come home to, a family to distract him from the stresses of being the youngest, least experienced head coach in the league? And, worst of all, why, when he saw Kade and Mac with their women, did he feel, well, squirrelly, like something, maybe, possibly, was missing from his life?

Nah, it was gas or indigestion or an approaching heart attack—he couldn't possibly be jealous of the happiness he saw in their eyes... Besides, Cal had only suggested marriage, not the added extras.

It was a normal reaction to not wanting to be alone, he decided, reaching for the shampoo and savagely dumping far too much in his open palm, cursing when most of it fell to the floor. He viciously rubbed what was left over his long hair and his beard and swore when some suds burned his eyes. Turning the jets as far as they could go, he ducked and allowed the water to pummel his head, his face, his shoulders. Marriage, family, kids—all impossible. Seven years ago, during a routine team checkup, he'd been told by the team doctor and a specialist that his blood tests indicated there was a 95 percent chance he was infertile. Further tests were suggested, but Quinn, not particularly fazed, hadn't bothered. He'd quickly moved on from the news and that was what he needed to do again. *Like, right now. Is it time for you to grow up, Rayne?*

His friends' lives were changing and because of that, his should too. Quinn swore, his curses bouncing off the bathroom walls. But, unfair or not, the fact was that his liaison with Storm, his daredevil stunts, his laissez-faire attitude to everything but his coaching and training of the team, had tarnished the image of the Mavericks and Bayliss didn't want him to be part of the deal. If Kade and Mac decided to side with him and ditch Bayliss as an investor, there was a very real chance that the Widow Hasselback would sell the franchise to Chenko. And that would be on Quinn's head.

His teammates, his friends, his brothers didn't deserve that.

He didn't have a choice. He'd sacrifice his freewheelin' lifestyle, clean up his mouth, tone down the crazy stunts, exhibit some patience and stop giving the press enough rope to hang him. Mac and Kade, his players, the fans—everyone needed him to pull a rabbit out of his hat and that's what he would do. But how long would it take for the press to get off his ass? Three months? Six? He could behave himself for as long as he needed to, but it would mean no stunts, no women...

No women. After Storm's crazy-as-hell behavior, he was happy to date himself for a while. And the new season was about to start. With draft picks and fitness assessments and training, he wouldn't have that much spare time. Yeah, he could take a break from the sweeter-smelling species for a while, easily.

What he wouldn't do is get married. That was crazy talk. Besides, Cal had been joking. She had a weird, offbeat sense of humor.

Quinn shut off the jets, grabbed a towel and wound it around his hips. He walked out of his bathroom and braked the moment he saw Cal sitting on the edge of his king-sized bed, a beer bottle in her hand.

"Just make yourself at home, sunshine," he drawled, sarcasm oozing from every clean pore.

"We should get married," she told him, a light of determination in her eyes.

He recognized that look. Cal had her serious-as-hell face on. "God, Cal! Have you lost your mind?"

Possibly.

Cal watched as Quinn disappeared into his walk-in closet and slammed the door behind him. She eyed the closed door and waited for him to reemerge, knowing that she needed to make eye contact with Quinn to make him realize how desperately serious she was.

Dear Lord, the man had a six-pack that could make a woman weep. Callahan Adam, get a grip! You've seen Quinn in just a towel before. Hell, you've seen him naked before! This should not—he should not—be able to distract you!

Right. Focus.

Them getting married was a temporary, brilliant solution to both their problems, but she'd have to coax, persuade and maybe bully him into tying the knot with her. If she and Quinn married, she would be killing a flock of pesky pigeons with one supercharged, magic stone. She just needed Quinn to see the big picture...

The door to the closet opened and Quinn walked out, now dressed in a pair of straight-legged track pants and a long-sleeved T-shirt, the arms pushed up to reveal the muscles in his forearms. He'd brushed his hair off his face, but his scowl remained.

Cal sat cross-legged in the middle of the bed and patted the comforter next to her. "Let's chat."

"Let's not if you're going to mention the word *marriage*." Quinn scowled and sat on the edge of the bucket chair in the corner, his elbows on his knees and his expression as dark as the night falling outside. Oh, she recognized the stubbornness in his eyes. He wasn't in any mood to discuss her on-the-fly proposal. If she pushed him now, he'd dig in his heels and she'd end up inheriting Toby's tainted $200 million.

Being a little stubborn herself, she knew that the best way to handle Quinn was to back off and approach the problem from another angle.

Cal rubbed her eyes with her fist. "It's been a really

crazy afternoon. And a less-than-wonderful day. I spoke to my dad's doctor about fifteen minutes ago."

Quinn's demeanor immediately changed from irritation to concern. He leaned forward, his concentration immediately, absolutely, focused on her. It was one of his most endearing traits. If you were his friend and he cared about you and you said that you were in trouble that was all that was important. "And? Is he okay?"

"He looked awful, so very old," Cal said, placing her beer bottle on his bedside table. Her father would be okay, she reminded herself as panic climbed up her throat. The triple heart bypass had been successful and he just needed time to recover.

"The doctor says he needs to take three months off. He needs to be stress-free for that time. He's recommended my father book into a private, very exclusive recovery center in Switzerland."

"But?"

"According to the doc, Dad is worried about the foundation. Apparently, there are loads of fund-raisers soon—the annual masked ball, the half-marathon, the art auction. The doctor said that if I want my father to make a full recovery, I'll have to find someone to take over his responsibilities."

"There's only one person he'd allow to step into his shoes," Quinn stated, stretching out his legs and leaning back in his chair.

"Me."

"You're an Adam, Red, and your father has always held the view that the foundation needs an Adam face. I remember him giving you a thirty-minute monologue over dinner about how the contributors and the grant recipients valued that personal connection. How old were we? Fifteen?"

Cal smiled. "Fourteen."

"So are you going to run the foundation for him?"

"How can I not?" Cal replied. "It's three months. I spent three months building houses in Costa Rica, in Haiti after their earthquake, in that refugee camp in Sudan. I say yes to helping strangers all the time. I want to say yes to helping my father, but I don't want to stay in Vancouver. I want be anywhere but here. But if I do stay here, then I can help you, Q. Marrying me will help you rehab your reputation."

If this wasn't so damn serious, then she'd be tempted to laugh at his horrified expression.

"I'm not interested in using my association with you, sullying my friendship with you, to improve my PR," Quinn told her in his take-no-prisoners voice.

And there was that streak of honor so few people saw but was a fundamental part of Quinn. He did his own thing, but he made sure his actions didn't impact anyone else. His integrity—his honor—was why she couldn't believe a word his psycho ex spouted about their relationship. Quinn didn't play games, didn't obfuscate, didn't lie. And he never, ever, made promises he couldn't keep.

"I can rehabilitate my own reputation without help from you or anyone else."

Cal didn't disagree with him; Quinn could do anything he set his mind to. "Of course you can, but it would be a lot quicker if you let me help you. The reality is that, according to the world, I am the good girl and you're the bad boy. I don't drink, party or get caught with my panties down." God, she sounded so boring, so blah. "I am seen to be living a productive and meaningful life. I am the poster girl for how filthy-rich heiresses should behave."

"Bully for you," Quinn muttered, looking unimpressed.

"I know—I sound awful, don't I?" Cal wrinkled her nose. "But my rep, or the lack of it, can work for you, if you let it. Being seen with me, spending time with me will go a long way to restoring your reputation and, right now, it needs some polishing. The Mavericks are in sensitive discussions around the future of the team and, from what I can gather, your position within the organization is unstable. Your fans are jittery. You're about to start a new season and, as the coach, you need them behind you and you need them to trust you. They probably don't at the moment."

A muscle ticked in his jaw. She was hurting him, and she was sorry for that. His job—his career—was everything to him and her words were like digging a knife into a bullet wound.

"If we're married, the world will look at you and think, 'Hey, he's with Callahan, and we all know that she has her feet on the ground. Maybe we've been a bit tough on him.' Or maybe they'll think that your exploits couldn't have been that bad if I'm prepared to be with you. Whatever they interpret from the two of us being together, it should be positive."

"I cannot believe that we are still discussing this, but—" Quinn frowned "—why marriage? Why would we have to go that far? Why couldn't we just be in a relationship?"

Cal took a minute to come up with a response that made sense. "Because if we just pretend to have a relationship, then it could be interpreted as me being another notch on your belt, another of your bang-her-'til-you're-bored women. No, you have to be taken seriously and what's more serious than marriage?"

Quinn frowned at her. "Death? Or isn't that the same thing?"

"I'm not suggesting a life sentence, Quinn."

"And would this be a fake marriage or a let's-get-the-legal-system-involved marriage?"

Cal considered his question. "It would be easier if it was fake, but some intrepid journalist would check and if they find out we're trying to snow them, they'll go ballistic. If we do this, then we have to do it properly."

"I'm over the moon with excitement."

Cal ignored his sarcasm. "I'm thinking that we stay married for about a year, maybe eighteen months. We act, when we're out in public, like this is the real deal. Behind closed doors we'll be who we always are, best friends. After the furor has died down, after the Mavericks purchase is complete, we'll start to go our own ways and, after a while, we'll separate. Then we'll have a quick and quiet divorce, saying that we are better off as friends and that we still love each other, all of which will be true."

Quinn narrowed his eyes at her. "That's a hell of a plan, Red. And why do you want to do this?"

And that's where this got tricky, Cal thought. Without a detailed explanation, he wouldn't understand her wish to walk away from so much money. She'd have to explain that accepting Toby's money would stain her soul and Quinn would demand to know why. She couldn't tell him that the debonair, sophisticated, charming and besotted-by-his-new-bride Toby turned into a psycho behind closed doors.

She simply couldn't tell anyone. Some topics, she was convinced, never needed to see the light of day.

"Being part of a couple provides me with a barrier to hide behind when the demands of my father's high-society world become too much. I need to be able to refuse invitations to cocktail parties and events, to not go to dinner with eligible men, to do the minimal amount of socializing that is required of me. In order to get away with that without offending anyone, I need a good excuse." Her mouth widened into a smile. "My brand-new husband would be an excellent excuse."

Quinn closed his eyes. "You're asking me to marry you so you can duck your social obligations? Do you know how lame that sounds?"

It did sound lame, even to her. "Sure, but it will stop me from going nuts."

"The press will be all over us like a rash." Quinn said.

"Yeah, but, after a couple of weeks, they will move on to something else and will, hopefully, leave us alone."

Quinn didn't look convinced and stared at the carpet beneath his feet. "What happens if we do get married and you meet someone who you want to spend the rest of your life with?"

Jeez, she was never getting married—in the real sense—ever again. She'd never hand a man that much control over her, allow him to have that much input into how she lived her life. She'd been burned once, scorched, *incinerated*—there was no way she'd play with fire again. Marrying Quinn was just a smoke screen and nothing would change, not really. They had everything to gain and little to lose.

"Don't worry about that. Look, all I'm asking is for you to provide me with a shield between my father's world and the pound of flesh they want from me," Cal stated. "It's taking the lemons life gives you—"

"If you say anything about making lemonade, I might strangle you," Quinn warned her in his super-growly, super-sexy voice.

Cal grinned. "Hell, no! When life gives me lemons, I slice those suckers up, haul out the salt and tequila and do shots." She stretched out her legs. "So, are we going to get married or what, Rayne?"

He stood up and stretched, and the hem of his shirt pulled up to reveal furrows of hard stomach muscle and a hint of those long, vertical muscles over his hips that made woman say—and do—stupid things. Like taking a nip right there, heading lower to take his...

Cal slammed her eyes shut and hauled in some much-needed air. Had she really fantasized about kissing Quinn...*there*? She waited for the wave of shame, but nothing happened. Well, she was still wondering how good those muscles and his masculine skin would feel under her hands, on her tongue.

She had to get out of his bedroom. *Now.* Before she did something stupid like slapping her mouth on his. Her libido wasn't gently creeping back; it was galloping in on a white stallion, naked and howling.

Maybe getting hitched wasn't the brightest idea she'd ever had. She should backtrack, tell Quinn that this was a crazy-bad idea, that she'd changed her mind.

"Okay, let's do it," Quinn said. "Let's get hitched."

Oh, damn. Too late.

Three

Three weeks later...

Cal, yawning, stumbled up the stairs, her eyes half closed and her brain still in sleep mode. A cool wind from an open door whirled around her and she rubbed her hands over her arms, thinking that she should've pulled a robe over her skimpy camisole and boy shorts. Coffee time, she decided.

Cal looked to her right, her attention caught by the silver-pink sheen as the sun danced on the sea. Maybe she wouldn't go back to bed. Maybe she'd go up onto the deck and watch the sun wake up and a new day bloom.

"Morning."

Cal screeched, whirled around and slapped her hand on her chest. Quinn stood in the galley kitchen, a pair of low-slung boxers hanging off his slim hips, long hair pulled into a tail at the back of his neck. Oh, God, he was practically naked and her eyes skimmed over the acre of male muscles. His shoulders seemed broader this morning, his arms bigger, that six-pack more defined. She—slowly, it had to be said—lifted her eyes to his face. Her heart bounced off her rib cage when she realized his eyes were on her bare legs and were moving, ever so slowly, north. She felt her internal temperature rocket up and her nipples pucker when his eyes lingered on her chest. When their eyes met, she thought she saw desire—hot and hard—flicker in his eyes and across his face. But it came and went so quickly that she doubted herself; after all, it wasn't like she'd had a lot of experience with men and attraction lately. Lately, as in the past five years.

Her libido had picked a fine time to get with the program, she decided, deeply disgusted. It was a special type of hell being attracted to your fake husband.

"Do you want coffee?" Quinn said as he turned his back to her. Cal heard an extra rasp in his voice that raised goosebumps on her skin. His back view was almost as good as the front view—an amazing butt, defined and muscular shoulders, a straight spine. There was also a solid inch of white skin between his tanned back and the band of his plain black boxers.

Cal placed her hand on her forehead as she tried to convince herself that she wasn't attracted to him, that she was being ridiculous. She forced herself to remember that she'd seen him eat week-old pizza, that he was revolting when he was hungover and he sounded like he was killing a cat when he sang. She told herself that she'd never felt even marginally attracted to him so whatever she was feeling was flu or pneumonia or typhoid.

Her libido just laughed at her.

"Red, coffee?"

Quinn's question jolted her back and she managed to push a *yes* through her lips. Cal crossed her arms over her chest and felt her hard nipples pressing into her fisted hands. Dammit, she needed to cover up. She couldn't walk around half-dressed. Cal looked toward the salon and saw a light throw lying across the back of one couch. She quickly walked across the room to wrap it around her shoulders and instantly felt calmer, more in control.

Less likely to strip and jump him in the kitchen...

"Here you go."

Cal turned and smiled her thanks as Quinn placed a coffee mug on the island counter. Keeping the ends of the throw gathered at her chest, she walked toward him and pushed her other hand through the opening to pick up her cup. She took a grateful sip and sighed. Great coffee.

"I'm surprised to see you up and about so early," Quinn said, turning away to fix his own cup.

"Couldn't sleep," Cal replied.

Quinn lifted his mug to his mouth and gestured to the short flight of stairs that led to the upper deck. "Let's go up. It's a nice place to start the day."

On the deck Cal sat down on the closest blocky settee, placed her coffee cup on the wooden deck and wrapped her arms around her bent legs. She turned and watched as Quinn walked up the stairs, cup and an apple in his hands. He'd pulled on a black hooded sweatshirt and disappointment warred with relief.

Quinn sat down next to her, put his mug next to hers and took a big bite from his apple. They didn't speak for a while, happy to watch the sun strengthen, bouncing off the tip of the mountains on one side and the skyscrapers on the other.

She'd forgotten how truly beautiful Vancouver could be. And sitting here, feeling the heat radiating off Quinn's big body, she enjoyed the quiet. When they decided to marry, they'd stepped into a whirlwind of their own creation. Between dealing with the press, her responsibilities to the foundation and the beginning of the new hockey season for him, they had barely touched base since their quick Vegas wedding. And, despite her moving into the guest cabin downstairs, she hardly saw him.

That could be because he was already gone when she woke up and the nights when she knew he was in, she made a concerted effort to be somewhere else.

Cal had the sneaking suspicion that he was also avoiding her and wondered why. She knew what her reasons were—she'd prefer that he didn't realize that she lusted after him, that she spent many nights in her cabin imagining what making love with him would be like. She didn't want to complicate this situation, make it any more uncomfortable than it already was and, man, it was complicated enough already.

Cal lifted her cup to her mouth, the diamond in her engagement ring flashing despite the still-low light. Then again, at ten carats, the ring could be seen from space.

"How are things?" Cal asked Quinn, noting his tired eyes. "I haven't seen you since we attended that art exhibition two nights ago."

"Where we spoke to the press more than we spoke to each other," Quinn said, his expression enigmatic.

Cal shook her head, disgusted. "I expected some interest around my return, but this is ridiculous. And, if I'm out alone, they're always asking where you are."

"How do you answer?"

"I say that you're at home, naked, waiting for me to ravish you," Cal joked, but, instead of laughing something indefinable flashed in his eyes. Cal felt her mouth dry up. She waved her coffee cup and brushed the flash of whatever that was away. "I tell them that we both have very busy lives, that you're working."

"Well, that's the truth. I do little else but work. It's the start of the season and I have a young team who need extra practice."

"I saw that you have some new players on board. They any good?"

"If they weren't, they wouldn't be there," Quinn replied. "I might not take much seriously, but I don't mess around with the team."

Cal lifted her eyebrows at his touchy tone. Quinn was normally easygoing, tolerant and charming. Hearing him snap was always a surprise. She understood his frustration. Quinn didn't function well when he was bound by rules, when he felt like he had clipped wings. Wren, the Mavericks' PR whiz, had carefully choreographed every aspect of their fake marriage, from the leaked photographs of their quickie wedding to their appearances on the social scene. Someone having that much control of his personal life would rub Quinn raw.

Their marriage grounded him, but Quinn desperately needed to fly. Unfortunately, he'd been flying too close to the sun for far too long. "It's not forever, Quinn. You'll be rid of me before you know it."

Beneath his beard, Quinn's white teeth flashed. "Honey, I saw more of you via Skype when you were halfway across the world than I do now and you're living on my damn yacht. Though, in some ways, that's not a bad thing."

Okay, she was not touching that cryptic statement with a barge pole. "Maybe you and I need to reconnect, *as friends*. We need to remember that before we were caught up in this craziness, we enjoyed each other's company. Let's make some time try to be who we always were."

And if they managed to reconnect as friends, maybe

this ridiculous need to touch him, to taste him would disappear. God, she could only hope. "When are you free?"

Quinn frowned, thinking. "Tonight I have plans. Tomorrow night I'm having drinks with some potential sponsors. Thursday is poker night."

Once-a-month poker night with Kade and Mac was sacrosanct. Even Brodie, Kade's fiancée, was under strict instructions to not go into labor until Friday morning.

Boys.

"Friday?" Quinn asked, lifting his startling eyes back to her face. God, she loved his eyes.

Friday? *Really?* "That would work except for one little thing."

"What?"

"Friday is the Adam Foundation Masked Ball. It's only the most important social event on the city's calendar."

Quinn pulled a face. "And I suppose I *have* to be there?"

"Q, I'm the official host and you're my husband!"

"I'll be masked. How will they even know that I'm there? I could be anyone," Quinn protested.

"Yeah, there will be so many six-foot-three ripped men there with long blond hair and beards. C'mon, Quinn, you *knew* about this. I sent you an email about it last week."

"Ugh."

"Have you got a mask yet?"

Quinn sent her a get-real look and Cal sighed. Of course he hadn't; he'd heard the words *mask* and *ball* and tuned out. "Leave it to me."

"Plain black, as small as possible," Quinn growled. "Do not make me look like an idiot."

"The point of the masked ball is to be masked, as much as possible. Not knowing who is behind the mask is part of the fun," Cal protested. Knowing that choosing a mask would be pure torture for him, she'd already purchased a plain black affair that covered three quarters of his face. It was, she and Wren agreed, as fussy as Quinn would tolerate. "Relax. Plain black tuxedo, black tie and the mask. That's it."

Quinn made a sound in the back of his throat that sounded like a rhino going into labor. She patted his shoulder and smiled. "Quinn, it's a masked ball, not a root canal."

Quinn reached out and tugged her ponytail. "So what are you wearing?"

Cal looked down into her empty coffee cup, wondering if she should tell him about the dress she'd found in a tiny boutique in Gastown. Maybe not, because she still wasn't sure whether she'd have the guts to wear it. It was a kick-ass dress and not something her husband's friends and acquaintances would expect her to wear.

It would make heads turn and tongues wag and probably not in a good way. But no one would mistake her message: Callahan Adam-Carter had died with her husband, but Cal Adam—or Cal Adam-Rayne to be precise—was back in town. "I'm not sure yet," she hedged.

"Whatever you wear, I know you'll look fantastic. You always do."

Cal tipped her head and flushed at his words. It wasn't an empty compliment or a line. Quinn said the words easily and with conviction. He genuinely believed them. God, it was such a silly thing, but such easy acceptance meant the world to her.

"So what time do you want to leave for the ball?" Quinn asked.

Cal lifted her wrist to look at the face of his high-tech watch. She was going to be late for her early meeting if she didn't get cracking. "I'll find you there, somewhere. I

have to be there early to check on everything, so you can
get there later. Or come with Mac and Kade. Anyway,
I have to go," Cal told him, leaning sideways to place a
kiss on his cheek.

She inhaled his scent and instantly felt calmer, his
arm under her fingers tight with muscle. God, her best
friend—her fake husband—was all heat and harnessed
power. Their eyes clashed and an emotion she didn't recognize flashed between them. Quinn's eyes dropped to
her mouth and she touched her top lip with the tip of her
tongue.

Quinn lifted his hand, bent his head and for one brief,
red-hot second Cal thought that he would, finally, give
her the kiss she was aching for. She waited, but Quinn
just sucked in a harsh-sounding breath, pulled back and
abruptly stood up.

Cal bent over to pick up both their cups, stood and
walked to the stairs. "I'll see you at the ball, okay?" she
said, her voice wobbly as she tossed the words over her
shoulder.

"Sure," Quinn answered, sounding absolutely normal.
So why did she sense—wish—that he was looking at her
butt as she walked away?

It was later in the morning and Mac warbled a horrible
version of the "Wedding March" tune as Quinn walked
into the conference room at the Mavericks' headquarters. He handed Mac a sour look and frowned at Kade.

"What?" Kade asked, looking confused. "What did
I do?"

"You instituted the ban on getting physical anywhere
other than the ice or the gym," Quinn complained, dropping his helmet onto the seat of an empty chair. "If it
wasn't for you, then I could shut him up."

"You really should see someone about those delusions, dude." Mac smiled.

Standing opposite Mac, Quinn placed his hands flat on the table, leaned across it and got up in his face. "And I swear, if I hear that stupid song one more time, I will rip you a new one, Kade's ban be damned."

Mac just laughed at him. "You can try, bro, you can try. So how is married life?"

Quinn pulled back, blew out his breath and tried to hold onto his temper. He had this conversation at least once a day and he was thoroughly sick of it. *What type of question was that anyway?* he silently fumed. What he and Cal got up to behind closed doors—which was nothing that would make a nun blush—was nobody's business but their own. Yet their marriage fascinated everybody, from his friends to the general public.

And why was Mac asking? He knew that their marriage was as fake as the tooth fairy. Quinn sent Mac an assessing look and decided to play him at his own game. "Actually, Cal and I had hot sex on the deck in the moonlight."

"Seriously?" Mac's face lit up with amusement.

"No, butthead, we didn't." Quinn looked at his helmet and wondered if he could use it to bash some sense into Mac's thick skull. He dropped into a chair, placed his elbows on the table and shoveled his hands into his hair. *"Dude,"* he moaned, feeling a headache brewing, "I don't know how else to explain this to you... Cal and I have been friends since we were in kindergarten. We are not going to sleep together. This is a sham marriage, one we entered to achieve a very specific objective. Remember?"

"What's the point of being hitched if you don't, at the very least, get some fun out of it? And by fun I mean sex."

Quinn didn't respond, knowing that Mac was just looking for a reaction. And they had the temerity to tell him that *he* needed to grow up?

"The point of their marriage was to rehab his reputation and that is going exceptionally well." Wren's cool voice brought a measure of intelligence to their conversation and Quinn could've kissed her.

"Really?" he asked.

Wren sent him a sympathetic smile. "Really. The press has definitely warmed up to you and Bayliss doesn't think you are the spawn of Satan anymore."

"Yay," Quinn said, hiding his relief under sarcasm.

Once he agreed to sell his soul to the devil—aka Wren and her publicity machine—he'd placed his life into Wren's very capable hands. She'd organized every detail of their wedding and made it look like a hasty, romantic, impulsive affair. The woman was damn good. No one suspected that it was a highly orchestrated con.

"And, despite some initial reservations about you and Cal, and how good you will be for her, the public sees your marriage as a positive thing." Wren's eyes left his face and dropped to the sheaf of papers on the table in front of her and Quinn knew there was more she wanted to say and she was debating whether she should or not.

Quinn rubbed the space between his eyebrows. "What, Wren?"

Wren lifted one shoulder in a shrug. "A good portion of the public is just waiting for you to mess it up."

Quinn threw his hands up in the air. "What can I mess up? You've banned me from doing anything that might raise an eyebrow. I'm married so I can't date." Quinn shook his head and looked at the broad band on his left hand. "That sounds insane."

"You do have a knack of complicating the hell out of your life, Rayne," Kade agreed.

That was the thing. He really didn't. His life, as he saw it, was uncomplicated: he went to work, coached the hell out of the Mavericks and got results that nobody expected from a young coach with little experience. So why couldn't they keep their hands, and their opinions, off his personal life? He kept it simple there too: he did what he wanted, when he wanted.

Well, except for this episode of his life. He really hadn't wanted to get married…

You're temporarily *hitched,* temporarily *grounded and for a damn good reason.* When he remembered what was at risk, he would stay married and well-behaved forever if that was what was required of him.

He would not be the reason the deal with Widow Hasselback failed. He would not give Bayliss a reason to pull out of the deal. He'd protect his team, his players, the brand. He'd protect the Mavericks with everything he had.

Because this place, this team, these men were his home. Yeah, technically, he had a family, but he hadn't spoken to any of them for years. A lack of understanding, communication and, okay, kindness had forced him to distance himself from them and it was a decision he did not regret. Kade and Mac, as annoying as they could be, were now his brothers and he would, at some point— *soon!*—go back to thinking of Cal as the sister he'd never had.

Cal, Mac and Kade were all the family he needed— the only family he'd ever have. He wasn't going to risk Cal not being part of his clan, part of his life, by acting on what was a frequent and annoying fantasy of stripping her naked and making her scream.

Quinn scowled up at the ceiling. His simmering attraction to Cal was unexplainable and ludicrous and it would pass—he just had to keep avoiding her as much as possible until it did—and their friendship would survive. This craziness would pass. Everything always did.

Quinn rolled his shoulders and felt like the walls were closing in on him. He imagined himself on his bike, leaning into a corner, the wind blowing his restlessness away.

"Oh, crap, he has that faraway look in his eyes. The one he gets when he's feeling caged in."

Mac's words penetrated Quinn's fog and he snapped his head up to glare at his friend. "What are you talking about?"

"It's one of your tells," Mac informed him. "You get glassy-eyed and we know that you're considering doing something crazy."

"I'm not going to do anything." Quinn pushed the words out. He wanted to. He wanted to burn some of this excess energy off. But he wouldn't. Not today anyway.

"Don't mess up, Rayne. Please don't jeopardize our hard work." Kade's words felt like bullets from a machine gun.

Ben is studying, Quinn. Don't disturb Jack.

Try to be more considerate, Quinn.

Why can't you toe the line, Quinn? Be more like your brothers, Quinn? Why do you have to be so much trouble, Quinn?

It was stupid and crazy and childish, but statements like *don't rock the boat, Quinn* and *be good, Quinn* just made him want to do the opposite. He loathed being told what to do. Quinn bit the inside of his lip and jammed his hands into the pockets of his leather jacket so his friends couldn't see his clenched fists.

He wasn't in control of his own life and he despised it and, yes, Kade was right—he did want to run.

It's not for long, Quinn told himself for the umpteenth time. In six months he could start, to a certain extent, living life on his own terms again.

"Sit your ass down, Rayne, and let's get to work," Kade told him and it took Quinn a moment, or twenty, to obey.

The Adam Foundation's masquerade ball was touted as "A sexy, masked Venetian affair" and Quinn thought most of the guests were taking the suggestion that they come disguised a little too far.

Elaborate wigs and masks effectively hid identities, allowing their wearers the anonymous freedom to indulge in some hard-core flirting and, if they wanted to, to go beyond flirting in the dark corners of the lamp-lit room.

It was behavior he excelled at, reveled in. Behavior he couldn't indulge in because, hell, he was *married*. And finding his wife in this packed ballroom was like looking for a particular piece of hay in a haystack. Full-face masks were the norm and he hoped that Cal hadn't bothered with a wig. Her red hair would be a great way to identify her. Damn, he thought as he turned in a slow circle, he should've insisted on knowing exactly what she intended to wear.

But, in his defense, he was still amazed that he'd been able to carry on any type of conversation that morning on the deck. Cal's tiny barely there shirt and tight shorts just skimming the top of her thighs put his brain in neutral. He'd removed every type of lingerie imaginable—from silky negligees to crotchless panties—from a lot willing female bodies, and her plain, white pajamas hadn't been anything extraordinary. But her in them? *Dynamite*.

Quinn shook his head. This was *Cal* he was thinking about. *Stop it!*

You're only thinking about her, like that, Quinn rationalized, *because you're a red-blooded man and she was wearing next to nothing. And, because you haven't been laid for nearly six weeks, pretty much any woman will do. Even Cal. It's normal. It didn't mean anything.* He had a fake wife; their marriage was a con they were pulling on the world. Nothing between them would change.

Ever.

Quinn adjusted his mask and did another scan of the ballroom. With so many people here, he'd probably only find Cal after they were allowed to remove their masks around midnight. Quinn looked at his watch. Two and a half hours to go.

Hell.

He noticed a bar at the far end of the room and was about to head in that direction when he saw two of his favorite women standing to the left of him. Rory's mask barely covered her eyes and Brodie's huge stomach made identifying them easy.

Making his excuses, he walked over and quickly dropped a kiss on each of their cheeks and he briefly touched Brodie's pronounced baby bump.

"Ladies, you both are looking spectacular," he said, his compliment absolutely heartfelt. He genuinely liked the women his friends were in love with.

"How is my favorite girl?" he asked Rory.

Rory smiled, her eyes softening. Both she and Mac doted on their baby daughter, Rosie, as did they all. "She's fine, at home. Troy is babysitting."

"Good man, Troy," Quinn said, meaning it. He really liked Rory's best friend and the fact that a super-qualified nurse was looking after their precious Rosie made them all feel more at ease. He turned to Brodie and looked down at her bump.

"You look like you've swallowed a bowling ball, Brodes."

"I feel like I've swallowed a bowling ball," Brodie replied, reaching up to touch his smooth jaw. She lifted his mask and sighed before dropping the mask back onto his face. "But let's talk about you, sexy guy. We didn't recognize you until you spoke. Looking hot, Quinn. I very much like the new look."

Oh, yeah, that. Cutting his hair and shaving off his beard had been an impulsive decision. There was a salon next to his dry cleaners and when he'd picked up his tux, he'd popped his head in and saw that the place was empty. He'd intended to trim his hair, shorten his beard, but the stylist, who turned out to be young, pretty and very persuasive, charmed him into going short. He'd agreed, partly because she was cute but also because everything else seemed to be changing in his life so he thought he might as well change his looks too.

In for a penny and all that.

"What prompted the makeover?" Rory asked.

Quinn frowned at her. A makeover? He'd had a haircut and shaved his beard off. Why was she busting his chops? She'd obviously been hanging around Mac for far too long. "It's *not* a makeover."

"It's a dramatic change—long hair to short and spiky, no beard. When you end up looking ten times better— which, I have to point out, should be illegal in your case—it's a makeover." Rory started to lift his mask again, but Quinn gently pushed her hand away. "Those lips, that jaw."

"Those eyes," Brodie added.

Quinn felt the tips of his ears growing hot. He ran a

finger around the edge of his collar. "Will you two stop? Please?" he begged.

"Yeah, please stop," Mac said as he joined them, his arms instantly going around Rory's waist. "I think I might gag."

"He just looks so different," Rory explained. "This new you is, well, hot." She fanned herself.

"Okay, honey, enough now," Mac said, an edge creeping into his voice.

Kade walked up to them with three glasses of champagne and ignored Brodie's dark look when he handed Rory and Kade a glass each and kept one for himself. "Hi, Quinn. Sorry, I didn't know you were here. I've ordered you a sparkling water, honey."

Brodie's frown deepened. "Oh, joy. Can I have a sip of champagne, at least?"

Quinn hid his smile as Kade monitored just how big a sip of alcohol Brodie was taking. When she went in for a second sip, Kade yanked the glass away. "That's enough."

Quinn smiled at Kade's protectiveness. His friends adored their women and Quinn was thrilled that they were so happy. Yet he also felt a little like a third wheel, a thought that would horrify them all. But it wasn't an unfamiliar feeling. In his parents' house he'd always felt on the outside looking in. Despite his ability to shoot the breeze, to charm blood out of a rock, or the panties off nuns, he'd seldom connected on an emotional level with people and shared very little of himself, even with his friends. Not because he didn't trust them—he did—it was just a habit he'd cultivated when he was a kid and one that still served him well.

He wasn't a talker, preferring to work his inner world out on his own. Cal was only the person he'd opened up to as a kid…

Quinn felt the energy in the room change, heard the low buzz of voices that indicated something was happening. He slowly turned and looked toward the door to see a woman walking into the ballroom.

Her dress left him—and every other male in the room—in no doubt as to how close to perfect her body was. If he could actually call what she was wearing a dress. The word *dress* implied fabric and there was little of that. It could only be designer and, like three quarters of the dresses in the room, it was black. Unlike the other dresses, it was ridiculously sexy.

The best way Quinn could think to describe it was that someone had painted her torso with fabric swirls. One started at her neck and covered a breast, while another ran under her arm and across her other breast and covered some of her stomach, meeting in a perfect point at her hip. A slit revealed a long, toned leg ending in a strappy, sky-high black-and-silver sandal. Quinn forced his eyes up and took in the blunt-cut, chin-length, jet-black bob. He could see little of her face beneath the complex gold mask made from feathers, chains, beads and fake gemstones. Gorgeous skin, a pointed chin and lips painted a bright, siren, sexy red completed the picture.

She was exactly his type: sophisticated, sexy, mysterious. Hot enough to melt glass. Yet, she was missing… *something.*

Quinn looked at Mac and then at Kade, deeply amused that their mouths were open and that their eyes had glazed over. He watched, laughing quietly, as Brodie and Rory exchanged eye rolls.

He understood, intellectually, that she was the sexiest thing on two feet and, yeah, if he was single and acting like himself, he definitely would not say no if she suggested a little bed-based fun, but…

The memory of Cal, dressed in her simple white pajamas, sporting a messy head of red curls and sleepy, dark eyes, was infinitely more tempting and so much sexier than the smokin' body in a barely-there dress.

It was official—along with his long hair and his beard, he'd also lost his mind. No, Cal was *not* sexier than this babe. Cal was *not* sexy at all. She was his friend! Friends and sexy did *not* go together.

"I so need a drink," Quinn muttered. Or a brain transplant.

He barely felt Brodie's hand on his arm, didn't realize that she was trying to get his attention until her nails dug into his skin.

"I wanted to tell you how much I enjoyed meeting Callahan," Brodie said, her expression sincere. "She's so down-to-earth."

Oh, yeah, right. He remembered hearing something about Rory and Brodie inviting Cal to lunch last week. Quinn flicked another glance at the hot woman—she was definitely worth another look—before answering. "She always has been. Despite their wealth, her parents are too. Well, her dad is. Her mom passed away a long time ago."

"And you've known each other all your lives?" Rory asked.

Quinn nodded. "I met her when I was eight. She lived a few doors down from me. For the next decade I treated her home like mine."

Rory sipped her wine, interested. She looked around, made sure that no one outside the group could hear her question. "And there's never been anything between you?"

Quinn tossed his hands up, frustrated. "You've definitely been living with Mac for too long. We're friends. We've always been friends. Why does everyone keep asking that?"

Rory, the meddler, just smiled at his heated response. "Maybe, my darling Quinn, it's because it's a question that always gets a heated reaction from you."

"I *definitely* need a drink," Quinn growled. He leaned forward and dropped his voice. "Fake marriage. Friends. Nothing has changed. Status quo. What else can I say to convince you? Should I go over and flirt with Miss Swirls over there to prove it to you?"

Quinn flicked a look across the room and noticed that her back was to him. That view was almost as luscious as the front, just acres of creamy skin from the base of her neck to low on her buttocks. Whoever designed that dress had to have a degree in engineering because Quinn hadn't the foggiest idea how it was attached to her body. When he went over to talk to her, to flirt with her—he was still allowed to flirt, wasn't he?—he'd try to work out how it all stayed tidy.

Kade's laugh rolled over him. "Sure, go ahead if that's what you want to do. But maybe, *possibly*, it's not *us* you're trying to convince."

Four

Her *husband* had stood her up, Cal realized, standing in the shadows on the terrace, taking a break from the busy ballroom. It was past eleven and she'd yet to find Quinn.

Okay, there were two hundred men at the ball, but it wasn't like Quinn, masked or not, would be hard to find. Long hair, heavy beard, taller and broader than most. She hoped he made an appearance by midnight. People would be expecting him to stand at her side when she thanked her guests for attending, when she called for their masks to be removed. If he wasn't, then there would be questions—questions neither of them needed, especially since the world seemed to be buying their fake marriage and the interest in their personal lives seemed to be waning.

From the shadows, Cal had an unrestricted view of the ballroom and she scanned the room, idly noticing that the dance floor was packed. Nope, couldn't see him...
Dammit, Rayne!

She did another slow scan of the room, ostensibly to look for Quinn but knowing that she wouldn't mind taking another long look at the guy she'd been trading glances with all evening. She first noticed him early in the evening, soon after she arrived, and while she couldn't really make out his features—*damn these masks!*—she instinctively knew that he was six foot something of coiled power, radiating testosterone, heat and… God, sex.

Hot, messy, slow, dirty, *sexy* sex.

The kind of sex she'd never experienced since all her lovers had been more of the this-is-about-me-not-you type. And Toby had been their king.

Jerk…

Anyway, she was just so grateful that she felt sexually attracted to someone besides Quinn. That proved to her that her long dormant libido had come out of hibernation and she was attracted to good-looking men in general and not Quinn in particular. Her lust wasn't directed at Quinn specifically so that was a relief.

Such a relief.

Cal inhaled the gently fragranced night air. She'd escaped to the balcony partly because she needed a timeout but mostly because she'd felt Hot Guy's eyes on her at various times during the evening. It started with a prickle between her shoulder blades and then heat traveled from her coccyx up her spine and she knew that HG was looking at her, that he was the reason for the sudden bump of her heart, the fact that the air had disappeared from the room. She'd turn and, yeah, as she suspected, he'd been looking at her. Yet he never made a move to approach her; he'd just kept his brooding, intense gaze on her.

Animal magnetism—she suddenly understood that concept. Totally, absolutely, innately. It didn't matter that she hadn't seen his face, heard him speak—those details were inconsequential. All she knew was that she wanted to get her hands on that body, to explore that wide chest, those big shoulders, the muscles of those long, long legs.

Her attraction to him and, she supposed, to Quinn made her feel happy. The throb between her legs and the flutter in her stomach made her feel normal again. For the first time in Vancouver, in nearly a decade, she felt strong and confident and in control. During her marriage, events like this had felt like minefields and she'd tiptoed her way through the evening, fumbling her way to the end. She constantly monitored her words, checked her responses, made sure that nothing she did or said could cause offense.

Amazing what a few years and being Toby-free could do, Cal thought. She was wearing a dress that Toby would never have allowed her to wear, had slapped on siren-red lipstick that he would've hated and she'd spent the evening gently flirting with every man who'd approached her. She'd had *fun*.

Cal heard the beat from the band and as the vocalist belted out the first line of a new song, she shimmied her hips, lifting her shoulders in a sensuous roll.

Dancing alone, in the moonlight, Callahan?

She heard Toby's sneering voice in her head and smiled as she raised her arms over her head and did a slow, sexy, shimmery twirl.

Yep. It's my ball and I can dance if I want to...

Big hands landed on her waist and spun her around. She sucked in an astounded breath but didn't resist when Hot Guy walked backward, stopping when her back rested against the cool wall behind her.

Cal's eyes widened as his long form pushed her into the stone and blocked out all the light in this already dark corner. She could taste his breath—whiskey and pepper-mint—and her heart threatened to climb out of her chest. She should be scared, she thought, but she wasn't. She was just utterly, comprehensively turned on.

"You smell like wildflowers...*ah, crap!*"

God, she recognized that voice; she knew that voice as well as she knew her own. *"Quinn?"*

So Hot Guy was Quinn and her libido, dammit, was still only attracted to one guy, the *wrong* guy.

Quinn's curse flew over her head, but she didn't care. She didn't want to think about who he was, *what* he was. His hands on her hips made her heart race; his thigh between her legs made her hot. She'd never wanted anyone's lips over hers as much as she wanted his, here on this terrace with four hundred people inside dancing and chatting.

The moment hung, heavy with expectation, vibrating with intensity. Caught up in passion and in the fantasy of the moment, she put her fingers on his lips and shook her head, not wanting the fantasy to evaporate.

They were both masked and they could pretend... God, she needed to pretend.

"Kiss me."

Cal couldn't see his expression beneath his mask and it was too dark to see the emotion in his eyes. She felt his hesitation and worried that he would back off, that he'd yank them back to reality, to their lives. When his mouth softened and his thumb drifted over her ribs, she knew that he was as tempted as she was, that she wasn't the only one wanting to visit Fantasy Land.

He finally ducked his head and his mouth hovered over hers, teasing, tempting. She waited, knowing he would get to it, in his own time. He wasn't a man who could be rushed and she didn't want him to. She wanted the anticipation, the headiness, the bubble, the fizz. She wanted it all.

Minutes, hours, eons later, he lowered his head and his mouth brushed hers. Her hands trembled as she pushed her fingers into his hair. His fingertips dug into the bare skin at her waist, and by their own volition her hands parted his jacket to touch the muscles at his waist, to echo his hold on her.

As he kissed her, as she lost herself in him, the world faded away, melting in the joy his mouth created. In this moment, as his mouth invaded hers, she wasn't the good girl, Cauley's daughter, the do-gooder with the sterling reputation. She wasn't the heiress, the widow, the fake wife, the princess.

She was Cal. Quinn holding her was all that was important. When they kissed, her world, for the first time in far too long, made sense. Here in this moment, there was perfect clarity, absolute understanding…of everything.

Then the universe shifted as he pushed his hips into hers, rocking his long erection into her stomach. Now his kisses weren't enough and she made a sound of desperation deep in her throat, groaning as his hand left her hip to cover her breast, his thumb finding her nipple and teasing it to a point that was almost painful. In response she dropped her hand and tried to encircle him, frustrated by the barrier of his pants.

Quinn murmured something, his words too low to make out, but she knew they were hot and encouraging so she fumbled for the zipper of his fly as he pushed away the clingy fabric covering her right breast to reveal her bare skin. Then his amazing lips sucked her bottom lip into his mouth and she stumbled on her heels, utterly off balance. A broad hand on her butt kept her upright and his other hand dipped into the slit high on her thigh, found the tiny triangle of her thong and pushed the silk aside. As he touched her intimately, knowingly, she found him, long and hot and jerking with need. She rubbed his tip and he stroked her clit and she started to free-fall...

"Please, please, please. Don't stop," she begged, arching her back as he pulled her nipple against the roof of his mouth. She needed him to push her over the edge, needed him to take her there...to that magical place that had always, always been just out of her reach. "That feels so damn amazing. God..."

It took Cal a little while to realize that he had, in fact, stopped, that he was statue-still, that his fingers had stopped creating magic and that his mouth had left her breast. It was a couple more seconds before it sank in that his fingers were leaving her body, that he'd—

That he'd stopped at a crucial point. He was going to leave her high and dry and throbbing with need.

What? Why? What had happened? Cal sucked in air, trying to get her bearings, trying to get her noodle-like knees to lock.

When she thought she could put words together, she looked up at him, adjusting her mask so she could see through the slit-like holes. "Why did you stop?"

"Because making love to my best friend up against a wall just outside a ballroom with her guests inside was never part of the freakin' deal!"

Twenty seconds ago he'd had Cal's nipple in his mouth, his fingers on her—oh, God, he couldn't go there. He'd been a minute away from pushing her dress up to her hips and sliding home. He'd been lost, in the best way possible, in the heat of her—deaf, dumb, blind and crazy with lust...

For Cal!

For his best friend!

Quinn stepped away from Cal, zipped up his pants and pulled his stupid mask from his face, throwing it onto the floor at their feet. He heard Cal's gasp and looked at her through narrowed eyes. She'd pushed her mask up into her wig and he saw desire blazing from her eyes.

He felt the jerk in his pants and closed his eyes. He still wanted her, still wanted to take the...the...*situation* to its natural conclusion. Judging by her rapid breathing and her squirming, so did she.

He was not about to take Callahan up against a wall. He wanted to, but he wouldn't.

And the frustrations just kept rolling in, Quinn thought, pushing his fingers through his short hair. He walked away to grip the edge of the balcony, trying to get his labored breathing under control. He was only out here because he was annoyed at not finding Callahan in the ballroom, frustrated because he wanted to see her, talk to her, laugh with her.

Bothered because his thoughts kept wandering to his fake wife, and wondering where she was, he'd deliberately turned his attention to Swirls and, admittedly, that hadn't been a hardship. He'd hoped that she'd distract him from his current obsession with his fake wife.

She hadn't, so, needing a break from the perfume-scented air inside, he'd wandered onto the balcony. When he saw Swirls swaying in the moonlight, he'd stepped up to her, thinking he'd dance with her, needing distraction from the bubbling sexual tension and frustration living with Red caused.

Then all hell broke loose...

"You shaved your beard, cut your hair," Cal whispered, her fingers against her mouth. "I didn't recognize you."

Quinn placed his hands behind his head and stomped down the terrace, staring into space. He didn't like feeling so off balance so he took refuge in an emotion he did understand: angry frustration. He spun around and glared at her. "So you allowed a stranger to put his hands on you? Do you know how dangerous that is? God, I could've been anyone! A predator! A rapist!"

Cal's mouth fell open. "Are you seriously lecturing me? Right now?"

Quinn was about to respond when he realized that her right breast—her perfect, perfect breast—was still on show, the fabric of her dress pulled to the side. He dropped his hands and waved his hand in the general direction of her torso. "Will you please cover up?"

Cal looked down and gasped. She hastily pulled the fabric back in place and he almost groaned in disappointment.

"You don't need to be such a jerk," Cal muttered.

"You don't need to be so damn tempting," Quinn retorted without thinking. He closed his eyes and tipped his head back, praying for sanity. Or a lightning strike. Or a time machine to roll them back to an hour ago, to earlier in the evening, to birth.

Except that he couldn't quite regret kissing Callahan. Kissing Cal had been...man, so wonderful. Even worse was the fact that he wanted to do it again, and so much more. God, he was in trouble.

"Let's take a couple of breaths and calm down." Quinn rolled his head in order to release the knots of tension in his neck and when he felt marginally calmer, he spoke again.

"Look, Red—" he deliberately used his childhood nickname for her "—the fact remains that you're you and this was...wrong."

Well, not wrong per se but wrong for them. They were best friends. He didn't want to lose her. Lose that.

"Wrong?"

Quinn ran a finger around the edge of his collar and wondered where all the air had gone. Damn, if this was anyone else, he'd have managed to charm his way out of this situation, but she wasn't a stranger and he was living with her, *married to her.* Fake married but still…

"Well, not wrong but…weird."

"Weird?"

Why did she keep throwing his words back in his face?

Quinn shook his head and prayed for patience. He was trying to think, dammit! But his brain refused to work properly because it was still processing how Cal felt, tasted…

He took a step forward, wanting to kiss her again and abruptly stopped. Closing his eyes, Quinn told his libido that finishing what they'd started would be a very bad idea.

Very, very crazy-bad idea.

Sleeping with her would be the equivalent of dousing the friendship bridge with napalm before igniting it with a surface-to-missile rocket.

Best friend, living together, fake wife. The complications were crazy.

He needed to fix this, now, immediately. And to do that he'd have to stay calm—and keep his hands off her—because the situation was amped enough without any more drama.

He needed a joke. He and Cal had always been able to laugh together. It would be a way to lighten the mood.

Except that he couldn't think of anything remotely funny to say. And God, this silence was becoming even more awkward. And tense. And…hot. Cal gnawed her bottom lip and placed her hand behind her back and in-advertently lifted her chest and he wished that she hadn't covered up.

Okay, he *had* to get them back on track. "Look, I don't want this to cause awkwardness between us."

"I think we are way beyond awkward, Quinn."

"I'm sorry." It was all he could think of to say.

Cal drilled him with an intense look. "What, exactly, are you sorry for?"

Quinn covered his eyes with a hand and rubbed his eyes. "Why can't you see that I'm just trying to not make the biggest mistake of my life, Cal?"

He dropped his hand, blinked and his heart felt like it was in free fall as he waited for her response. And when she spoke again, she sliced his heart in two. "Of all the mistakes you've made, and you've got to admit that there have been some zingers, I'm devastated that you think that almost making love to me was your biggest."

Quinn watched Cal walk away and wished he could find the words to explain that his friendship with her was, possibly, the only thing he'd ever done right. That was the reason why making love to her would be such a mistake. He couldn't risk losing the best, purest relation-ship he had in his life for a quick orgasm.

Orgasms were easy to find; somebody who under-stood him wasn't.

Cal kept a healthy distance between her and Quinn as they walked down the dock toward his yacht. Cal looked to her left and saw that Quinn was staring straight ahead, his jaw tight.

They hadn't exchanged a word since leaving the ball-room and the silence between them was heavy and saturated with tension. They'd had their fights before—all friends did—but this situation wasn't that simple.

It wasn't simple at all.

She'd had her hand around his... Cal lifted her hands and rubbed them over her face, no longer concerned about dislodging her wig or smearing her makeup. She'd had her hand in his pants...

Cal shivered again and this time it wasn't from humiliation; it was because she wanted to touch him again. That and more. She wanted to kiss him, needed to feel his mouth on her breasts, needed to feel that pulsing build between her legs. She wanted him to take her over the edge, to make her scream as he filled her, stretched her.

Cal groaned and stumbled. Quinn grabbed her bare elbow and his fingers dug into her skin and Cal just managed to keep her frustrated moan behind her teeth. She stopped walking and stared at the ground, not wanting him to see her face because if he did, he would know how much she still wanted him, how close she was to begging—*begging!*—him to finish what he started.

"Are you okay?" Quinn, asked, his voice low.

Cal nodded, conscious that his hand was still holding her arm and sending sparks through her. "Fine."

"You're cold." Quinn placed his hands on her bare upper arms and rubbed her skin and Cal had to stop herself from purring. "Where is your coat?"

She had no idea. In his car? At the ball? Who knew? "Uh…"

Quinn shrugged out of his tuxedo jacket and draped it around her shoulders. Cal pulled her wig off, handed it to Quinn and pushed her arms into the sleeves of his jacket, still warm from his body. His scent—sandalwood and citrus—mingled with the smell of the sea and she felt that buzz in her womb again, was conscious of the beat of butterfly wings in her stomach. God, she was definitely going off the deep end.

She heard Quinn's heavy sigh. "Let's get home, Red. It's been a hell of an evening."

It really had. Cal folded her arms across her chest, bunching the fabric of his beautifully tailored, designer jacket. They continued in silence, climbed the steps to the main deck and Cal waited while Quinn unlocked the sliding doors and flipped on some lights. She stepped inside and shrugged off her shoes. She slipped off his jacket and handed it to him, aware that his eyes seemed to be taking a long time to move off her chest. She looked down and was thankful to see that everything was properly covered up.

But Quinn still seemed fascinated by her dress.

"That dress. It's a damned miracle I can string a sentence together," Quinn drawled, his eyes hot but his expression rueful as he dropped his jacket on top of her mask and wig. "There were more than a few eyebrows raised when your guests realized that you were behind that getup."

"I assumed there would be," Cal told him, heading for the kitchen. Leaving the lights off, she opened the fridge and pulled out a bottle of water and lifted it up in a silent offer. Quinn nodded and she pulled out another one, handed it to him. Quinn, always a gentleman, cracked the lid, handed the bottle back to her before opening his own. Cal sipped and looked at the inky water outside, lights from skyscrapers behind them tossing golden ribbons across the water.

"Want to explain that?" Quinn asked, taking a seat across the island from her, his elbows on the granite.

In the light spilling from a lamp she took her first long look at Quinn, clean-shaven and sexy. His beard was no longer a distraction; she could see the line of his strong jaw, the smooth skin of his neck, the tiny dimple in his right cheek, the scar on his top lip. She'd given him that scar, she remembered. She'd smacked him with a metal photo frame for dismembering four of her favorite Barbie dolls.

It had taken three weeks for her to talk to him again. At seven, she'd been more stubborn than most.

"By the way, I like seeing your face." She tipped her head. "But you'd look better with some stubble."

That was the type of comment Cal-his-friend would make, the Cal she was trying to be.

Quinn ran his hand over his smooth jaw. "Thanks. It's a change. And why do I suspect that you are trying to change the subject?"

Cal sighed. She'd forgotten that Quinn wasn't that easily distracted. "Back to my dress, huh?"

"Would you prefer to talk about what happened on the terrace?" Quinn asked, his voice low but resolute.

Cal scrunched her nose. "No," she admitted. She wanted to do it again, but she most certainly did not want to talk about it.

"Then back to the dress," Quinn told her, looking determined. And remote and nothing like the crazy-with-need man who'd kissed her with such skill on the terrace. Where had he gone? She'd like him back.

"Though we will have to discuss what happened between us at some point."

"Does never work for you?" Cal asked, feeling the heat rise up her neck.

Quinn just sent her a steady look and her shoulders slumped.

"You were never very good at being an ostrich," Cal complained. "Sometimes you've just got to shove your head in the sand and wait for the storm to pass over."

"Not the way I work, Red," Quinn said. "So, your dress. I think you wore it to make a statement."

"And what statement might that be?" Cal demanded.

He was perceptive and so damn smart. Oh, she knew he didn't think so; he'd been compared to his brilliant brothers all his life and that made him think that he was less than. Unlike them, he wasn't a genius, but he had something his brothers didn't: the ability to read people, to look below the surface and work out what made people tick. Quinn was intelligent, but, more than that, he was street-smart.

"Your dress was a declaration of independence, a way to tell the world that you are your own person, fully adult and fully responsible. That you are, finally, making your own choices."

Yeah, *that*. Her dress had also been a silent way for her to send a message to Toby's world that she wasn't the polite, meek pushover she once was. It was her act of rebellion, years overdue, and she didn't regret her choice.

Dancing in the dark, allowing a stranger to put his hands on her, had been another little rebellion, her way to walk on the wild side. Except that the stranger wasn't a stranger…

Cal placed her elbows on the cool granite of the island and massaged her temples with the tips of her fingers. Why couldn't she stop thinking about his lips on hers, the way he tasted—sexy, dark, sinful?

"God, Cal, don't look at me like that," Quinn begged, his fists clenched at his sides. "This is hard enough as it is."

"I've never been attracted to you in my life. Why now?" Cal moaned.

"I'm choosing to believe that it was because it was a masked ball and because everyone is encouraged to misbehave," Quinn replied, his voice sounding strangled.

Cal lifted her head and met his eyes. "So if I walk around the island and kiss you, you're going to push me away and tell me that the attraction only lasted as long as we were masked and in the dark?"

Quinn stared at her and she saw the thin line of his lips, watched his eyes narrow. She knew that he was considering whether to lie to her, to tell her exactly that. He opened his mouth and the lie hovered between them, silent but powerful. Then his shoulders slumped and he rubbed his big hand over his face.

"I want to say that," he admitted, his voice rough. "But I've never lied to you and I won't start now."

"And?"

Quinn stared up at the ceiling. "I want you, but I don't want to want you. So what are we going to do about this, Callahan?"

Well, frankly, she'd like to get naked and hit the nearest horizontal surface and let him rocket her to an orgasm. She'd been so close on the terrace and she still felt unsettled, grumpy... She sighed. Unfulfilled. Horny.

Cal wanted to suggest one night—one crazy, hot, steamy, uninhibited night of passion. They had a few hours until the sun came up, before life intruded and they could spend that time exploring their attraction, giving and taking pleasure. They could step out of their friendship and pretend the past and the future didn't exist, live entirely for the moment. Wasn't that what you were supposed to do? Carpe diem and all that? The past was gone and the future was still on its way...

They could start off with her sitting on this island and then they could move onto that blocky couch. After that they could shower together; she'd seen his massive shower—all sorts of things could happen in that oversized space. Then they could nap before he woke her up for round three, or four…

"I think we should go to bed, separately, and get our heads on straight. Forget this ever happened."

Cal's eyebrows slowly pulled together as she made sense of his words. That sounded suspiciously like she wasn't going to get lucky. Not tonight or anytime soon. There would be no couch or shower or nakedness and definitely no orgasms.

Forget this happened? How was she supposed to do that? He'd had his hand between her legs, for God's sake!

"Sex is easy, Cal. Friendship is not. I'm not tossing a lifetime of memories away because we want to scratch an itch. This stops here, tonight. We are friends and we are not going to color outside the lines."

Cal blinked. She definitely wasn't getting lucky tonight, dammit.

"Uh…okay?" It definitely wasn't okay! There was nothing remotely okay about this stupid situation!

"We're going to forget this ever happened. We're going to wake up tomorrow morning and we're going back to being friends, easy with each other, the way we've been for the last twenty years. Clear?"

Cal glared at him. "Stop being bossy. I heard you the first time. You don't want me and we're going back to being friends."

"I never said I didn't want you!" Quinn threw up his hands and climbed off his stool, slapping his hands on his waist before dropping his head to stare at the floor. He always did that when he thought that his temper was slipping away, when he felt like he was losing control of the situation. Good, she wanted him to lose control. She wanted his reassurance that she wasn't the only one whose world had been rocked by their kiss, by the passion that had flared—unexpectedly but white-hot—between them.

"Go to bed, Cal," Quinn said. "Please. I don't want us to do something we'll regret. Sex has a way of changing everything, of complicating lives. My life is complicated enough and I'm trying to do the right thing here. Please, I'm begging you, go to bed."

Her libido, long neglected, whimpered in protest, but her brain, slowly regaining control, insisted that he was right, that she had to be sensible. Cal pursed her lips, hitched up her skirt and walked away. Being sensible, she decided, was no fun at all.

Five

Quinn watched Callahan run down the stairs to the lower deck and when he heard her bedroom door slam shut, he grabbed his jacket and slipped into the night. He walked to the promenade, the popular walkway empty at this late hour. Most of the boats were dark, he noticed as he shoved his hands into the pockets of his pants. Ignoring the bite of the wind and the mist brushing his face with wet fingers, he walked to the nearest pier. At the end of the pier he rested his arms on the railing and took a deep breath of the cold, briny air. Three in the morning, the loneliest, most honest hour of the day, he thought.

Situation report, Quinn decided. He'd friend-zoned Callahan. He'd said no to some hot, bedroom-based fun with the woman he liked best in the world. He was as proud of himself as he was pissed off. Was he out of his mind? Or was he, for once, thinking with his big brain?

A little of both, he admitted, staring at the awesome

views of the Vancouver skyline. He had the same views from his yacht, but because he didn't trust himself not to run down to her room and sneak into bed with her and lose himself in the wonder that was Callahan, he was standing on a dock freezing his ass off instead.

Resigned to the fact that he was going to be cold for a little while still, Quinn watched the lights reflecting off the water and tried to make sense of the evening, trying not to imagine how it would feel to explore that luscious mouth, how she would look after he peeled that sinful dress off her equally sinful body…

Quinn's groan bounced off the water and he gripped the railing, dropping his head between his taut arms. He couldn't, shouldn't, wouldn't. Apart from what he had with Mac and Kade, his friendship with Callahan was the only relationship in his life that was pure, uncomplicated, based entirely on who he was as a person and not on who people expected him to be.

The rest of the world saw the pieces of him he allowed them to see. Depending on whom he was with, he could be the charming rogue, the life and soul of the party, the daredevil adventurer, the tough and focused coach.

Cal saw the big picture of who he was and he, in turn, knew what made her tick, understood what drove her. Well, he had up until she got engaged to her now-dead husband.

Quinn's hands tightened on the railing. He still had no idea why she'd married Carter and why she still, to this day, refused to discuss him. Carter was firmly off-limits and Quinn wondered why. It wasn't like Cal to keep things to herself.

Then again, Carter had always been a touchy subject between them. From the first moment Quinn heard she was dating the forty-year-old businessman, he'd mishandled his reaction. He'd told her, in fairly salty language, that Carter was an idiot and that she needed to have her head examined. Cal had told him to keep his opinions to himself. He'd tried, but when they announced their engagement, he'd told her, stupidly, that he wouldn't watch her throw her life away and that if she married Carter, he was walking out of her life. In his youth and arrogance he'd thought that nothing could come between them, that their friendship was that solid, that important.

She'd married Carter anyway.

Carter, her marriage and his death were still taboo subjects. Was it because the pain ran too deep? Because Carter was—God forbid—her one true love, someone who couldn't be replaced? Quinn hoped not. Unlike him, she wasn't cut out to be alone, to flit from casual affair to casual affair, from bed to bed.

Hearing that it was extremely unlikely that he'd ever be able to father a child—amazing what routine blood tests could kick up!—just cemented his resolve to be alone, to choose when and how he interacted with people, with women. He'd trained himself not to think about what he couldn't have—a wife, a family—and he'd never allowed himself to take a relationship further than a brief affair. What was the point? It couldn't go anywhere...

But being attracted to someone who knew him so well scared him.

Cal was an essential part of his ragtag, cobbled-together family and you did not mess with family. She was his best friend and you did not try and play games with something that had worked so well for so long. You did not break what worked...

It did not matter if she had a body to die for and a mouth made for sin. It didn't matter that their kiss had been hotter than hell, that he'd been rocked to the soles of his feet. That he'd never felt so…

Quinn closed his eyes. He'd never felt so out of touch with himself, so caught up in the moment. A bomb could've dropped next to him and he wouldn't have noticed and that…well…freaked him out. Callahan—dark eyes and a steaming-hot body, the only woman he'd ever kissed who made him forget who he was, who made the world recede, caused his brain to shut down as soon as their lips met—was an impulse he could not act on, a risk he could not take. Because he could not, *would not* mess with the only family he had…especially when he'd never been part of the one he'd originally been given and he was unable to create his own.

Fact number one: Quinn was a good-looking guy.

Fact number two: he was a superbly talented kisser.

Fact number three: he was her best friend.

Fact number four: she'd acted like an idiot last night. Worse, she'd acted like a desperate puckbunny who'd throw her mother under a bus to get it on with a Maverick.

She was mortified.

Cal wiped the perspiration off her face with the back off her wrist and waited for her heart rate to drop. She'd pushed herself jogging this morning, trying to outrun her embarrassment. It hadn't worked. Now she had to face the music. Frankly, she'd rather have her eyes pecked out by a starving vulture.

If she was really, really lucky, then Quinn would've left the yacht already to do whatever he did on Saturday mornings and she could delay the inevitable for twelve or fourteen hours or so.

Cal heard the hiss of the coffeemaker, the bang of a cupboard door and realized that bitch Luck was laughing at her. Maybe if Cal slipped her trainers off, she could sneak past him...

Cal sighed. Running away from a situation—or running into another situation because she was running away from another—was how she made things worse. She was a grown-up, and she faced life head-on. She took responsibility for her actions, for her choices, for her life.

But she just didn't want to, not this morning. Cal lifted her foot to take off her trainers.

"Avoiding me, Red?"

Busted. Cal stared down at her multicolored trainers and eventually lifted her eyes to meet his. He was wearing his inscrutable mask, but his eyes expressed his wariness and more than a little confusion.

"Morning. How did you sleep?" Cal asked with false cheeriness.

Quinn lifted one mocking eyebrow. "About as well as you did."

Which would be not at all. If she had the same blue stripes under her eyes as Quinn did, then there wasn't enough makeup in the world that could do damage control.

"Coffee?" Quinn asked.

"Please."

Cal walked over to the window and placed her hand on the glass, looking at the low, gray clouds. The wind whipped up little peaks of white on the waves and, under her feet, the yacht rocked. She longed for a day of pure sunshine and she felt a sudden longing for a clear, hot day in Africa, the sun beating down on her shoulders, the shocking blue sky.

Quinn cleared his throat and she turned to see him holding out a mug. Cal took it and her eyes widened when a zing of pleasure shot through her as their fingers connected.

Their attraction hadn't dissipated in the cold light of morning.

Dammit.

Quinn leaned his shoulder into the glass and stared broodingly out of the window, his mouth a grim line. "We have a problem."

Of course they did.

Cal took a large sip of coffee before wrapping her hands around the mug. "What now?"

Quinn gestured to his tablet on the island. "Your dress caused a stir with the press."

Oh, that. Cal looked at the large clock on the wall behind him. "I haven't even had breakfast yet and you've been online already?"

Quinn snorted. "As if. No, Wren emailed me the highlights. That woman is a machine."

"I'd say," Cal replied. "So, what are they saying about my dress?"

"A lot. Some columnists said it was good to see you pushing the envelope. Others said it was too much. One suggested it was a dress more suited for a…" Quinn's words trailed off and he looked uncomfortable.

Ah, she'd expected that too. "A hooker?"

"A high-class one," Quinn clarified.

Like that made a difference.

"It was on the Celeb Chaser blog. Don't read the article—it was vicious."

"Give me the highlights," Cal demanded, her coffee sloshing in her stomach.

"You looked like a slut. Carter would be so embarrassed to see you like that. You're a disgrace to his name." Quinn scowled. "It also mentioned your dress is the first indication that my dissolute lifestyle is rubbing off on you."

Come on, how could anyone be rude enough to write that? "Moron," Cal stated, rolling her eyes.

"I'll get my lawyers to demand they write a retraction," Quinn told her, his lips thin with displeasure.

"I appreciate the gesture, but it's not worth the time or the effort," Cal said. "Were you embarrassed by what I wore?"

She didn't give a damn about Toby and his opinions—being dead, he had no say in anything she did or thought anymore. But she did care what Quinn thought. She'd always trusted his judgment. Had she gone a little overboard in an effort to assert her independence?

Quinn looked puzzled. "Are you really asking me if I was embarrassed to be seen with you wearing that dress?"

Well, yes. Cal nodded, hesitant.

"Why the hell would I be? Yeah, it was—let's call it minimalist—but you looked incredibly sexy." Quinn's mouth tipped up at the corners. "Hence me kissing the hell out of you on the terrace. I just wanted to get you out of it."

Cal waved his words away. "Okay, I get that, but was it too much?" She took a deep breath. "Did I look, well, tarty?"

Quinn's smile was a delicious mixture of reassurance and male appreciation. "Red, you don't have a tarty bone in your body. You are all class, no matter what you wear."

Something hot and wicked arced between them and Cal found herself looking at his mouth, licking her lips. His eyes turned a deeper green, heated by desire, and she knew he was mentally stripping her, his hands on her skin, his mouth tasting her. God, she wanted him. Quinn broke their stare and she heard his long, frustrated sigh.

"Something else caught the press's attention last

night," Quinn said. His worried voice broke the tense, sexually charged silence between them.

In the past eight hours, she'd kissed and groped her best friend and they'd upset the apple cart that was their relationship. She'd had no sleep and she wasn't sure how much more she could take.

Cal hauled in a deep breath and rolled her hand. "Hit me."

"Some reports are questioning whether there is trouble in paradise."

"Our paradise? Meaning our marriage?" Cal clarified. Of course there was trouble in paradise but nobody should realize that but them. "Did they catch us groping on the terrace?"

"There's nothing too unusual about a man and wife getting hot and heavy, Callahan. If anything, that would've reinforced the fact that we are crazy about each other."

Oh. True. Cal wrinkled her nose, puzzled. "Then what?"

"I didn't join you on the stage when you gave your thank-you speech. When you told the guests that they could take their masks off, I was, apparently, scowling at you and looking less than happy. And we didn't dance and weren't as affectionate as we usually are toward each other."

Cal thought back and realized the reporters were right. She and Quinn usually had no problem touching each other. They'd always been affectionate. It meant nothing for her to hold his hand, for him to put his arm around her waist, to tuck her into his side. They enjoyed each other's company and the world noticed that. Toby had certainly noticed and he'd loathed her friendship with Quinn.

Last night, she and Quinn—after leaving the terrace with the memory of what they'd done fresh in their minds—hadn't known how to act around each other. She'd been both angry and turned on, both discombobulated and annoyed, and she knew Quinn well enough to know that, behind his cool facade, he was as unsettled as she was. The easiest course of action—the only way to get through the rest of the evening—was to ignore each other, to pretend they hadn't just tried to swallow each other whole.

"We have no choice but to ride the storm. And, according to Wren, that means arranging another outing to show the world that we are happy and in love and that all is well with our world," Quinn stated quietly.

A raindrop hit the window and Cal watched it run down the glass. "Except it's not."

"Yeah, but nobody knows that but us," Quinn stated. "We have to do this, Cal. We can't back out now."

She had to ask, she had to find out where they stood. "And what about last night? What do we do about what happened on the terrace?"

"That," Quinn said behind gritted teeth. "Now *that* we are going to simply ignore."

Quinn sat on the corner of Wren's desk, picked up her pen and twisted it through his fingers as Wren typed. After five minutes, she leaned back in her chair and crossed her legs.

"They can take potshots at me, Wren, but saying that Cal looked like a hooker is not, and never will be, acceptable," Quinn stated, still fuming despite the fact that it was Monday and he'd had the weekend to work through his anger. "I want them to write a retraction or else I will sue them for libel."

Wren placed her hand on his knee and gave it a reassuring squeeze. "Hon, you know that won't work and that it will just add fuel to the fire. Let it go."

He couldn't. He'd seen the worry in Cal's eyes when she'd asked him whether her dress had been inappropriate, had seen that she was questioning her taste, her own judgment. He was so angry that one article—two hundred badly written words—had caused her to question herself.

"Trust me, there's nothing you can do and you reacting to it is exactly what they want you to do." Wren patted his knee again.

Quinn knew she was right and that still irritated the hell out of him. He wasn't the type to walk away. He always preferred action to negotiation, doing to thinking. "Do you know who this Celeb Chaser is?" he asked, still not ready to let it go.

Wren didn't answer him. "Do you want what's best for Cal?" she demanded, her feminine face turning tough.

What kind of question was that? She knew he did.

"Not responding, in any way, to this article is what's best for Cal," Wren told him. "And that's not negotiable."

Wren just cocked her head when his curse bounced off the wall. Quinn swiped his palm across his face and sent her an apologetic look. "Sorry. Frustrated."

"Sure you are, but I don't think it's the article that's the true source of your frustration."

When he didn't ask her what she was implying, Wren shrugged. "So, I made reservations at Sylvie's for eight tonight for you and Cal. After Sylvie's, you are going dancing at Beat. Try to look like you are having fun, like you are in love. We need the press to believe that."

Beat? He'd never heard of it and he thought he knew all of the trendiest clubs in the city. "Is that the new club we invested in, the one in Sandy Cove?"

Wren shook her head. "That's Cue, as in billiards.

No, Beat isn't a club. I suppose it's more of an old-fash-ioned dance hall, sexy music, low lighting… It's very romantic."

Yay, romance. Exactly what they needed because they weren't sexually frustrated enough already.

Oh, this just got better and better. Quinn rubbed the back of his neck. He understood Wren's need to do some damage control after the ball—he and Cal had looked like anything but the newly married, blissfully happy couple they were supposed to be—but was a romantic dinner and dancing really necessary? Surely they could just hit a club, let the press take a couple of photos of them look-ing happy and the balance of the universe would be re-stored. If they went to a club, then they wouldn't have to talk much and that could only be a good thing because talking to Cal had suddenly become hard work.

For twenty-plus years conversation had flowed be-tween them easily. One kiss and a hot grope and they were tongue-tied, desperately awkward.

He hated it. They needed to resolve it, and quickly. He couldn't imagine going through the rest of his life, this marriage, this *week* not being able to talk to Cal. Cal was his sounding board, his moral compass, his reality check. Although she was living in his house, it felt like she was back in Africa and they had no means to communicate.

And when he wasn't thinking about all the things he wanted to discuss with her, then he was thinking about their kiss, the way she tasted, the softness and scent of her endlessly creamy skin. He wanted to kiss every freckle on her face, wanted to see if her ridiculously long eye-lashes could tickle his cheek, how her hands felt wrapped around his…

"You two need to look like you're in love. Sylvie's is

romantic and Beat is a sexy, sexy place." Wren's cool voice interrupted his little fantasy.

"I've given a few of my more trustworthy press contacts the details. They'll be there to snap you looking hot and happy. Do not mess it up," she warned, drilling a finger into his thigh.

"Why do you automatically assume that I'm the one who'll muck it up?" Quinn grumbled.

"The best predictor of future behavior is past behavior," Wren replied, her voice tart. "You threw the first punch in that bar two years ago. You BASE jumped off that building and got arrested for trespassing because you had no right to be there. You were caught flying down the highway on your Ducati. You—"

Quinn held up his hand. "Okay, point made. I will be a good boy and act like a besotted fool."

Wren cocked her head and frowned at him. "Is that what you think love is? Foolish?"

Quinn looked at her, caught off guard by her question. "Sorry?"

"I'm just curious as to why you think that love is foolish. You make it sound like a waste of time, like it's boring, almost annoying."

"You get all that from one word?" Quinn lifted an eyebrow, hoping that his expression would dissuade her from pursuing the subject. Unfortunately Wren wasn't, and never had been, intimidated by him.

"The definition of *foolish* is *lacking good sense or judgment*. Pretty fitting coming from the man who has sold a million papers thanks to his lack of judgment. I find it interesting that you'll take physical risks but you won't risk your heart. That you think bailing off a building with just a parachute to break your fall is acceptable but falling in love is dangerous."

"I never said it was dangerous. I said it was foolish."

Wren snorted. "Because it's dangerous. Because your heart could get hurt."

"This is a ridiculous conversation," Quinn muttered, standing up. "And it's over. Will you email Cal the details about tonight or should I?"

"It's your date. You do it." Wren crossed her legs and smiled. "Feeling a bit hot under the collar because I mentioned love, Rayne? It's not so bad, you know—your buds seem to be stupidly happy as they go about creating their families."

Creating their families... Quinn hauled in a deep breath, hoping the air would blow away his resentment. He couldn't have what everyone else did—not in the way they had it—and he was trying to do the best he could with what he did have. Why couldn't anyone see that?

Ah, maybe because you've never told a soul about what you're missing?

"Are you done?" he asked Wren, his voice tight with annoyance.

"I just want you to be happy, Quinn," Wren told him, her voice soft but sincere.

Quinn stood up and jammed his hands into the back pockets of his jeans. "The thing is, Wren, I am happy."

"Could've fooled me," Wren muttered as he left the room.

Six

Sylvie's was a luxurious, upmarket restaurant serving traditional Italian cuisine in the fashionable Gastown area of Vancouver. It had been a while since she'd eaten at the award-winning restaurant and on any other night she would be looking forward to the evening in the steel-and-glass, exposed-brick restaurant with its incredible wine selection and innovative dishes.

Before the ball, Quinn would've been her favorite person to dine with. They would spend ages discussing the menu and deciding what they would eat, arguing about who ordered what because they would, inevitably, end up swapping dishes halfway through. Or she would eat a third of her meal and Quinn would polish off the rest. But that would be dining with the old Quinn, her best friend, not the Quinn who'd pinned her to a wall and kissed the hell out of her, who'd stroked her to the point of overheating and then backed away.

The Quinn she still wanted and couldn't have.

Cal, dressed in a thong and a tiny strapless bra, glared at her bed and the pile of clothes she'd tossed onto it. What was she supposed to wear on a date that wasn't a date with a husband who wasn't actually a husband, with a man who was your best friend but whom you really wanted to get naked with?

Did that make any sense at all?

Cal placed her hand behind her head and groaned. Should she wear the fire-red shift dress with cowboy boots for a country-chic look? Or should she pair it with heels for an urban-chic look? But the long sleeves might be too hot for dancing. Designer jeans and a bustier? Nah, too sexy. Maybe the halter-neck, vintage 1950s, black-and-white, floral dress with her cherry-red stilettos? She had to make up her mind sometime soon—Quinn would be knocking on her door and she still had to do her makeup and her hair.

All she wanted to do was pull on a pair of yoga shorts, her Feed Me Ice Cream T-shirt and veg in front of the TV, eating pizza and drinking red wine. She wanted to watch a horror movie with Quinn, both of them mocking the special effects and providing commentary throughout. She wanted to put her head on his shoulder, or her feet in his lap, have him swipe the half-eaten piece of pizza from her hand.

She wanted him to pick her up and lay her on her back, lean over her and slide his mouth over hers, have his hand drift up her waist and encounter her breast, his thumb swiping her nipple. Cal closed her eyes, imagining him pushing her pants over her hips, exposing her to his hot gaze. His finger sliding over her, testing her, groaning when he realized she wanted him as much as he wanted her...

"Red, have you seen my wallet?"

Cal's head snapped up as her door opened. It took her a moment to realize the object of her fantasies was standing in her doorway, athletic shorts riding low on his hips, his broad chest glistening with perspiration. He'd been for a run, Cal remembered. They'd passed each other on the dock as she'd arrived home. He'd been wearing a shirt then and hadn't bothered to talk to her except to snap out a brief "See you soon."

Cal bit her bottom lip, her eyes traveling over those long, muscled, hair-roughened thighs; up and over that ridiculously defined abdominal pack; across his broad chest. God, he was hot. When she reached his face, she realized his eyes were still south of the border. Cal lifted her hand to touch her chest and encountered the soft lace of her strapless bra, the warmth of her breast spilling over the top.

She wasn't exactly wearing much, just a brief pair of panties that matched her bra. And Quinn seemed to like what he was looking at. Should she pick up her dress and cover herself or just stand there? Before their kiss, before the madness, she would've mocked him, told him that he looked like a goldfish with his open mouth and sent him on his way.

The only place she wanted to send him was into her bed, to get naked under her covers.

God, she was in so much trouble.

Cal watched as Quinn placed his hands on his hips and closed his eyes. Her eyes looked south again and, yes, there was a ridge in his pants that hadn't been there before. "God. This, you..."

Cal cocked her head, intrigued. Quinn was never disconcerted, was never at a loss for words. He always had a witty comeback, a way to diffuse tension, a smart-aleck comment. Right now he looked as flustered and, judging by the steel pipe in his pants, as turned on as she was.

"Uh... I'll find my wallet and I'll see you downstairs."

Cal released the breath she was holding as he spun around and walked away. She forced her legs to move across the pale floor to shut the door he'd left open.

When she'd proposed this marriage, she'd thought Quinn to be a safe bet, someone who wouldn't disturb her calm, orderly life. How could she have been so wrong? He was supposed to be the one man in her life, the one relationship that was stable, solid and unchangeable. Platonic, dammit.

She'd never believed that she would spend her nights— and a good part of her days—flipping between imagining what making love to Quinn would feel like and reminding herself that sleeping with Quinn would not be a good idea.

Having sex with Quinn would make their situation even more complicated; it would be another layer to disassemble when they split up. They were risking their friendship, something that was incredibly important to both of them.

When she felt brave enough to be very honest, she knew she was also terrified that if she slept with Quinn, she could open the portal to feeling something deeper and more intense than she did right now. Those emotions had the potential to be too powerful and if she surrendered to them, she felt like she was granting someone else— Quinn—control over her heart, her life.

She couldn't do that, not again. Not ever. No one would have control over her again.

Until something changed, until they managed to navigate their way back to friendship, they were caught in sexual purgatory, Cal realized. Unable to be lovers but definitely more than friends. It was, she noted, a very short walk from purgatory to hell.

"Let's talk about us sleeping together."

Cal had been concentrating on her *fritto misto di mare*, thinking that the food at Sylvie's was utterly delightful, when Quinn dropped his bombshell statement. She swallowed her half-chewed prawn, washed it down with a sip of fruity white wine and leaned back in her chair. Quinn carried on eating, slicing into his roasted monk fish and lifting his fork to his mouth. He chewed, looked pensive and went back to his dish to prepare another bite.

"After an hour of laborious conversation, how can you toss that across the table and then continue eating?"

Quinn shrugged. "I've tried ignoring it, but it isn't going away so we need to discuss it. And I'm still hungry. And this fish is delicious."

Cal leaned across the table and kept her voice low, not wanting to take the chance that there was someone in the restaurant who had brilliant hearing. "*It?* Are we talking about sex in general or you and me in particular?"

"Both." Quinn gestured to her plate and leaned across, jabbing his fork into a piece of her squid. "Your food is getting cold." He ate her squid and pointed his fork to her plate. "Damn, that's good. Do you want to swap plates?"

"No, I want you to explain your comment."

Quinn reached for his wine and wrapped his big hand around the bowl of the glass. Candlelight cast shadows across his face and turned his hair to gold, his eyes to a deeper shade of green. The skin of his throat and his forearms, exposed by his open-collar gray shirt and rolled-back sleeves, was tan. He looked fantastic and she wanted to jump him...

The urge just kept growing in intensity.

"What we did, that kiss...it's changed us," Quinn quietly said.

She couldn't argue with that. Of course it had.

"The question is, what are we going to do about it?" Quinn took a sip of his wine. "Are we going to do what we're both thinking about?"

Cal felt the need to protest, to hold her ground. "What makes you think I'm thinking about sex with you?"

"The fact that you stare at me like you want to climb all over me and do what comes naturally." Quinn looked impatient. "C'mon, Red, we've always been honest with each other, brutally so. Let's carry on doing that, okay?"

Cal wiggled in her chair, ashamed. "I know. Sorry." She bit her bottom lip and placed her forearms on the table. "I've always known that you were a good-looking guy. I've known that since you were thirteen and Nelly Porter grabbed you and dragged you behind the gym to kiss you senseless."

Quinn smiled. "She shoved her tongue in my mouth and I nearly had heart failure. She was my first older woman."

"She was thirteen and a half." Cal's smiled died. "But the point is that I know that women like you, that they are attracted to you, that you're hot. Intellectually, I understood it, but it never translated."

"Translated?" Quinn frowned.

Cal tapped her temple. "I got it here, but lately—" she placed a hand on her sternum and stumbled over her words "—I get it, physically." Cal dropped her head and felt the heat creep up her neck, into her cheeks. "I never expected to be attracted to you, to feel that way about you."

"I didn't either, Red, and it's growing bigger and bolder. I don't think we can carry on the way we have been living. It's driving me crazy." Quinn tugged on the open collar of his shirt. "I keep telling myself that you are my best friend and that our friendship is too important to mess up. But you have no idea how close I came to tossing you on the bed tonight when I saw you in your sexy lingerie."

Cal saw the heat in his eyes, the desire. Nothing more or less, just pure attraction untainted by manipulation or punishment. "But how could one kiss, one grope change everything?"

"Who knows?" Quinn drained his glass. "But I know that I've relived that kiss a million times, wanting and *needing* more.

"Aren't you curious?" he asked after a short silence. "If that kiss was so good, don't you wonder how good we'd be in bed?"

Cal felt hot…everywhere. The heat pooled between her legs. "I'm crazy-curious," she admitted.

"Of course, that could be because I haven't had sex since Toby," she added. Oh, how she wished she could blame her current obsession with Quinn's body—with Quinn—on the fact that she'd been in a long, dry spell.

It took a moment for those words to sink in. "You haven't had sex in five years?" he clarified.

Okay, he didn't need to look so horrified. "No. Anyway, let's change the subject."

"Let's not." Quinn lifted their joined hands and nudged her chin so she had to look at him. "Five years since you last had sex tells me that you could take or leave it. That suggests your experiences in the bedroom weren't that great. Not surprising since you were married to the biggest asshat on the west coast."

"It's not nice to speak ill of the dead," Cal told him, eyes flashing.

"I spoke ill of him when he was alive so I can when he's dead. So, am I right? Okay, I know you won't answer that, but I'll take your nonanswer as a yes." Quinn shook his head. "What an idiot."

"Can we go back to talking about risking our friendship for sex?"

"And it is a risk," Quinn said, his chest rising as he pulled in a huge breath. "I want you, but every time I think about losing you because of sex, I start backpedaling like crazy. I want a guarantee that if we sleep together, we won't let our friendship get weird."

"It's weird right now, and we haven't even slept together," Cal pointed out.

Quinn leaned back in his chair and looked stubborn. "I want the sex and I want my friend."

"There is only one thing I'm sure of when it comes to relationships, Quinn, and that's there are no guarantees. It is never how you think it's going to be."

"Is that what happened with your marriage, Cal? Did it not turn out to be as great as you expected?"

Cal forced herself to meet his eyes.

"Every time I refer to Carter or your marriage, you shut me down. You don't talk about it and you talk about everything. Especially to me. Which means that you're either still mourning him because you were crazy in love with him or you had a really bad marriage."

Cal couldn't help the shudder and she winced when Quinn's eyes sharpened. "That's it. It was bad, wasn't it?"

Oh, he saw too much, knew her too well. "Maybe I don't talk about it because I know you never liked him, because you never wanted me to marry him," Cal protested, voicing the first excuse she thought of.

"Rubbish! I never wanted you to work overseas, in dangerous countries and situations, but you did and we still talk about your work. Your marriage is over. Your husband died. Okay, so it wasn't great, but why won't you talk about it? It's not like you're the first person in the world to make a mistake."

Because she still, years later, felt like an idiot. Because she'd found herself—a strong, independent woman—in an abusive relationship and not sure how she was going to get out of it. Toby had brainwashed her into thinking she couldn't make it in the world alone. Up until the day he died and she had to make it on her own. And then she proved him wrong by surviving and then flourishing.

She'd never allow a man to do that again, to climb so far inside her head to control how she felt about herself. To control anything she did or thought. No matter how much she wanted Quinn, she'd never let him control her, dominate her. And wasn't sex a manifestation of dominance?

Or was she just projecting her memories of Toby and sex onto Quinn?

Cal tapped her finger on the stem of her wineglass, deep in thought. Quinn had never, not once, tried to control her, dominate her or manipulate her, so why did she assume he would be like that in bed? Quinn wasn't Toby...

Quinn. Was. Not. Toby. And she was not the woman she'd been with Toby. *Everything* was in her control. She could choose whether or not to have sex, how much to give or take, how much to allow. This was her life, her body.

Her heart...

She could do this.

"Talk me through it, Quinn. Sleeping with you, I mean." Her heart knew that sex with Quinn would not be like sex with Toby but her brain still needed a little convincing.

Quinn pushed his plate away and reached for the wine bottle, dumping a healthy amount in both their glasses. He smiled and it was a potent mixture of slow and sexy. "I could make it good for you, Cal... No, I would make it amazing. You need amazing. You'd leave my bed boneless, satisfied, happy. I'm a good lover."

She didn't doubt it.

"And that's not because I'm experienced but because it's important to me that my lovers enjoy it as much as I do. And you are a hundred times more important to me than anyone I've ever taken to my bed before."

Cal heard his sincerity, his growly voice sparking a firestorm over her skin.

"Sex, to me, is about so much more than my orgasm." Quinn's eyes on hers dried up all the moisture in her mouth. "It's about discovering the exact texture of your skin. Is it as creamy, everywhere, as it looks? I've always loved your freckles and I need to know if you have freckles in unusual places."

His voice was grumbly and so freakin' sexy as he continued. "I want to feel your hair tickle my stomach. I want to know whether you smell of wildflowers between your legs. I want to drown in the heat of your mouth. You have the sexiest mouth. I bet you don't know that."

He was killing her, Cal decided. Her hands and panties both felt damp with excitement. "I want to hear your moans, your breathy voice in my ear telling me what you like. I want to hold you as you shudder, feel you as you go over the edge. I want to find out what it's like making love to you, with you, Cal."

She couldn't stay here, not for one more minute. His voice had whipped her up until all she could think about was allowing him to do everything he mentioned and anything else he thought of.

"So let's find out."

Hunger, hot and hard, flared in his eyes. He stood up and reached for his wallet. "Yeah, let's."

She pushed her chair back and tossed her napkin on the table as she stood up. She looked up at him and nodded once, slowly. This was about sex, about physical relief, nothing more. She could do this…

This wasn't about control or deeper feelings or the future. Or her past. This was about walking on the wild side, tasting the storm, riding the wind. This was about Quinn.

This was about tonight. The future could look after itself.

Quinn whipped open the sliding door and placed a hand on Cal's back, urging her inside. He slammed the door shut behind him, wincing as she jumped. If she changed her mind, he'd cry like a little girl. He needed this…

He needed her.

Please don't let her change her mind.

Quinn stepped toward her, searching her face. In her eyes he saw a bit of what-the-hell-are-we-doing but nothing else that would make him back off. She wanted this, wanted him, and his heart swelled.

Quinn put his hands on her hips, swallowing a relieved sigh when her breasts flattened against his chest, when her hands slid over his pecs to his shoulders and up to his neck. He kissed her, slid his tongue into her open mouth and resisted the urge to squeeze her tighter, to suck her into him. Cal's hand dropped down his back and yanked his shirt up, trying to find the skin of his lower back. Impatient, he grabbed the back of his collar and pulled his shirt off in one vicious yank. He heard Cal suck in a hard breath and a second later her mouth was on his chest, tasting his skin above his heart with the tip of her tongue.

Such a small gesture, he thought, closing his eyes. Yet it sent a spark of pure light straight to his groin. Quinn took her face in his hands, bending his head to kiss her. He devoured her, pouring the frustration of the last few weeks of wanting her into his kiss. Cal moaned in his mouth and Quinn thought he was feeling far too much fabric and not enough skin.

He walked her backward until the back of her calves hit the sofa. "I wish I had the patience to slowly undress you, but I don't," Quinn said, his mouth against her neck. "Get naked, as quickly as possible."

Quinn yanked off his shoes as she stepped out of her heels and when his hands went to unsnap his pants, she released the ties holding up the bodice of her dress and then pushed the fabric down her hips. Her sexy dress dropped to the floor and she stood in front of him, pink lingerie and most of her endlessly creamy skin on display.

"I don't see any freckles," he murmured, his finger sliding across the tops of her round breasts.

"You're not looking closely enough," Cal replied. She nodded to his still-buttoned pants. "Need some help getting those off?"

"I can manage." Quinn smiled as he pushed his pants and boxers over his hips revealing himself to her curious gaze. Her eyes deepened to black and her body flushed.

With need. For him. Quinn felt a hundred feet tall, Hercules-strong. Unable to wait any longer, he unsnapped her bra and her breasts fell into his hands. Quinn skimmed over her breasts, across her nipples, his eyes falling to her flat stomach. He smiled when he saw her belly button ring. He dropped his hand and touched it, rolling the small diamond between his fingers.

"I remember when you got this. You were sixteen and mad at your mom because she wouldn't let you get a tattoo," he whispered.

Cal smiled. "And you bought me a chocolate milk shake and told me jokes to stop my tears." She touched his cheek and then his chin. "You hated it when I cried."

"I still hate it when you cry," Quinn told her, kissing the fingers that drifted over his lips.

Cal sucked in her bottom lip. "Please don't let this be a mistake, Quinn."

Quinn's hand lay flat across her lower stomach, warm and solid. "No matter what, Red, we'll always be friends. Nothing and nobody, not time and not this, will change that."

"Promise?"

"Promise. And I promise that I'll make this good for you."

"It's already amazing," Cal stated as his fingers slid under the lace of her panties and touched the most feminine part of her.

Man, she felt marvelous. Wet, hot, girly. God, he was rock-hard and he wanted nothing more than to slide into her, feel her engulf him, hot and ready. But this wasn't about him; this was about Cal. He'd promised to make sex wonderful for her, to allow her to feel what she never had before. He wanted to make this special, to build her up, to let her experience the magic that was fantastic sex. It felt right that he was sharing this with her, that he was showing her how hot, dirty, crazy and wonderful sex could be. They'd done so much else together, had experienced so many firsts, that it seemed, well, fitting that he should show her how amazing sex could be.

Reminding himself to go slowly, he pushed her panties down her smooth thighs and gently lowered her to the couch. He bent down, dragged his wallet out of his pants pocket and found his emergency condom. He ripped the packaging open, slid the latex on and turned to face Cal, lying on the couch, open to his gaze. With her red curls, dark blue eyes, luscious skin and that made-to-sin-with-him mouth, she was the most beautiful woman he'd seen in his life.

"God, Cal," he whispered and then moaned when her thighs opened as he settled on top of her, his erection finding her hot, secret, girly opening.

"You haven't found any more freckles yet and you don't know if I smell like wildflowers," Cal whispered into his ear as her nails dug into the skin of his butt and she lifted her hips in that age-old invitation to come on in.

"I'll do that later," Quinn promised. He needed all of her, as much as he could get, so his tongue invaded her mouth and his cock pushed into her, finding her soft and hot and silky and perfect.

Cal wrenched her mouth away and whimpered. He stopped, looking down at her in concern. "You okay?"

A strand of red hair covered her cheek and her eyes blazed up at him. "Just don't stop. Please!"

Quinn wanted to reassure her, but he couldn't—it was all too much. He felt both honored and terrified that she needed him as much as he needed her. She was too much. So responsive, so sensitive.

Quinn pumped his hips, Cal moaned and he never wanted to stop. "Quinn! Please…"

Quinn pushed himself up on one hand and reached between them to touch her, his fingers immediately finding her special place. She bucked, moaned and her internal muscles clenched around him. She bowed her back and slammed her hips up, taking him deeper. He felt her vibrate, felt her release and, having no willpower left, let go, pulsing into her.

Quinn felt her hands running up his butt and his back. He listened to her breathing. Instead of rolling right off as he usually he did, he took the moment to inhale her sex-and-flowers scent, enjoying the feel of her lips as she dropped tiny kisses on his jaw, her soft hands roaming his body.

When he finally lifted his head to look at her, her eyes were languid and soft and oh-so-satisfied.

"Well, that was fun. Want to do it again?" she asked with a husky laugh.

Hell yes.

Seven

Quinn looked across the picnic area at Ferguson Point in Stanley Park and noticed that Cal was surrounded by kids. She had a toddler leaning against her shoulder, another in her lap and an older girl had a slim arm around her neck. Six or seven kids, all of different ages, were sitting on the grass in front of her, fascinated by whatever she was saying.

This event—a picnic for children who'd survived a life-threatening illness—was another of the foundation's annual events. Quinn didn't mind joining her and supporting the event. He believed in what they were trying to achieve. And spending the day sitting in the sun and eating junk food in Stanley Park was good for anyone's soul, sick or not.

Kade and Brodie sat on a park bench with him, watching the activity. Some of the older kids were throwing a Frisbee. There were kids on the swings. Toddlers were chasing bubbles and squealing.

"What is she doing?" Quinn asked Brodie, gently nudging her with his elbow, wincing when he connected with little Cody's foot instead of Brodie's side. Her and Kade's brand-new son was asleep in her arms. "Sorry, sorry... Did I wake him?"

"It would take a bomb to wake Cody," Kade replied. He sat on the other side of Brodie, his arm around her shoulder. "And, from what I gathered when I walked past, Cal is telling them a story, something to do with the animals in the forest."

"She's really good with kids," Brodie said, twisting to put Cody into Kade's spare arm and snuggling into her husband's side. Cody's eyes flicked open as he was resettled, looked up at his dad and fell back asleep, utterly content.

Kade was a good dad, Quinn realized and his heart bumped. He looked across at Mac who was talking to Wren, his arm across Rosie's small chest, holding her between his legs, her back to his stomach. He was oblivious to the fact that his daughter was drooling over his hand. Kade and Mac had made the transition from bachelors to husbands to fathers easily and happily, taking the added responsibility in stride.

Quinn was proud of them for stepping up to the plate, for putting their women and their children first, for making them a priority in their lives. They'd embraced love and this new stage of their lives with enthusiasm and joy and Quinn was happy for them.

He would never make that transition, would never have to rearrange his life to make room for a family and he was okay with that. Wasn't he?

Of course you are! And really, why do you want to borrow trouble thinking like that? Don't you have enough

problems dealing with your attraction to your temporary
wife and best friend?

Quinn pulled his gaze off Cal to look at the panoramic
view of English Bay. Yet the amazing scenery was no
competition for the woman sitting on the grass, her bright
hair in a long braid, freckles scattered across her nose
and cheeks. God, he loved her freckles, loved that lush
mouth, the fascinating dark blue of her eyes. The gorgeous dip of her back above her butt cheeks, her elegant
toes, the perfection of her breasts, her pretty—

"So, is there any chance of making this fake marriage real?"

Quinn's head snapped around and he looked across
the empty space where Brodie had been sitting. He'd
been so focused on watching Cal he hadn't noticed Brodie leaving the bench.

His frustration with himself, and his discomfort over
the fact that Cal had him under her spell, made him
scowl. "What?"

"You and Cal."

"What about me and Cal?"

"You look good together, you enjoy each other's company and you're more real with her than you've ever been
with any of your previous women—"

"*Real?* What does that mean?"

Kade didn't react to Quinn's hot tone; he just kept
his steady gaze on Quinn's face. He tried not to squirm.
"With her, you're you. The real you."

"I'm exactly the same person whomever I'm with,"
Quinn protested.

"You are degrees of you," Kade replied, tipping his
head. "You can be charming, the life and soul of the
party, a daredevil, all determination and hotheadedness.
You are also a don't-give-a-toss bad boy."

Quinn thought about arguing and then realized that he couldn't think of anything to say that would counter Kade's argument.

"When you are relaxed, quieter, not trying so hard to show everyone that you're such a bad ass—that's who you are when you are with us, when you are with Cal. The real Quinn."

Right now he was the wanting-to-punch-Kade version of himself. The truth always hurts, he realized. He did use different elements of his personality to navigate different areas of his life, but that didn't mean he liked to be called on it.

"Doesn't everybody pull on different sides of their personality to get through the day? To get them through life?"

Kade nodded as his finger slid down Cody's nose, his expression contemplative. "Sure. But it's important to have a person you can relax with, who you can drop the pretense with. Cal is your person."

No, she wasn't. Not like that. Well, maybe like that but not in a happy-ever-after way. She was his best friend and the person he was sleeping with. He was temporarily, legally bound to her and when they were done being married, they'd still be best friends.

They had to be. It was what they'd promised.

"It isn't like that," Quinn protested.

"It's like that," Kade insisted. "Why won't you see it?"

Everything was changing, Quinn thought, ignoring Kade's question. A few short months ago his life made sense. He'd been wild and free, but he was now married and sleeping with his best friend. He'd spent more time thinking about kids and families in the past weeks than he had all his life.

His world had shifted off its axis and he didn't know

how to move it back, or if he even wanted to. Being a husband, having a family wasn't something he could wrap his head around, but, somewhere and somehow, he'd stopped dismissing the notion for the nonsense he'd always thought it to be.

Irritated with himself, he watched as Cal stood up. His heart stumbled as she scooped up the smallest toddler and easily settled the dark-haired boy on her hip. The child dropped his head onto her shoulder and shoved his thumb into his mouth. Cal patted heads, squeezed shoulders and started to walk toward Quinn, her cheek against that small, dark head.

God, she'd be a good mom. Even if he could imagine a life with her, he could never give her children. He'd want to give her children. Kids, for Cal, would be a deal-breaker. He knew Cal wanted a big family one day and he would never be able to give her what she truly deserved.

Sometimes he thought that he should tell her, just blurt it out and get it done. Didn't she deserve to know? He should have told her years ago, as his best friend. Then again, he hadn't told Mac or Kade. He hadn't told anyone...

Sometimes, like now, he felt like he wanted to tell Cal. That could be because he was feeling connected to her, dammit—*emotionally* connected. Great sex had the ability to create those connections and usually, when that happened, he distanced himself from the source of the connection. That couldn't happen with Cal thanks to their friendship and the wedding band on his finger.

Quinn wiped his hand across his forehead. He was being too introspective; he was overthinking and overanalyzing. *Take a step back and pull yourself together, Rayne.*

He and Cal were friends who were having sex. It wasn't something to fret over. And his secret was his to keep...

"Hi," Cal said as she approached them and patted a chubby leg. "Meet Lee, who is a cutie-pie." She flashed a smile at Kade and looked down at Cody. "God, he's gorgeous, Kade."

Kade's smile was pure pride. "Isn't he? I do really good work."

Cal grinned. "I think Brodie might have helped a bit."

Kade patted the seat beside him and stood up. "Have a seat. I'm going to put my guy in his stroller and then I might start a game of soccer." He looked in Quinn's direction. "Do you want to play?"

Quinn shook his head. "Maybe later."

Quinn watched Kade walk off and then stretched out his long legs and tipped his face to the sun. "You've had a good turnout. There are a lot of kids here."

"Yeah." Cal sat down and the little boy curled up against her chest. "My mom started this event a couple of years before she was diagnosed. She loved kids."

"As you do," Quinn said. He half turned in his seat and gripped the end of her braid between his thumb and index finger. "During your marriage, I kept expecting to hear that you were pregnant."

Distaste flashed across Cal's face and Quinn frowned, puzzled. "You didn't want kids?"

"Not then," Cal muttered. She shuddered and her arms tightened around Lee's small body. Quinn looked down and saw the child's eyes had closed. He'd stopped sucking his thumb.

Quinn ran his finger down her cheekbone, along her jaw. "I'm presuming that you'd like a family one day?"

More family talk? There was definitely something

wrong with him. Quinn watched as Cal captured her bottom lip between her teeth and nodded. "Yeah, I really, really would."

He pushed the words past that expanding ball in his throat. "Then, after we're done, you're going have to marry again, find a good guy who will give you a kid or three or four."

Cal rolled her eyes. "C'mon, Quinn, since when do I need to marry to have kids? Hell, I don't even need a man to have a baby. Have you heard of sperm banks?"

Quinn looked at her horrified. "Are you insane? You can't pick the father of your children out of a database!"

"Why not?"

"Because he could be a psycho?"

"I'm sure they weed out the psychos in their screening process."

Quinn wasn't sure if she was yanking his chain or not. "No sperm banks, Cal. Seriously."

"Well, what are my other choices?" Cal demanded, leaning into his shoulder. "I suppose I could have a series of one-night stands with men I think would be good genetic material but that seems, well, tacky."

Okay, that sounded even worse than the sperm banks. The thought of another man's hands on her body made Quinn want to punch someone. "No one-night stands, Callahan."

"Well, I'm not going to fall pregnant by wind pollination, Rayne. Anyway, I'm not nearly ready to have a kid and when I am, I'll make a plan. I might even ask my best friend to donate some of his boys. He's my favorite person, is stunningly good-looking, smart as a whip and I like him. But don't tell him that."

Quinn stared at her. He blinked, trying to make sense of her words. There was no way she could possibly be asking him for the one thing he couldn't give her. No way, no how.

Life couldn't possibly be that much of a bitch.

"Take a breath before you pass out, Rayne. Jeez," Cal said, patting his thigh with his free hand. "It was just an idea that popped into my head."

"Cal—"

Cal's fingernails pushed through his jeans and dug into the skin of his thigh. "Okay, I get it, that's a solid hell no."

Hurt flashed across her face and dropped into her eyes. Her chin wobbled and Quinn felt like a toad. He pushed the words up his throat. "I'm sorry, Cal, but I could never do that."

Quinn looked at her profile and sighed. He had to tell her, had to give her the reason for his refusal. Besides, if there was anyone whom he would share this secret with, it was Cal. He might be stupidly, crazily attracted to her, but she was still his best friend. Her friendship was still more important to him than the fantastic sex. He liked and respected her. She'd trusted him to show her how amazing sex could be; he could trust her with his biggest, darkest secret.

He took a deep breath and forced the words out. "There's little I wouldn't give you, Red, but I can't give you—what did you call them?—my boys."

"I get it. You don't want to be a dad, have a family, be tied down."

Quinn pinched the bridge of his nose with his thumb and forefinger. "God, Cal, shut up a sec. Okay?"

Cal jerked her chin up, but she stopped talking and Quinn sighed. The best way to say this was just to get it out as quickly and painlessly as possible. "I can't have kids, Cal. I'm infertile."

Cal frowned. "No, you're not."

"Yeah, I am. Every couple of years the Mavericks players have a full medical, where the team docs check us out from tip to toe. The results indicated that I am infertile."

"Did they do a sperm test?"

"No, just a blood test. Apparently it's quite a rare condition, but I've got it."

"What's the condition called?"

Quinn shrugged his shoulders. "Hell if I can remember."

Cal's fist thumped his thigh. "When did you find out and why didn't you tell me?"

Quinn covered her fist with his hand. "They told me a couple of weeks before your wedding. I picked up the phone to call you, but then I remembered that you weren't talking to me." He looked at her distraught face and sighed. "Look, Cal, this isn't a big deal—not to me anyway. I've never wanted kids, never wanted the whole picket fence deal."

Cal leaned sideways and dropped a kiss on his shoulder. He felt the heat of her lips through the fabric of his hunter-green T-shirt. "I'm so sorry about that whole no-talking thing. That was my fault and it was wrong of me."

"I did call your husband a first-class moron and threatened to kidnap you to stop you from marrying him," Quinn conceded.

Cal kept her lips against his shoulder and her words whispered up to him. "Sometimes I wish you had." Before he could ask her to explain her cryptic statement, she pulled away and spoke again. "I understand why you don't want kids and marriage, Quinn."

He lifted his eyebrows. "You do?"

"It's not quantum physics. You were hurt and ignored as a child and you're scared of being hurt again. Because your parents let you down, you are reluctant to take another chance on being loved."

"Whatever," Quinn growled, hating that she was right, that she'd put his deepest fears into words and made him face them. "My not being able to have kids is not a big deal, Cal."

He wasn't sure who he was trying to convince. Himself or her?

"It is, to me," Cal stated, her tone fierce. "It's a big deal because I think you would be an amazing dad, an amazing husband. If you dropped that shield, that fear of being hurt, and allowed yourself to love, you'd be a wonderful family man."

Cal lifted her hand from his thigh and rubbed the back of her neck, her eyes on his face. "Look at you, all puzzled and weird, thinking I've lost my mind. I haven't. I just know you, Quinn, better than anybody. *I. Know. You.* You're a wonderful friend and you'd be a great husband.

"Listen," she continued, "you need to investigate this condition, find out what you can do. There are other options for you to have a family. Adoption, surrogate sperm—"

"Cal, enough!" The words shot out like bullets. He shook his head and lifted his hands. "I'm good. This is my life. I'm okay with not being able to have kids. I always have been."

Cal shook her head. "I don't buy it. You could have it all, Quinn."

Quinn shook his head and gripped her chin in his hand. "Don't you dare feel sorry for me, Red."

"This so-called infertility is just another excuse for

you not to commit, not to get involved," Cal said, her expression mulish.

Okay, he wasn't going to waste his time trying to convince her. "That's your perception, Callahan. Discussion closed."

"No, it's not."

"Let's talk about Carter, your marriage and his death."

Her face closed up and her eyes turn cool. "Let's not. Ever."

"Why won't you—"

Cal stood up and the child in her arms opened his eyes and blinked at the sudden movement. "Don't do this, Quinn."

"Why are you allowed to prod and pry, but I'm not? Why don't you trust me with the truth?" Quinn demanded, following her to his feet and pushing his hands through his hair. Why did he need to know about Cal's life with Carter? The man was long dead and he didn't affect Cal's life anymore, so why did her secrets about him bother Quinn so much?

God, this was confusing and annoying. This never happened when he slept with women he didn't talk to. Quinn jammed his hands into the pockets of his jeans and rocked on his heels, frustrated. She might trust him with her body, but she didn't trust him with her past.

And that stung.

Conversations like this—hell, any conversation with Cal lately—made him feel like he was standing in a basin on six-meter swells, desperately trying to keep his balance. Too much was happening, all at the same time. He was married, living with and making love to his best friend. His marriage would end at some point in the near future and, he assumed, sex as well. Would their friendship also end?

And if it didn't, could he still be her friend without remembering the spectacular sex? Could he forget that she had three freckles on the inside of her thigh, would the memory of her breathy moans fade?

He'd said that sleeping together would cause difficulties, but he'd underestimated how many and he certainly hadn't realized the degree to which the sex would mess with his head.

Cal was now, without doubt, his biggest complication.

"Coffee."

Cal buried her head in her pillow and felt Quinn's eyes on her. She was lying on her stomach, naked, the white cotton sheet skimming the top of her butt. She felt him rolling to his side and she turned her head sideways. He was supporting himself on a bent arm and his other hand played his favorite game, joining the dots on her shoulders. He loved her freckles as much as she hated them.

"Where's my coffee?" Cal whined and he laughed.

"Good morning to you too, Red." Quinn skimmed his hand down her back and over her butt. "Did you sleep well?"

"No, because you kept waking me up," Cal muttered, squinting up at him. He had a crease in his face from the pillow, hectic stubble and bed hair and he'd never looked more beautiful.

"If I recall, you woke me up the last time." Quinn pushed a strand of hair out of her eyes and off her forehead.

She blushed and Quinn laughed. "Don't feel embarrassed, Red. Not with me."

Cal closed her eyes, turned her face back into the pillow and let out a long groan. She couldn't help it. She became an uninhibited, wild woman with him, happy to go wherever he led her. It was the only place where she allowed Quinn a measure of control over her. In every other sphere they were absolute equals.

He never questioned where she was or what she was doing and when she did explain, he listened to her activities with interest and trusted that she'd been where she said, doing what she said. He allowed her, without any fuss, to contribute to the expenses living on the boat and when she'd purchased some jewel-toned cushions to add color to the neutral palette, it had taken him three days to notice. He told her he loved whatever she was wearing but insisted he loved her birthday suit best.

He was easy to live with, but their friendship had always come easy.

Cal rolled over, pulled the sheet up to cover her breasts and pushed her hair off her face. "This is weird. Don't you think this is weird? When do you think it'll stop being weird?"

"What is weird, exactly?"

"You and I naked. Together. Friends don't get naked."

"We have, we do," Quinn replied. "Don't overthink this, Cal. We're lovers in the bedroom, friends outside of it. It doesn't have to be more complicated than that."

Cal tipped her head and seemed to consider his words. Simple, no drama. So refreshing. She yawned and when she lifted her arm he traced the words of her white-ink tattoo across her rib cage.

"'She flies by her own wings,'" Quinn read the words aloud. "Why that phrase, Red?"

It was a statement of her independence, but, like so much else, she couldn't find the words to explain.

"When did you get the tattoo, Red?"

"About a year after Toby died."

There, she'd said his name out loud. It was, she supposed, some sort of progress.

"I like the white ink," Quinn commentated. "It's feminine, pretty."

She still found it difficult to talk about her past, so she lowered her eyes and sent him a hot look, dropping her gaze to his biceps and then his chest. "You are the baddest bad boy around and, sadly, the only one without any ink. How can you still be scared of needles?" she teased.

"I'm not scared," Quinn shot back. "I just don't see the point."

Cal rolled her eyes. "I was there the night you tried to get your first tattoo, Quinn. You passed out when the guy sat down next to you and lifted the tattoo machine. Wuss. Repeat after me, I'm a scaredy-cat." Cal sang the last word in an effort to distract him.

Quinn didn't take the bait. "Why those words, Cal?"

Aargh! Stubborn man!

"I have another one."

"You're avoiding the subject and I'll let you, for now. But at some point, sometime soon, I want to know why. So… Where? I thought I'd explored every inch of your body."

Quinn pulled down the sheet and his eyes skimmed over her torso, down her belly. Her heart thumped and her skin prickled. Occasionally she forgot that he was her oldest friend. Sometimes he felt like a tantalizing mixture of new and old, of excitement and comfort.

"Where's the second tattoo?"

"Here." Cal lifted a slender foot and twisted her ankle so he could see the tiny feather on the instep of her foot. It was beautifully rendered, a subtle white and silver shot through with gentle pinks.

Quinn cupped her foot in his hand and swiped his

thumb across the tattoo. "It's in memory of your mom. She always picked up feathers, wherever she went."

Cal bit her bottom lip, touched that he'd remembered. "She said they were messages from angels. I've started looking for feathers now too."

Their eyes met and, through them, their souls connected. "And do you find them?"

Cal smiled. "Yeah, I do. All the time. I choose to believe they are my mom's way of telling me she is still around, watching over me." She pulled her foot from his hand and wriggled, suddenly uncomfortable. "I suppose you think that's silly."

"Why would I?"

"Because the dead are supposed to be dead, gone." Cal spat out the words like they were bitter on her tongue.

Quinn rolled off the bed, stood up and grabbed a pair of jeans from the back of the chair in the corner. He pulled them on, left the buttons undone and walked over to a chest of drawers, pulling out a T-shirt for Cal to wear. He handed it to her and Cal pulled it over her head, the soft blue cotton swallowing her smaller frame. She'd never quite realized how much bigger than her he was until they'd started sleeping together.

Big but gentle, in control of his strength.

Quinn lifted his shoulders to his ears before dropping them abruptly. "I think you are mentally, and spiritually, tougher than anybody I know. Anybody who lost their mother and husband within the space of two years and managed to keep going, to keep it together, has to be. And if finding feathers gives you comfort, then who am I to judge?"

Cal knew she shouldn't compare, but if this had been a conversation with Toby, then she would've been ridiculed and mocked, disparaged and called a child. God, Quinn was Toby's exact opposite.

"I'm not sure the feathers are a message from your mom, but I know how much your mom loved you, so if finding feathers makes you feel close to her, then I'm not going to judge that, Red. I have no right to."

Cal's eyes filled with tears and she felt comfortable showing him her pain. "I miss her so much, Quinn. Still."

"I know, Red. I do too."

Cal knew that to be the truth. Her mom had been his because his own mother had been so bad at the job. Rachel had celebrated his achievements with him, the sports awards, the very-impressive-but-not-brilliant report cards. She'd accompanied Cal to watch his hockey games. She'd attended his graduation. She'd been a strong and loving presence his whole life and Cal knew he flat-out missed her too.

"What do you think she'd think about this?" Quinn asked, his voice sounding strangled. "Would she approve of you and I doing this?"

Cal took a moment to respond. "I'm not sure. I mean, she loved you, but she might think it was strange, like I sometimes do. Don't you ever look at me and wonder what we are doing?'

"All the time." Quinn scratched the back of his head. "Do you want to stop?"

Hell, no! Cal dropped her head, inspected her nails and when she lifted her head again she grinned. "It's not *that* strange."

Quinn laughed and dropped a hard kiss on her mouth. "Talking about strange… My mother left a snotty voice message saying they'd expected us to visit by now, to explain why we eloped, why there wasn't a wedding, why they had to read about my marriage in the press."

Cal frowned. "You didn't tell them? Quinn! It's been nearly three months. What were you thinking?"

"I was thinking that, since I haven't spoken to my parents or my brothers for years, I didn't need to tell them anything," Quinn replied, defensive.

"Why haven't you spoken to them?" Cal asked, swinging her legs so she sat on the edge of the bed. "Did you have another fight?"

Cal remembered their last major dustup—they'd objected to his career as a professional hockey player and he'd told them he no longer gave a damn what they thought—and after that fight, she knew his relationship with his parents and, consequently, his brothers had cooled.

"Nope. We just faded away." Quinn shrugged. "Anyway, they suggested that we have supper. To be honest, I think they want to see you, not me."

"Why? Your parents never had much time for me."

"They never had much time for anybody who didn't have an IQ of 150 or above, so don't take it personally." Quinn pushed a hand through his hair. "And I have no idea what's behind the invite. I gave up trying to figure out my family a long time ago."

"Do you want to go?"

Quinn gave her his are-you-mad look and Cal wrinkled her nose at him. "I think we should go."

Her mom was dead and her father had nearly died; family was important!

"God." He sighed and scrubbed his face with his hands. "I am quite certain I was swapped at birth. You're going to be stubborn about this, aren't you?"

"Yep."

"I'll see when we can go over," Quinn capitulated and she smiled.

Cal shook her head. "Let's not eat there. You know your mother burns water. Why don't you invite them here and I'll cook?"

"You can't cook either," Quinn pointed out. "And grilled cheese sandwiches don't count."

"Hey, I happen to be a very good cook...now."

"Then why haven't you cooked for me, *wife*?"

Cal mock-scowled at him. "Because we're frequently not home to eat. And when we are, you bring food home. Or we eat at Mac's or Kade's."

"When did you learn to cook?" he asked, obviously curious.

Cal dropped her head and her hair hid her face. Cooking had been another of Toby's efforts to turn her into the perfect wife. "Toby sent me on a couple of cooking courses." And that was all she was saying on *that* subject!

Before he could ask her to elaborate, Cal stood up and walked over to the en suite bathroom, putting a little extra sway in her hips, hoping to move him off the topic. His eyes, as she'd hoped, moved to her chest and then headed south.

"I'm going to take a shower," Cal told him. "Call your folks, your brothers, invite them to dinner. It'll be fine."

"Ack. That's too much wishful thinking for so early in the morning," Quinn grumbled.

"Right now, I'm also wishfully thinking about coffee," Cal said from the doorway of the bathroom. "Feel free to make my wishes come true."

Quinn grinned at her. "I thought I did, last night."

Yeah, he had and did. Every night.

Cal shut the bathroom door behind her, caught a glance of the happy-looking woman in the mirror and did a double take. She barely recognized her bright eyes, her naughty smile, the sheer contentment on her face. *Don't do this, Cal,* she warned herself.

Don't set yourself up for a fall.

Quinn was temporary, their marriage was temporary—it was all so very temporary. Being with Quinn, being happy like this was a wonderful treat.

But it wasn't real life and it would end.

Happiness always did.

Eight

When Quinn returned from walking his family back to the promenade, he stepped into the main salon and dropped his head to bang it against the glass door.

"I think you're right. I think you were swapped at birth," Cal said, standing next to the dining table and looking at the remains of the meal she'd spent hours preparing. The filet of beef was virtually untouched, the blueberry cheesecake was intact and there was still half a dish of rosemary-and-garlic-roasted potatoes. "Could they not have told you they are now all vegetarians? That three of them are on a raw food diet?"

Quinn stepped away from the door. "On the plus side, they did polish off the steamed vegetables."

"And a bottle of ten-year-old whiskey and three bottles of your best red wine." Cal sniffed, thoroughly annoyed.

It had been over twelve years since she'd shared any time with the Rayne family, but Cal soon remembered why she and Quinn had spent most of her childhood hanging out at her house. His relatives were, quite simply, hard work and after an interminable evening Cal understood Quinn's need to keep his distance.

Why couldn't they see the man she did? The smart, funny, successful man who would love them, spoil them, if they gave him half the chance. He didn't need to be a genius. Being Quinn—loyal, funny, responsible and mentally tough—should be enough.

"Jeez, why did they bother to come to dinner?" Cal demanded, stacking the dirty dinner plates and taking them to the kitchen. "They spent most of the time talking to each other and barely spoke to us."

Quinn picked up the dirty wineglasses and placed them on the counter next to the dishwasher. "Ah, but they did express their reservations about our marriage and Ben did tell me that I am flaunting my wealth because I'm living on a yacht."

"Ben is still the idiot I remember." Cal rolled her eyes.

Quinn did another trip to clear the dining table and after placing some serving dishes in the dishwasher, he leaned against a counter and frowned. "Jack was more reserved than normal."

Cal bit the inside of her lip and wondered whether she should express her opinion of his brother's relationship with his long-term partner. Maybe she should just let sleeping dogs lie…

"He and Rob want to get married," Quinn told her, pouring wine into two clean glasses. Cal took the glass he held out to her and smiled her thanks. Jack and Rob marrying would be a very bad idea, especially for Jack.

"Cal? Have you got something you want to share with me?"

Dammit. The man had a master's degree in reading

her body language. Cal slowly turned around, still not sure whether she had a right to say anything.

"Spit it out, Red," Quinn commanded.

She'd never told anyone about the reality of her marriage to Toby and if she didn't shut down this conversation, she'd end up telling Quinn her dirty little secret.

This wasn't a conversation she could dip her toe into and back out of when the water got a bit chilly. This was sink or swim. She didn't want to do either.

Why couldn't she keep her big mouth shut around Quinn? Surely, by now, she would've learned to? "Cal, talk to me."

"I think Jack is being abused, possibly physically, definitely verbally by Rob," Cal quietly stated.

"What?"

"You heard me," Cal replied, crossing her arms.

"Why do you think that?" Quinn asked. Cal could see he was caught between denial and disbelief. "I thought Rob was the most reasonable, rational person at the table tonight. Apart from you and me, naturally."

Cal tapped her finger against her wineglass. "He's charming, I agree, and he made an effort to talk to us, to you," Cal replied. "He was civil and we needed civil tonight to balance out the crazy."

"Then why would you think he's beating up on my brother?" Quinn asked, genuinely confused. "Either physically or verbally?"

Cal looked around the kitchen and sighed. She didn't have the energy to tidy up, but, unfortunately, the kitchen elves were on strike. And her pride wouldn't let her leave it for Quinn's cleaning lady to sort out in the morning. She put down her glass and started to rinse the dirty plates so she could place them in the dishwasher.

"I agree that nothing about Rob's behavior suggests

that he's an abuser, but everything about Jack's behavior does," Cal said, keeping her voice low. God, why had she even opened up this can of rotten worms?

She was okay. She could still walk away from this subject. She *would* walk away if it got too intense. Talking about abuse made her heart race and it made her remember why she never wanted to be embroiled in a relationship again.

You're in a relationship with Quinn...

No, she wasn't, not really. They were legally married, friends outside the bedroom and lovers within it.

She'd only married Quinn to sever the last cords tying her and Toby together. But talking about abuse felt like she was surrendering a little of the confidence she'd fought so hard to regain. She was overreacting. This was Quinn! The only person she could trust with this information. He was, first and most importantly, her friend. Her oldest, and best, *friend*.

Quinn flipped open the dishwasher and held out his hand for the wet plate. Quinn still looked expectant and Cal knew he wasn't waiting for another dish. "Jack looked at Rob every time he voiced his opinion, wanting his approval. He served Rob his food, kept asking if he needed anything. Agreed with everything he said."

"Jack's always been needy, a fusser," Quinn stated.

"This goes deeper than that. He was nervous, constantly looking for Rob's approval."

"Isn't it natural to want approval from the people we love and who love us?" Quinn asked, confused.

Cal sighed. She understood that it was difficult to accept that his tall brother was being abused by the much shorter, less bulky Rob, but she also knew that abuse had nothing to with size. Like Toby, Rob needed to have the upper hand, needed to be in control, and he knew exactly what buttons to push to get Jack to dance to his tune.

"Beneath the facade of charm, I heard Rob's patronizing condescension, the I'm-not-entirely-sure-why-I-put-up-with-him attitude. I wanted to lean across the table and smack his smarmy face," Cal said. "Trust me, Rob's a snake."

"You don't have to like him, Red, but it's a big jump from being a jerk to being an abuser."

"It's not as far as you think," Cal muttered, not entirely under her breath.

Back off, Cal. Now!

Quinn frowned at her. "Sorry, what?"

Cal shook her head and waved her words away. "Trust me on this, Quinn. Your brother is in an abusive relationship." She closed the dishwasher and, hoping to move off the subject, she nodded toward the cheesecake. "Do you want a piece?"

Quinn laid a hand on his heart and tapped his chest. "God, yes. It looks fantastic."

Cal opened the drawer to take out a knife. Cal cut two slices and placed them on a plate. He took the fork she held out and dug in.

"Poor Ben. I saw him eyeing the filet. The guy is jonesing for a steak and fries." Cal scooped up her cheesecake and slipped it into her mouth, the tart berries a perfect complement to the creamy filling and the sweet base. "Damn, that's good."

"I would never have believed that you made this if I hadn't seen you whipping it up earlier," Quinn admitted, going back for a bigger forkful.

"I'm a girl of many talents."

"You so are." Quinn looked at her and her stomach

did that swirly, jumpy, bats-on-speed spin it always did when Quinn looked at her that way.

Quinn took another bite of cheesecake and frowned at the rest of the dirty dishes. "Leave the mess. Let's take the cheesecake and wine up onto the deck."

Cal followed Quinn up the stairs as he walked toward the large, square ottomans next to the Jacuzzi. Sitting down, he patted the cushion next to him. Cal sat, tucking her feet under her bottom and resting her glass on her knee.

"Jack's an idiot if he's being abused," Quinn stated as he put the plates on the coffee table in front of them. "Seriously, one slap and he should lay charges."

He made it sound so easy, Cal thought. So black and white. He had no idea how words could be twisted and used as weapons, how cruel loved ones could really be. Abusers could win acting awards, easily able to play the victim, always stating that they couldn't understand why they were so badly treated when they loved so much. Few people understood what it felt like to live with the fear, the crazy scenarios, the accusations and the recriminations.

By the time Toby started slapping her, her confidence had been smashed to smithereens. Regaining her sense of worth and finding herself again had been a battle of epic proportions.

"I just don't understand how someone can put up with that crap," Quinn said, leaning back and lifting a forkful of cheesecake to his mouth. "It doesn't make sense to me."

It never made sense to anyone until they were walking through the sludge of an abusive relationship, not sure how they got into this swamp and having no way to get out. And to Quinn, who was so self-reliant and confident in who and what he was, it was an anathema.

Quinn waved his fork in her direction. "So, tell me why you think Rob is abusing Jack."

Cal looked into her wineglass, thinking furiously. This was a watershed moment and she had to decide whether to own it. She either had to tell Quinn about her rotten marriage and her abusive husband or she had to shove it back in the corner and pretend it had never happened. She either had to trust him with all of the truth or nothing at all.

Quinn would…what? Hit her? Disparage her? Mock her? Of course he wouldn't. Quinn wasn't that type of man. Hadn't she told him that she knew him? And she did. Quinn wouldn't lose his temper. He'd control his reaction and she'd be safe.

Of course he would—this was *Quinn*.

Besides, telling Quinn wasn't about how he'd react but about whether she had the strength to do this, the courage to face her past. She'd grown so much in the past five years and she was a new Cal, a better version of the girl she'd been before she'd met Toby.

Telling somebody, telling Quinn, meant freedom. She would be shining a light on her dark past.

Releasing her pain would heal her. It would give her closure.

Didn't she deserve that? Cal finally acknowledged that maybe she did.

Her decision made, Cal lifted her eyes. "Before I go into that, I need to tell you something…and it's linked, in a roundabout way, to your question about Jack."

Quinn looked puzzled. "Okay."

"I asked you to marry me for a reason."

Quinn frowned, confused. "Yeah, I needed to look

better in the press and you needed some distance from the social swirl."

Cal shook her head. "All true, but there was another reason, one I haven't told you."

"Okay, that sounds ominous. What?"

Cal explained about the inheritance, told him how she needed to be free of Toby. "I don't need his money. My mom left me a trust fund and I stand to inherit a bundle from my dad."

Quinn looked astounded. "You walked away from $200 million?"

"I couldn't take his money. It was…" Cal hesitated. "It was tainted. I'll explain why, but let me go back to my comment about Rob's abuse of Jack." Cal sucked in a deep breath, looking for her courage. "The thing is, Quinn, I can recognize controlling behavior from a hundred yards away. I was married to a man who controlled everything I did, everything I said."

Quinn cocked his head. It would take a moment for the truth to sink in—it always did.

"I was Toby's possession, just like Jack is Rob's," Cal continued.

Cal watched as his protective instincts kicked in and anger jumped into his eyes. "Go on," he said, his jaw tight.

"In hindsight, there were subtle hints of his controlling streak when we were engaged, but I thought he was just trying to protect me. After we married it got progressively worse."

Quinn bounded to his feet and loomed over her, his hands on his hips and his face suffused with anger. Cal felt a touch of panic, but she pushed the feeling away and pulled in a deep breath. This was Quinn. Quinn would *never* hurt her.

"Why the hell did you stay with him? Why didn't you divorce him? Why didn't you walk?"

He made it sound so simple; yet, at the time, it hadn't been.

Quinn looked down at her, now bewildered as well as furious. "Why didn't you call me? Jesus, Cal, why the hell didn't you tell me about this? I would've—"

"You would've punched him and caused a scene," Cal told him, her voice firm. "Then he would've pressed charges and you'd have ended up in jail, convicted for aggravated assault. I couldn't do that. I couldn't allow you to destroy your career."

"My career isn't that fragile."

Toby had ruined so much that she hadn't been prepared to take the chance.

Quinn pushed his fingertips into his forehead, upset and angry about something that had happened years ago. Cal reminded herself that he wasn't angry with her but at what had happened to her. He had such a good heart and he was incredibly protective of the people he allowed into his life. She loved that about him. She loved him…

Cal felt fear roll over her, hot and terrifying. She couldn't love Quinn—that wasn't part of the deal. Anything other than being part time lovers and full time friends wasn't part of the plan. She couldn't love Quinn. It wasn't safe to love Quinn.

She couldn't think of that now. Maybe she wouldn't think about it again at all.

She had to tell him the rest of her story or she never would.

"He was also physically abusive."

It would take a moment for the truth to sink in.

"What did you say?"

"Toby liked to use force to get his point across."

"Carter hurt you?" Quinn's roar was louder this time and Cal winced. Oh, God, he was losing it. Anger, dark and dangerous, sparked in his eyes and every single muscle in his body was taut. She had to bring him down; she had to diffuse the situation.

"It wasn't that bad, Quinn." Cal placed a hand on his arm. "He slapped me a couple of times. It was mainly verbal—"

"Don't you dare defend him!" Quinn linked his hands behind his head, incandescently angry. "He raised his hand to you—there is no excuse!"

It was important for her to keep calm. Arguing with him wouldn't help.

"I'm not defending him, Quinn, I'm trying to explain what happened."

"When did he start hitting you?" Quinn demanded, the cords in his neck tight.

Dammit, he would have to ask that question. "About six months after we married," Cal admitted.

"And you stayed with him for another year?" Quinn shouted. "I don't understand this, you! Why didn't you bail?"

"Because, by then, I had no self-confidence. He told me he would destroy me and my father if I walked out on him."

"And you believed him? Come on, Red, you are smarter than that!"

Cal wrapped her arms around her bent knees and tried not to feel hurt. Quinn didn't understand. "I used to judge women who stayed in abusive relationships too. It's easy to stand on that pedestal, but Toby knocked me off it with a single slap."

Her gentle rebuke hit its mark. The fire went out of

Quinn's eyes, but the tension in his body remained. He pulled in a deep breath and then expelled the air and rolled his head. After a few minutes he walked back to the daybed and sat down next to her.

Quinn picked up her hand and threaded his fingers between hers. The anger was still there, but it was under control. "So, explain it to me. Why did you stay with him, Cal? I can't understand why you didn't leave the first time he hurt you. You know, you *knew*, better than that."

Shame and embarrassment rolled through her. "I told myself I didn't want my big, fancy, expensive wedding to be a waste of money—a stupid reason—and I didn't want to admit that I'd made a huge mistake. Pride and stubbornness played a part."

"Oh, Cal."

"Mostly, I didn't want to look like a fool," Cal admitted and wrinkled her nose.

"Did you ever think about leaving him?"

"I was leaving him," Cal said. "The day before the accident I told him that I was filing for divorce. We had a huge fight and he told me he would destroy me. Destroy my father. Then he punched me, really hard, in the ribs."

She saw anger roll through him again, hot and powerful. "God, I so want to find Carter's grave, dig him up and beat him back to death."

"He broke three ribs. After his death, the press reports said that I was too shocked to cry, that I was beyond tears. All I could think about was that he couldn't hurt me again. I wouldn't have to deal with a messy divorce, with the drama that would follow. I felt like I'd received a get-out-of-jail-free card." Cal looked at him with wide eyes. "Is that wrong?"

Quinn shrugged. "Not from where I'm sitting." He

squeezed her hand. "You could've called me, Cal. I would've helped."

"I know, but I felt..."

"Like a fool?"

"Yeah. I thought that since I'd gotten myself into the situation I needed to get myself out." Cal pulled their joined hands into her lap and leaned against his shoulder. "I was very young and very dumb. I was grieving my mom's death and he made me feel bright and beautiful and, I guess, safe. Protected."

"I was also there. Didn't I make you feel like that?" Quinn demanded,

Cal shook her head. "Toby spoiled me. You've never done that. You treat me like an equal, like an adult. Toby promised that my life would be drama-free with him. After Mom died, I wanted that."

"Life is never drama-free."

"I know that now," Cal said. "I'm sorry I didn't tell you, didn't ask for your help, that I haven't told you about this before. It was my ugly little secret."

"We all have secrets, Cal, but nothing about you—not even your secrets—can ever be ugly." Quinn turned toward her and placed his hand on her cheek. The tenderness and regret in his eyes made her heart trip. "I wish you'd come to me."

Cal tasted tears in the back of her throat. "I do too. I know now you would've been there for me, Quinn, just like I know that you would be there for Jack if he allowed you to be." Cal mimicked Quinn's action and put her hand on his rough, stubbled jaw. "You're such a good man, Q, even if you don't believe it half the time."

"Not so good," Quinn said, his voice rough with emotion.

Cal shook her head. "You'll never convince me of

that. You are both tender and strong and that combination floors me."

Tenderness flared in Quinn's light eyes, along with desire and protectiveness.

She couldn't resist him.

Nine

"Red—God, why can't I resist you?"

His eyes roamed over her face, looking at her like he was seeing her for the first time. And Cal knew that, even if it was just temporary, their friendship had retreated to make room for a blazing love affair.

It might only last the night or it might be strong enough to withstand the passage of time. No matter how long it lasted, she would enjoy him, as much as she could.

"I need you. I need to love you right here, right now, in the dark, in the cold night air," Quinn told her, his hands reaching for the belt that held her rich purple wraparound jersey together. His hands pulled the fabric apart and he skimmed her torso, cupped her breasts while his tongue invaded her mouth, sliding against hers in a dance that was as exciting as it had been the first time he kissed her on the terrace at the masked ball.

"You taste so good." He broke the contact with her mouth to murmur the words.

Cal moaned and her hands slid over his chest, down his waist to grip his hips. He hadn't bothered with a coat so she had easy access to the buttons on his shirt and she went to work on them. She soon felt the contrast of the chilly night air and his superhot skin. Cal felt his hand under the cup of her bra and she shivered, excitement skittering over her. These were hands that knew her, knew what she liked, knew how to touch her.

Quinn pushed Cal's shirt down and off her arms and he groaned when he pulled his head back to look at her lacy bra barely covering her creamy breasts. He dropped his head to pull her nipple into his mouth, tasting her through the barrier of the lace. Cal linked both arms around his head and held him to her. She needed this, needed him to need her, to crave her. She felt powerful and feminine, confident and sexy. Strong.

God, she felt strong.

Quinn's hands dropped to her stomach, fumbling as he tried to open the buttons on her jeans. He cursed, sounding uncharacteristically impatient. "I need you. I need to be inside you, loving you."

Quinn groaned, his mouth on hers as he pushed her jeans and thong down her legs. She kicked the garments off and moaned when his fingers stroked her with exquisite care. "So hot, so warm. Mine."

God, she was. *His, only his.*

Cal snapped open the button to his jeans, tugged down his fly and Quinn sighed when her hand found him, long, strong and so hard. She couldn't wait, couldn't cope with his drive-her-crazy foreplay tonight. She just wanted him inside her. Completing her.

Quinn shucked his clothes and pushed her down onto the ottoman. With his hands on her thighs, he gently pushed her legs apart. He leaned over her, his expression hot and hard and intense and, with a lot of passion and little finesse, he entered her with one long, fluid, desperate stroke. She was wet and ready for him. He stopped for a moment, his arms straight out as he hovered above her, her astonishment at how in sync they were reflected in his eyes. He was rock-hard and ready and she was very, very willing.

She could feel every luscious inch of him, skin on skin, her wet warmth coating him, his head nudging her womb. He felt amazing and... *God!*

"Quinn!" Cal smacked his shoulder with her fist and he pulled his head back to look down into her face.

"What? What's wrong?" he demanded, his voice hoarse with need.

"Condom! You're not wearing one."

Quinn pushed himself up on his hands to hover over her. She really didn't want him to pull out. She loved the intimacy of making love to him without a barrier. It felt real...

"I'm clean and I'm—" he choked on the words "—you know...a genetic dead end." He supported himself on one hand and she saw the muscles in his shoulders and biceps bunch as he lifted his thumb to caress her cheekbone. "If I have to run downstairs for a condom, I will, crying all the way. But I've always used a condom and I was tested last month. I'm clean, there's no chance of you falling pregnant and I just want to make love to you, feel every inch of you, with no barriers between us. Because, God, you feel amazing."

She clenched her internal muscles, involuntarily responding to the emotional plea beneath his words. His jaw was rigid and she could see he was using every speck of willpower he had to stop himself from plunging into her.

"Okay, yes," Cal said and her hands flew over his ribs, down his hips and over his butt, pulling him deeper into her. "Move, Quinn, I need you."

"Not as much as I need you, baby," Quinn growled as he forced himself to keep the pace slow. Cal whimpered with need, slammed her hips up, driving him deeper inside.

"Harder, deeper, faster," Cal chanted.

Quinn had no problem obeying that particular order and he pistoned into her, his hand under her hips to tilt her pelvis up so she could take him deeper. She suspected he was a knife's edge away from losing it and she wanted him sharing this with her.

Cal lifted her hands between their bodies to hold his face. She stared into his eyes, blue clashing with green, and smiled. "Let's fly together, Quinn."

Quinn nodded. "Now?"

"Now."

Cal let herself dissolve around Quinn, her body shaking with her intense orgasm. Love, hot and powerful, roared through her as Quinn groaned and threw his head back. She felt him come deep inside her.

His, Cal decided. Only his.

Cal rolled over and, not finding Quinn, put her hand out to pat his side of the bed. Frowning, she opened her eyes. Hearing the sound of water running, she looked at the closed bathroom door. Cal sat up, grateful for a moment alone, a little time to think.

Last night she suspected that she might be in love with Quinn. In the cold light of morning she knew it to be true. She'd fallen head over heels in love with her oldest friend.

Idiot.

Had she really been stupid enough to think he was

a safe bet, to think she'd be immune to his charm, his quirky sense of humor, to that luscious body and to-hell-with-you attitude? He was the least safe person in the world to love. Yet here she was, feeling all those crazy emotions she'd swore she'd never feel again. She wasn't supposed to be thinking of him in terms of commitment and forever. Quinn didn't do commitment and he had no concept of forever. He married her because he needed an out, a way to mend some fences. He married her because he trusted her to not make waves, to not make demands on him that he wouldn't be able to meet.

Quinn wasn't perfect, but she didn't need him to be. He was perfect for her. He was strong enough to allow her to be strong. They argued, but he didn't overpower her. He didn't force his opinion on her. He trusted her to be the best version of herself, was strong enough to deal with the broken bits of her, adult enough to know that everyone had their quirks.

He knew her, flaws and all. Better than that, he accepted her, flaws and all.

For that reason, and a million others, she loved him. In a soul-mates, be-mine-forever way.

The way he'd made love to her last night, both on the deck and later in this bed—the way he'd held her like she was precious and perfect—gave her hope. She felt excitement bubble and pop in her stomach. Maybe they had a shot...

"You're looking a bit dopey, Red."

Cal jerked her head up. Quinn's shoulder pressed into the door frame and a white towel around his hips was a perfect contrast to his tanned skin. He looked as gorgeous as ever—and as remote as the International Space Station. Unlike her, Quinn wasn't having a warm and fuzzy, I-love-you moment.

"Hi."

Quinn lifted an inquiring eyebrow. "What's up?" he asked, stalking into the room. "You have your thinking face on."

Damn, he knew her so well.

"You might as well spit it out, Red. You know you want to."

She did. She wanted to tell him how she felt, wanted to admit to him—and to herself—that she wanted a real marriage between them, something that would see them through to the end of their lives. She wanted to be the brave, strong, confident woman she'd worked hard to be and ask him if he felt the same, ask him whether he could love her like she needed to be loved.

Cal wrapped her arms around her knees, biting down on her bottom lip. "I could tell you, but I don't know if you want to hear what I have to say."

Quinn's eyes hardened and turned bleak. "Are you going to tell me something else about Carter that I won't like?"

"No. I told you about the abuse and the inheritance and that's it," Cal replied.

"Then what is it?" Quinn asked, looking at his watch. "And, sorry, I don't mean to rush you, but I need to get to headquarters for a strategy meeting with Mac and Kade."

She couldn't just blurt this out on the fly. They needed time to talk about it. Cal blew air into her cheeks. "Leave it. We can talk later."

Quinn gripped the bridge of his nose, obviously frustrated. "Cal, just say it."

Well, okay then. Cal kept her eyes on his as she spoke her truth, her voice shaking. "I'm in love with you and I want to spend the rest of my life with you. I want this marriage. I want you."

Happiness flared in his eyes but quickly died as confusion and fear stomped over that fragile emotion. Quinn rubbed his hand over his jaw and then moved it to rub the back of his neck. "God, Cal. That was not what I expected to hear."

"Yeah, I figured."

"I'm not sure what you want me to say…"

Cal pushed her curls off her face. "It's not about what I *want* you to say, Quinn. I'd just like to know if you think it's a possibility…whether you might, someday, feel the same."

Quinn disappeared into his walk-in closet and when he reappeared five minutes later, he was dressed in track pants and a Mavericks hoodie. He carried his shoes to the bed, sat down on the edge and slowly pulled on his socks.

Cal waited for him to speak and when he did, his words were precise and deliberate. "I think this is all going a bit fast. Last night was emotional and I realize that talking about Carter was difficult for you. The floodgates opened and you released a lot of feelings and I think you might be confusing that release with love. Could that be possible?"

Cal considered his words. Nope, she decided. She was definitely in love with him. "Sorry, that's not it."

Quinn bent over and stared at his sneakers before tying the laces. "The sex between us is amazing, Red, and we're good friends. That doesn't mean we are in love." Quinn sat up and looked at her, his expression determined. "*If* this is happening, then we need to take a step back, figure out what the hell we're doing before we make plans and promises that will blow up in our faces."

Cal nodded, conscious of the slow bruise forming on

her heart. "You still haven't told me if you love me or not."

Quinn stood up and slapped his hands on his hips. He didn't speak and when Cal finally looked up, she saw fear and confusion in his eyes. "I don't know, Cal. I don't know what I feel. This—*you*—it's all a bit too much." He glanced at his watch and grimaced. "Let's think about this, step away from the emotion and consider what we're doing. What we're risking."

Cal clearly heard what he wanted to say but couldn't because he didn't want to hurt her: *What you're doing, what you're risking.*

He was giving her an out, a way to go back to sex without the messy complication of love.

Quinn picked up his wallet and cell phone and jammed them into the pockets of his hoodie. "I have a...thing... this evening. You?"

Cal lifted her chin, knowing damn well he didn't have plans since they'd discussed seeing a movie tonight. But her pride wouldn't let him see her disappointment, wouldn't permit her to ask for anything more. "I have a *thing* too."

Quinn nodded and walked to the side of the bed. Cal kept her face tipped, waiting for his customary see-you-later, open-mouth kiss, but he kissed the top of her head instead.

It was the age-old, you're-looking-for-more-than-I-can-give-you brush-off.

Message received, Quinn. Message received.

A week passed and Cal wasn't sure why she was at the Mavericks arena midmorning, especially since she had work piling up on her desk back at the foundation. If pressed, she supposed she could say she'd come to talk to Quinn about their upcoming schedules, whether he could attend a theater production with her later in the month. There were a dozen questions she could ask, but nothing that couldn't be resolved during a two-minute phone call or later that day when they touched base back at home…

Home. It might be a good idea if she stopped thinking of the yacht in those terms.

Coming to the arena had been an impulsive decision but one that was rooted in her need to see Quinn. She wanted to talk him into having lunch with her, to try and push past the barrier her impulsive declaration of love had created between them a week ago. They were still living together, still sleeping in the same bed, still making love. But they weren't communicating. They were two people who were sharing his space and their bodies and nothing else. She didn't think she could live like this for much longer. She was back in purgatory, except this time they were lovers but not friends. She felt angry and sad and, yes, disappointed.

They were acting exactly how they'd said they never would and they were hurting each other. They needed to break this impasse. One of them had to be brave enough to walk away before they destroyed their friendship. She'd raised the subject of love; she'd changed the parameters of their marriage by uttering the *L* word so it was her responsibility to fix what was broken.

While she waited for Quinn to call an end to the practice session, she thought how much she loved to watch him skate. Cal propped her feet up onto the boards that lined the rink. He was poetry in motion, at home on the ice just as he was on land. Dressed in jeans and a long-sleeved T-shirt with a sleeveless jacket over his broad chest, he looked bold and determined.

And utterly in charge.

His players took his direction easily and quickly and, while they respected him, they certainly weren't scared of him. It was obvious they gave him a thousand percent all the time. You didn't work that hard for someone unless you were inspired to do so.

He pulled no punches. No one was spared his praise or his sharp tongue. Even Mac, his partner, was treated exactly the same as the rest of the players. On the ice there was only one boss and Quinn was it. That amount of intensity, that power was…well, it made her panties heat up.

Cal, digging into a bag of chips, looked up when she heard the click-clack of heels. She smiled at Wren, who was making her way to her seat in the first row back from the rink. On the ice, Quinn was barking orders to his squad, short blond hair glinting in the overhead lights.

"I heard you were here," Wren said, bending down to kiss her cheek before dunking her hand in the bag of chips.

"Sneaky thief," Cal muttered as Wren settled into the chair next to her.

"You can't eat a mega-sized bag of chips by yourself. You'll get fat," Wren told her. "I'm just being a good friend, helping you out."

"Yeah, yeah," Cal replied and placed the bag between them. She nodded to the thick envelope on Wren's knees. "And that?"

Wren patted the envelope and popped another chip in her mouth. After swallowing, she passed the envelope to Cal and smiled. "That, my darling, is the measure of our success. You actually did it."

"Did what?" Cal asked, opening the envelope and pulling out a sheaf of papers.

"The rehabilitation of Rayne. Those are the photocopies of every article mentioning you or Quinn over the past month and every single one is positive. Quinn is redeemed. By the love of a good woman."

Cal started flipping through the papers, stopping now and again to read a headline, to look at a photograph. There was one of them kissing outside the coffee shop close to her office, another of them in Stanley Park at the picnic, walking hand in hand and laughing. Old Friends, New Lovers read one headline. Are Quinn and Cal Vancouver's Most Romantic Couple? Is It True Love?

"The Mavericks brand is stronger than ever and trust in Quinn, as a person and as a coach, has been restored. Instead of baying for his blood, the press is now baying for babies." Wren's hand dipped into the bag again and she stood. "I'll leave you to take a look through those. Thanks, Cal. I could never have whipped him into shape on my own."

Baying for babies? Cal felt her heart tighten. That was never going to happen and it made her feel sad, a little sick.

If Quinn wanted a family or marriage, if he wanted *her*, he would've initiated a discussion about their future. He would've asked to talk about her ill-timed and unwelcome declaration seven days ago.

His silence on the subject said everything she needed to hear: he absolutely wasn't interested in anything more than what they had.

He'd married her for a reason and since that goal had been achieved, there was no rationale for staying married. It was time to cut her losses and try to move on.

Cal tipped her head to look up into Wren's lovely face. "Does this mean we can start, uh, dialing it down?"

"Sorry?" Wren asked, confused.

Cal shoved her fingers into her hair, lifting and pushing the curls back. "That was the plan—we make it look good and then we start drifting apart."

Wren waved at the papers in Cal's lap. "If you faked everything, then I commend you on your magnificent acting." Wren placed her hands on her hips and scowled. "But I've been doing this for a long time and I know fake when I see it. This isn't one of those times."

"We're friends."

"Pffft. You are so much more than that. You are good together. Damn, girl, you are the best thing that's happened to that man in a very long time. You don't seem unhappy either, so why on earth do you want it to end?"

She didn't, but what she wanted was beside the point. "It will end, Wren."

"Then you are both idiots," Wren told her before bending down and kissing Cal's cheek. "I hope you both change your minds because yours could be an amazing love story."

Wren touched Cal's shoulder and gave her a sad smile before walking away. Cal gathered the articles together and pushed the papers back into the envelope and laid it face down on her lap.

She had to start controlling her attraction to Quinn instead of letting attraction control her. If she didn't, she would find herself in the same situation she'd been in years ago, hopelessly in love with a man who didn't love her, without any emotional protection or power.

Oh, wait…that horse had already bolted from the stable; she already loved Quinn. She loved him like a friend; she loved him as a lover. She simply, deeply, profoundly loved him, in every way a woman could.

Okay… She loved him, but that didn't mean she couldn't protect herself. She was not prepared to let all rational thought disappear and capriciousness rule. She'd learned her lesson well.

Unlike her younger self, she could now look at relationships, and men, and see them clearly. Quinn didn't love her, not romantically in a I-want-to-spend-the-next-sixty-years-with-you type of way. He loved making love to her. Maybe because she was handy and she was the only person he could—without making waves and headlines—have sex with. Quinn was also exceptionally good at separating his emotions from, well, anything and she knew he could easily separate their friendship from making love.

She didn't have any desire to change Quinn. Yeah, her goal had been to rehabilitate his reputation, but she had no desire to rehabilitate him. She'd always loved him for who he was, the adrenaline junkie who'd jump off buildings with a parachute strapped to his back, who laughed like a maniac on roller-coaster rides, who leaped from one crazy stunt to another in order to feel alive. Because he'd spent his childhood hoping to be noticed, and she understood his need to feel alive, to feel free. She understood what motivated his crazy…

She loved him. She understood him. She would feel like she'd had her limb amputated when they parted, but they had to end this. Her heart was already battered and bruised, but that was better than having her psyche and her soul decimated.

She and Quinn needed to have a serious talk about splitting up. They needed to come up with a plan for how to navigate the next couple of months. They had to start winding down their relationship, start spending some public and private time apart. They had to be strategic in how they drifted away from each other.

She didn't want the public to blame Quinn. She didn't

want to reverse the current wave of good press he was receiving. Her father wanted to return to work and so could she; there were problems with the projects in Botswana, India and Belize she needed to attend to. They could blame her work, distance and time apart for the breakup of their marriage. Everyone understood that long-distance relationships never worked…

Cal pulled a bottle of water from her bag and twisted the cap. She took a long swallow and replaced the cap as Quinn called a break.

Quinn's eyes met hers across the ice and he lifted a finger to tell her he'd be with her shortly. Happy to wait, Cal watched as the players glided across the ice, most of them in her direction. As they removed their helmets, she recognized some faces from the barbecue on Quinn's yacht last weekend.

"Hey, Cal."

Cal dropped her feet and leaned forward, smiling. "Hey Matt, Jude. Beckett."

Beckett sent her a bold smile. "*Mrs.* Boss Lady."

Cal leaned back and crossed her legs, amused when six eyes followed the very prosaic movement of her denim-covered legs tucked into knee-high leather boots. God, they looked so young, so fresh-faced. Compared to Quinn, they looked like boys. These boys still had a lot of living to do. They needed to experience a little trouble, needed to have their hearts broken and learn a couple of life lessons. Then their pretty-boy faces would become truly attractive.

Cal jerked her attention from her thoughts to their conversation.

"So, what are we doing tonight?" Beckett demanded, sliding guards onto the blades of his skates before swinging open the door that would take him off the ice. He walked between Cal and the boards and dropped into the chair next to her, sending her an easy, confident grin. "FOMO's, Up Close or Bottoms Up?"

"What's FOMO's?" Cal asked, interested. She knew that Up Close was a club and that Bottoms Up was a sports bar owned by Kade, Mac and Quinn.

Beckett stretched out his arms and his hand brushed Cal's shoulder as he rested it against the back of her chair. Not wanting to give him any ideas—he was far too slick for his age—Cal leaned forward and rested her elbows on her knees.

"It's a place downtown," Beckett replied. "Want to come?"

Matt flicked a glance toward Quinn and shook his head. "Uh, Beck, not a great idea. Boss man wouldn't like it."

Cal frowned. The comment sliced a bit too close to the bone. "Last time I checked, I was a grown-up and I make my own decisions. Quinn doesn't do that for me."

Jude pinched the bridge of his nose. "Seriously, Cal, he really won't like you…"

Beckett's laugh was rich. "If she wants to come, let her. We'll be there from around ten."

Who went out at ten? Ten was when most people were thinking about bed, or sitting in their pj's eating ice cream. "Ten?"

Beckett picked up the end of her braid and rolled it in his fingers. "Maybe you are too old to party with us." Cal almost didn't notice the sly look he sent Quinn, the smirk to his fallen-angel mouth. "Maybe you should just be a good wife and stay in. Quinn *definitely* won't like it."

She knew she was being played, but she couldn't bear the thought of this young whippersnapper thinking anyone had control over her.

Cal jerked her braid out of his fingers. "For your information, Quinn has no say about what I do or who I do it with."

Beckett lifted an amused eyebrow. "Okay then, *Mrs. Rayne*. FOMO's, at ten. Do you want us to collect you?"

"I think I can get there under my own steam," Cal told him, her tone slightly acidic.

"Get where?"

She hadn't heard Quinn's silent approach, but Matt and Jude's tense body language should've given her a hint. Beckett's sly smirk deepened and Quinn's fierce frown didn't intimidate him in the least. "Hey, boss. Just to let you know, Callahan is joining us at FOMO's tonight, if you want to hang out."

Quinn's eyebrows nearly disappeared into his hairline. "At FOMO's?" He folded his arms across his chest and scowled. "No, she's not."

Beckett stood up and shrugged. "I told her you wouldn't like it, but she said you're not the boss of her."

"Hey, I'm right here!" Cal stated.

"You are *not* going to FOMO's."

Cal tilted her head. Right, this was just one small reminder as to why she shouldn't want to stay married. Nobody was allowed to make decisions about any aspect of her life but her. "I am. And you are not going to stop me."

Cal stood up as Beckett, Jude and Matt made a tactical retreat.

Quinn looked like he was making an effort to hold on to his temper. "Cal, listen to me. FOMO's—"

"You can't tell me what to do, Rayne! We're sleeping together and that's it." Cal pulled her bag over her shoulder. "You are never going to control me, tell me what to do or how to do it. I will never allow a man that measure of control again."

"I'm not trying to control you! I'm trying to tell you that FOMO's is—"

"Save it! I'm not going to listen!" Cal wasn't interested in anything more he had to say, her temper now on a low simmer. What was it about men and their need to control the situation, control how their women acted? Was it ego? Stupidity? A rush of blood to the head? Whatever it was, she wasn't going to play his game. She might like his bossy ways in the bedroom, but everything else—her money, her clothes, what she did and how she did it— was strictly off-limits.

She loved him and he didn't love her. It was that simple. But even if he did fall to the floor and beg her to spend the next sixty years with him, she would never grant him the right to dictate her actions.

"I'm done with this conversation," Cal told him, her voice quiet and cold. She picked up the envelope and slapped it against his chest. "Wren dropped these off. When you see them, maybe you'll agree that we need to talk. We need to start thinking about dialing this down."

"What are you talking about?" Quinn raised his voice as she started to walk up the stairs to the exit. "Come back here, I need you to understand why I won't allow you to go to FOMO's."

Cal half turned and raised one shoulder, her face flushed with anger. Did he really use the word *allow*? After everything she'd told him? Seriously? "*Allow?* You won't allow me to go? Who the hell do you think you are? I don't answer to you, Rayne. I am not one of your players or one of your bimbo girlfriends who will roll over at your command!"

"Callahan!" Quinn growled.

Cal just kept on walking.

Yeah, they really needed to put some distance between them.

Ten

Black and pink and purple, Cal thought as she walked into FOMO's. Lots of black and pink and purple. Not her favorite color combination. Cal slid into a small space near two guys standing at the bar. Between attempts to catch the eye of a bartender, she looked around for Beckett or any of the Mavericks players. She couldn't see them and she wondered, not for the first time, what she was doing here.

Clubs weren't her scene; the repetitive thumping of the music gave her an earache and the flashing neon lasers gave her a headache. The smell of liquor and cologne and perfume clogged her nose and she felt claustrophobic from the bodies pressing her against the bar.

"What can I get you?" the barman shouted at her, his white teeth flashing and his dreadlocks bobbing in time to the beat.

A taxi? An oxygen mask? "A club soda and lime. Hey, have you seen the Mavericks players in here tonight?"

His hands deftly assembled her drink, but his eyes gave her an up-and-down look. "Honey, you're a little old and a lot overdressed to catch their eye."

"Thanks," Cal said, her tone dry. "Have you seen them?"

He nodded toward a floating staircase in the corner. "They are upstairs." He slid the glass toward her. "You look really familiar. Do I know you?"

"No," Cal quickly answered, but she didn't kid herself that she wouldn't be recognized sometime soon. Not everyone in the club was drunk or stoned and she could guarantee that the vast majority of those who were still sober were Mavericks fans.

"I have that type of face," Cal told him. She reached into the pocket of her tight skinny jeans and pulled out a bill. Before she could hand it over, she felt a hard body press her into the bar and a hand shot past her face, strong fingers holding a twenty-dollar bill.

Cal sighed when the bartender took the man's money and not hers. She frowned, waving her money at him. "I want to pay for my own drink. No offense intended."

"I've been offended all damn day," the familiar voice growled in her ear. "I was offended when you flounced away, when you wouldn't answer any of the ten calls I made to you, when you didn't come home before coming here."

Dammit. Quinn had tracked her down and he was here, stalking her. Not that his presence was too much of a surprise. Quinn wasn't one to walk away from a fight.

"Quinn and his missus!" The bartender held up his knuckles for Quinn to bump. "Haven't seen you in here for ages, man!"

"Yeah, wives tend to frown on their husbands visiting FOMO's, Galen."

"That's the truth, dude."

He knew the bartender, which meant he was very familiar with this club. Cal looked at the raised dance floor to the right of the bar and sighed at the skimpily clad women—girls—writhing and grinding. It was probably one of his favorite hunting grounds.

"What are you doing here, man? And why did you bring your woman?"

"Cal and I were on our way to dinner and I wanted to stop in and check on my boys. They behaving themselves?" Quinn asked.

Galen nodded to the floating staircase. "They're upstairs, blowing off some steam. No paparazzi up there, no dealers, just some of their regular girls."

Quinn nodded. "Let me know if that changes."

"Will do, boss man."

Galen passed Quinn a beer and he wrapped his fingers around the neck of the bottle and the other hand around her wrist. She tugged at his hold and he bent his head toward hers. She was sure that anyone watching him would think he was whispering something sexy in her ear, but his words were anything but. "You. Stay."

"I am not a dog! You don't get to tell me to sit and stay!" Cal shot back, wondering how she could be so annoyed with someone who smelled so good and turned her insides to mush.

"Callahan, I am on the edge of losing my temper with you and you won't like it when I do. Do not push me."

Cal bit her lip and looked up at him, suddenly, inexplicably, scared. Toby always used the same words—*do not push me*—before his hand shot out, sometimes stopping and sometimes connecting. Sometimes the slap turned into a punch, sometimes a tap; once or twice his palm left finger marks on her cheek. Even worse was when the slap morphed into a caress, into foreplay, into sex she didn't want to have.

Cal bit her bottom lip and tried to get her racing heart under control. Quinn wasn't Toby; he would never, ever hurt her. So then why did she feel like she was being controlled by a bigger, stronger personality than herself?

Oh, God, this had little to do with Toby and everything to do with Quinn and the fact that she'd allowed herself to be vulnerable again. Once again she'd handed over her love, her most precious gift, and once again it had been rejected. Everything she'd worked for—her independence, her sense of self—was slipping away... It felt like *she* was fading away.

She couldn't control the sudden surge of overwhelming anxiety. Feeling like she couldn't get any air, she lifted her hand to her throat and patted her skin, trying to tell herself to breathe. But it was too hot in the club, too noisy and her heart was pounding so hard she felt like it was going to jump out of her chest.

Panic attack. She hadn't had many—she'd started having them in the month before Toby died—but she instantly knew what was happening. Dizziness, a tingling body and ice running through her veins. She wanted to run away from Quinn, this place, her life, but she couldn't. She held onto Quinn's arm, hoping his heat and warmth would pull her back from that dark, horrible place.

"What the—" she heard Quinn's words from a place far away and felt her knees buckling. Then Quinn's arm was around her waist and he pulled her into his embrace, his hand holding her head to his neck, his voice in her ear.

"I've got you, Red. Just breathe. C'mon, baby, just breathe, in and out."

Cal concentrated on his soothing voice, on his

strength, on the warmth of his body, his smell. His heat. She pulled in air, slowly, as he suggested, and the ice in her blood melted and the world stopped whirling. She managed to move her arms so she held his hard waist, her hand clutching the fabric of his black button-down shirt. His fingers in her hair massaged her scalp.

"C'mon, Red, get it together. I'm here and you are fine. You just need to breathe, suck in the disgusting air."

His words caused her to let out a snort of laughter and Quinn's arm around her hips tightened a fraction. "There we go. You're getting there."

Cal pulled in a deep breath, felt her head clearing and nodded, her nose bumping into his jaw.

"If I put you down, will you be able to stand?" Quinn demanded, his lips on her cheek.

"Yeah."

Cal wobbled when her heels hit the floor, but Quinn stabilized her. She stared at the open patch of tanned skin revealed by the collar of his shirt and struggled to make sense of what had just happened. Oh, God, if this wasn't another sign that she had to put some emotional distance between her and Quinn, then she didn't know what was. She couldn't be in a relationship with him, with anybody. If just a couple of words could send her into a tailspin, and his touch could bring her back from the edge, then she needed to get out.

He made her want what she couldn't have, what she wasn't prepared to give. She didn't want to cede that much control over her heart, her thoughts, her life. A relationship meant sacrifice; it meant losing control. It meant bouncing between love and trepidation, between hope and despair.

Love meant being vulnerable.

"Let's get you out of here." Quinn cradled her head

between his hands and rested his forehead on hers. She felt his breath, minty fresh, on her cheeks, her nose, whispering across her forehead. "God, Red, what's happening to us?"

Back on the *Red Delicious*, Quinn watched Cal as she carefully sat down on the edge of the sofa's square cushions and stared at the maple floor beneath her feet. They needed to talk, but was she up to it?

He'd always prided himself on being forthright and honest, but this week he'd been anything but. He knew, better than most, how under-the-surface emotions could fester. He'd seen the looks Cal had sent him, the confusion on her face when he made love to her and then emotionally retreated. He was being unfair, but he wasn't sure how to resolve their stalemate.

"I'm going up onto the deck. I need some air."

Quinn nodded and went into the kitchen to pull two wineglasses from the cabinet. He dropped to his haunches and quickly scanned his wine collection before deciding on a robust red. As he reached for the corkscrew, he noticed the thick envelope he'd tossed onto the counter earlier. He'd been so angry with Cal that he hadn't bothered to look inside, but now he was curious. Putting the corkscrew down, he opened the flap and spread the papers on the counter. He sucked in his breath at the photographic documentation of the past few months with Cal.

God, they looked happy, in love, crazy about each other.

There was a photo of him watching her at that art exhibition and he saw love and lust, pride and affection written all over his face. In every photo, the world could see their crazy chemistry, knew their thoughts weren't far away from the bedroom. Some of the photos managed to capture their genuine liking for each other, their trust in each other. He could easily see why the city assumed they were in love.

A camera had flashed in the club earlier, capturing him holding Cal's face in his hands. When that photo appeared online or in tomorrow's social column, they would see a man looking at his woman, adoration on his face.

Because he did adore her—he loved her—but did he love her like *that*? Did he love her enough to walk away from the safety of his lone-wolf lifestyle, enough to give her what she deserved, what she craved? A home, a family—through surrogacy, through adoption, through some nontraditional way—and the love and commitment and fidelity she deserved? Could he put her first, forever and always? Could he build the family he now knew he wanted with her? Could he trust her to put him first, to be the rock he wanted to lean on?

It would be easier to walk away from her right now, tonight, to let whatever they had die a natural death. But if they ended it now, it would take months or years for their friendship to recover, if it ever did. Could he risk that? Could he risk losing her to keep his heart safe?

He didn't know...

Quinn picked up the wine bottle and glasses and took them up to the deck. Cal stood at the railing looking up at the skyscrapers of downtown Vancouver. He loved the deck at night, dark and quiet despite the hectic light show above and behind them.

Cal kicked off her shoes and his eyes traveled along her legs in those tight jeans to her tiny waist, displayed by her snug coat. He put the glasses and wine down and walked toward her, placing his front to her back, pulling aside her hair to place a hot kiss on her elegant neck.

He knew they needed to talk, but he wanted this first, the magic and wonder of her under him. He wasn't sure where they were going, but he needed to love her one more time before words got in the way.

Because words always did.

Early the next morning Cal felt Quinn's kiss on her neck, heard him pull in a deep breath as if he were trying to inhale her. His arm was tight around her; his thigh was flung over hers as if he were trying to hold her in place. It meant nothing, Cal reminded herself; him holding her was a conditioned response.

Cal opened her eyes as Quinn rolled away from her, leaving the bed without speaking to visit the bathroom. She hoped he'd come back to bed, but she didn't really expect him to. Her instinct was proven correct when he walked over to the large window and placed his arm on the glass above his head, his expression disconsolate.

"What caused your panic attack last night?" Quinn asked, without turning around.

Cal didn't bother to pretend that she was asleep. Neither of them had slept and, instead of talking, they'd reached for each other time and time again, as if they knew this conversation would change everything between them. Well, dawn was breaking and the night was over...

Cal pushed back the covers and stood up. She pulled a T-shirt from the pile of laundry on his chair and pulled it over her head. She walked over to the large porthole to stand next to Quinn. He'd pulled on a pair of sleeping shorts and a T-shirt while he was in the bathroom and Cal was grateful. She didn't think they could have this conversation naked.

"You told me you were on the edge of losing your temper," Cal replied, placing her hand on the glass.

She felt Quinn's penetrating look. "And you took that to mean...what? That I would hurt you?"

She lifted a shoulder. "Intellectually, no. Emotionally, I rolled back in time. I have issues about being controlled."

"Because of Carter." Quinn rubbed his hand over his jaw. "But you do know I would never, ever lay a finger on you?"

"I know that, Quinn, I do." Cal looked at him, so big and bold and so very pissed off. "I don't respond well to orders anymore and I didn't like you telling me what to do."

Quinn linked his hands behind his neck, his biceps bulging. "And I had a damn good reason for that. You didn't know what you were walking into last night," Quinn snapped. "FOMO's is, on the surface, a pretty normal club."

"Then why did you have a problem with me going there?" Cal demanded, sitting on the side of the bed, surprised when Quinn sat down next to her, his thigh pressing into hers.

"I said that it's normal on the surface. Girls looking for rich guys, guys looking for pretty girls. I'm on good terms with the bartender, as I am with at least ten others throughout the city, because I pay them to keep an eye on my players, especially the younger ones."

Cal frowned at him. "What? You pay them to spy on your players?"

"I pay them to keep me informed. There are lots of temptations out there for young kids with too much talent and money. Those bartenders and bouncers tell me when they think a player might be in danger of going over the edge. I try to stop it before it gets that far."

"How?"

Quinn looked grim. "Suspension, random drug tests, threats, bribery, coercion. I'm not scared to use what works. I will not let them throw their talent away, throw their future away because they are young and dumb."

"Oh." Cal turned his words over. That was so like Quinn, deeply honorable and innately protective. "Your players were upstairs…so what's upstairs?"

"Strip joint, men and women. Lap dances. Men on men, women on women and any combination thereof. It's a cool place to hang out, to show that you have no issue with your sexuality. I don't care who does what to whom, but the drugs flow through there like water through taps," Quinn stated in a flat voice. "If you had gone up there, on your own, without me, and you were photographed, it would've gone viral."

"I was on my way up there," Cal admitted.

"Yeah, I know. We ducked a bullet. It would've been pretty hard to explain why you were in a strip joint when we are so happily married," Quinn said.

"Except that we are not happily married. Or even properly married."

"No, we're not." Quinn rested his forearms on his thighs, his hands linked. "I looked at the photos, the articles. It seems as if we've done a great job of convincing the public that we are in love."

"But we're not, are we?" Cal asked, her heart in her throat. Well, she might be, but he wasn't.

Quinn pushed an agitated hand through his hair. "It's become complicated, exactly what we didn't want it to be."

He was looking at her as if he expected her to drop another conversational atomic bomb. She could see the trepidation in his eyes, the tension in his hard jaw. He was bracing himself for begging and tears.

She wouldn't do that, Cal decided. She wasn't going to beg him to love her. She'd rolled that die already and lost. She wasn't going to do it again.

But, God, it hurt. Cal sucked some much needed air and looked for a little bit of courage.

For the first time she made the conscious decision to lie to him. It was, she rationalized, for their greater good.

"I love you. I always have. But I won't let myself be in love with anybody, Quinn, not even you." She couldn't keep sleeping with him, couldn't keep up the pretense. Because she knew with every day she spent with him, every night she slept in his arms, she would fall deeper in love with him and leaving him would become impossible. She needed to save herself and to do that she had to leave. Now.

"Maybe we should—" Cal stopped. She didn't want to say the words because once they were said, she couldn't take them back. Nothing would ever be the same between them again. If she said what she needed to, she'd lose him, lose what little of his love she had. God, she'd had no clue this conversation would be so difficult.

Quinn moved so he sat on his haunches in front of her, his arm on his knee, his fingers encircling her ankle. "Maybe we should stop, Cal. We absolutely should play it safe, be sensible. Sleeping together complicated what was supposed to be a simple arrangement."

And so it starts…

No, don't think about how much it hurts. You can fall apart later. When you are alone. You've been through worse than this, Callahan. You can cope with a little heartbreak.

Focus on the practicalities. They still had a role to play, a marriage to act out.

"And the press? How do we handle them?"

"We don't do so many public appearances together and when we do, we make sure that we aren't acting so affectionate," Quinn suggested, his voice rough with an emotion she couldn't identify.

Cal tucked her legs under her bottom and pulled his shirt over her knees. "It might be easier if I left...the city, the country."

Besides, being away from him would give her the distance she needed to patch her heart back together.

Shock and denial flashed across his face and Cal lifted a shoulder. "That would be the best option, Quinn. The easiest way to do this."

Quinn muttered a curse and drummed his fingers on his thigh, obviously upset. "Okay, tell me what you're thinking."

"My dad is bored with being idle. He's itching to come back to work and if I give him the smallest excuse, he'll be home in a flash."

"Is he well enough to work?"

"It's been three months so I think so." Cal raked her hair back with her fingers and twisted it into a loose knot at the back of her neck. "And I should get back to my own work. There are problems everywhere that I need to sort out, some I can only fix by being on the ground." Cal nodded as a plan started to form in her head. "I suggest we issue a press statement, saying that I need to return to work, that we're going to do the long-distance marriage thing until I wrap up some projects. Except that the projects take longer than expected and, as a result, we start drifting apart."

Quinn's face gave nothing away and Cal had no idea what he was thinking. Damn, she'd always been able to read him, had always known what he was thinking until recently, when he kept his thoughts hidden from her. She hated it. Despite their best efforts, the last three months had changed their friendship.

They'd chosen the situation; they'd known the risk. Now they had to deal with the fallout.

"That could work," Quinn agreed. "When will you—"

"Go?" Cal finished his sentence. She didn't think she could live with Quinn and not touch him, not make love to him. If she moved anywhere else, then a lot of questions would be asked. The best solution was to leave, as soon as possible.

She just needed to find the courage to walk away, to do what was necessary. For both their sakes.

"ASAP, Quinn. I don't want to draw this out, make it harder than it needs to be." Cal dropped her gaze so he couldn't see how close she was to losing it.

Quinn's arm around her shoulders, him hauling her into his side, told her he'd already noticed. He kissed her temple and rested his head on hers. "We really should've kept this simple, Red."

Cal placed her arm around his neck and closed her eyes, feeling his heat, his hard body and ignoring the throb between her legs, her blood roaring through her veins. "Yeah, we really should've. We weren't very smart, Quinn."

It was the second game of the season and Quinn stood in their newly acquired owners' box in the Mavericks arena looking down at the rink. The seats were starting to fill and there was a buzz in the air.

The fans were excited and he could understand why. Yesterday he, Mac and Kade had signed the final papers giving them a majority ownership of the Mavericks and fulfilling their biggest dream.

Kade and Quinn stood next to him and he saw, and ignored, the long look they exchanged. He took a sip from his coffee cup. He grimaced. The coffee, like everything else over the past month, tasted like crap.

"We are now the official majority owners of the Mavericks," Kade said, a goofy-looking grin on his face. He bumped fists with Mac, who was also wearing a stupid-ass grin. They were still on a high from yesterday, still assimilating the knowledge that the deal was, finally, done.

The Mavericks, as they'd planned ten years ago, was theirs. They'd worked like crazy, taking financial risks, pouring their hearts and souls into the team and it had finally, finally, paid off. Quinn part-owned a professional hockey team, the *only* hockey team.

He should feel happier.

Mac's fist plowed into his shoulder. "I've seen you more excited over a pizza, dude."

Quinn looked across the ice, guilt closing his throat. This was a turning point, a major achievement, and he was sucking the life out of the party. Normally, he'd be the one celebrating the hardest, but little was normal since Cal left.

Everything felt strange, out of place. It was as if his life was now one of those fun-house mirrors, everything distorted, unfocused. But that wasn't his friends' fault; it wasn't anyone's fault but his. He made his choices and was living with the very crappy consequences.

Suck it up, Rayne. He dragged a smile onto his face and lifted his cup in a salute. "Here's to us. We kicked ass."

Kade's small smile acknowledged Quinn's effort to get into the swing of things. "Good try, but your level of enthusiasm still sucks. So, let's talk about it."

"Might as well," Mac agreed.

Oh, God. What was with his friends and their desire

to talk things through? They were guys. Guys didn't talk stuff to death.

"Nothing to talk about," Quinn snapped and frowned at Mac. "And we need to get down to the locker room."

"We have time," Mac replied.

Kade removed a stick of gum from his pocket, unwrapped the paper, keeping his eyes on Quinn. "Nothing to talk about? Really? Except Callahan, that is. How is she?"

So it looked like they were going to discuss Quinn's absent wife and his nonmarriage. "She arrived safely in Lesotho. I haven't spoken to her recently."

"Why not?" Kade asked.

"She's in a mountainous region with a bad signal," Quinn snapped.

"Wren manages to talk to her every couple of days, so do Brodie and Rory," Mac commented, his face and tone bland.

Busted. How could he worm his way out of this? What excuse could he use? Quinn rubbed his temple and decided he was too tired to look for one. Besides, these were his best friends, his safety net.

"It's just easier not to talk to her." Quinn took another sip of coffee and grimaced. He placed the mug on a high table and pushed it away.

"You miss her."

Miss her? That was such a stupid, tame, word for what he felt. He couldn't sleep, couldn't concentrate, couldn't think for missing her.

He absolutely missed his lover, missed his friend. "Yeah, I miss her."

"Why did she leave again?" Mac asked.

Quinn rubbed the back of his neck. "We decided that the…situation was getting out of control."

"Out of control how?"

Kade looked at Mac; Mac shook his head and echoed Kade's look of confusion. Really, was Quinn going to draw them a picture? "Neither of us wanted a happily-ever-after deal. Neither of us wanted to commit so we dialed it down before we…before we found ourselves doing that."

Kade tried to contain his mirth, but Mac just let it rip, his laughter rumbling over them. Quinn felt his fist clench and wondered if he would be forgiven for punching his best friend shortly after they realized their biggest professional and business triumph. And before a game.

Probably not.

"Glad that I amuse you. Moving the hell on—"

"How can you not realize that you and Cal are in a committed relationship, that you have been for years?" Kade asked, bemused.

"What are you talking about?" Quinn demanded.

"Moron, you've been friends for twenty years. That's commitment right there. Easy, natural, something that just is."

He'd try to keep this simple and maybe they'd understand. "Yeah, we were committed to a friendship, not a love affair."

"You worked to keep your friendship alive. You wanted to keep that connection. It was very damn important to you. And to her. You've been more committed to each other than anybody else in your lives. Your commitment to each other is longer than our friendship, longer than your career with the Mavericks, so much more meaningful than your relationship with your family. And you're both wusses, running away from each other," Mac bluntly said.

Oh…hell. Quinn wanted to deny his words, wanted

to argue, but he couldn't find anything to say. There were reasons why he couldn't have a be-mine relationship with Cal.

"It's not as simple as that," Quinn croaked the words out.

Two sets of eyebrows lifted. God, he'd never felt so exposed, so completely vulnerable. How could he tell them, these two masculine, *virile* men...

He rubbed his temple and when he looked up at them, his eyes reflected his anguish. "Cal wants kids. I can't give her any."

Kade and Mac stared at him for a long time and while he saw sympathy on their faces, he didn't see pity. Thank God. If he had, he would've handed in his man card. Kade tapped his fingers on the table, a sure sign that he was thinking. "Why do you think that?"

Quinn explained and they listened intently. Kade frowned and shook his head. "You need to get a second opinion. I don't think you can rely on one blood test years ago as a definitive diagnosis."

Mac nodded. "And, if it turns out you can't have kids, then there are other options. Adoption, surrogacy, sperm banks. Hell, I'll even donate some of my magnificent boys to the cause."

Kade choked on his beer and Quinn's mouth dropped open. Then humor—unexpected but welcome—bubbled to the surface. He shook his head. "It's bad enough working with you, training you—having to raise a mini-you would do my head in."

"The point is, there are options. But—" Kade sent him a hard, cool, assessing look "—before you get there you have to decide whether you want Cal in your life or not. Separate and apart from the giving-her-kids issue."

"Which he does," Mac interjected.

Which Quinn did. More than he wanted to keep work-ing, coaching, *breathing*. His life without her in it had no meaning, no color, absolutely no direction. And even less joy. Kade was right: he'd never been able to commit to anyone because he'd always—even if it was only on a subconscious level—been committed to Callahan. He loved her. He'd always loved her. His subconscious knew what it wanted and it had been waiting a damn long time for his body and his brain to catch up.

"Yep, he's getting there." Mac gripped Quinn's shoul-der, their equivalent of a girly hug.

Quinn felt he should say something, should express his gratitude that he had these two guys solidly in his corner. But hell, what could he say that didn't make him sound like he'd grown a pair of ovaries?

"Thanks," he eventually muttered.

Mac grinned. "Well, you know that we'd take a bullet for you. Not in the head, or in the heart, but maybe like in the ass…or the big toe."

Quinn, for the first time that night, for the first time in a month, laughed. As his laughter rumbled out, he felt his mobile vibrate. He pulled it out and swiped the screen with his thumb.

His laughter died and something that felt like hope took its place. "I need to go."

Mac snatched the mobile from his hand, read the message and handed the phone to Kade. Quinn was too shocked to object to them reading his messages. All he cared about was going home.

Kade slapped the phone back into Quinn's hand.

"I have to do this," he said, hoping they'd understand. "Cal and I need to talk."

Neither Mac nor Kade said anything for a while and Quinn's heart sank. He understood their reluctance, he was, after, running out on his responsibilities. The Mavericks, the game…they were important, sure, but Cal was his *life*.

Then they grinned and he knew that they'd been messing with him. Jerks.

"Go, we'll handle your responsibilities here," Kade told him. He grinned. "I mean, really, how difficult can coaching be?"

Quinn shoved a hand through his hair and narrowed his eyes at Kade. At the door he turned and sent Kade a withering glare. "Payback is a bitch, Webb."

Kade just laughed. "Get the hell out of here, Rayne, before we change our minds."

Quinn bolted.

Eleven

Living her life without Quinn was like trying to make the world spin in another direction. It simply didn't work. It made her feel dizzy and ditzy and…sad. Bereft. Alone.

She'd tried. She'd given it her best shot and, after a month, she was over living on the other side of the world, trying to remember why it was better that she and Quinn were apart. The only thing that was true, real, important was that they stay linked, that he remain a part of her life, in any way she could get him.

She didn't know how that would work, what role she was going to play, but they could work it out. They *would* work it out. He'd been the biggest part of her life for most of her life, the person she'd loved best all these years, and while she loved him, fiercely, she'd take him any way she could get him.

Cal opened the door to Quinn's home and dropped her overnight bag to the floor. Although she knew Quinn would be at the arena, preparing for a Mavericks game, she tipped her head, listening for movement, hoping she'd hear him upstairs. Hoping she could see him, drink him in.

Cal played with her cell phone as she walked toward the huge windows. She placed her shoulder against the glass and stared out at the water; she'd missed this view, missed his home.

Missed him with every atom of her being.

She'd always thought that love was something ethereal, an emotion that made you happier, prettier, smarter, more worthwhile. She'd dived into a marriage with Toby in order to feel safe and protected, in the hope that he'd take her to a place where grief didn't exist, where nothing could hurt her. She'd miscalculated there. Toby had hurt her and she'd been slapped in the face with everything she'd been running from.

His death had released her and, instead of trying to work through her issues with men, commitment and marriage, she'd dismissed both the species and the tradition, choosing to go it alone.

Only to find all she wanted and needed in the man who'd always been her rock, who made her laugh, who'd always encouraged her to fly but who would catch her if she crashed.

Because love wasn't perfection. It wasn't big houses and gourmet meals, designer clothes and fake smiles. Love wasn't the storybook kiss in the rain. It wasn't red roses or deep, soulful conversations.

Love was messy. Love was imperfect. Love was sarcastic text messages and two-minute phone calls, buying takeout and eating it on the bed before making love. Love was arguing and sharing the shower, stealing his cup of coffee when you were running out the door, morning kisses before teeth were brushed. Love was a friendship set on fire. Love was not running when things got tough; it was having the courage to reach out for more.

Love was traveling across an ocean from one continent to another to tell her best friend, the man she loved best, that she wanted everything he could give her, whether that was a little or a lot.

Cal took a deep breath, felt her heart kick up. She couldn't call him. He was preparing for a game and he wouldn't answer. Quinn had tunnel vision when he was in the zone and he was never more in the zone than when he was preparing for a Mavericks game. But she could send him a text. He'd get it when the game was over and that would give her some time to think about what to say to him.

For the first time ever, she couldn't find her words with Quinn, couldn't explain what she was thinking and feeling. Maybe it was because this time the words she needed to say were too important, the feelings too scary. She typed and erased four messages and cursed herself.

Keep it simple.

Hi, I wanted to tell you that I miss you, that I miss us. Maybe you can give me a call and we can chat about us, our marriage? Please?

Cal pushed the send button on her phone and bit her bottom lip. What if he didn't reply? What if he came home and was upset to see her back? Oh, God, what if he'd moved on? What if he came home with a puckbunny groupie on his arm?

Maybe coming back to Vancouver was a bad move, she thought, staring at the ocean, fighting back her tears.

Maybe she should leave. Go back to Africa and then onto India, bury herself in her work.

Except she'd done that, had tried to push him away, had tried to forget him, but she'd failed spectacularly. No, she wouldn't run. She'd wait, talk to him, repair whatever she could of their friendship.

She realized that he would never love her, not the way she wanted him to, but they could be friends and maybe that would be enough.

So she'd stay here and wait.

Thank God he was one of the bosses because blowing off an important game, leaving the stadium before his team was about to go on the ice, would get his ass canned if he were an employee, Quinn thought as he swung his Ducati in and out of traffic. As soon as he got to the yacht, he'd call Cal back, find out where she was. Then he'd call the team's pilot and tell him to file a flight plan for their company jet.

He needed to grab some gear and his passport—God, he couldn't forget his passport. Quinn steered his bike into his parking spot at the marina, ripped off his helmet, shoved it under his arm and started jogging toward the access gate and the *Red Delicious*. As he ran, he looked down at his cell, his thumb hovering over the green button to call Cal back. What would he say? How could he express everything that was in his heart?

Why did this have to be so damn difficult? He didn't want to spill his soul on a telephone or via an internet connection. Nope, if he was going to make an idiot of himself, then he was going do it properly, face-to-face.

And if that meant flying halfway around the world, then that was what he would do. Besides, he knew he could persuade her to his way of thinking—a proper marriage, love, staying together, being together—by kissing her, helping her get naked. Hey, a guy had to use whatever worked.

Quinn stormed onto the yacht, belted up the stairs and whipped open the door. He threw his helmet onto the chair at the door and thundered down the stairs to his cabin. He pushed the green button and the call rang as he yanked open the door to his walk-in closet. Stepping inside he grabbed some T-shirts and tucked them under his arm.

One ring, two, three, four—God, she had to answer.

He tossed the shirts onto his bed and dropped to his haunches next to his nightstand. He stared at the small wall safe in the table and couldn't remember the code. What if she didn't answer? What if he couldn't get ahold of her? What would he do? Where would he go?

"Hello?"

Quinn stood up abruptly, swore and rubbed the back of his neck. "Hi, sorry. I didn't think you were going to answer." He spat the words out, hardly able to hear his own voice above the thundering of his heart.

"Hi. Shouldn't you be at the game?"

"I should. I'm not." Just hearing her voice made sense. *She made sense.* "Where are you?"

"Why?"

"Because wherever you are, I'm on my way there." God, he sounded like an idiot. "I mean, I'll get there. Give me some time. You're right—we need to talk."

"You're coming to me?"

He thought he heard amusement in her voice but dismissed it as a figment of his imagination. It wasn't like he was thinking straight at the moment. "Yeah, the company jet is at my disposal. It'll get me where I need to go. So, can you text me directions?"

"I can do that. But it's pretty simple, I can tell you over the phone."

"God, Red, I can't think straight, and I definitely won't remember anything you say. Just text me. I'll get to wherever I need to be as soon as I can." And he prayed it wouldn't take more than a day or two.

"Okay, um, great. See you soon." Cal disconnected and Quinn stared at his blank screen, a frown on his face. Dammit, that was it? That was all she had for him? He was flying out to see a woman he loved and all she could say was *see you soon*? God, she was the most infuriating, crazy, annoying brat he'd ever laid eyes on. The only woman he'd ever loved, would ever love.

And, yeah, two days was better than two weeks, two months, two years, never. So he'd be a man and suck it up...

His phone flashed and Quinn swiped his thumb across the screen. He read the message, frowned and read it again.

At your bedroom door, turn right. Walk up the stairs and look for the girl holding the bottle of wine and two glasses.

Holy, holy, *holy* crap.

Quinn thundered back up the stairs, skidded into the lounge and stopped by the cream-colored sofa, his hands gripping its back with white-knuckled fingers. Cal noticed that his chest was heaving and his breathing was erratic. She was amazed, thrilled, that her presence could raise the heartbeat of this superfit man.

Her man. Maybe...

She looked for something to say, some witty comment

to break their charged silence, something to slice through the tension. She had nothing so she lifted her half-full glass of wine. "Want some?"

"Wine? No." Quinn's voice, deep and dark, rumbled across her skin as he walked toward her, his eyes a little wild and a lot determined. Her throat closed up as he narrowed the distance between them and she allowed him to pull the glass from her hand, watching as he placed it on the coffee table in front of her. "That's not what I want."

"What do you want?" Cal asked, tipping her head back to look at him, wishing he would touch her, kiss her.

"You. Any damn way I can get you." Quinn's gaze dropped from her eyes to her mouth, where he lingered as if he was fighting the urge to kiss her. Cal sighed when his hand cupped her shoulder, skimmed up her throat, her jaw, stopping when his palm rested on her cheek, his fingers in her hair.

Cal needed to touch him so she placed her hand on his chest. "Your heart is racing," she murmured.

The corners of Quinn's mouth kicked up. "Yeah, it started doing that when I saw your name on my screen and it went into overdrive when I realized you are here, in my home, and not a continent away. Why are you here, Cal?"

She tried to tell him why, but the words wouldn't come. Instead of telling him that she loved him, that she wanted a lifetime with him, she bit her lip.

"Why were you going to hijack the company jet to come to me?" she whispered, hoping he was braver than her.

"I was going to fly over there and beg you to come home. To me." Quinn's voice was saturated with emotion. "My life…is not that exciting anymore. Not without you in it."

She needed clarity, needed to know what he meant by that statement. "As a friend? As a lover?"

"As my everything," Quinn whispered the words against her lips and the last, tiny kernel of fear dissolved. "You're the only woman I've ever loved, the only person I fully trust."

"Quinn." Cal bunched the fabric of his shirt in her hand, closing her eyes when his lips touched her temple, her cheekbone, the lids of her eyes.

"Nothing gives me as much of a thrill as I get when I wake up with you in my arms, when I come home and you're here. Nothing gets my heart racing like making love to you. Nothing feels as good as watching you shatter when I'm inside you. You are my highest peak, my biggest wave, my fastest ride."

Cal linked her arms around his neck and stood on her tiptoes to brush her lips against his mouth, to push her breasts into his chest, her hips into his. If she could climb inside him, she would. "Quinn."

Quinn kissed her and she felt his love in his lips, in the way he tasted her. His lips sipped at her; his tongue traced the fullness of her bottom lip, the edges of her teeth, before it slid inside to tangle with her tongue. It was a kiss that promised, that soothed, that excited. It told the story of their past and painted a picture for the future, of a friendship set on fire.

Then his kiss slowed, he hesitated and pulled back to look at her, a question in his eyes.

"Why did you come back?" he asked, his hands on her hips, the tips of his fingers digging into her skin. Cal touched his cheek and realized there was doubt in his eyes, and fear. Fear that he was the only one feeling this way...

Cal swallowed, humbled by the fact that this strong, brave man was insecure, that he needed her reassurance, that he wasn't the only one who was risking his heart. "I came home because you are, simply, my home. You have always been my deepest connection, my best friend. You bring out the best in me. You make me want to be better, do better."

Quinn's eyes softened, turned a brighter green. "Are we saying that we love each other?"

Cal nodded her agreement but didn't drop her eyes from his. He just looked at her, waiting for her to verbalize her thoughts, to make them real. "I do love you." But she'd always loved him, so she thought clarity was needed. "I am so *in love* with you."

"As I am with you," Quinn replied, resting his temple against the top of her head, hugging her to him. "God, baby, I've missed you so much."

"I've missed you too. I never knew how long nights could be without you beside me," Cal said, snuggling in as her tension drained away. "I didn't think you could love me, but I knew I had to be near you, if only as a friend."

Quinn's hand squeezed her butt in a way that was anything but friendly. "Like we could be in the same room without wanting to get each other naked. Talking about getting naked..."

"Were we? I thought we were going to spend the next couple of hours being all mushy," Cal teased him, not quite able to imagine her adrenaline-seeking man being ridiculously romantic.

"I do my best romancing naked," Quinn assured her,

his hand tugging on the hem of her flowing, rust-colored sweater.

Cal lifted her arms and he pulled the sweater over her head and tossed it to the floor. Instead of reaching for her, Quinn held her away from him, his face questioning. "Is that what you need from me, romance?"

Cal cocked her head. "Would you give it to me?"

"I will try to give you whatever you need to make you happy. Fidelity, respect, love—that's a given. I'm not a romantic guy, but if that's what you need to feel secure, I'll try."

His sincerity hit her in the gut and her jumpy heart settled, sighed. "I don't need the gestures of romance, Quinn. I just need you. The Quinn I've always known is the Quinn I want in my life. I just need you to tell me you love me occasionally and to get me naked as often as possible, and I'm grand."

"I have no problem with telling you I love you. I always have and it seems to be as natural as breathing."

"Me too."

Sadness dimmed the happiness in his eyes. "What about kids, Cal? I can't give you kids."

Cal hastened to assure him that her love wasn't conditional. "I'm still not convinced about that, but we'll work it out. You and I, we can work anything out, as long as we do it together."

Cal's eyes drank him in. His beautiful eyes, his jaw rough with stubble, his relaxed mouth. His hair was longer and not so spiky and...

Cal laughed and she lifted her hand to a spot just above his ear.

Quinn raised an eyebrow. "What?"

Cal tugged the white feather out of his hair and held it up for him to see. "I think my mom approves."

Quinn touched the feather with his index finger before pulling Cal into his arms and dropping his face into her neck. "I do love you, Red."

Cal felt his heart thudding under her hand and knew her happy-ever-after had arrived. Their life together, she decided, was going to be an amazing ride.

Epilogue

Three months later...

"Now tell me this wasn't a grand idea," Mac demanded, lifting a champagne bottle to refresh Brodie's and Rory's champagne flutes. The six of them, with Rosie and Cody, were sitting on the veranda, having just come back to the luxury house after an afternoon spent on the beach.

Cal had no problem telling Mac that his impetuous decision that they spend a week at the house they jointly owned in Puerto Rico was a fine idea and she lifted her untouched glass in his direction. "Fantastic idea, Mac."

"Wait until you live through a hurricane here," Rory muttered, but her eyes laughed at her husband.

Mac took his toddler daughter from Rory and dropped a kiss on her puckered lips. "It was just a little wind, Rorks, and you took shelter in my big, brawny arms."

"Well, one arm. The other was fairly useless at the

time," Rory corrected him. "God, you were a terrible patient."

Their friends laughed when Mac scowled at her. Cal leaned back in her chair and picked her feet up to tuck her heels on the edge of the chair, thinking that it wouldn't be long before she wouldn't be able to sit like this. She was surprised Quinn hadn't noticed her rounder shape.

For the last day or so, since they'd left Vancouver, she'd been wondering how to tell him he was going to be a dad, probably in around thirty weeks or so. He'd be surprised and, she hoped, ecstatically happy. Even happier than they presently were…if that was even possible.

Quinn, sitting next to Kade, picked up Cody's foot and bent his head to gently nibble the baby's arch, causing Cody to chuckle heartily every time. They'd been playing this game for ten minutes and neither of them was bored with it yet. Cal felt her eyes fill with tears and after she'd blinked them away, she caught Kade's gaze and saw him tip his head, his eyes quizzical.

Kade always seemed to sense a secret just as it was ready to be divulged. And what was she waiting for? These were Quinn's best friends—her best friends— their family. Quinn wouldn't care how he heard that he was going to be a dad, and they'd get a kick out of seeing his happiness.

Cal flicked her eyes to Cody, gave Kade the tiniest nod and his eyes flashed with understanding and joy.

"Quinn—" she started to speak, but her words drained away. She bit her lip, her mind a blank. It was such good news, crazy-good news, but her throat had closed from too much emotion.

"Hey, butthead—" Kade jumped into her silence, winking at Cal "—did you ever go back to the doctor to redo those fertility tests?"

Quinn looked up at him and scowled. "I'm playing a rather excellent game with your son and you have to spoil the moment by raising *that* subject? Thanks, Webb."

Kade wasn't remotely chastised. "Well, did you?"

Quinn reached out and took Cal's hand in his and she felt the tension in his fingers. "Cal and I decided that we'd do it when the season ended, when we had a moment to breathe. We're taking a little time for ourselves before we go down that road."

"But you do want kids?" Kade demanded.

Cal saw Quinn's Adam's apple bob and the slow, definite nod of his head. "I want whatever we can have. As long as Cal is at the center of our family, I'm good."

Tears, silent and powerful, rolled down Cal's face. Her small sob had Quinn whipping his head around to look at her and his eyes widened in shock. "Crap! What did I say? Red, don't cry—jeez! I'm sorry, I know it's a sensitive subject and Kade is a moron for bringing it up."

"I agree with that," Mac chimed in.

Cal let out a laugh and placed her hand on Quinn's cheek, pulling his frowning face back to hers. "Stop looking at Kade like you want to thump him, darling. He's actually being a good guy, trying to help me out here."

"Told you so," Kade said with a smirk, rubbing his unshaven chin across Cody's fuzzy head.

Quinn frowned. "What do you mean?"

Cal blinked away her tears and smiled. She reached past Quinn and tapped Cody's foot. "We're going to have one of these." She looked at Rosie, who was dipping her fingers into Mac's beer glass and shoving her wet digits into her mouth. "Or maybe a pink one, like Rosie. Um…maybe you should move your beer glass out of your daughter's reach, Mac."

Mac picked up his drink and Rosie let out a yell of protest.

Rory covered her eyes with her hand. "Oh, God, she's definitely a Maverick. Heaven help me."

Quinn shook his head, still confused. "I don't understand. What are you trying to say, Red?"

Cal smiled and pulled his hand to her stomach. "Do you remember I asked you for some of your boys?"

He was still confused. "Yeah, and I told you that I don't have any."

Cal laughed. "Four pregnancy tests and a scan the day before yesterday says you do, my darling. So, do you want to come on an adventure with me, Q? You, me and our munchkin?"

Quinn lowered his forehead to hers, his eyes glistening with hope, excitement and undiluted joy. "Red, I love you to distraction and you should know by now that I would go anywhere with you. You, and them—" he jerked a thumb toward his friends "—are my family, but I'm thrilled, ecstatic, that we're making it bigger."

"We're halfway to having our own junior Mavericks team, men," Mac drawled. "Another from each of us and we can put a team on the ice. But, really, to make an impact, we'd need a couple more..."

* * * * *

LET'S TALK

Romance

For exclusive extracts, competitions
and special offers, find us online:

f facebook.com/millsandboon

◎ @millsandboonuk

𝕏 @millsandboon

Or get in touch on 0844 844 1351*

For all the latest titles coming soon, visit
millsandboon.co.uk/nextmonth

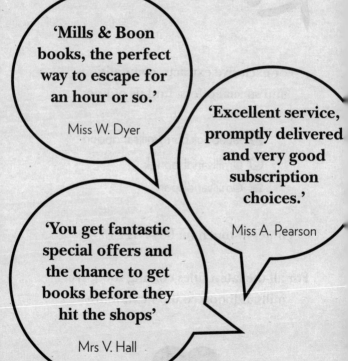